ASSOCIATES OF SHERLOCK HOLMES

Edited by
GEORGE MANN

TITANBOOKS

Associates of Sherlock Holmes
Print edition ISBN: 9781783299300
E-book edition ISBN: 9781783299317

Published by Titan Books
A division of Titan Publishing Group Ltd
144 Southwark Street, London SE1 0UP

First edition: August 2016
10 9 8 7 6 5 4 3 2 1

A CIP catalogue record for this title is available from the British Library.

Printed and bound by CPI Group (UK) Ltd, Croydon, CR0 4YY

CONTENTS

THE RIVER OF SILENCE

Lyndsay Faye

Stanley Hopkins, who makes his canonical debut in "The Adventure of Black Peter", is described as a young police inspector so newly minted that he still retains the posture of a roundsman wearing an official uniform. In all the cases in which he appears, he evinces the utmost regard for Holmes, professing "the admiration and respect of a pupil for the scientific methods of the famous amateur". Holmes, in turn, seems rather paternally amused by Hopkins, often attempting to steer him in the right direction without entirely giving the game away. This is the story of their first encounter.

—Lyndsay Faye

Letter sent from Inspector Stanley Michael Hopkins to Mrs Leticia Elizabeth Hopkins, Sunday April 29th, 1894

Dearest Mum,

Thank you for the new muffler and fingerless gloves – you're dead to rights in supposing a promotion calls for a fellow to look smart, and right to consider that I should have my hands free to boot! You worried over the colour, but it's *just* the ticket. A nice, dignified navy will do very well with my brown ulster.

How strange and freeing it is to be out of blue livery and stalking the shadowed streets in neat tweeds! The lads from H Division hooted over my plainclothes at first, saying I looked a smug breed of pigeon, but there was no malice in it and they toasted me plentiful times calling out, "Three cheers for our own *Inspector* Hopkins!" down at the Bull's Head last week. (I didn't myself join in enough to mar the solemnity of my new station, I promise you.)

My musty cubby at the Yard is well-outfitted now, with maps and reference volumes, plentiful ink and paper, and a flask of brandy should any females be forced to consult me in a state of distress – you understand I'd never hope for such a thing, but we live in a dark city, and I mean to shed some light on it. My resolve has impossibly redoubled since the news came down I was to shed my uniform, and when I've already thought of nothing else since... well, you know best of anyone to what I refer.

Enough dark reflections. Probably you've read of this, but *Sherlock Holmes himself* has returned as if by miracle from the dead and is to practice independently again in London. What a weird and wonderful world! Before I'd any inkling of joining the Peelers, I admired his brilliant methods ("idolised" Dad used to tease, remember?) and now to make inspector during the very week of his triumphant return from the depths... what an absolute corker. I can't but think it providential, Mum, truly.

On that note: dare I surmise that the gloves and muffler suggest you're at peace with my occupation, and your disappointment over my not becoming a clergyman like Dad has faded?

Trusting I interpret your kindly gifts aright, as I'm now to become a professional at reading the subtlest clues, I remain,

Your Stanley

Letter sent from Inspector Stanley Michael Hopkins to Mrs Leticia Elizabeth Hopkins, Tuesday May 1st, 1894

Dearest Mum,

I'm sorry for thinking the muffler and gloves suggested you had come round to the notion of my being a policeman. Rest assured that I intend to prove you needn't simply make the best of a bad business, and can instead feel as proud as you would if I were delivering sermons (a task at which I've many times told you I'd be *dismal*). Remember all the occasions when Sherlock Holmes's exploits led to God's justice being served?

Thank you for the dried sausages – they arrived quite safe, and I wrapped them against mice just as you said. Must beg pardon for brevity, as a strange teak box was just dredged from the Thames with something terrible in it. The other inspectors seem not to want to touch the business – dare I hope that I might have the chance to test my mettle, and so soon?

In haste,
Your Stanley

Telegram from SCOTLAND YARD, WHITEHALL to BEXLEY, Tuesday May 1st, 1894

CONTENTS OF TEAK BOX MOST DISTRESSING STOP THANKFULLY CASE ASSIGNED TO ME STOP WILL FULLY APPRISE YOU AS SOON AS POSSIBLE STOP DUTY CALLS STOP YES I WILL BE CAREFUL - STANLEY

Entry in the diary of Stanley Michael Hopkins, Tuesday May 1st, 1894

Too much has happened to set it all on paper – but I must put my thoughts in proper order, no matter if I'm grasping at snowflakes only to watch them dissolve. Here at Scotland Yard I feel as if I'm starting my career afresh, and in a sense I am, and a warm glow lodges at the base of my spine whenever I'm reminded of my new responsibilities. But Lord, it would be something fine to have one of my trusty H Division boys to natter with. Here the inspectors call out obscure jokes to one another I can't begin to savvy, and their eyes slide off the newly promoted when we pass in the crowded corridors. I don't blame them. They're overworked, and soon so shall I be. Headquarters smells of wearied sighs tinged with whiskey, shirt collars too long worn over interrogations and the filling out of forms.

And I've no one to consult with over this confounded box.

But I mustn't pity myself, for that isn't quite true – Inspector Lestrade visited me in one of the evidence lockers as I went through the contents, and though I know him to have been ensuring that a raw detective wouldn't botch the matter, I was thoroughly grateful.

"All right, Inspector… Hopkins, I think it is. What have you got yourself into on your first day that has everyone buzzing like an upturned hive?"

Sweeping off his bowler, Inspector Lestrade frowned at me. I think he frowns to impart his words with weight rather than signal displeasure, though, and he needs all the gravitas he can muster, since the little fellow can hardly weigh more than eleven stone. He has brown hair and eyes, both several shades darker than mine, and I tried not to seem to be looking down at him even though I couldn't help it – hardly anyone can.

Clearing my throat nervously, I began to answer.

"But you're already through writing it up, I see," he said, interrupting me. "Just pass that over and I'll check your form is correct."

I obeyed. Lestrade stood in full view of the peculiar – not to say ghastly – contents of the box, both objects resting upon the table, but he'd every right to supervise my paperwork on my first go of it. The other sight seemed not to disturb him, as indeed it couldn't by this time shake me either.

A grunt emerged as the senior inspector scanned my notes:

Item: one large carved box
 — _teak wood (foreign origin)_
 — _decorated with stylised lotus flowers (suggests Chinese import)_

Contents: one severed forearm with hand: human, female
 — _white flesh, decomposition not yet set in (recently amputated, not an outdoor worker)_
 — _mild swelling and discolouration (indicating submersion in river water for not more than five hours)_
 — _clean nail beds (respectable)_
 — _actual nails thin and cracked (poor health or nutrition)_
 — _no sign of ever having worn a ring (unmarried)_

Lestrade raised his eyebrows, seemed about to speak, and frowned instead.

"Something wrong, sir?"

"On the contrary."

"Have I done well, then?"

"Not bad for a greenhand," He returned my report. "Don't forget to sign and date everything. And I can tell you that although the brass latch is equipped with a lock, it wasn't used — merely fastened. I opened it myself without a key."

Hastily, I bent to record this fact.

Lestrade rubbed at one temple fretfully. The arm looked

much more poignant adrift on the sea of the large table than it had cradled in the ornate box. "You came to us from H Division, I hear."

"I did."

"Well, we don't want any repeats of that business."

"No, sir." If it sounded like a vow and not a mere reply, there was nothing to be done about it.

"What are your plans?"

Straightening, I rubbed my palms together. "Obviously, first we must ensure it's not some wretchedly coarse jest, and I've already sent wires to all the major hospitals asking after autopsies performed during the last twenty-four hours. In a moment, I'll circulate word for dockside police to look out for any similar objects, God forbid. Next I'll canvass businesses that import Chinese goods, particularly small furnishings such as this box, down Stepney way. If that fails, I'll scour both Yard files and the newspapers for missing persons, and enquire at local cemeteries to see whether she might have been the victim of a grave robbery. That ought to hold me for a day or two."

Lestrade's bright eyes narrowed in comprehension.

"How old were you when you joined the Force, Hopkins?"

"Twenty-five. I'm only thirty now, sir."

"Eighteen ninety-nine, then. You read *The Strand Magazine,* don't you?" He crossed his arms, tapping a finger against his sleeve.

"I, that is… yes," I stammered.

"Can't be helped, I suppose."

"No, sir."

"Inspired you, I shouldn't wonder, or some such rubbish."

"I confess so. This matter at hand… you mentioned

H Division yourself, inspector, and not wanting another catastrophe. Bearing in mind the severed limb, I... I wonder whether Mr Holmes would be interested?"

A bona fide snort quashed my fondest hope. "Mr Holmes goes in for the grotesque, not the gruesome."

"That doesn't surprise me, considering the stories. They're marvellous. I've read every one." The words were spilling like water from an upturned jug, and I'd no notion how to staunch them. "Is he just as Dr Watson says he is? Impossibly tall, impossibly brilliant, all of it?"

"Impossibly irritating? Yes. Everything about Sherlock Holmes is impossible," Lestrade huffed.

"You arrested Colonel Moran, you must have seen him again – so the roundsmen are gossiping. Is he much changed? I mean – not that you didn't solve Adair's murder yourself, inspector, I only –"

Lestrade made a motion as if shooing a fly. "It's all true. He's alive, he collared the colonel, he's even more impossible than previously. And he'll be back to his mad antics, I shouldn't wonder, with me left to tidy up the shrapnel."

"You must be so pleased he's miraculously safe home."

I blurted this knowing it was true, not only from the fact they'd worked extensively together, but also from the half-rueful, half-wistful smile hovering over Lestrade's features. They twisted in surprise, but then he shrugged narrow shoulders.

"Of course I am. He's good for the city, and it's the city I serve. Well, I must be –"

"Dashed if I can think of anything on Earth I want more than the chance to work with him."

"Take that back," Lestrade advised with a sour grimace, returning his hat to his head.

"Why?"

"Because working with Mr Holmes means you failed."

A shadow from the open door fell across his face.

And then he was gone, and I alone again, wondering how a mere mortal could trace a box with a poor and (presumably) dead girl's limb in it. I've every confidence of filling my hours meaningfully upon the morrow, and yet... it is difficult to be optimistic.

Everything is difficult, under the circumstances. Lilla's letters are still in the drawer of my night-table. Every day I try to move them to my battered trunk of keepsakes, and every day I fail. I check the post with fingers crossed and heart equally as twisted, the same weird curling feeling inside as I sort through mail never finding her name as I'd used to, and always hoping against sense a new missive may appear.

Letter sent from Inspector Stanley Michael Hopkins to Mrs Leticia Elizabeth Hopkins, Thursday May 3rd, 1894

Dearest Mum,

I can't do as you ask and no amount of cajoling will budge me − it's *impossible* for me to pen you details of an open investigation. For open it still is, and I'm nigh ready to start banging my pate against my desk. The trail grows colder every instant, and all I can do is tilt at windmill after windmill. When I solve the case, for I *will* solve it yet, you can scold me for bragging. Meanwhile, my nose must be to the grindstone and not hovering over correspondence, and I hope you'll forgive me.

I'd not thought of the question before you asked, but under these glad circumstances, I'll be dashed if there aren't more *Strand* stories to come, now you mention it! How could Dr Watson resist? The mince pie you mailed arrived only the *slightest* bit crushed, and I'm leaving it in my desk to have with my tea.

Still in haste,
Your Stanley

Entry in the diary of Stanley Michael Hopkins, Friday May 4th, 1894

And now I know what Inspector Lestrade meant by warning me against working with Mr Sherlock Holmes. Today was simultaneously the best day of my life since 1889, and the worst to boot. If someone asked after the whereabouts of the sky, I'd hardly know which way to point.

No warning was given for his appearance. I don't suppose there ever is – do God's angels send cards announcing their arrival, or do they simply appear, frightening shepherds (to say nothing of sheep) out of their wits? One moment I was writing up futile reports at my desk – *no indication of desecrated graves, no missing persons providing leads, no similar Chinese boxes sold in Stepney discovered,* etc. – and the next moment I heard Lestrade say, "Oh, what luck he's right where he's wanted. Mr Sherlock Holmes and Dr John Watson, meet our newest detective, Inspector Stanley Hopkins."

Whirling in my chair, I fished for words and caught none.

Sherlock Holmes is both identical to and nothing like the man in the magazine. Every physical characteristic is correct (frightfully tall, sinewy, pale, and so forth), but his bearing and movements defy description. The vast intellect in his grey eyes is hooded behind affected languor, like a sheathed sword, and dying must take its toll on a fellow, for plentiful cats'-whisker lines fanned from their edges I did not expect to find. And there I was, first week as a proper detective and my first case at that, already a failure, goggling at him as if he were the risen Christ. (Wouldn't Mum and dear departed Dad pitch a fit if they ever read *that* comparison.)

Dr Watson (a sturdy, handsome gentleman with a soldierly bearing and moustache) thrust his hand out after I'd sufficiently embarrassed myself. The act galvanised me and I sprang to my feet.

"An honour, Dr Watson, an absolute honour."

"Likewise," he affirmed warmly.

"I've followed your biographies very closely indeed. You might even say I've made a study of them. And the internationally celebrated Mr Sherlock Holmes – I hardly know what to say. What does a chap say when Orpheus is standing in his office? I, that is – hang it – the world is thankful for your return. Welcome back to London, sir."

Lestrade half-turned to cover a sneeze I suspected was not a sneeze at all. Dr Watson merely smiled and rocked onto his heels and back again, tilting his head to see what reply his friend would make. Mr Holmes examined my hand for an instant too long before gripping it.

"France is hardly Hades," he demurred – but I know the look of a man who has seen prolonged hardship and danger, and it was the look he wore. Come to that, the doctor likewise appeared a touch left of centre, eyes continually darting at his friend as if to ensure he was really there.

"Inspector Hopkins, I believe you've something unpleasant to show me."

"Growing more unpleasant every hour. But Lestrade, I thought –"

"If we wait any longer, there will be nothing to find," he interjected tersely. "Mr Holmes did more than his part during the dark times, and agreed to come down. Follow me, gentlemen."

I knew this already, knew everything about his involvement with Saucy Jack that could be gleaned from the gutter press, though I also knew better than to trust so much as a word written by a yellow journalist. But the H Division lads had confirmed Mr Holmes was in the thick of it when I joined their ranks, would mutter *'twas its own special hell and not another word I'll speak on the subject.* Snatching up my paperwork, I hurried after the trio.

Mr Holmes visited the arm, which had been preserved as best we could in glycerin, but pronounced there was little to see, glancing at Dr Watson to determine whether his medical companion agreed. Then we strode in his long-legged wake towards the evidence lockers and I located the box, watching as the great detective circled the table like a panther. Suddenly he froze. Somehow his stillness appeared more electric than his motion.

"I'd hardly any hope of being able to assist when you wired me so unforgivably late, Inspector," he admitted, glancing up at Lestrade. "Happily, I was guilty of rash pessimism. Your box, Hopkins, will be of immense help to us."

This surprised Lestrade, and Dr Watson likewise blinked. Staggered as I was, my pleasure took precedence. "I'm glad you think so, sir. Here is my initial report."

Mr Holmes took the paper with a bored air, but his eyes flicked back to the page almost instantly. A faint dusting of colour had appeared on his wan face. When through, he passed the page to Dr Watson and quirked a brow at Lestrade.

"Hopkins here reads *The Strand*," Lestrade pronounced with an air of martyrdom.

"Good heavens! He certainly does," Dr Watson exclaimed.

"And provided me with three clues I should have lost otherwise due to the arm's inevitable decay." Mr Holmes's tenor remained clipped, but an icicle twinkle appeared in his eyes.

"Did I really?" I cried, overjoyed.

"It's going to be utterly intolerable around here from now on," Lestrade sighed. "I'm requesting a transfer to Wales."

"Best pack a muffler," Dr Watson suggested, biting his lower lip valiantly.

This elicited a soundless laugh from Sherlock Holmes. "Come, Lestrade, you needn't despair. He's missed absolutely everything to do with the box. So have you, but we can hardly be shocked over that occurrence."

Lestrade ignored this jab. "By Jove, splendid! You've really found something?"

"What have I missed?" I protested. "The teak wood and lotus flowers strongly suggest foreign origin, likely Chinese. Lestrade informed me that the lock was not used, the hinges are quite normal, and… and I don't see anything else."

"Wrong again, I'm afraid. You do not *observe* anything else." Mr Holmes flipped the box onto its side with long fingers. "What is this?" he asked, pointing.

"A chip in a lotus petal." Mentally cuffing myself, I moved to examine it.

"Why should that have happened, I wonder?"

"The box must have been subjected to violence in the Thames. A boat or a piece of driftwood struck it."

"That may well be true, but it is not remotely what I meant."

"What did you mean?" I questioned, mesmerised.

"What do you conjecture?"

"I can think of no other answer."

"If you give up so quickly on your first case, I shudder to think what will daunt you six months from now. Astrological impediments? The state of Parliament, perhaps?" When I flinched, he continued in the same ironical tone, "What do you know about teak wood?"

"Very little," I admitted, my face heating.

"Teak has an average weight of forty-one pounds per square foot, rendering it extremely hard, and thus resistant to stress and age. It also contains a high level of silica, which often causes instruments used on it to lose their sharpness. A direct blow to this box while in the river could cause this chip, but not without cracking considerably more of the body. Thankfully, this is not *tectona grandis*, however. This is *alnus glutinosa*, which is remarkably helpful and ought to narrow our search considerably."

"Beg pardon?"

"Dear me, I've considered writing a monograph regarding the fifty or so commonest woods in daily use hereabouts, and I see I've been sorely remiss in delaying the project. It is European alder, indigenous to our fair isle and, might I add, a fairly soft wood. Observe the scratches covering the surface – this vessel was knocked about by flotsam, but as you noted, Hopkins, the limb was not waterlogged enough to have been very long in the Thames, and teak could never have suffered such myriad injuries in so short a period. It is stained in the expected dark reddish manner, and there its resemblance to the Chinese product ends. This is a sham," he concluded, pressing a small pocketknife into the wood. A faint but clear mark immediately resulted.

"Thank God. You think it a hoax made by some perverse anatomist?" Dr Watson ventured.

"You misunderstand me, my dear fellow. Deteriorated as the limb we just viewed was, the cut severing the arm was never made with any medical precision – you must have determined as much yourself."

"Certainly. I would hazard our subject used either a small axe or a large hatchet."

"I concur." Mr Holmes had produced a notebook and pencil and made short work of recording something. "No, the arm is quite real. The conveyance is the sham, and we must be grateful for its abnormality."

"Severed limbs are abnormal enough," Lestrade muttered.

"Would that were true, but this serves our purposes better." Sherlock Holmes's eyes glinted with enthusiasm despite our sobering mission. "What sort of person would create a false Chinese box?"

I couldn't answer. None of us could. But when Mr Holmes spun on his heel and glided through the door, we understood that we were about to find out.

As it happened, the sort of man who would create a false Chinese box was a skilled woodcarver who lacked access to the high-quality lumber of his homeland and yet wished to ply his trade, or so Mr Holmes deduced most convincingly as we four hastened from the slate monochrome of Scotland Yard into the colour and chaos of London's busiest thoroughfares. I'd been sniffing about the wrong neighbourhood, though I was as close to the mark as was possible without having the faintest notion of what I sought, the sleuth claimed (this seemed to be meant as neither censure nor condolence). Apparently, I didn't want the gritty straw-strewn byways of Stepney, with its deafening markets and echoing warehouses and mountains of imports.

"You wanted Limehouse, my good inspector," Mr Holmes finished, clapping me on the shoulder as he stepped down last from the four-wheeler. "The single neighbourhood hereabouts where Chinese culture thrives in corporeal rather than merely imported form."

Air thick as soup filled our nostrils, the tarry odour of the docks combined with roasting meats, simmering vegetables, and unfathomable spices. Beneath all skulked the reek of strangely foreign refuse – for whatever they were discarding, it wasn't potato peelings and apple cores. Chinese with glossy queues teemed along the pavements, and intermingling with them loitered grizzled career seamen and leather-skinned stevedores making deliveries. Lestrade flipped up his coat collar against the chill breeze.

"Are we to communicate what we're looking for through pantomime, or learn Mandarin?" he asked dourly.

Mr Holmes smirked, flipping open his notebook to reveal three Chinese characters. "I rather think the signature of the maker might be of greater immediate use."

"Capital, my dear fellow!" Dr Watson approved, grinning.

"How the devil did you find that out?" I cried.

"It was a positive tour-de-force of inferential reasoning," Mr Holmes drawled. "When I flipped the box on its side, I discovered the mark had been scratched very subtly into the base."

Dr Watson had the decency to study a stray cur worrying at an oxtail as my face flamed, but Lestrade gave a low whistle.

"Oh, come, none of that." Mortified as I felt, I was grateful that Sherlock Holmes sounded impatient rather than pitying. "*Ut desint vires, tamen est laudana voluntas*. You mistook the characters for more ill-use visited by the Thames – resolve to do better during your second case. Now. I'm acquainted with one or two nearby apothecaries in this warren, and I'd wager a fiver my friend Wi Cheun will do right by us. Do wait here, for the poor fellow suffers from a tremendous sensitivity to strange Englishmen."

We watched his gleaming black hat bob away in the throng of men fully a foot shorter than he. Or I did, while Lestrade and Dr Watson complacently lit cigarettes under a mud-spattered gaslight, as if they had waited for Sherlock Holmes to consult Chinese apothecaries some dozens of times. Decades seemed to pass. I'll be dashed if glaciers didn't melt.

"I feel such a fool," I confessed.

"That was nothing," Lestrade scoffed.

"It wasn't nothing. My father was a clergyman – I do have some Latin, enough for Ovid anyhow. I suppose it's too much to hope he'll forget about it?"

The men continued smoking. I forced my jaw not to clench in dismay.

"Never mind, Inspector," Dr Watson offered along with a genuine smile. "If everyone were Sherlock Holmes –"

Lestrade mock-shuddered, and the doctor chuckled gamely.

"I say, if everyone were Sherlock Holmes —"

"Then my career would be ruined," the man himself finished, fairly vibrating with energy as he materialised in our midst. "I've traced the box, and we've a brief trudge. I'll tell you on the way that I dislike Wi Cheun's account extremely for the hypothesis it suggests to my mind, and yet — well, we refuse to draw conclusions before the evidence is scrutinised. Quick march!"

We set off briskly towards the Limehouse basin and soon were crossing its dingy footbridge under the octagonal hydraulic tower, surrounded by the clatter, shouts, and bangs of the lifeboat manufactory. As we walked, Mr Holmes shared what he had learned.

Five years previous (according to Mr Holmes's druggist acquaintance) the mark, which read "Wu Jinhai," would have designated Wu Jinhai himself, an immigrant from the outskirts of Shanghai who had once made his living carving teak. Upon arriving in London, he discovered that he could procure a few shillings by foraging driftwood along the riverbank, creating landscapes and animal menageries and the like on the flotsam's surface, and afterward staining the piece to a high sheen. In time, he earned enough not merely to buy wood and commence crafting boxes, for which there was a perennial demand, but to marry a beautiful young Chinese woman and set up both shop and household in Gold Street near to Shadwell Market.

"A single domestic canker blighted this idyllic scene," Mr Holmes explained. "Wu Jinhai and his wife were childless, and no amount of visits to the local physicians could banish their infertility."

So distraught were they over their lack of progeny that one day, when Mrs Wu was scattering wood chips and sawdust over the ice in the back alley and spied a pair of white children on the brink of starvation, she did not chase them away as most would have done with street arabs, especially those of another race – she invited them in for soup. The Wus did not lack for money, and she saw no harm in gaining a reputation for both status and generosity amongst all manner of neighbours.

"In Chinese society, benevolence is often a way to reach across social boundaries and forge acquaintances that would otherwise be impossible," Mr Holmes continued. "In this case, however, there was a catch which manifested almost immediately."

Mrs Wu by this time spoke good English and discovered over empty bowls of dumpling soup that the children were mudlarks – the most wretched of the destitute, scouring the riverbanks for scraps of rag or coin or metal, as her own husband had once been forced to scrounge for wood. Far worse, the girl suffered from a spinal deformity – possibly brought on by polio, Wi Cheun had theorised to Mr Holmes – and the boy, though a few years older, was simple, only speaking in monosyllables. The girl revealed that they were siblings escaped from the cruelties of a nearby orphanage, and neither knew who their parents had been nor where they had lived before the bleak institution.

"The Wus took them in," reported the detective. The intersections we now crossed, though no less cramped nor refuse-strewn, were populated with as many Italians and Jews as Chinese, though queerly picturesque Oriental writing remained slashed across many ashen shop placards. "As employees at first – or so Mrs Wu presented them –

but later, apparently they were indistinguishable from her children save for their skin. The sister, Liza, worked on accounts and answered supply orders after learning her sums and letters from a paid neighbour. Arlie, the brother, never learned eloquence, but showed an immense aptitude for carving once Wu Jinhai taught him technique."

"What happened five years ago?" I inquired breathlessly, for our pace had been set by the man with the longest stride.

"Five years ago," he reflected. "Yes, five years ago Mr and Mrs Wu passed away from an influenza outbreak, leaving Arlie and Liza alone to run the family business as best they were able. And that, gentlemen, is the part I do not like, though I decline to make inferences in advance of tangible data."

A chill stroked my spine, and my companions' faces froze, for we had all seen Mr Holmes's mind. A doltish brother, a defenceless sister who might have been thought a burden, a frail white arm hacked away and consigned to the Thames. None of us wanted to contemplate such a thing, and I'll be dashed if the world-famous problem-solver did either.

"You're right, Mr Holmes. We know too little as yet to condemn anyone," I declared.

The sleuth's steely jaw twitched. "Are you being fawning or optimistic?"

"Neither. I'm being magnanimous, or attempting it. I was meant to become a clergyman like my father," I said wryly.

"Disinclined to resemble the patriarch?"

"On the contrary, I admired him more than anyone I've ever known. Didn't share any of his talents, more's the pity. Always stammering my way through catechisms. Dreadful.

He passed some eight years ago and Mum thought I'd finally see the light, but all I saw was the noose in the prison yard. When my cousin took the cloth, I gave him Dad's Bible with heartiest blessings and a helping of good riddance."

Dr Watson nodded sympathetically as Lestrade sniffed in mild amusement. A flicker of a smile ghosted across Mr Holmes's lips and vanished.

Then we had arrived, and I'll never forget it as long as I live: the crooked house in the middle of the row, runoff trickling down Gold Street, rivulets sparkling despite their leaden colour. The Wu residence's steps had not been cleaned since the last snowfall melted, streaks of soot painting black waterfalls down them, and one of the windows was patched with four or five layers of rotting newsprint.

Mr Holmes and Dr Watson approached with the bearing of men who've looked into the abyss and lived to tell about it, Lestrade close at their heels. Trailing only slightly, though my nerves hummed and sparked, I watched as the independent detective whipped out his pocketknife again and bent to one knee at the top of the steps.

"We haven't any warrant, Mr Holmes!" Lestrade hissed.

"You directed my notice to a trail old enough to be considered positively historical, and now you're quibbling about warrants?" the detective snapped in return, fiddling with the lock and producing a sharp *snick*. "Supposing we find anything, claim you investigated because the door had been forced. It would even be true."

Lestrade struck his palm against the rusted iron rail, but made no further protest. Indeed, we were all about to burst into the house when Mr Holmes flung his arms out, causing Lestrade to stumble and Dr Watson to catch his friend's shoulder.

"Enter, and then don't move a muscle," Sherlock Holmes ordered. "I must read the floor."

We crowded inside and my senior edged the front door closed. We were in a murky room, lit only by the undamaged windows, with a thin haze of wood particles tickling our throats. Stack after stack of carved boxes filled the chamber, only interrupted by a deal table with an unlit lamp resting upon it, and next to it a bowl of soup with dried broth staining its lip. Mr Holmes tiptoed along the walls, hands hovering in midair, reading the sawdust as we watched in silence.

"All right, come in." Mr Holmes's brows had swept towards his hawklike nose. "There's been traffic within the past day or two, but –"

He cut himself off and stalked across the room, staring down at a row of boxes piled six and eight high. When we followed him, it was plain to see that a single column had recently vanished, for its rectangular outline was printed clearly in the dust on the floor.

"Dear God," Dr Watson breathed.

The trio sprang into action, opening doors and cupboards, urgently seeking more evidence. My efforts to assist soon bore morbid fruit when I took the corridor leading to the back area and discovered a bloodied hatchet lying on the ground.

"Mr Holmes!" I shouted (though I ought to have called for Lestrade). "In the rear yard!"

Both men were there in seconds, gathering around my hunched form. Mr Holmes's eyes darted hither and thither over the cornsilk-hued grass and the chipped flagstones but, seeing nothing he deemed important, he sank to his haunches next to me, peering at the dull blade with its encrustation of gore.

"What do you see?" he asked. Lestrade opened his mouth. "No, no, my dear fellow, let us test his mettle a bit further. Inspector Hopkins, tell me what you observe."

A needle of panic shot through my breast, but I soon rallied. "The blood is not more than five days old, which fits our timeline – it rained on the twenty-eighth, which would have washed much of this away, and the arm was found on the first, quite fresh. Additionally, there is not a large amount of it. While it coats the edge of the hatchet, the ground beneath is spotted, not soaked."

"Meaning?"

"The body was moved."

"Or?"

This required thought, but I soon had it. "The body had been dead for long enough for the blood to begin to coagulate."

"Top marks." Mr Holmes stood. "This is manifestly the scene of the crime, and it would do to call in –"

"Holmes!" Dr Watson's face appeared in the door, his pleasant features sombre and still. "You had better see the bedchamber."

Not twenty seconds later, we were standing in the queerest room I'd ever encountered.

Two beds nestled against opposite corners, indifferently dressed in stale bedclothes. The single round table hosted dirtied teacups and several amber bottles, which the doctor shifted to study.

The rest of us gazed in astonishment at the walls, which were entirely covered with maps. Maps of the world, maps of Great Britain, maps of our dozens of colonies. Maps of America and its southern neighbours, maps of Arabia and Brazil and the Sahara, maps of Japan and the Bering Sea, maps showing entire constellations of islands I'd never heard of before. Stuck into these scores of maps were pins of every colour, some with notes – *"tropical, parrots and pineapple trees!"* – and some without, creating a dizzying spectacle of a smashed globe spread out flat and fixed to the plaster.

"Well, someone's taken an interest in geography," Lestrade muttered.

"This was recently a sickroom," Dr Watson reported. "Here is a willow bark tonic, elderberry syrup, yarrow extract, ginger… whoever was being treated had a severe fever."

"By George, Liza was taken ill," I realised. "And only her brother left to care for her. But did he speed it along, or –"

"Hsst!" Mr Holmes lifted his palm.

I heard nothing, and from their faces neither did the others. But an instant later, dashed if Sherlock Holmes wasn't out of the room and already halfway down a flight of steps. Quick as we ran, he had the advantage of us, and we reached the cellar (which housed a single combined workshop and lumber room) just as a guttural moan reached our ears.

"Stop! Slowly, now," Mr Holmes said in a calm, clear voice, and we proceeded at a more measured pace. "Watson, I need you."

Mr Holmes was half-kneeling with his forearm resting on his upraised thigh, looking for all the world as if he'd happened upon a friend in a quiet lane on a summer's day. The lad cowering behind a stack of alder planks looked to be around eighteen years old, his face streaked with tears and sawdust, his sandy hair matted into a squirrel's nest, his blue eyes round and anguished. His lip bled where he gnawed at it, and the boy was thin enough to be a wraith.

Lestrade cursed as we stood aside for the doctor to pass.

"Your name is Arlie, I think," Mr Holmes said with a voice like warm syrup. "I am Mr Sherlock Holmes, and this is my friend, Dr Watson."

"She don't need a doctor no more," the boy replied, almost too thickly to be understood.

"I know she doesn't, but do you think that you might?" Mr Holmes continued. Dr Watson sat unobtrusively on a crate to Arlie's left. "We'd be grateful if you allowed my friend to take your pulse. He's a very good sort and would never dream of harming you."

Arlie was too far gone to protest when Dr Watson slipped his fingers around the lad's wrist. Tears continued to stream from his eyes, his wasted body shaking.

"He's dehydrated, in shock, and in considerable need of food, but otherwise healthy." Pulling a brandy flask from his coat pocket, the doctor offered it. "Take a sip, if you please. That's right! Good man – you'll feel calmer in a moment. You say that your sister needed a doctor but doesn't anymore?" he added, casting a tense glance at Mr Holmes.

Arlie nodded, choked on more tears, and swallowed them back. "All she wanted were to see more'n that back room. For a long spell we managed on our own, but a week ago my sister done showed signs o' the sickness, and I'd nary a choice save hiring meself out for the medicines and tonics. It were too soon for her to be ill, too soon by far. She didn't want to stay in London, in that room, not *forever*."

"Do you mean to say your sister was too weak to leave the house?" Mr Holmes prompted softly.

"Aye." The boy winced. "These ten years she has been, for all the poultices and teas the Wus tried. Me, I done brung all such maps as I could find, and she'd tell me what it were like there, in other lands. Dragons and beasties and tigers ten foot tall. She wanted to see 'em with 'er own eyes. Liza said as the Thames don't look like much, but the Thames can take you anywhere in the world, *anywhere*, and one day we'd sail down it together and see something other than Limehouse. But then she stopped breathing. For *hours*." Racking sobs did violence to the boy's lungs. "I done sent her off to the islands and the deserts like she wanted. Down the Thames, she said. She always said as that were the way to get there. She knew the way. I were careful never to lock the boxes. When she lands, she'll be worlds away from London."

Horror had spread like a plague across our faces, Lestrade standing with a hand over his mouth and Dr Watson and I staring as if somehow the force of our sympathy could undo what had been done. Only Mr Holmes remained impassive, his skin marble-white and his eyes positively metallic.

"Did anyone notice you?" he asked in the same hypnotic tone. "Packing the boxes, or perhaps carrying them?"

"Not I. I went by night down to the river steps."

"Hopkins, run and fetch us a constable," Lestrade commanded with uncharacteristic gruffness.

"No, not on my life," Mr Holmes growled fiercely.

"Can you be serious?" Dr Watson demanded of my senior inspector.

"Now who's theorising in advance of facts?" Lestrade snapped, brushing an angry hand over his face. "Get this Arlie lad to his feet, come with me, and we'll find a cab. Hopkins here is about to report that an abandoned building has been broken into. Aren't you, Hopkins?" he added meaningfully.

"Yes, sir," I answered with some passion.

"What of the bloodied hatchet?" Dr Watson wondered as he and Mr Holmes together helped the distraught youth to stand.

"The family had just killed a hare for supper when they suddenly vanished," I supplied at once. "It's a great mystery as to where they went. I daresay it's possible they left a letter of intent somewhere, however, and I daresay I can bring it to the constable's notice."

"Right, that's settled." Lestrade shook his head in despair. "Lord have mercy. Doctor, can you find him a place?"

"I've a friend with a thriving practice for neurotics in the Kent countryside." Dr Watson sighed. "It'll be temporary, but I'll wire him at once. Arlie, we're taking you to our home in Baker Street where you'll have a bath and a warm meal, all right?"

Arlie made no sound, but leaned on the doctor and nodded his tangled head.

"Good," Lestrade approved. "Gentlemen, are we all in complete agreement?"

After a pause, Mr Holmes said, "Poe referred to the Thames as the River of Silence. Ever since reading that, I've thought of it so."

"Very well," said my fellow Yarder. "Let no more words be spoken on the subject, then. *Ever.* Inspector Hopkins, I regret to say that your first case remains unsolved."

So my first case was a failure twice over, and I am glad of it.

It was the right thing to do. It was the only thing to do, and the best thing to do.

Yet my heart has been tugged in so many directions today that it feels quite unravelled, loosened sinews and arteries now doing their utmost to weave themselves back together again inside my chest.

Letter sent from Inspector Stanley Michael Hopkins to Mrs Leticia Elizabeth Hopkins, Saturday May 5th, 1894

Dearest Mum,

My first case, once so bright in its promise of removing a villain from our streets, turns out to be the basest of hoaxes. A rogue medical student was guilty of chopping a body into seven parts and setting them adrift. Women of your constitution don't shirk at such macabre news, yet I loathe telling you, for it means after all that there is nothing of importance to relate. I am nonetheless weary for this having turned out to be a prank, however, and so will write you properly tomorrow or the next day. The bubble and squeak turns out to travel *very well indeed* in wax paper, and will serve as my breakfast.

Exhausted but hale,
Your Stanley

Entry in the diary of Stanley Michael Hopkins, Tuesday October 9th, 1894

Six months after the business of the false Chinese box, three cases total logged working with the incomparable Sherlock Holmes (and the estimable Dr Watson), and today I received the shock of my life when he arrived at the Yard with fresh evidence for Inspector Bradstreet. Mr Holmes never vacillates once a course is set, sails ahead like a schooner with an aquiline prow. But he paused before my alcove as if he'd expected to find me there.

"A word when I'm through, if you please, Inspector Hopkins," he decreed, whisking off without awaiting a reply.

I'd no notion of whether to feel excitement or anxiety and settled on a queasy combination by default. Meanwhile, I had need of a case file and thought a brief dash to the archives might settle me. It would have worked, too, had Sherlock Holmes not been seated in my chair when I returned, his fingers steepled and his stork's legs crossed in front of him. Greeting him as cheerily as I could, I dropped the papers and leaned against my cubby's dividing wall.

"Can I help, Mr Holmes?"

Inspecting me with hooded grey eyes, the detective considered. "That depends entirely upon your response to a query of mine. Three possible outcomes present themselves. Either you'll give me a satisfactory answer, an unsatisfactory answer, or you'll refuse to answer altogether, as I've no right to wonder what I've been wondering of late."

"You may ask me anything, Mr Holmes."

"In that case, I wonder that you didn't try for another profession," he observed idly.

"By George, I don't... why... what do you mean by that, sir?" The effort not to appear slighted was excruciating.

"Dear me, no, put the thought from your head. You've a natural talent for police work." Mr Holmes made a lazy figure eight of dismissal with his forefinger. "It's the income, you see. Detection doesn't pay the official Force well, not when they're honest, which you are, and rewards are rare – maybe more so than you'd hoped. You could easily have been a City clerk with your acumen and risen accordingly, but instead you live week to week, probably because you are forced to support someone who is not in your immediate family but is nevertheless dear to you, following a tragedy which affected that person gravely."

Someone who's never spoken with Mr Holmes might think they'd anticipate his omniscience, maybe even expect he's about to throw open the curtains of their lives and survey the mess in broad daylight. Well, I record it here for posterity: no one save Dr Watson himself fares any better than I did.

"Heavens, lad, sit down!" Mr Holmes tugged me towards my own chair, pivoting so his lean body rested against my desk. "Upon my word, I didn't imagine you'd react so strongly. The brandy flask I once observed in your top left drawer —"

"No, thank you." I chuckled weakly as Sherlock Holmes of Baker Street offered me both my own chair and my own brandy. "I'm surprised at myself. Forgive me."

"Pray don't ask such a thing. It's hardly the first time I've staggered a stout fellow. Recently, at that." He glanced away, an unreadable look briefly warping his perfect suavity. "I did you a disservice. Let us abandon the topic in favour of —"

"Not a bit of it!" I exclaimed, recovering. "Now you explain how you knew. I shall catalogue every detail."

Mr Holmes did not smile, but his wintry eyes warmed. "There were a number of small indications, so many that I must take a moment to sort them. Yes, first I noted that the button on your left ulster sleeve is cheaper than that on the right, and mended in a slipshod fashion by a man unversed in the art of tailoring. Clearly, that man is you, and while you are impeccably neat in appearance, you neither bothered to match the expense of your lost button, which was made of polished horn like its brethren, nor to match the thread colour, using instead whatever you had to hand. That you are a bachelor would have been obvious from your hat brim, but your financial straits speak more clearly through your buttonhole."

"I'll have to be more meticulous in future. Why need there have been a tragedy?"

Mr Holmes jutted his bold chin at my torso as he lit a cigarette. "Your watch chain is an old family heirloom, but the type of locket hanging from it with the scalloped edge was in fashion some five years ago, before I met my untimely demise."

"Thankfully very untimely indeed."

"Your servant. The locket is a memento, and five years is approximately the amount of time it takes to lose a well-sewn button and for one's hat colour to pass out of style. No offence intended."

I shrugged. "None taken. So I have financial problems, and you say they point to a tragedy. Supposing I merely had onerous debts?"

"You'd have pawned the locket or the watch chain or simply the watch to ease your path."

"What if they were all too dear to me?"

"After having gifted your beloved late father's Bible to a cousin? Please. You aren't a man driven by foolish sentiment, and your high expenses haunt you monthly, which is why you know better than to squander your keepsakes at a jerryshop. Economy is the only solution. Your mother posts you dinner, for heaven's sake, or at least so the writing on your many savoury-smelling packages indicates. No, don't ask, it's too obvious and I've glimpsed the addresses – you write a male version of her penmanship."

Despite my distress, I smiled ruefully. "The tragically afflicted – you said not a family member? It might be my sister."

"If your sister were impoverished or afflicted, she would live with you and reattach your buttons, or live with your mother and eat her mince pies," Mr Holmes said so smoothly that his tone might nearly have been called kind.

"Quite so." I cleared my throat. "Mr Holmes, what is this about?"

Sherlock Holmes's head swivelled to regard me fully, a bird of prey ruminating over a hapless mammal.

"You joined H Division at the age of twenty-five in the immediate wake of the Ripper murders," he said with clinical detachment. "Why? Men spat at the uniformed constables in the streets, women refused to look at them. I was acquainted with canines that wouldn't so much as bark in a bobby's direction. You are intelligent, active, and approachable, and even if you'd no desire to be a clergyman, the world was still your oyster, and you chose to join an institution that had been hung out to dry. Pray refrain from telling me it was all thanks to *The Strand*, though the doctor has every right to be flattered *some* good has come out of his melodramas. There is another, darker reason, and if I am to rely upon your sober judgement, as I wish to do in future, I request you tell me what it is."

Despite my reluctance to reveal the source of my heartache, there is nothing quite so persuasive as Sherlock Holmes urging a man to prove himself trustworthy. I straightened my shoulders, tugged down my waistcoat, and set to.

"I was engaged to be married in eighteen eighty-eight to a Miss Lilla Dunton. She was – is – a woman of finest character, and I'd known her if only peripherally since childhood. The suburbs in southeast London aren't populous, Mr Holmes, and she attended my father's congregation. I regret to say that her family life was not a happy one. Her father was born in West Africa to colonial parents and saw much hatred and degradation along the Gold Coast and as a young man in Freetown.

"Mr Dunton told Lilla tales, even as a little girl, which invested her with waking nightmares, and as her mother died in childbirth, there was no one at home to offset this morbidity save a doddering old nurse. When the Ripper crimes commenced, she was merely appalled, as we all were, but when they continued… she was reminded of brutal stories she never imagined would be brought to life here in England. Tribal massacres, soldiers ruthlessly quashing native unrest. By the time Mary Jane Kelly was left in shreds," I finished hoarsely, "her mind was in a similar state."

It's obvious from Dr Watson's writing that Mr Holmes can be affected by misfortune and grief – dashed if I hadn't already seen it myself, when we encountered Arlie in Limehouse. On this occasion, his iron expression did not harden so much as it melted before snapping back into that perfect equilibrium he so famously maintains.

"My dear fellow. What steps did you take?" he asked softly.

"She lives at an asylum in the Sussex countryside – a humane and peaceable one, much lauded by both locals and professionals. The expense is… significant. My locket containing a miniature silhouette is all I have left of her, though I often dream she'll write me one day. Despite our geographical proximity, during our engagement we used to exchange love letters absurdly often. I'd still give anything to see her handwriting in my post. Meanwhile, I promised myself I'd do everything possible to prevent such a monster from ever desecrating our streets again."

"You may yet hear from her," he observed as if making a remark about the weather.

My answering smile was one of thanks and not joy. "That's past praying for, I fear, Mr Holmes. Highly improbable."

"But not impossible." The sleuth stood fully, gathering up the hat and gloves he had laid upon my desk. "Thank you for the candour of your reply. Inspector Hopkins, I intend to make a detective of you."

"I... just a moment, you..." I trailed off, reduced again to a blithering neophyte, as appears to be my natural state when in the presence of Sherlock Holmes.

"One cannot help but agree that you would make an execrable clergyman, and so we must see what we can do about making you a crack investigator." He winked, and for the first time I was granted a glimpse of the impish humour Dr Watson had so often recorded in early adventures.

"Do you really mean it?" I whispered in awe. "You'll share your methods, allow me to ask questions, that sort of thing?"

"I'll teach you the whole art of detection myself, only supposing you don't mistake wheelbarrow tracks for bicycle tracks again as you did last —"

The unfortunate Mr Holmes was interrupted, for I was wringing his hand so hard he must have been in some pain.

"All right, all *right*," he gasped, laughing. "I ask a single favour in return, mind."

"Name it, please," I urged, half delirious with happiness. "Anything you like. I am yours to command. I was before, anyhow."

"The name of this bucolic hospital in Sussex. Tut, tut!

This is not about your former fiancée, whose health I hope improves by the hour – I've been struck by a sudden inspiration, one the doctor will enjoy tremendously, and keeping Watson in good spirits has direct bearing upon the quality of my living arrangements."

Deeply puzzled, I wrote down the address. "It has nothing to do with me, then?"

"I did not say that either," Mr Holmes chided, declining to meet my questioning eyes as he tapped his cigarette out against his boot sole and then flicked it into my rubbish bin. He took the paper with a flourish. "Good day, Hopkins. Until you have need of me."

Dunce that I am, it took me all evening to work it out. What an ass I've been, and what a worthy hero I've chosen to guide me on my chosen path. As mired in penury as Mr Holmes and Dr Watson were in *A Study in Scarlet*, now they are internationally celebrated and sought after – and wealthy to boot.

Of course his asking after the asylum had nothing to do with my poor, precious Lilla.

It had everything to do with Arlie, however.

Telegram from SCOTLAND YARD, WHITEHALL to BEXLEY, Tuesday October 9th, 1894

```
INCREDIBLE NEWS STOP AM TO TUTOR WITH THE
GREAT DETECTIVE SHERLOCK HOLMES STOP WHO
KNOWS BUT THAT YOUR BOY MIGHT NOT FIND
HIMSELF IN THE STRAND ONE DAY STOP WILL
BE HOME FOR SUPPER TOMORROW WITH CHAMPAGNE
                              - STANLEY
```

PURE SWANK

James Lovegrove

The character of **Barker**, Sherlock Holmes's "hated rival on the Surrey shore", appears in only one Conan Doyle story, "The Adventure of the Retired Colourman". He is also a private detective and happens to be investigating the same mystery as Holmes. Their paths cross, and they set aside their differences and agree to work on the case together. Barker cuts such a striking figure in the tale, from his military bearing to his heavy moustaches to his grey-tinted sunglasses, that there is clearly a great deal more to him than meets the eye, and I felt it would be fun to fill in some of the background detail. What sort of man would have the temerity to set himself up as a consulting detective while Sherlock Holmes is around? Why does Holmes consider him a rival, and a hated one at that? Are there greater depths to their relationship than Watson knows (or is letting on)? When I was asked to contribute to this anthology, Barker was the first "associate" that sprang to mind, and my questions about him started swirling and coalescing in my mind. I envisaged an antagonism much like that between Mozart and Salieri in Peter Shaffer's *Amadeus*, the bonafide genius and the pretender to his crown, and the story just unfurled from there.

—James Lovegrove

S ome day the true story may be told.

How I laughed when I read those words in the latest edition of *The Strand* this morning, and it was a laugh that was scornful and knowing in equal measure. The esteemed Dr Watson, ever the diligent chronicler of the adventures of Mr Sherlock Holmes, has once again set down in print the full facts of a case solved by his remarkable colleague. Yet, in his slavish conviction that nothing Holmes does or says is incorrect, that his long-time friend is infallible, Watson cannot have dreamed that, far from telling the "true story", he has told only half of it.

Hence I, Clarence Barker, have taken up my pen in order to convey my own account of the same events, one that is accurate in every part. I do not intend to copy Watson's example and submit this manuscript for publication in a journal with a national readership. That would be a grave mistake. These words are for my eyes only. As I enter my fifty-sixth year, with my faculties dimming daily, this is perhaps a confession, perhaps also a settling of scores, but perhaps most of all an attempt to enshrine a reminiscence before it slips entirely from my memory. By this means I may, as it were, pin the episode in place like a mounted butterfly, so that I can later and at my leisure admire its beauty.

The just-published tale to which I am alluding is one that Dr Watson has entitled "The Adventure of the Retired Colourman". It recounts a crime that took place nearly three decades ago, back in 1899, and which caused a scandal and gave rise to many a prurient, melodramatic headline but has since faded into obscurity – at least until now, when Watson has decided to exhume it from his notebooks and dish it up for public consumption. I have already received some telephone calls today from friends and acquaintances wondering whether I am the Barker referred to in the story. Anyone who knows of my past as a consulting detective may be able to infer that I am indeed he whom Holmes is seen disparaging as his "hated rival upon the Surrey shore" but none the less collaborates with quite readily in order to resolve the mystery. The deduction is, for want of a better word, elementary.

I do not feel that I emerge too badly from my portrayal in "The Retired Colourman". I am described as "tall, dark, heavily-moustachioed, military-looking", none of which I can gainsay. Thirty years ago I did favour luxuriant facial hair, in the fashion of the day, and prior to that I did see service in the Lancashire Fusiliers during the late 1880s which bestowed upon me the straight back and square shoulders of an infantryman. "Stern-looking" and "impassive" are other epithets Watson applies to me, neither of them uncomplimentary, and he notes my grey-tinted sunglasses, an item of apparel I still wear, not through vanity or to correct any defect in my visual acuity but to ameliorate a sensitivity to bright light which has afflicted me most of my adult life.

There is more to me, however. What Watson was oblivious to, although it is hinted at very heavily by his friend in the story, is that I was formerly a member of that band of young ragamuffins whom Holmes used to employ as spies and errand runners in London. "His methods are irregular, no doubt," Holmes says to Inspector MacKinnon at the dénouement of the case. "The irregulars are useful sometimes, you know." He could hardly have been more explicit, could he? And, for that matter, how else could he have commanded my loyalty and complicity so easily – "… as to Barker, he has done nothing save what I told him" – had we not already had an established relationship as employer and employee?

I remember well the sixpences and half-crowns with which he would reward us Irregulars for services rendered. They made all the difference to a poor, homeless, famished orphan such as myself. Sometimes they were the only thing that stood between me and the workhouse. I remember how I and Wiggins, the leader of our merry gang, would sprint from Baker Street to the nearest bakery with our gainfully-gotten bounty and stuff our bellies with Chelsea buns until we felt sick. Moments of bliss in an otherwise miserable existence.

As an Irregular I grew to love and admire Mr Holmes. He was abrupt with us, stern, sometimes even harsh, but you never once doubted that he was on the side of the angels and therefore, by extension, we were too. I came to regard him as the father I never knew.

It was he who, when I reached my majority, advised me to join the army. "They are looking for young men such as you, Barker," he said. "Stalwart, well-built, with a natural intelligence and aptitude, capable of following an order. A spell taking Her Majesty's shilling could be the making of you."

In a way it was. I enjoyed the physicality and uncom-plicatedness of military life, and I could cope with the deprivations easily. I had grown up accustomed to hardship and become inured to it. Camp beds and mess rations were luxury compared with the bare floorboards and meagre snatched meals of my youth. Further, I was given the opportunity to learn to read and write, which I seized with both hands. I gained an erudition and a vocabulary that belie my humble, deprived origins. No, I did well by the army, and I think the army did well by me.

I was stationed in India for a time – the Nicobar Islands. The heat was lethal, the natives only a little less so. There was the penal colony at Port Blair to keep an eye on. There were mosquitoes that ate you alive and stomach ailments that hollowed you from the inside out. Worst of all there were the Sentinelese, savage Andaman Islanders who arrived at regular intervals in canoe-borne raiding parties to give us merry hell.

What I recall most, though, is the hour upon hour of guard duty, standing watch in the relentless, glaring tropical sun. It is to this that I ascribe the problems with my eyes. Those ferociously bright rays, reflecting off the ocean, seared and scarred my retinas. Only sunglasses brought relief.

I discharged myself from the Lancashires in 1892, whereupon I set about pursuing my true ambition, the vocation that I had had a hankering to follow ever since my stint as an Irregular under Holmes. I wished to be a consulting detective, like him. I wished to emulate his exploits and gain some of the wealth and celebrity he had accrued.

It came as a surprise when I returned to England to discover that Sherlock Holmes was dead. News of his demise had not reached us in our far-flung outpost of the Raj. He had perished the previous year in a life-and-death tussle with the arch-criminal Professor Moriarty in Switzerland.

I was shocked. I had harboured the hope that Holmes would at least mentor me in the early stages of my career, or even engage me as an apprentice.

Yet I saw it also as a sign. Holmes was gone. There was a vacuum left by his absence. Who better than I to fill it?

Using what scant savings I had accumulated from my army pay, I set up a practice south of the river in one of the cheaper corners of Brixton. The first few months were dismal. I had barely a trickle of clients, and none of them were what one might call illustrious, and certainly none of them had deep pockets.

I persevered, however, and built up a reputation, and gradually more work came my way. I took it upon myself to join the Freemasons, and it was a productive move. Through the Brotherhood I broadened my social circle. Fellow members of my Lodge, the Camberwell, came to consult me on matters that bedevilled them, and I was recommended by them to members of other Lodges, and thus my renown spread through the tendrils of that not so secret society.

It was thanks to a Mark Master Mason of the Supreme Order of the Holy Royal Arch, no less, that I was brought in to investigate the notorious Park Lane Mystery. This was, of course, the murder of the Honourable Ronald Adair, who was found dead in his home on the aforementioned thoroughfare, shot in his second-floor sitting room. The door to the room was fastened on the inside. No gun was discovered anywhere on the premises. It was all perfectly baffling.

Adair had belonged to the Grand Temple, like the gentleman who engaged me. I took it as a personal mission to unmask his killer, in a spirit of Masonic solidarity. And it was in the execution of this quest that I first came to the notice of Dr Watson and cropped up in one of his tales. The irony is that he did not realise who I was.

The story in question is "The Empty House", and any alert follower of Watson's writings will recall his mention of "a tall, thin man with coloured glasses, whom I strongly suspected of being a plain-clothes detective". Watson overheard me, amid the crowd that had gathered outside Adair's house, delivering my theory about the murder to those around me. He does not vouchsafe what that theory was, and I cannot myself recall it exactly, but I believe it involved a rigged gasogene, primed to fire a bullet into the head of the first person who used it to add soda to their whisky.

The real answer – an air-gun – eluded me at the time. I had not yet been able to view the crime scene and was merely giving vent to informed speculation. I would doubtless have come to the correct conclusion had I been given the liberty to inspect the sitting room and its environs for myself, but a wiser, better man than I got there first and the mystery was cleared up before I could even begin work on it.

Why did Dr Watson not recognise me as an erstwhile Irregular? For the same reason he did not recognise me four years later when he encountered me outside Josiah Amberley's house in Lewisham, as recounted in "The Adventure of the Retired Colourman". As a boy I had been just one of a dozen scruffy, smudge-faced urchins who passed through the door of 221B Baker Street. He probably had not even known my name. I was merely an Irregular, anonymous, part of a horde. Also, I had grown considerably since, my features lengthening and hardening with the onset of adulthood, although still retaining their slightly swarthy cast. I believe my father, whoever he was, must have come from the Levant or North Africa. Perhaps he was a sailor passing through Tilbury, who used his shore leave profitably and departed never knowing he had conceived a son whose mother neither wanted offspring nor cared for the one who arrived nine months later.

At any rate, it was Sherlock Holmes who inferred that Adair's murderer had shot him from afar with an air-gun loaded with expanding bullets. The culprit, moreover, was Professor Moriarty's own henchman, that old shikari Colonel Sebastian Moran, whom Adair had accused, not without justification, of cheating at cards. I did not know any of this back then, and neither did anyone else, for Dr Watson did not see fit to publish "The Empty House" until 1903.

What mattered most, however, was that Holmes was alive! He had not died in that lonely spot on a Swiss mountainside. He had survived his struggle with Moriarty and was back to re-assume his crown as the country's foremost consulting detective.

This turn of events – Holmes's reappearance – left me in a quandary. I realised I would only ever be second best, now that he was back. Who would go to Clarence Barker when the great Sherlock Holmes was once again available? I wondered whether I should carry on regardless, tenaciously ploughing my furrow, or present myself to Holmes and suggest we set ourselves up in a partnership.

I opted for the latter. I plucked up my nerve and paid a call on him in his rooms at Baker Street. How small and cramped and cluttered the place seemed to me then, as I returned to it some half-dozen years after my last visit.

To my boyish eyes it had been a sprawling wonderland of books, chemistry apparatus, knickknacks and oddments. Now it was like some queer museum of intellect, admirable but stuffy, bewildering in its chaotic disarray. Holmes's landlady Mrs Hudson had not allowed his lodgings to be let during his three-year absence. She had kept the place untouched and undisturbed, almost as a shrine. Perhaps, through some preternatural womanly instinct, she had known he was not really dead. Or could it be that she was privy all along to the fact that he was alive, as was his brother? She must at least have wondered why Mycroft Holmes continued to pay the rent on the rooms.

Holmes greeted me warmly enough. He was alone, Watson elsewhere. He performed his customary trick of evaluating details of my recent past from my appearance and attire. He was spot-on in his assessments as always. He was even aware that I was now pursuing the same line of work as he.

"I do not mind another detective in my orbit," said he as we smoked a pipe together. "London is a vast, populous city. There is surely room for two of us. There will be plenty of clients to go round."

"Indubitably," I said.

He must have registered a hesitation in my voice, for he then said, "But that is not the reason for your visit, pleasant though it is for the two of us to catch up and compare notes. You are wishing to propose an alliance, are you not? A merging of the streams. Holmes and Barker, Consulting Detectives, no?"

"Astute as ever, sir. It would seem sensible. Where one man can achieve great things, two together can achieve still greater."

"Out of the question." This was accompanied by an airily dismissive flap of the hand.

"You will not even consider the idea?"

"I already have a partner, Barker. You may have heard of him. Name of John Watson. Physician, ex-serviceman, courageous, trustworthy."

"Yes, but with all due respect, Holmes, Dr Watson is not a peer. He is your scribe. Your amanuensis. He trots at your heel as faithfully and eagerly as any dog. You snap at him, you belittle him, you mock him openly, yet his obedience to you remains undimmed. By all means he should remain at hand, taking notes about your exploits to turn into reading fodder for the masses. But I could be more useful than him by far. I could be a sounding-board, an accomplice to share ideas with, a chess player of near equal skill with whom you may hone the excellence of your own game."

"Excellence at chess," said Holmes, "is one mark of a scheming mind."

"It was merely a metaphor. You are rejecting my overtures outright, then, I take it. That is your final judgement on the matter."

"Watson is all I need or could ask for in a cohort, Barker. I do not require any other. I nonetheless wish you luck in your career. May you flourish to the best of your abilities. May you prosper to the extent that you deserve."

To anyone else's ears it would have sounded like encouragement, but I could read between the lines. Holmes was exhorting me to accept my limited prospects. He was telling me the scraps from his table were mine to scoop up and devour. He was consigning me to the fate of forever living in his shadow. London would lavish its acclaim on one consulting detective – and it would not be me.

* * *

That settled it. I resolved there and then to stick at the job. I would take whatever cases I was offered. I would not be proud. I would be content even if any clients came to me and said they had chosen me because Mr Holmes had refused to help them; or Mr Holmes charged too much; or Mr Holmes was too busy to accommodate them; or they simply did not like the cut of Mr Holmes's jib.

Over the next few years, dozens of clients turned up at my door saying just that. Many even told me that Holmes had evinced no interest in their problem but had referred them to me with the suggestion that I, being more modest in my outlook and accomplishments, might be of avail. I do not know if he used that precise verbal formulation, but it certainly seemed to be implied. I had called Dr Watson a dog, but I was the dog now, the abandoned stray to whom Holmes threw a bone every now and then.

My respect for him abated further, curdling little by little into resentment. He, meanwhile, went from strength to strength. To his door travelled nobles and royals and industrialists and the landed gentry, presenting him with their concerns and conundrums, some outré, some involving affairs of state, some with consequences that reached far beyond Britain's borders, none tawdry or lacking in depth. To my door, by contrast, came the dregs, with their lost baubles and missing pets and gossipy concerns about neighbours and grievances about embezzling employees. It was more than galling. But it was a living.

His "hated rival upon the Surrey shore" indeed! Such airs and graces. Trying to imply that between us there was a mutual antipathy, when all too obviously the hatred went one way: I loathed him, he was indifferent to me. He was trying to convey that he somehow regarded me as an equal, a threat to his position, a pretender to the throne, when he and I both knew I was not and never could be.

My Masonic brethren kept me supplied with a few cases of sufficient merit and intrigue that I did not completely succumb to despair and become eaten away by envy. Every so often I performed what I considered a sterling piece of deduction. For example, the time I identified a sign-writer as a blackmailer through his use of stencils in his demands for payment, and the time I ascertained that a draper was the one who had stolen certain legal deeds thanks to the saw-tooth pattern of the pinking shears with which he cut through the ribbon of a portfolio. These were victories but, next to Holmes's, pale ones. Still, they instilled in me enough gratitude to my fellow Masons that I took to wearing a tie-pin with the set square and compasses on it as a symbol of pride.

Dr Ray Ernest was a Mason too. We ran into one another by chance one evening in a West End pub. My tie-pin announced to him our shared affiliation. A handshake – forefinger applying pressure to a certain of the other's knuckles – sealed our bond. We were both "on the square". We both paid homage to Hiram Abiff, the Widow's Son. We had that instant commonality and camaraderie.

We talked. We drank. Then Dr Ernest happened to mention casually that he had of late entered into a friendship with a certain Josiah Amberley, a retired manufacturer of artistic materials, junior partner of the Brickfall and Amberley brand. In his early sixties, Amberley had taken up with a spinster some twenty years younger than him, and married her. She was a comely woman, Dr Ernest said, and too good for Amberley, who was a tyrant and a miser, niggardly both with his affections and his money, despite having ample of the latter.

Amberley did not deserve the woman, that was the long and the short of it. Ernest did. Moreover, he desired her and she him.

He confided this intelligence to me when we were both fairly inebriated. I proposed, only half in jest, that he should do something about the situation. Woo Mrs Amberley, gain her trust, then elope with her. In addition, he should inflict some other punishment on Amberley. He should not be content with simply absconding with the man's wife. He should hit him where it really hurt.

I do not know what motivated me to say all this. The devil may have got into me. The drink undoubtedly had.

Ernest, for his part, alighted on my suggestion with delight. "Capital idea!" he declared. "Being cuckolded is something Amberley might well recover from. The shame and ignominy would pass. But he would never get over the loss of that which is truly dear to him, his money."

I left it to Ernest to concoct a method for depriving Amberley of the competence that was keeping him so comfortable. Ernest was a chess player. It was a hobby he and Amberley shared and the mortar that bound their friendship together. And what was it Holmes said about excellence at chess? I could tell Ernest had a scheming mind. He was, too, just unscrupulous enough to get whatever he set his cap at, however immoral the means or the goal.

I was keen to get my hands on some of that money myself, though, so I volunteered to aid Ernest in his undertaking by cunningly deflecting any suspicion of guilt away from him. This I would do by offering myself to Amberley to investigate the theft and, through misdirection and misguidance, steering him onto a wholly erroneous path. When I was done with him, Amberley would believe his wife and her beau to be innocent of the crime. I would use my wiles and whatever evidence presented itself to pin the blame on, say, some hapless vagrant or a passing Lascar. In return, I would expect a cut of the proceeds.

Ernest agreed. We haggled but settled on a two-to-one ratio. I would get one third of whatever he managed to steal. He and Mrs Amberley would keep the rest.

The compact was sealed. The wheels were set in motion. Ray Ernest and I had become, in one fell swoop, a mirror image of Sherlock Holmes and John Watson – a detective and his medical confederate whose aims were not noble and benevolent but dark and illicit.

A week passed.

Then I learned that both Ernest and Mrs Amberley had vanished, and with them a large proportion of Josiah Amberley's pension fund.

At first I was outraged. I knew just what had happened. I had been double-crossed. I had been betrayed. The pair of them had taken off with Amberley's money and decided to keep it all for themselves. I had been cut out of the deal. Masonic solidarity clearly meant nothing to the treacherous wretch Ernest.

Perhaps I ought to have anticipated that Ernest would stab me in the back. He was, after all, a man to whom the fundamental tenet of his Hippocratic Oath – "First do no harm" – did not extend to his private life. How could I have trusted someone so patently ruthless?

I went to Ernest's home and his surgical practice as well, but he was to be found at neither. His housekeeper and his receptionist had seen neither hide nor hair of him for several days and professed themselves baffled and concerned.

Clearly, then, he had gone to ground elsewhere, along with his paramour, and would not be showing his face publicly any time soon.

So, out of desperation more than anything, I started staking out the Haven, Amberley's house in Lewisham. The criminal sometimes returns to the scene of the crime, does he not? I reasoned that Ernest at least might pass by the property at some point, if only to gloat. Failing that, I might be able to insinuate myself into Amberley's life and learn more about the circumstances of the theft and possibly glean some insight into the whereabouts of the guilty parties.

That was how I became apprised of Holmes's involvement in the affair. I saw Dr Watson arrive at the Haven – an incongruously grand edifice, set in its own grounds yet surrounded by humble suburban terraces – and enter via the gateway. He spotted me but, of course, had no idea who I was or what my purpose was for being there. He did not even correlate me with the fellow he had seen on Park Lane less than half a decade ago. How can Sherlock Holmes ever have borne the company of such a plodding, unobservant clod? It is almost as though Holmes enjoyed having someone present that he could look down on from his lofty intellectual height; and the duller-witted that person was, the more superior he might feel to him. That would surely be why he had not wanted me as a partner. He could not view me with quite the same Olympian disdain as he did Watson.

Having watched Watson go into Amberley's house and then an hour or so later leave, I was led to intuit that there was more going on here than met the eye. I went away and did some surreptitious asking around. I spoke to various police contacts at my Lodge. It soon became apparent that Amberley was not the tragic dupe he seemed. Something sinister was afoot.

While I was attempting to discern what that something sinister might be, who should I run into but Sherlock Holmes? I had returned to Lewisham and, having ascertained that Amberley was out, was contemplating the best means of breaking into his house in order to look for clues. As I crossed the unkempt, overgrown garden, I saw to my startlement that someone else had had the same idea. A man was crawling out of a ground-floor window.

Amusingly, I did not realise who it was at first. His face was hidden from me, and I took him to be a common-or-garden cracksman. I seized him by the collar while he was still halfway through the window and yelled, "Now, you rascal, what are you doing in there?"

There followed a scuffle, in which Holmes managed to turn the tables and get the better of me, depositing me prone on the lawn in an arm lock. Him and his deuced *baritsu*. Underhand tactics, if you ask me, using an Oriental martial art. What's wrong with a man's own strength and good old-fashioned fisticuffs?

Be that as it may, once he saw who I was, he released me and we dusted ourselves down and had a good laugh. Two detectives independently investigating the same case – or such was the situation as far as Holmes was aware – and we were battling each other like a pair of rogues. Absurd!

"How about this?" Holmes said. "Why not forge a temporary alliance? Two heads are better than one, as the saying goes. I do not necessarily ascribe to that principle, but on this one occasion it might pertain. Let us pool our resources and work together."

I should have said no, but in all honesty how could I? Although I had come to nurse a deep-seated grudge towards this man, he remained my boyhood benefactor, my exemplar, even my hero. Here he was, offering to conduct an investigation side by side with me. It was, in many ways, a dream come true. If only for a while, we would be Holmes and Barker, Consulting Detectives after all. A fusion of talents. Greatness squared.

Saying yes to his proposal would also deflect any hint of suspicion away from me, for Holmes gave no sign of perceiving my true motives for being at the Haven. His assumption that I had come there in the course of my enquiries would only be reinforced if I consented to co-operate with him. It would have been out of character, and risk arousing his curiosity, were I to have refused.

Josiah Amberley, Holmes confided to me, was not a victim. He was the perpetrator of a heinous crime. It was as plain as the nose on your face.

"It is?" I said, thinking that for a man with a nose as prominent as Holmes's, everything must be plain.

"It most certainly is."

He reeled off the facts he had unearthed about the case. There was the Haven's strong-room, where Amberley kept his cash and securities. There was the malodorous green paint Amberley had been using to carry out some redecoration. There were the peculiar pair of words written in purple indelible pencil just above the skirting: "We we". Most of all there were the tickets for two upper circle seats at the Haymarket Theatre, one of which Amberley had presented to Watson as his alibi for the night Dr Ernest and Mrs Amberley went missing. It transpired that neither seat had been occupied during the performance, according to the theatre's box-office chart.

I must have still looked perplexed, for Holmes said, "Tut, man! Think about it. Consider the data. Data, data, data. What does it all add up to? You style yourself a detective. You have studied my methods. Apply them."

I did. "The strong-room, you say, has an iron door and window shutters. It is all but hermetically sealed. That is suggestive."

"Suggestive at the very least."

"As for the paint, its smell may have been intended to disguise another smell."

"May have been, Barker? Was!"

"A smell such as that of gas."

"A-ha! Very much so."

"He killed them – Dr Ernest and Mrs Amberley. He gassed them to death in the strong-room."

"But how?" said Holmes. "How did he manage it?"

"Do you not know?"

"I have an inkling, but tell me your thoughts."

"Well, I imagine he set the jet for a lamp going, without lighting it. Then he inveigled the two of them into the room on some pretext and slammed the door on them. Unable to escape, they would have asphyxiated within minutes."

"My interpretation precisely, Barker. And the 'We we'?"

"I cannot but think that it was scribbled by one or other of the doomed couple as they lay gasping their last on the strong-room floor. It represents a desperate last-ditch attempt to leave a clue for anyone who might inspect the room looking for signs of foul play. The first 'we' is an abortive attempt to write a sentence. The second 'we' likewise met with failure."

"Or," said Holmes, "the second 'we' is part of a new word, which was left unfinished: 'were'."

"As in 'We were here'. 'We were innocent'."

"Or 'We were murdered'."

"That seems plausible," I said, nodding, even as a slight chill ran through me. "And if Amberley was not at the theatre as he maintains..."

"Then his alibi crumbles like a sandcastle before the incoming tide," said Holmes. "He may be diabolical, but he is not as clever as he thinks he is. We have him. All that remains is for us to extract a confession out of him. Would you, pray, care to assist me with that?"

"Holmes," I said, "I should like nothing better."

It seemed I would not be getting the portion of Amberley's worldly wealth that I had been hoping for. That was a source of great regret. I would, however, be on hand to see a double murderer brought to justice and play a significant role in his apprehension. The glory would be an almost adequate substitute for the money.

Events played out more or less as Watson has described in the closing passages of "The Adventure of the Retired Colourman". Amberley attempted suicide by poison pellet when Holmes confronted him with an accusation of murder. Holmes's extraordinarily swift reflexes prevented him from cheating the hangman's noose, and together we wrestled that great brawling brute of a man to the floor, subdued and secured him. Inspector MacKinnon took him into custody. In all, it was a satisfactory conclusion to the proceedings.

Save in one respect.

There was still the question of where the money and securities had gone. If they were not in the strong-room, where were they? Dr Ernest and Mrs Amberley had, obviously, not made off with them. Their bodies were revealed to have been buried in the garden of the Haven, down a disused well whose opening was concealed by a dog-kennel. In the breast pocket of Ernest's jacket was a purple indelible pencil. One can only presume Amberley tucked it there after finding it on the strong-room floor and failing to spy the truncated message Ernest had scrawled with it on the skirting.

Holmes submitted that Amberley must have hidden the cash and documents elsewhere in the house, in a safe place, as part of his scheme to frame the adulterous couple as thieves and throw the police off the scent. Accordingly, constables searched the Haven the following day and found a bureau with a secret drawer capacious enough to hold all those papers and sheaves of pound notes. The drawer, however, proved to be empty, and although they continued to comb the house from attic to cellar, they discovered no other suitable potential location.

Amberley himself refused to divulge where he had concealed the items. Throughout his trial, all the way to his appointment with the scaffold, he kept the secret. I think that, even to the bitter end, he felt there was a remote chance he would escape justice. He anticipated that he might somehow receive a custodial sentence instead of a capital one, on grounds of diminished responsibility perhaps, the balance of his mind disturbed by jealousy, that sort of thing. He might even − for all that it was an almost impossibly unlikely outcome − be exonerated.

He was not. Amberley went to his grave knowing that the bulk of his competence was not where he had stowed it but believing that it was still recoverable should he ever be set free. The cash might be forfeit but the bonds would be impossible to sell through any legitimate outlet and would fetch a tiny fraction of their worth on the black market. Even if they were disposed of somehow, it would not be beyond the bounds of feasibility to track them down and through them trace a path back to the original seller, the thief.

This, I am sure, was his logic. In his imagined future, where he was released at some stage to resume life as a free citizen, Josiah Amberley would hunt down the individual who had raided the bureau and its secret drawer and exact a terrible vengeance upon him.

That I am sitting here writing down these words is proof, if proof were needed, that Amberley did not get to fulfil his desire. He was hanged that autumn, after a trial in which the jury took no more than ten minutes to return a guilty verdict. He never knew who it was that had made off with his fortune.

The securities that I extricated from the bureau, I burned. I could not take the chance of them being found in my possession, and trying to sell them posed an even greater risk.

As for the few thousand pounds, I eked it out and made the most of it. I spent it carefully and judiciously, little by little, a bit here, a bit there, using it to prop up my finances during lean times when business was not good. I was not rash with it. I did not make any extravagant or ostentatious purchases, lest this alert someone – specifically Sherlock Holmes – that I was living beyond my means. It was Holmes whom I feared, above all else. He, more than anyone, might deduce where the loot had gone. He might work out that I had broken into the Haven the night after Amberley was arrested. He might realise that I had, as a change from solving crimes, elected to commit one.

Because Holmes never troubled himself to enquire further into the matter, I can only assume that the mystery of the missing lucre was too petty for him. Maybe he felt it was beneath his dignity to follow up on a case he had so triumphantly cracked. The money was a minor loose end. Why not leave it to the police to tie up? He, the mighty Sherlock Holmes, had bigger fish to fry. It is highly likely that the subject slipped his mind altogether, for soon after the Amberley case another problem engaged his attention, the vexing affair of Lady Eva Blackwell and "the worst man in London", the blackmailer Charles Augustus Milverton.

I do wonder, though, whether he actually knew all along that I had taken the money. By all accounts he lives in Sussex now, near Eastbourne. He is in his dotage, keeping bees. Does he ever think of me, down there in his retirement cottage by the sea? Does he smile fondly, perchance, as he recalls his former Irregular and one-time collaborator Clarence Barker?

Does he ruminate on how he let me get away with an audacious act of thievery?

If so, why did he not pursue me at the time? Why did he not apprehend me, as he did so many other wrongdoers?

I like to think that he felt I had earned the money. I deserved it. It was due to me not because I joined forces with him and went unpaid for my efforts, but rather because he was ashamed by the way he spurned me when I approached him with my offer of a partnership. He felt guilty that he did not take me on as a protégé and help me make the most of my talents. Deliberately allowing me to slip through the net was his penance.

Perhaps. Perhaps.

At least he never knew that I had urged Dr Ernest on in his romantic pursuit of Mrs Amberley and his bid to steal from her husband. He never learned about that.

In that one regard, I am unequivocally Sherlock Holmes's better. I got away with something that virtually no one else has: pulling the wool over the great detective's eyes. I outwitted him. He failed to see through me, as he did so many others, Josiah Amberley among them.

There is this sentence in one of the final paragraphs of "The Adventure of the Retired Colourman":

"Pure swank!" Holmes answered. "He felt so clever and sure of himself that he imagined no one could touch him."

The subject is Amberley, of course, and it is as apt a description of that fiend as any.

But it could just as easily be me.

Signed,
Clarence Barker
January 1926

HEAVY GAME OF
THE PACIFIC NORTHWEST

Tim Pratt

When I was approached to write a story for this project, I immediately wanted to write about **Sebastian Moran**, but was *sure* some other writer would have snatched him up. Imagine my delight to find he was still available. Moran first appeared in "The Adventure of the Empty House" (1903), and was arrested in the same story, but Doyle implied a lot of backstory, with Moran named as Moriarty's lieutenant, "the second most dangerous man in London."

I confess, though, that Moran made a bigger impression on me with his roles in the works of other authors. He appeared as vile blackmailer "Tiger Jack" Moran in George MacDonald Fraser's *Flashman* series; as hired killer and adrenaline junkie "Basher" Moran – the narrator of Kim Newman's marvellous *Professor Moriarty: The Hound of the D'Urbervilles*, where Moran plays a dark Watson to Moriarty's "consulting criminal"; in a minor but memorable role in Anthony Horowitz's novel *Moriarty*; and even as the profoundly damaged narrator of Neil Gaiman's Lovecraftian Holmes story *A Study in Emerald*. In all those stories, Moran is a formidable man of great courage, who happens to possess no moral compass at all – a fascinating figure, psychologically. The fact that he is canonically the author of at least two autobiographical volumes about his time as a hunter made it obvious that my story should be a memoir of a hunting trip, too.

—Tim Pratt

M emoirs are a poor substitute for sport, but with little else to occupy my time in this dreary cell, I may as well take up my pen again. My earlier literary efforts, *Heavy Game of the Western Himalayas* and *Three Months in the Jungle*, were well received by their intended audience, but I daresay the recent notoriety inflicted upon me will lead to a wider interest in whatever I write now. I'm sure many would be eager to read about my career with the late professor, but that work never interested me much beyond the technical challenges and the generous remunerations. I'm minded instead to begin these reminiscences with the last time I took up rifle against heavy game in the forest... and the extraordinary, and, to some degree, inexplicable manner of my survival in those circumstances.

It was June 1892 when my old comrade-in-arms Major Fraser sent a missive asking me to join him for a big game hunt in the forests of Washington State, in America's remote Pacific Northwest. He planned an expedition to pursue what he described as a deadly and unique creature, the killing of which would prove us hunters mightier than Nimrod or Orion, and enshrine our names among sportsmen for a thousand years. Fame has never interested me, and indeed I have sought to avoid it, but the challenge appealed to me, and Fraser's choice to withhold details was clever: he knew how to tempt my curiosity. The thought of taking up my long gun again was alluring. Playing cards is a pleasing pastime, but it does little to stir the blood.

I hesitated for two reasons. First, the journey would be expensive, with only glory at the end, rather than riches. My late employer had paid me on the order of six thousand pounds per year, excluding bonuses, but I lost a fair bit at cards and other wagers immediately following the professor's death, having little else to occupy my time following his tumble from the falls. (I could have pursued his killer across Europe and Asia, but saw little dividend in such outsized expressions of loyalty, contenting myself with a promise to kill the great detective if he ever returned to London; you all know how that vow ended.) Soon enough I altered my manner of play to improve the odds in my favour, and my purse refilled, so my accounts were healthy enough. After some calculation I supposed I could stand the cost of the journey.

My second hesitation regarded the location. The prospect of visiting America was appalling. I have journeyed with delight to the wildest and most barbarous places in Asia and Africa, so some find my great distaste for America confusing. To those I say: no one pretends the natives of the western Himalayas or the dark continent are anything other than savages and subhumans, but the rebellious Colonials fancy themselves sophisticates of a sort and equals of their former masters. I find their pretensions as vulgar and laughable as the sight of a pig in a crinoline.

Still, Fraser was a reliable man for a Scot, and if he said there was something special to hunt in those woods, I believed him. (You may be acquainted with one of my past exploits: when I pursued a wounded tiger into a drain in order to dispatch the beast. You likely don't know that it was Fraser who prompted that act, by betting me a sovereign I didn't have the wherewithal to do it.) I resolved to join his party.

I won't go into the tedium of the journey to America. There were fools with cards on the ship, so that was all right, and the passages west on the Transcontinental Railroad and then north on the Northern Pacific were only made horrible by the number of Americans on board the trains. My "accent", as they called it, excited so much comment from my fellow passengers I scarcely spoke a word after the first day.

We reached the last station of my journey late in the morning, remarkably on schedule, and I was astonished by the flood of people who disembarked, since from what I could see this was a crude pioneer village with little to recommend it beyond mud and trees. I gathered my personal effects and committed myself to the wilderness.

"Colonel Moran!" a voice shouted. I looked around and saw Fraser standing beside a horse-drawn wagon, waving his hat at me. I trudged towards him through the muck, followed by the boy I'd paid to carry my trunk.

"Major. You're looking well." I would have lied, but it wasn't necessary. Fraser was a few years older than myself, in his late fifties, but still hale and fit, with a bit of brown yet peppering his hair. He wore a black patch to cover the scar from the knife wound that took his left eye in Sherpur, which gave him a roguish, piratical air.

"You look fit yourself, Moran." He directed the boy to load my things into his wagon, then tossed the child a coin and invited me to join him up front. Fraser flicked the horse's reins, and it set off plodding along the thoroughfare.

I'd travelled in worse circumstances, but not since the

war. Water drizzled down on a canvas canopy rigged over our heads, and everything around us was hazy and grey. After a time we left all signs of habitation behind, following a rude dirt track between towering evergreens. I shivered, even in my coat. The damp penetrated.

We chatted about this and that, with Fraser not yet broaching the subject of the hunt. I was growing weary of the suspense, but chose not to press the issue yet. "Beastly weather," I commented at one point.

Fraser chuckled. "I saw a flash of sun through the clouds this morning, so this counts as a beautiful day by local standards. The whole place squelches most abominably as a rule."

After longer than I care to recall, we reached a good-sized wooden lodge, the walls furry with moss, a mountain of split wood heaped against one side of the house. "Here is my stately home," Fraser said.

I looked at the rude cabin, and the encroaching woods, and finally at Fraser. I shook my head. "How ever did you end up in this place, Major?"

"All will be revealed. Come in out of the wet." He led me onto the porch, pausing to scrape the mud off his boots before going inside. The interior was as rustic as I'd expected, but it was warm and dry. I settled into a cushioned armchair while he saw to the fire, and once the flames were dancing, he presented me with a very serviceable brandy and took his own chair across from mine.

Those preliminaries settled, he leaned forward in his armchair and fixed me with his one good eye. "Did you ever hear tales of the ape-men of Nepal?"

I grunted. "My time in the Himalayas was in the west, mainly, but I recall a few stories. Great hairy beasts, bigger and stronger than a man, said to stalk the high passes? A lot of rot, I always thought."

"Perhaps not such rot." Fraser's tone was amused. "The native peoples of the Himalayas all tell similar stories of man-bears, wild men, and similar fearsome creatures. After I left the First Bengalore Pioneers I spent a bit of time in the region, following the rumours, and even tried to arrange a hunt, but it all fell apart when I had to return home to see to the disposition of my father's estate. Blasted inconvenience. You asked how I ended up here – my father had sizeable shares in some timber and mining concerns in the region, and I travelled out to oversee their liquidation, as I had debts to repay. In those days this was the Washington Territory of course, though I can't say the recent promotion to statehood has altered things much for the locals. During that first visit, I heard stories startlingly similar to those I'd encountered in Nepal, and came to believe the ape-man of the Himalayas has an American cousin."

I took a sip of brandy to keep from expressing any impolite opinions about that conclusion.

Fraser went on. "I travelled from here to London and back a few times, before settling here for an extended stay just over a year ago. By then I felt I'd done sufficient research and was ready to pursue my prize. For an expedition like this, I wanted a good man by my side. There's no better shot than you, Colonel, and no more indomitable tracker. I have every confidence our hunt will succeed."

I nodded thoughtfully, and said, in a remarkably level voice, " I can't say I share your confidence. You invited me to this damp abscess of a place to hunt an imaginary ape-man. Have you lost your wits, Fraser?"

He shook his head. "I knew you'd be sceptical, which

is why I didn't offer details when I invited you. But is it really so far-fetched, Colonel? The orang-utan of the Malay peninsula was considered a myth when the natives first described them as 'people of the forest.' You yourself heard tales in Africa of monster apes that kidnap and kill tribesmen. The creature they describe has not been conclusively identified, but it surely exists. Is it so improbable that in the wilds of the American forests there lurk similar beasts?" Fraser warmed to his subject, or perhaps it was just the brandy. "I have travelled here and in Canada and down to California, hearing stories that use different names for the same beast – *skookum*, *oh-mah*, *gougou*, *tsiatko*, or just 'big man' – but all describe the same thing: a beast that stands up to ten feet tall, covered all over in coarse hair, with feet as much as eighteen inches long. These creatures sometimes kidnap the unwary, perhaps to eat them, and perhaps for more terrible purposes. There are also tales of the creatures acting to help those lost in the woods, but I don't much credit those. These *oh-mah* are cunning, elusive, and feared and respected by the locals... but no specimen has ever been recovered, intact or in part. To go into the forest and bring back the body of such a thing... what a triumph!"

"Indeed." Clearly Fraser had been seized by a fervour for some imaginary beast, and we might as well be setting out to hunt dragons or manticores. "What makes you think we'll find one of these 'big men' of yours?"

"I have many recent reports of activity in the forest not far from here." He tapped a map laid out on the table, but I didn't bother to look at it closely; it showed a great tract of trackless woods, more or less. "There have been recent sightings of immense, shambling creatures, and verified accounts of two small children being snatched away from a local village, with a third taken while you were en route. The big man of the woods is here, Moran, and we can kill it."

My disappointment was vast, but perhaps something could be salvaged. In a forest like this, surely there would be some beast worth shooting. Perhaps we'd encounter a grizzly bear. They were supposed to be formidable quarry, and taking one would salvage something of this trip. "When do you propose we set out?"

He chuckled. "Tomorrow before first light, unless you need more time to settle in."

"I'm settled enough. I just need time to clean my guns. Are we to be the whole of the party?"

He waved his hand. "I have a man-of-all-work, named Newman, to fetch and carry and perform other tasks as needed. He's mute from an old throat injury, and illiterate besides, which makes him more discreet than most men."

"Where's he lurking about, then?"

"Oh, I sent him out to procure some essential supplies. I'd hoped to employ an Indian tracker from one of the local tribes, but my approaches were rebuffed. They don't believe we should trouble the 'big men', it seems. No matter. We're up to following the signs ourselves, I daresay."

"If there's anything to track, we can track it." I thought we'd find nothing at all, or else discover some filthy madman of a hermit with a long beard. As long as the brandy didn't run out, I supposed I could stand the indignity.

We let the subject of the wild men of the woods lapse, then, reminiscing instead about our campaign days, and hunts we'd both enjoyed over the years. After so long enmeshed in the professor's plots, it was pleasant to return to thoughts of a simpler time. We ate a dinner of roasted game birds, moved along from brandy to port, played a bit of cards (for negligible stakes, and there aren't many two-handed games worth playing anyway), and then I retired early to a bed that felt stuffed with equal parts hay and loose pebbles.

In the first glimmerings of dawn, we stepped into the damp air. A thin fellow with stringy grey hair stood waiting placidly outside, an overstuffed pack resting by his feet. Fraser nodded to him. "Newman, this is Colonel Moran. Heed his words as you would my own." The man nodded solemnly. There were scars all around Newman's lips, down his chin and on his throat, leading me to speculate on how he'd become mute.

We clambered onto the cart, Newman perched in the back with the camping gear and supplies, and we set off along a rutted logging road, bouncing abominably.

Fraser said, "I've tracked the sightings, and particularly the disappearances of children, and have a good sense of the monster's territory. We'll get as close as we can by road, then hike in and look for signs."

"If these 'big men' of yours leave eighteen-inch long footprints, it shouldn't be hard to find some trace of them in this muddy ground. Indeed, it's remarkable one has never been tracked before."

"I understand your scepticism." Fraser's voice was low and calm. "Surely a creature like this couldn't escape capture for so long. If it were real, there would be a specimen by now. But the forests here are vaster than you realise, and more thinly peopled. Even so, there have been scores of sightings in recent decades and old tales from the indigenous savages going back centuries. The beasts are wily, that's all. As cunning as any tiger, and hard to capture."

I looked at my one-time fellow soldier for a long time. I'd known him as impetuous, but never credulous, or prone to fancies. "You've seen one, haven't you?"

He bowed his head for a moment, then nodded. "I have. I was walking in the forest, three years ago, when suddenly the birds fell silent, and a great hush descended. I stopped because I know when the prey fall silent, the predator is often near. I had the most peculiar sense that someone was watching me – you know the feeling, when you can *feel* a sniper has you in his sights?"

I didn't reply. I'd fired my rifle at enough unsuspecting targets to know the ability to sense a watcher was unreliable at best.

"I turned my head, and there it was, not ten yards away. A figure standing at least nine feet tall, with long arms, covered all over in thick hair, watching me. After a long moment it darted out of sight, faster than I could credit. At first, I feared it was circling to attack me, but soon the birds began their song again, and I knew it was gone." Fraser shrugged. "What had been mere curiosity became my singular passion after that encounter. Still, I'm not without a sense of proportion. I don't wish to become Ahab, pursuing my obsession even to death."

"Eh? Ahab?"

"From an American novel, written, oh, forty years ago, about a sea captain obsessed with a great white whale."

I grunted. I'd never hunted whales. Seemed like too much mucking around with boats, though there were no heavier game, I supposed. "I don't read Americans."

Fraser chuckled. "I have missed you, Colonel. This expedition will either see my passion satisfied or disappointed, and either way, after this I am done pursuing the *oh-mah*. I'll return to London either way, be it empty-handed or covered in glory."

I was glad to hear he hadn't lost all his sense. Only most of it. "Let's hope for the latter, then."

The sun was well up by the time he stopped the cart, at the end of a grassy track that didn't merit being called a road. We were surrounded on all sides by evergreen forest, dense and damp and scented with the astringency of pines.

Newman unhooked the horse from the cart and hung packs on it, then took the animal's tether and nodded his readiness. "Lay on," Fraser said cheerfully, and we set off through the trees. I had one of my favourite long guns (a four-bore that had once taken down a charging elephant) slung over my back, a revolver at my hip, and a walking stick made of stout black wood (among other things) in my hand.

"Newman scouted ahead and found a suitable campsite," Fraser said, and the truth of that was revealed in due time. We settled in the lee of a house-sized heap of mossy boulders, on a level stretch of ground still relatively bare from the depredation of some past fire. It was hard to imagine a forest as sopping as this one could ever burn, but ashes do not lie. We set up our tents and secured our food in the branches of a nearby tree to stymie any bears attracted by the scent. After that, we checked our weapons, and declared ourselves ready to begin.

Newman lifted a coarsely woven sack from the back of the packhorse – and the sack whimpered audibly. The man froze, staring at me, and in turn I looked at Fraser.

He cleared his throat. "I haven't been entirely

forthcoming about my plans for the hunt, Colonel, for fear you'd disapprove, I suppose. The particular *oh-mah* we're hunting has shown an interest in children. As I mentioned, three have been stolen away in recent months, and in all cases a huge, hairy figure was sighted in the vicinity shortly before the disappearance. With that in mind, I sent Newman to secure… bait."

I looked at the sack, judging its size. "You've stolen a child."

"We'll set him free when we're done," Fraser assured me. "We'll fill his pockets with money, too, to dissuade his parents from making any complaint. He's only four – it's unlikely he'll even remember this excursion, particularly given the dose of laudanum Newman administered to him last night."

"You intend to tether the child, as we used to tether goats beneath a tree to lure tigers, is that it?"

He nodded. "Yes. Then we'll lie in wait, rifles at the ready, as the boy's cries attract the *oh-mah*."

I could tell Newman was waiting for either my approbation or censure, but I merely shrugged. The discomfort of some American child, doubtless at least half-savage just by dint of living in this benighted place, hardly concerned me. "Let's prepare, then."

Newman shouldered his burden and led us through the forest to the spot he and Fraser had chosen. I had to admit, it was well suited to the task at hand: a small depression of low ground, with ample higher cover on all sides where we could settle in with our rifles, enjoying clear sightlines and waiting to see if the bait attracted any notice.

The mute man carried his sack of child to a tree in the centre of the hollow and let the boy out of the bag. The child was ragged and wretched, with a thatch of unruly black hair, and he complained in a slurring but uncomprehending voice as Newman lashed him to the tree with stout ropes. We stayed out of sight, neither Fraser nor I openly acknowledging that it was better if the boy didn't see our faces, but acting according to that principle. A four-year-old is an unreliable witness, and perhaps unlikely to be believed in any case, but Fraser and I were foreigners, and thus more prone than most to the suspicion of the locals.

Once the boy was secured, Newman joined us behind the cover of some large rocks. The boy began to weep, and then to wail, howling inconsolably.

Fraser beamed. "If the *oh-mah* is anywhere nearby, that noise will surely attract its attention."

I grunted. "And we're sure it won't attract the attention of anyone *else*?"

Fraser shook his head. "The nearest human habitation is miles away." He dispatched Newman to a point on the far side of the hollow to keep watch in that direction, then asked me where I'd like to settle.

"Here is fine." There was a sloping rock to lean my back against, and sitting on the stone was more appealing than squishing about in the damp soil. I had a good line of sight down to the child but was screened from his view by brush, and I was upwind besides, in case the "big man" had a keen sense of smell. Not that I believed there even *was* such a beast, but once a hunter, always a hunter.

Fraser clapped me on the shoulder and rose to take up his own position elsewhere on the rim of the hollow, whispering "Good hunting" as he went. Those were the last words Fraser ever spoke to me.

Much of hunting is waiting. I sat with my four-bore close to hand, and my walking stick laid across my knees, taking the occasional sip from a flask of warming whisky. The boy alternated periods of quiet whimpering with louder bouts of weeping and shouting, affirming the old maxim that children should be seen and not heard, though in this case, of course, the noise was theoretically useful. I expected nothing to come of this endeavour, and wondered how long we would be required to sit in the damp before Fraser gave up and let us return to camp.

Then, perhaps an hour before dusk, I saw movement in the trees: a towering figure, though probably closer to seven feet tall than nine, appeared briefly between the trunks of evergreens, and then disappeared. I let out a whistle, imitating the song of an English songbird, to alert Fraser that I'd seen something. I readied my gun, staring ferociously into the trees, alert to the slightest movement. The boy's wailing rose to a new and more irritating pitch.

I can't verify the exact order of events that followed and must indulge in a certain amount of speculation. After several long moments, there was a gunshot off to my right, the familiar boom of a large bore weapon. Then I heard Fraser shout and, shortly afterward, scream. I fancy I could make out a few words: "No," and "Please," and "You aren't," and "You mustn't" among them.

When he cried out I immediately began moving towards the sound, crouched low, long gun in my hands, the thrill of the hunt singing in my veins. A shame about Fraser, but when a predator is busy savaging its prey, you can often take it unawares, after all, and if the major were only injured, I might be able to save him.

I also dared to hope Fraser wasn't mad after all and that I would soon have the opportunity to kill a beast unknown to science.

By the time I reached Fraser, though, the predator was

gone, leaving only the mangled body of its prey. The old soldier was on his back, head twisted at an unnatural angle, eyepatch askew, his chest a bloody ruin. The major's weapon lay nearby, still stinking of its recent fruitless firing. I glanced around, and up, in case whatever killed him hunted from the trees like certain jungle cats, but saw no sign of any predator. I took a moment to examine Fraser's wounds, as they seemed strangely regular. I have seen many men killed, by all manner of animals and weapons, and it seemed to me these wounds were not made by teeth or claws. If called upon to make a wager, I would have bet my fortune they were caused by an axe.

A man, then, and not a beast, had killed Fraser. Had Newman gone mad or chosen this moment to redress some injury done him by his employer? I lifted my head and saw the boy was still tethered to the tree, his shouting having subsided into whimpers. Perhaps the gunfire had frightened him into something approaching silence.

Still holding my gun at the ready, I went in search of Newman, moving more silently than most would believe a man of my stature could.

I found Newman on the far side of the hollow, face down, his head nearly severed from his shoulders by an axe blow. Perhaps, being mute, he couldn't have cried out anyway, but I think he was taken entirely unawares. There was another person in these woods, then, armed with an axe. Perhaps the child's father, come to rescue him and punish his abductors? That seemed most likely. I could hardly blame the chap, if so, though I would shoot him, of course, rather than succumb to his ideas of justice.

I glimpsed movement in the hollow. A figure was approaching the boy... and I could see why the man had been mistaken for a great hairy beast of legend. He stood over seven feet tall, as broad-chested as an ox, his face three-quarters obscured by an unkempt dark beard, his hair a thatch of wild black liberally snarled with leaves and twigs. He wore clothes, though they were so mud-smeared they were barely recognisable as such. His feet were bare and black with mud, and quite large, though nowhere close to eighteen inches. The boy redoubled his screaming at the approach of this immense wild man, and who could blame him? This, doubtless, was the local thief of children: some sort of violent mad man.

(I learned, later, that my supposition was correct. I cannot recall the fellow's name now, but he was a Canadian hired to cut timber and was, by all accounts, a man of slow wit but even temper, and prodigious strength. One day, some months before I met him in the woods, a tree fell badly, and a passing branch struck him on the head hard enough to addle his brains. He lost the power of speech, and became prone to black and violent rages. He killed the camp doctor who came to tend him, reportedly breaking the man's neck with a single blow, and then snatched up an axe and disappeared into the forest. How this timber beast made his way to the vicinity of Fraser's camp, nearly fifty miles from the place he'd vanished, no one ever knew, but clearly his injury did little to diminish his woodcraft or survival instinct. No one knew why he took the children or what he did with them. The remains of those abducted were never found.)

The man – a big man, indeed, though not of the type Fraser sought – stood before the boy and lifted the axe. I took up my gun and sighted down on him.

My detractors do not like to credit me with any human

feeling, but it's true: I hesitated because I saw no way to kill the man without also killing the boy. My gun could put a good-sized hole in an elephant or a rhino, and I had no doubt, given my angle of fire, that the slug would pass through the man and hit the boy. My indifference towards the fate of the American child didn't stretch to a willingness to kill him myself, you see. I thought the wild man was going to slay the child with the axe, as he had Newman and Fraser, and if so, I resolved to kill him immediately after.

Instead, the big man cut the ropes with one blow of his long-handled axe, snatched the boy up under his arm as easily as I'd carry a newspaper, and loped away, vanishing into the trees. I almost wasted a shot, but chose to hold off rather than reveal my position. As far as I knew, the big man was ignorant of my existence, and I had no wish to alert him to my presence. I considered returning to camp, to the horse, to the train station, to London… but there might be some investigation by the local authorities, even in this uncivilised backwater, and my visit was hardly a secret. Many witnesses had seen me join Fraser at the station. I had managed to avoid entanglements with the law until that point, and while some involvement might be unavoidable in this case, I preferred not to be considered a criminal. If I killed the wild man and saved the child, I would be hailed as a hero, rather than suspected as a kidnapper or killer.

And, in truth, I'd travelled thousands of miles to shoot something, and hadn't yet fired my gun. I was eager to make *some* kind of kill.

Some say man is the deadliest creature to hunt, but that's balderdash. Hunting men is easy. In wartime there are ample targets and opportunities, and if they sometimes shoot back, that's only sporting. In peacetime, especially in a civilised city like London, people don't expect to be hunted, and as a result, they're as easy to pick off as a rabbit locked in a hutch. No, there are more dangerous creatures than man.

Nevertheless, I treated the big man with all the respect I would have given a tiger or any other formidable predator. He left little sign of his passage, but he could not entirely muffle the voice of the boy, and the occasional cry in the distance allowed me to correct my course and remain on their trail.

I fancied that I moved with the stealth of a big cat myself, but now I freely admit the wild man was my better in that regard. The child's cries grew louder, and I saw a flash of movement ahead. I thought the big man must have paused, perhaps for rest, or to kill or silence the child. I crept within range, then dropped my walking stick to the ground and readied my rifle.

Something felt wrong. Perhaps Fraser was right, and it is possible, sometimes, to tell you are being watched. It occurred to me that perhaps the wild man was aware of my pursuit and was playing the same trick on me that Fraser had tried to play on him: tethering the boy, and letting his cries act as bait, this time to draw *me*.

Apprehensive of ambush, I started to turn and look behind me, and so the wild man's axe struck me in the right shoulder instead of the back of my neck. The blow staggered me, the cold blade biting viciously into flesh and scraping on bone, but I did not fall. A few inches to the left and it would have chopped my neck and killed me.

I tried to turn and defend myself. My arm was numb below the agony of my shoulder, hampering my attempts to lift the long gun, which would have been useless at such close range anyway. The big man loomed over me, raising up the axe, his eyes bright and furious between the filthy mess of hair above and beard below.

I scrabbled for my revolver, reaching across with my damnable clumsy left hand, and dodged his axe swing at the same time. I managed to draw the revolver, but he slapped it out of my hand, sending it into the undergrowth. Then he struck me across the face so forcefully my vision went black.

I don't know why he didn't kill me, though I can guess. When my senses and vision returned, I was down in the dirt and saw the wild man running after the boy, who was attempting to escape. The wild man probably stopped short of finishing me off in order to go after the boy. I groped for my rifle, but it was gone; the big man wasn't entirely devoid of caution, and had hurled my gun away. I saw no sign of my revolver either.

My walking stick, however, was nearby. The wild man hadn't seen it as a threat, and why would he? It was well made but seemed otherwise unremarkable. Readers of this account are likely familiar with my famous air rifle, crafted for me at the professor's behest by the blind mechanic Von Herder, but they may not be aware that Von Herder made me other weapons, too. While the air rifle required some preparation to transform from walking stick to weapon, with some mechanisms to be attached and adjustments to be made, the walking stick I'd taken with me into the woods was a simpler device. Its body concealed a long barrel, and it contained a single slug and a single charge of powder. The boom-stick wasn't particularly accurate, and firing it even once would shatter the end of the stick, damaging the whole mechanism irreparably: it was a weapon of last resort. Indeed, since by design it could never be test-fired, I couldn't even be sure the boom-stick would work as promised, especially after so many years.

But what choice did I have? I crawled through the brush towards the stick, took it in my hands, twisted off the ornamental head to reveal the firing mechanism, and pointed the other end at the wild man as he crouched over the boy. There was still some chance I would hit the child, but by that point, the desire to harm the one who'd harmed me was greater than any other concern.

The boom-stick's recoil was vicious, but the results were most satisfactory. The large slug struck the man's head and very nearly disintegrated it, and his body fell into a bloodied heap. I let out a weak huzzah, but my consciousness was already ebbing; the blow to my head and the loss of blood from my shoulder conspired to draw me down into blackness. I called to the boy to go get help, but then realised the wild man had tied him up again. The child struggled against the ropes binding his arms and legs, weeping and wailing.

This would be my death, then. With a gun in my hands, and my prey dead along with me. A decent enough ending for an old *shikari* like myself. My only regret was that I wouldn't die on English soil.

I freely admit that the next portion of my account is unreliable. I can report only what I witnessed, or seemed to witness. I settled into a darkness that I fancy was death's anteroom, but a searing pain pulled me out of it. Someone was turning me over, lifting me up, and I complained bitterly, for death seemed preferable just then to agony. I smelled something musky, animal and pungent. I opened my eyes and looked around as best I could. Someone was carrying me over their shoulder, as easily as I'd carry a child. I looked at this stranger's back, which seemed to be covered in thick, coarse hair. The ground seemed far away from my face – at least three or four feet too far away, if the person carrying me was a man of ordinary stature. I turned my head and looked into the face of the kidnapped boy, who was slung over this figure's *other* shoulder, and gazing at me wide-eyed in fear or wonder.

Words in Fraser's voice drifted through my mind: *There are also tales of the creatures acting to help those lost in the woods, but I don't much credit those.*

I lost consciousness again, and when next I woke, it was to see an immense figure, something like the marriage of a giant and an ape and a hairy carpet, moving around the camp. This creature made the axe-wielding wild man look petite in comparison. The boy sat on a fallen log, chewing a bit of jerky, and when he saw my eyes open, he held out the food to me. But I was still grievously injured and passed out again. I think it was just minutes later that I opened my eyes and saw the back of the immense hairy creature as it departed the camp, taking long and somehow stately strides. Its feet were huge, at least a foot and a half long.

Some time later my consciousness returned properly, and I rasped out a request for water. The boy solemnly brought me a tin cup, and I gulped it down. Once I was able to sit up, I found that my wounded shoulder had been sealed over with mud. (When I eventually saw a doctor, he claimed not to recognise the leaves packed in the wound, but declared me remarkably free of infection.)

I looked at the boy. "What happened?" I asked.

The child shrugged. "You save me. Big man save you."

"Big man. You mean…"

"Big man." The boy held his hands apart. "Big *feet*." He grinned, and I let out a burst of laughter myself, giddy with the realisation that I might just live after all.

There was a bit of a fuss afterward, of course. When I took the boy to Fraser's cabin, what passed for the local police were waiting there, someone having seen Newman skulking around before the boy vanished. I professed to know nothing about any of that and spun a tale about going on a hunting trip with Fraser and Newman in search of bears, only to encounter a wild woodsman and this boy. When telling a lie, it's best to hew closely to the truth, and the wild man *had* killed my companions, and I *had* saved the boy, after all. The child said nothing to contradict my account, either because he lacked the sense to understand what had really happened, or out of loyalty to me for rescuing him. He did babble at length about the hairy "big man" who'd rescued us both. When questioned on that subject, I would only shrug and say I'd been injured, and that much of what happened after I dispatched the wild man was a blur.

I remain unsettled in my mind on this matter, I confess. Did one of Fraser's "big men" carry me to safety and treat my wound? Or was it just a benevolent woodsman, transformed by my battered mind into a figure from Fraser's fancies? Perhaps I'd carried the boy back to camp myself and slathered my *own* injury with leaves and mud, in a feverish delirium, and subsequently forgotten? I cannot definitively say. I wish the professor had not died, so I could ask his opinion.

I was obliged to sit in a cell while the authorities

investigated my story, but the condition of the bodies they found confirmed my account. The head of the constabulary told me those facts I related earlier about the origins of the wild man. There was some fuss about my being a foreigner, wandering about in the woods so heavily armed, with all those dead bodies in my vicinity. But in the end, it all came to nothing, as the only American citizen among the dead was Newman, who was well known locally and widely despised. The authorities set me free, kept my rifles and invited me to please never return to their state. I assured them that no prohibition had ever made me happier.

I returned to London and vowed that thereafter I would limit my sport to gambling at cards, as, for the first time in my life, the thought of holding a gun was somewhat distasteful to me. It occurs to me now that if I'd held firm to that feeling, I wouldn't have taken up arms to shoot that fool Adair, and then that cunning fiend of a detective wouldn't have contrived to capture me, and I wouldn't be in this cell now. But such reversals of fortune are all part of the sporting man's life, I suppose, and one never knows: I might have the great detective in my sights again someday, and give these memoirs a happier ending.

A DORMITORY HAUNTING

Jaine Fenn

When recalling women who acquit themselves well in Sherlock Holmes stories, most people think only of Irene Adler. **Violet Hunter** leaves less of an impression, perhaps because she does not best Holmes, although he does respect her quick and observant mind. Miss Violet Hunter appears in "The Adventure of the Copper Beeches", and my inclination to find out how she fared later in life became a firm decision when I realised that this story takes place within a few miles of where I live. Watson feels Violet Hunter might be a lonely person, with the implication that her intellect could be an impediment in finding a husband. At the end of the story Holmes comments that she ended up as head of a private school in Walsall where she "met with considerable success". That gave me all I needed: I couldn't resist having a go at mixing mystery and romance in a tale about an admirable and independent woman.

—Jaine Fenn

It is sometimes said – most often by men – that there is no more chaotic mental space than the mind of a girl on the cusp of womanhood. But whilst I have had to deal with my share of confusion, disruption and pigheadedness amongst my charges, the commotion that roused me that late October night was not of the usual kind.

The moon was half-full, hidden intermittently by racing clouds, and the first chill of winter had blown across the hockey fields during the afternoon's match with St Hilda's. We had lost, again: perhaps I should encourage Miss Simpson to take her well-earned retirement, but she is popular with the girls, and I pride myself that Rosewood Academy is a place that values pleasure in education above prowess in sport.

Lights had been out for a while, and I was dozing over some paperwork when a faint yet chilling shriek came from above. More cries followed, and I picked up the lamp and left my office, breathing a little hard. The dormitory is on the top floor and I was breathing harder still when I reached it. However, as the other teachers had all retired to bed, I was first upon the scene.

The occupants of the room were in a state of borderline hysteria. The lower school girls were shadowy shapes sitting up in their beds, some with covers drawn to chins; a couple were standing, but leapt back onto their beds when I entered. They had been looking down the length of the great attic room, towards the curtained alcoves where the fifteen senior boarders slept.

"Back to bed and back to sleep, girls. It appears you must set an example for your older schoolmates." For indeed, the upper school boarders all appeared to be out of bed, congregating in the centre of their dorm in a storm of over-loud whispers and gasps. As I strode forward and raised my lamp, white faces turned to stare. "What is going on here?" I demanded.

No one rushed to answer. Behind me, I heard a step on the boards, and caught a whiff of lilac eau de toilette – our French mistress, if I was not mistaken. I glanced behind to check and, supposition confirmed, called back, "Miss Fournier, please ensure that the younger girls settle without further fuss." I turned back to the seniors. "Well?"

"Please Miss Hunter," Jenny Miller put her hand up, presumably in response to the unexpected invasion of the girls' intimate space by the highest authority in the school; I tried not to be amused to see such a gesture from a girl in a nightshirt, "there's a ghost."

I raised my lamp higher. "An invisible ghost, presumably? How novel."

"Not in here," said Jenny, "out there."

She pointed to the arched window at the far end. Through it I saw a faint glow, as of the cloud-covered moon. Girls were slinking back towards their beds, and silence had returned to the dormitory. If left to their own devices, after a stern warning, everyone would no doubt calm from this latest fancy. However, the shriek had been imbued with genuine terror. "Well, I had best see it off then."

I admit that my steps as I approached the window might not have been as firm as those when I entered, but I believe the girls did not apprehend any hesitation on my part. I have no love of attic spaces, and kept my eyes upon the window, seeing only that faint, silvery glow. The girl in one of the two alcoves nearest the window had not been amongst the gossipy huddle that had greeted me. Rather, she sat on her bed, hunched over something in her lap. Mary Fraser. No doubt the scream had been hers. For a moment I considered asking her to put down her rosary and hold the lamp – to face the fear that, by her rocking motions and murmured prayers, patently gripped her – but I relented, and handed the lamp to Jenny, part of the cluster of girls one step behind me.

I eased open the catch on the window, drawing a gasp from the girls and a whimper from Mary. It loosened all at once, and I had to grab for the handle to stop the wind slamming the window back into the wall. I stuck my head out as the moon broke free of the clouds, flooding the world outside with silver. My heart, I admit, did beat a little fast, but I saw nothing more unsettling than the shadows of the trees upon the lawn. Certainly no ghost. I pulled the window to and fastened it shut then turned to my escort and held out my hand for the lamp. "Thank you Jenny. There is, you will be glad to hear, nothing untoward outside the window. Now, if you will all make your way back to your beds, no more will be said."

I did not have to tell them twice.

Turning back to Mary I found her looking up at me. "There was no ghost," I said gently.

"There was no ghost," she parroted back. Since moving up to the seniors she had taken to agreeing with the words of her elders, regardless of her own opinion. Whilst it made her pliant in class, it was not a healthy trait. I sighed, tempted to leave it at that. But she was a troubled young lady, and trouble untended only increases. I sat down on the end of her bed. "Mary, what did you see?"

Mary stared at the beads in her hands. "Nothing."

"All right. What do you *think* you saw?"

"A ghost." She flicked her chin up in brief defiance before dropping her gaze again.

"Not... some other kind of apparition?" When she first came to my school two years ago Mary had claimed to see the face of the Madonna in a stain that appeared on the refectory wall after some particularly damp weather. She had been teased for it, and at assembly the next week I had delivered a lecture on respecting the religious views of others, whatever variation of the Christian faith they favoured.

Mary shook her head, then in a low voice said, "It was a ghost, one of the unquiet dead, and it was white like bone and it flapped and beckoned to me and I was sure it was going to come through the wall and take my soul." She dropped her head, hugging her knees tighter.

I had an urge to touch the poor girl's hand, to comfort her. But that would not have been appropriate.

I would have liked more details, if not from poor Mary then from the other girls, on what they thought had happened here, but asking questions would give credence to what was most likely no more than the moon emerging from the clouds, or some piece of pale debris blown past the window. Instead, I asked Mary, "Would you like to move?"

"Move, miss?"

"Yes, to another alcove." When Mary became a senior at the start of term I had decided to put her in the end alcove because she was an asthmatic; being near the window would help her breathing when the weather allowed it to be open, and not being surrounded on all sides by other girls would make her unfortunate tendency to snore less disruptive.

"No, miss. I don't want to be any trouble, miss." Amongst her other challenging traits, young Mary Fraser can be very stubborn.

"I think Miss Hunter has a point."

"Thank you Mr Connor." I managed to hide my surprise at this unexpected support. The Walsall Historical Association can be somewhat resilient to change, and Chairman Stevens had devoted much of tonight's presentation to lamenting the loss of "traditional craftsmanship" in the area. I felt that these new industrial techniques might themselves be of interest to historians in a few hundred years time, but had waited until after the meeting to put this radical idea to our chairman. His uncharacteristic silence indicated that he was not impressed.

My new ally continued, "I believe Miss Hunter's own establishment was once a brewery?"

"A malt-house," I corrected, then regretted speaking out. Mr Connor had done nothing to deserve my ire. Chairman Stevens, however, was beginning to annoy me. But I bit my tongue. Even so, the esteemed leader of the Association gave his characteristic *harrumph*, and excused himself with a curt, "Good evening, then".

I turned to Mr Connor. "You came back." He had arrived unannounced at last month's meeting for the first time; late, greeted with frowns and stares and forced to claim the one empty seat next to mine. At the time I had ignored him save basic pleasantries, but I had noted his fine bearing, strong features and thick head of auburn hair, a shade not dissimilar to my own. This month he had arrived early and chosen to sit next to me, having asked permission and introduced himself first.

"I did." His voice had a faint burr, perhaps Irish. "And you would probably consider it forward of me to say this, but I came back partly in the hope that you might be here."

"I could consider that forward, yes. In fact I probably should." I glanced at his hand and saw no ring, but whilst the estimable Mr Holmes would no doubt deduce the potential existence of a wife, any offspring and the family income at a glance, all I could say with certainty was that this charming gentlemen was well turned out.

"So to state that it would be a shame to wait a whole month to see you again would be downright scandalous?"

He was keeping his voice low, but over his shoulder I saw the looks we got from the knots of townsfolk making their leisurely way out of the hall. As a person of status in the community, I would be expected to disengage from such shamelessly open attention at the first socially acceptable opportunity. "It would," I said curtly, but somehow failed to step away.

"But not so scandalous that you have discounted it."

I do, of course, have my reputation to think of. And that of the school. Yet sometimes I find myself wishing to do what is not expected and required, within acceptable boundaries. "It appears I have not."

"Then would the possibility of meeting me at The Singing Kettle this Saturday afternoon be one you would entertain?"

"I do believe I would, Mr Connor." People would gossip anyway. I might as well give them something to talk about.

* * *

Four days after the panic in the dormitory, and three days after I accepted Mr Connor's offer to meet for tea, there was another incident. The girls were at study in the library when, according to Miss Grainger the mathematics mistress, who was with them at the time, several textbooks "leapt off the shelf". Miss Grainger is not prone to exaggeration, but without being present myself I cannot say whether the books leapt, fell or were simply pulled down when Miss Grainger's back was turned. I can say that Mary Fraser was in the room at the time.

"A widower, you say?"

Mr Connor picked up the teapot. "As of six months ago. My dear Anna contracted a fever. She passed quickly, and in many ways she is still with me."

"My sympathies. Yes please, I will have more tea. And was she also, ahem, Irish?"

"Irish? Oh, the accent. I left Ireland when I was a boy, as so many of my countrymen do. I lived most of my life in America, where I met Anna and made business connections in the mining industry which have, whatever else, left me in a favourable financial position."

A man looking to turn a woman's head might make such a statement. But would such a man, a few breaths earlier, also imply he has not fully accepted the death of his wife? Either way, Mr Connor was nothing if not direct, and I decided to follow suit. "Strange, then, that you should leave the United States and choose to settle in a quiet town in the Midlands. Assuming, that is, you plan to stay in Walsall?"

"I've taken rental of a modest house on Ablewell Street. As to why: half my family went to the United States, the other half to work on the railways here. Those who came to England did well, and some still live in the area. With no wife or children in this world, I thought to try and reconnect with them. How long I will stay, I am not yet sure."

I took a sip of tea. "Ablewell Street is near St Matthews. I myself attend St Matthews for evensong most weeks, yet I have not seen you there."

"I worship at a different church."

I had thought as much. "Ah, your Irish roots perhaps?"

"I was raised a Catholic, but have drifted away from the faith of my fathers."

He had not, I noted, admitted which church he attended – if any; I would not put it past this unusual man to be an atheist. But his upbringing could provide knowledge relevant to the other matter on my mind. "Your familiarity with Catholicism still outstrips mine. May I ask a question?"

"Related to the Catholic faith? If you wish." He took a sip of tea.

"Where does Catholicism stand on the matter of ghosts? I had thought the Church of Rome's view not dissimilar to the Protestant one, but would welcome contradiction in this matter."

"Ghosts?" He put down his cup and cleared his throat. "In essence both branches of Christianity state the same view: ghosts are manifestations of the spirits of the dead."

"A view which, as we enter the twentieth century since Christ's birth, is hard to credit."

"Many do, Miss Hunter."

A suspicion was forming. "Including yourself, Mr Connor?"

He inclined his head.

"Then I am guessing," I said, "that Sunday may find you on Caldmore Road."

"You guess correctly. I am a Spiritualist."

"Ah."

"Does knowing this preclude our meeting again?" He sounded regretful.

My heart softened. "I think we may agree to differ on certain subjects."

He smiled. "I will take that to mean that tea next week remains a possibility."

"It does." Something about Mr Connor's company made me inclined to take risks.

Three days later the "ghost" made another appearance in the dormitory. Miss Langham dealt with the crisis this time, as I was sound asleep, having taken a draught to combat a minor chill. All the staff who live at the school had been made aware of the previous incident – and my judgement that the cause was youthful hysteria – so she did not wake me. But breakfast was a strained affair, and Miss Langham approached me for a private word. When I asked whether Mary had been the one to raise the alarm, she replied, "Why yes, Miss Hunter. The poor girl was terrified out of her wits."

The tense atmosphere persisted into the morning, with pupils and teachers alike on edge. I summoned Mary to my office after supper and told her that I was moving her to the alcove at the far end of the dormitory, next to the lower-school girls. She responded with a curt, "Yes, miss."

"Mary, is there anything else you can tell me?"

"I'm not sure what you mean miss."

"Were you asleep when you saw this apparition?" To confirm this was all in Mary's imagination would calm the situation.

"It wasn't a dream, miss! Jenny and Jane and Sarah saw it too."

Mary herself would give no further detail beyond insisting again that she had seen "an unquiet spirit". I spoke to the other three alleged witnesses. Whatever they saw had been directly outside the window, white in colour and had moved unnaturally. Only Sarah, the girl in the alcove next to Mary's, had caught more than a glimpse, claiming to have seen the ghost "flying off, up and away".

There was, of course, a potential expert close at hand. But whilst I found myself content, even perversely pleased, to endure a degree of gossip regarding my dealings with the town's newest resident, the idea of inviting a Spiritualist to carry on investigations at my school was unthinkable.

There was, however, another place to go for advice in matters this far outside my experience.

My dear Mr Holmes,

I greatly enjoy reading of your exploits as recounted by Dr Watson and am writing to you now in the hopes of some assistance. You may recall our brief acquaintance, some years ago, as immortalised by the good doctor. I suspect you remember every detail but in case you do not it concerned my brief sojourn as a governess at the Copper Beeches, a somewhat unwholesome house in Hampshire, and the deception perpetrated there of which I was an unwitting part.

I have since found my place in the world as headmistress of a modest school for girls of the upper middle classes. Most of my pupils are local, but we do have some boarders, and one of these has, on two occasions now, claimed to see a ghost outside the dormitory window, an experience that has left her greatly disturbed. Whilst she is unwilling to speak freely, I do not doubt that she believes she has seen something out of the ordinary, and knowing the girl in question well, I do not think this is behaviour designed to draw attention: on the contrary, she endeavours not to attract notice to herself. Whatever the case, the incident is causing considerable unrest at the school.

I know you for a rational man, and like myself you will seek for an Earthly explanation for these incidents, yet the girl in question's refusal to cooperate and the lack of reliable corroboration have brought me to an impasse.

Given your many commitments, and the unlikelihood of any criminal connection, I would not expect you to travel up to the Midlands, and my own position will not permit me to attend you in London. However, any advice or guidance you can give that might permit me to quietly resolve this mystery would be greatly appreciated.

Yours etc.,
Miss Violet Hunter

The letter was sent on Friday afternoon. On Saturday I again took tea with Mr Connor. I confess, I was looking forward to the meeting. This man caused feelings in me that I had thought myself long past.

We spoke of many things: of the seasonal changes in

nature, of the differences between American and English culture, of the life of the town and of possible walks to be had in the vicinity, although Mr Connor joked these would be tame compared to those he had experienced in the Rocky Mountains, where a walk might soon become a scramble or climb. I found myself picturing this rugged man on a rugged slope, and had to take a mouthful of tea to bring myself back to the room. We did not mention our differing beliefs, and I said nothing of the trouble at the school, relishing the chance to talk about matters outside my everyday responsibilities.

I had no problem promising to meet him again the next week. From our discussion I suspected he might ask for a less public meeting soon, perhaps a walk along the canal, or even a meal taken tête-à-tête and, though this would set tongues wagging further, had he asked, I might have accepted.

Out of his presence, however, my sense returned. Even if, as my heart insisted, I should make room for this man in my life, what would that do to my world? Even if, as my heart hoped, his intentions were what they appeared to be, what would happen to the school if − and here my heart skipped foolishly − I were finally to be married?

A telegram from Mr Holmes arrived on Monday morning.

```
Currently tied up in Sussex. Two pieces of
advice. Look to past history for matters
of note, most especially that of the girl
in question, and examine the scene with
utmost care.
```

His first suggestion sent a pang through me, for a hidden past had been the key to my own small mystery, nearly a decade ago now. The second was, now he mentioned it, obvious, though care would have to be taken, given the private space in question.

I started by interviewing Mary again. This time I took a different tack, asking her who she thought the ghost might be of, given the school had only been converted to its current use thirty years ago and so lacked any folkloric tales. She paled and shook her head, which I took to mean she had a good idea. After some coaxing she murmured that she feared it was her little brother.

"Did he pass away recently?" I asked gently.

Again she shook her head. Normally such slovenly manners would earn a reprimand, but I could tell the girl was fighting inner turmoil.

"As a young boy then?"

She nodded.

"I am sorry to ask this, but was his death… particularly unfortunate?"

She looked at her hands.

"You have no other siblings, I believe?"

Mary shook her head.

As far as I knew, the poor girl's only living relative was her mother, a thin flighty woman with an unsteady gaze whom I had met only a few times. Fees for Mary's education came direct from a small trust fund, administered by a lawyer in Birmingham. If I recalled rightly, at the beginning of this term Mary had been accompanied to the school only by a household servant. "So, it is just your mother and you. Your father is dead?"

Mary started, as though burned, then said in a harsh

whisper, "We do not speak of that."

A sad ending, then. Yet not one that Mary believed had resulted in this "ghost". But I had distressed the poor girl enough; I let her go.

Another matter I had not considered before Mr Holmes's missive was the relative proximity of Mrs Fraser's home to the school. She only lived in Blakenall Heath, close enough that she could have sent Mary to Rosewood Academy as a day girl.

This proximity provided my next avenue of investigation. Given Mary's attitudes and behaviour I surmised she had been born into her faith, and hence the family births, marriages and deaths would be recorded at their nearest Catholic church, rather than an establishment overseen by the Church of England.

Whilst my work is never done, I pride myself on the efficiency of my school, and so, should I wish to take a quiet Tuesday morning off and travel to a nearby town, I might do so. As I climbed into a cab I wondered if my fellow teachers thought this uncharacteristic behaviour related to the gentlemen I had been seen taking tea with. I would correct their misapprehension when and if it became important.

When I located the Catholic church in Blakenall Heath I found it in the process of renovation, with men working on the roof. The young priest in attendance was taken aback at a lone, veiled female visitor but soon recovered his composure. When I asked whether I might see records of his parishioners to resolve "a personal matter" he asked whether I was myself a Catholic. I considered lying to encourage cooperation, then chided myself. "No," I said, "but the individual whose welfare I am concerned about is."

"Most of our papers were removed for safekeeping when the restoration began. I would have to send for them."

"Ah, I see. I am putting you to some trouble."

"No, I mean yes, but… you must understand, I have to consider the welfare of my flock."

Though I am no expert in the moods of men, especially the clergy, I believe he found me intriguing. I smiled behind my veil, then said, "It is the welfare of one of them that concerns me."

"Ah. May I ask whom?"

A reasonable request, and, as it appeared I would be forced to return at a later date, I needed to be certain my errand was not futile. "A young lady called Mary Fraser," I said, watching his face.

He knew the name, though he regained control of his emotions quickly. "The Fraser family are of this parish, yes."

"So Mrs Fraser worships here?"

"When her health permits."

"She is unwell? Do you know what ails her?"

"My foremost concern is with the spiritual wellbeing of those under my care, although I pray for all their health."

His taut expression implied I would get no more from him on that. I tried another tack. "And Mr Fraser, he is buried here?"

The priest started. "Buried?"

"Yes. He has passed away, I assume."

"No. Mr Fraser still lives." The priest's lips thinned.

"Ah. But he does not worship here?"

"I can have the records here by tomorrow afternoon. Other than that…"

"… you cannot help me?" I try not to overuse the combination of steel and disappointment that has served me well with girls and parents alike, but it is second nature by now.

"I should not say anything." He forced his gaze back to me. "But whatever you find, or hear, please remember this: divorce is a sin. Now, if you will forgive me, I must prepare for mass."

"Of course. Thank you for your assistance." I made sure he saw the donation I put in the box by the door before I left.

A chance to put Mr Holmes's other suggestion into practice came the next day, whilst the girls were on the sports field. I resisted the temptation to borrow a magnifying glass from the biology mistress, and took only myself and − in accordance with Mr Holmes's practice − an open mind up to the dormitory.

The window opened easily, as it had on that first night. I examined the hinge, and found it well oiled, although whether this signified more than diligence by the housekeeping staff I could not say. There was no wind, but I secured the window with care anyway. The view was pleasing: across the busy playing fields, out beyond the town, and towards the higher land to the west.

I leaned over the sill and looked down. This side of the school has an impressive growth of wisteria but the branches were all but bare now, just a few yellow leaves clinging to them. I looked up, then cursed myself for a fool.

Above me, underneath the overhanging gable, was a hook. It was a great solid metal construction, left over from the days when the school had been a malt-house, when it must have been used to haul sacks of barley up into the drying loft. And there was something odd about the hook.

I dragged a chair over and stood on it, then peered upwards, into the shadow of the overhanging gable.

The chair rocked. I grabbed for the sill.

I allowed myself a moment to catch my breath then looked out again. There was something on the hook.

Without letting go of the sill I craned my neck. My thighs pressed against the window frame. I hoped the lower fifth were too busy with their hockey practice to notice their headmistress in such a precarious and undignified position.

Yes, there was something pale caught on the hook. I leaned harder. The chair creaked but held. I reached a hand up and snatched at the hook. My fingers found fabric, and I pulled it free. The chair rocked back, and I teetered for a moment, before steadying myself on the window frame. I climbed down with as much aplomb as I could manage.

Once safely on the scrubbed planks I opened my hand to find that I held a torn scrap of boiled cotton sheet, bunched up and tied with a light but coarse rope.

I was in two minds about returning to Blakenall Heath. After all, I now knew that poor Mary had nothing to fear: the "ghost" was a trick, most likely a bedsheet bunched up and tied to a rope threaded through the old hook. The sheet was a match to those in the dormitory; the rope, such as might be used by a local saddle manufactory. Both nights the "ghost" had appeared the wind had been strong enough to agitate such a prop, and Sarah had spoken of it disappearing upwards, as it would were someone below to pull on the rope, whisking the fabric up through the hook – or not, when it became caught. The explanation for the ghost was as mundane as I had thought.

But my curiosity over Mary's wider circumstances had been piqued. Therefore I returned to the Catholic church the next afternoon.

The priest was as good as his word, and even pointed out which pages in the great ledger might be relevant to the Fraser family, "Although," he added, "these entries only tell part of the story." I took this to mean that my enquiries still intrigued him.

I soon located records of Eileen Fraser's marriage, the birth of her daughter a scant and scandalous eight months later, then two years after that, of a son. The son's death was also recorded, four years ago, shortly before Mary came to my school. There was no other issue listed.

I found the priest tidying the votive candles outside the vestry and said, "I am afraid you were right."

"About what, madam?"

I did not correct his assumption about my marital status. "The records show only bare facts. I am not sure how helpful these will be to poor Mary."

He looked down at the candle in his hand and frowned. But he did not make his apologies or move away, so I prompted, "Though divorce may be a sin, separation is sometimes for the best, is it not?"

He looked up and placed a candle on the table. "I would not want to repeat hearsay. Gossip never does the Lord's work."

"In that we are agreed. I wish only for confirmation of the

facts. Mr Fraser does not live with Mrs Fraser, is that correct?"

"He does not, no."

"But he has not moved away?"

"It might be better if he had."

"Ah. So his continued influence is not a wholesome one. I am sorry, that takes us into the realm of gossip and opinion."

"No, it is a reasonable supposition. Mr Fraser was never a likeable man, especially when thwarted. By all accounts excess money and a lack of human contact have caused him to twist in on himself."

I suspected that the weight of confession, formal and otherwise, lay behind this young priest's willingness to open up to a stranger. His soft heart was a credit to his calling. "I imagine that knowing her husband is in such a dark place does nothing to help poor Mrs Fraser's health," I said.

"Indeed not. Though they have little contact, thank the Lord."

"And she lost her youngest, I see."

"Ah yes. A tragic accident."

"May I ask how it happened?"

"I should not say more." I understood his reticence, given the mother of the dead child was still one of his flock; I would exercise the same tact with my girls. But then he continued, "There has been an interesting recent development in the family that I can share, though I am not sure it is of relevance to young Mary's situation."

"Oh?"

"It concerns another family member, one who has slipped far from the faith."

I had a sudden, unpleasant, suspicion. "Please," I said, my throat tight, "do go on."

* * *

"Will you not sit down, Miss Hunter?"

"No, Mr Connor, I will not." I would rather not have had this conversation in public, nor did I wish to be alone with Mr Connor. Any townsfolk who chose to visit The Singing Kettle today in the hopes of seeing something of interest would not be disappointed.

"Please, what is wrong?"

"Why did you not tell me you were related to one of my pupils?" Though I kept my voice low, I would not speak names where they might be overheard.

"One of... oh, you mean my cousin's girl?"

"Yes, your cousin who was Eileen Connor before her marriage." When I had read Mary's mother's maiden name in the church register I had thought nothing of it, but then the priest told me of the cousin newly returned from America and it had all fallen into place. I had the *how* of the matter in that scrap of white fabric; the *why*, I admit, was still to come; but here, surely, was the *who*: a member of that ill-fated family, with some knowledge of my school, quite capable of scaling a wall covered in a knotty growth of a wisteria to hang a rope from that hook.

"I did not think it relevant. I was under the impression that the last thing you wanted to talk about with me was the school which takes up so much of your life."

Perhaps he had a point, but I would not be deflected. This man took an active interest in the so-called supernatural. Quite how faking a haunting would further his cause I could not yet say, but he had to be involved somehow. "Mr Connor, I am no more inclined to believe in coincidence than I am in ghosts."

"I'm sorry, but I am not sure what—"

"That is enough. I do not want to hear another word."
As I turned on my heel every eye was upon me. But I did
not look back.

When I took Mary aside and explained the matter of the
ghostly hoax she listened in silence. When I asked who she
thought might perpetrate such an unpleasant prank she
shrugged. I saw relief in her, but uncertainty too. I hoped
the truth would soothe her, but she was such a fragile thing,
and I did not want to press the point.

Perhaps, in a few weeks, I might be able to objectively
analyse Mr Connor's part in the affair, to work out what
he sought to gain or achieve. For now, I determined not to
think of him at all.

I interviewed Mary's senior dorm-mates individually, a
process carried out with some delicacy, as I wished both to
reassure them and to find out whether they had any more
to add to this not-quite mystery. They did not.

Similar tact had to be employed with the servants. It
would not do to act without evidence.

On Tuesday evening, to my surprise, Mary came to see
me.

I showed her into my office, and waited for her to speak.
She sniffed, blinked and said, "Please, Miss Hunter, don't
send me away."

"Why would I do that, Miss Fraser?"

"Because of the trouble I've been."

Aside from a complaint about her snoring, which
could hardly be helped, Mary had been no trouble at all
since moving beds. "The past is the past, Mary. And as I

explained, there was no ghost. All is well."

"So I can stay?"

"Of course you can. What makes you think otherwise?"

"The letter from Father."

"What letter? When did he write to you?" I looked over all post before distributing it to the girls. I had seen no letter.

"Yesterday, miss."

"Would you be willing to tell me what the letter said?"

"I... yes, miss. He said that seeing as how things were not working out here at the school, and how Mama's health is getting worse, I should come home to him."

"You live with your mother outside of term-time, yes?" Had Mrs Fraser gone through the process of a divorce from her unpleasant husband this arrangement would most likely have been overruled by the courts.

"Yes but... she is not well, and she's getting worse. Her nerves... When Peter died it was horrible, and she never got over it."

I quashed my unsatisfied curiosity at the circumstances of her little brother's death. What mattered was the family's current pain. "But you would still prefer to remain with her when you are not here, and not spend time with your father?"

"Miss, I would rather sleep in a ditch than enter that man's house!"

I tried not to let my surprise at her passionate words show. "I can assure you it will not come to that." But her desperate, if incomplete, account put a new light on the hoax that had disturbed my school.

I called the suspect to my office the next morning, having slept on the matter to ensure I had, as Holmes would

say "all the data". My suspect was Elizabeth Munton, a
lanky girl from a large local family who had worked at
the school for two years, reporting to the housekeeper.
I had spoken briefly to her, along with all the other
servants, when making my initial enquiries. At the time
she had claimed to "not know anything about no ghostly
prank" but had refused to meet my eyes, and the way she
said "ghostly prank" implied she knew more than she
was saying.

This time I tried a different tack. Having asked her to
shut the door and sit down, I asked, "Munton, what are
your usual duties?"

"Cleaning, laundry and whatever jobs Mrs Clews
requires, Miss Hunter."

"Including, on occasion, the distribution of the post to
the girls, I believe?"

Munton squirmed in her chair.

"Did you insinuate a letter that did not arrive by the
usual means into Monday's post?"

"I…" the girl's eyes darted round my office, looking for
escape.

"Did you, Munton?"

Her hands fluttered up from her lap, and she sobbed
once. "It wasn't my idea, miss!"

"Then whose was it?"

"It came from the same man, I think, though Ma didn't
say. She just gave me the letter to bring into work, told me
to get it to the Catholic girl, the nervy one."

"What 'same man', Munton?"

"I don't know his name, miss. He first called on Ma last
month, and they spoke in the kitchen. I didn't mean to
overhear…"

"What did this man say?" Mr Connor had arrived in the vicinity last month.

"Something about a prank at the school, and how he needed help with it."

"And why would your mother acquiesce to such a request? Did she know this man?"

"I don't know, ma'am." The girl's face reddened. "But Ma needs money, what with Pa gone and another baby on the way."

"And this man offered to pay if you carried out this 'prank'?"

"Ma never said but… yes, he must've. We've had meat on the table twice a week since."

"What precisely did you do, besides deliver the letter?"

"I got the sheet, and Jeb – my middle brother – he got the rope. I strung it up the night before the storms, whilst I was in there cleaning. Later on, he sneaked in below and tugged on the rope."

"Twice?"

"Aye, ma'am. Twice." From her face she knew how much trouble she was in. Why do people never consider the consequences of their actions?

"Did you also disrupt a study session in the library?"

"What study session, miss?"

"Never mind. The man who came to your house, did he speak to you?"

"No, just to Ma."

"But you heard him speak? Did he have an accent, perhaps an Irish one?"

"No, miss, he was local, by his speech."

"And his appearance: what colour was his hair?"

"His hair? Dark, though thin on top. Ma had me take

his hat when he arrived. Please, what'll happen to me?"

"I think you know what must happen to you now, Munton. I cannot have untrustworthy staff at my school."

"Yes, Miss Hunter." Though there were tears in her voice, I saw acceptance too.

"Kindly pack your things. I will not require you to work out your notice."

Her shoulders sagged and she whispered, "As you will, Miss Hunter."

"I would advise against telling any of the other staff why you must leave the school's service." Not that I minded if she did: knowing the mechanism behind the disruptive incidents might help restore calm. "Come back and see me before you leave."

When she was gone I sat back, then leaned forward and reached for my pen. I had two letters to write.

The first would be references for Munton, along with a bankers' draft for a week's wages. Foolish though the girl had been, she had been obeying her still-more-foolish mother. Up until this incident, she had been a competent housemaid and, although she could not stay here, I would not sabotage her future.

The second letter was harder. No one enjoys admitting they are in the wrong.

"You came, then?" I tried not to sound too relieved, but the maiden aunts who so enjoy my meetings with Mr Connor were not even pretending to address themselves to their Darjeeling today. After last week's show they watched us raptly, straining to hear the latest development in this low opera of emotions.

"I did. Please, Miss Hunter, sit down."

I did so, feeling a sigh escape as I did.

"I will come straight out and say this, Mr Connor. I am heartily sorry for the way I treated you last week."

"I accept your apology. You were applying that fine mind of yours to a problem without being in possession of the full facts."

"Quite so, to my chagrin. Perhaps coincidences are more common than I care to admit. Certainly, they are more common than conspiracies." I left it unsaid that I had wanted to think the worst of him rather than face the changes he might bring into my life.

Mr Connor nodded; graciously, I thought. I could imagine myself spending more time with this man. "And how is my cousin's girl doing?"

"She is nervous and scared, but that is, sadly, normal for her. I am not sure she will ever find happiness and ease, but for my part I will do all I can to help her."

"And for mine, I will ensure that her wretched brute of a father does not cause any more trouble."

"He strikes me as a man who will go to great lengths to get what he wants." And what he had wanted was his only child; thanks to his wife's faith, and her consequent refusal to agree to a divorce, there would be no other legitimate issue.

"Only if unchecked." Mr Connor smiled. "I have a purpose here now: to watch over what remains of my family."

"I am delighted to hear that."

"It is not a purpose that will take all of my time, Miss Hunter. I might hope, when spring comes, to explore the byways of the local countryside, with a suitable guide."

"That sounds like a pleasant diversion."

"More pleasant than chasing ghosts." I had given Mr Connor the gist of the affair in my letter.

"Now, you know there was no ghost, Mr Connor."

"Indeed not. But that is not the same as saying there are *no* ghosts, is it? 'There are more things in Heaven and Earth than are dreamt of in your philosophies… ' as the Bard puts it."

"Perhaps." Having been both right and wrong in recent weeks, I could concede that much.

Mary fell ill the next week. A bout of brain-fever was not unexpected after her recent traumas. She took to her bed, now out of sight of the fateful window, her rest aided by strong medication prescribed by our matron.

I had yet to replace Munton, so when autumn rain gave way, in the space of an hour, to winter's still and bitter cold, I took a spare blanket up to Mary myself. I found her dozing, rosary entwined in her fingers. As I unfolded the blanket over her she opened her eyes.

"Don't worry, Mary," I murmured, "just rest."

"I dreamt Father came for me."

"I can assure you that will not happen."

Her gaze was febrile and bright. "Are you sure? After Peter died, he said such terrible things."

"All untrue, I'm sure. Peter was your brother, wasn't he?"

"Yes." She looked past me, as though at something unseen. "He fell."

Whilst I did not want to cause the girl further pain, curiosity still pricked me. "An accident, yes?"

"Yes." Her gaze focused on me. "He fell from the attic window."

No wonder she had connected the flapping sheet outside with her dead brother! "Oh Mary. It must have been awful." I shivered; the cold had taken hold up here.

"It was." Her face twisted into an odd, feverish smile. "But it's all right. No one saw."

As I opened my mouth to ask what she meant a sharp bang resounded through the dormitory. I jumped to my feet, heart pounding. The noise had come from the far end of the room. I looked to the source of the sound, then, suspicions confirmed, hurried towards it.

The window was wide open. Before fear could get the better of me I leant out and grabbed the latch. My glimpse of the world outside was pure normality: a bright winter's afternoon, girls on the sports fields below, rooks in the elm trees.

When I tugged the window closed I half expected the catch to be broken, but it was not. Whoever last opened it must have failed to fasten it properly, leaving it to be caught by a stray gust of wind.

I walked back to Mary's alcove to find her sound asleep, that same peculiar smile still on her face.

THE CASE OF
THE PREVIOUS TENANT

Ian Edginton

Inspector Baynes of the Surrey Constabulary is something of an anomaly in that he appeared in only one Sherlock Holmes story, "The Adventure of Wisteria Lodge", but he's also the only police officer to have ever successfully matched wits with the great detective and come out on top. In fact, Holmes goes so far as to outright congratulate Baynes, remarking: "You will rise high in your profession. You have instinct and intuition."

It's something he's never said to poor old Bradstreet, Gregson or Lestrade, despite their best efforts.

Baynes is described as being on the stout side with florid cheeks but possessing extraordinarily bright eyes hidden beneath the heavy creases of his solid, yeoman features. The intimation is that there's a keen intellect at work behind that everyman exterior. Given that he's also a provincial policeman, there's the temptation to write him off as an almost comic aside, but that's where you'd be wrong. He's very much a precursor to Columbo, in that his appearance, methods and mannerisms often lead people to underestimate his abilities. Even Holmes himself is a little taken aback when Baynes spurns his offer of help and successfully solves the case in his own way.

I would have loved to have seen Baynes and Holmes cross paths in a few more stories, which is why I jumped at the chance to use him.

—Ian Edginton

"Well, Doctor, what is your diagnosis?"

"Of what?" I asked.

"Why me of course." came the curt reply. "For a full thirty minutes now, you have been perusing me from behind the horizon of your newspaper."

Before I could respond, he brandished an index finger in my direction. "Do not deny it. You may as well have been sending out a semaphore for all your interminable rustling."

I sighed and patiently folded my newspaper. I knew too well from past experience how Sherlock Holmes railed against inactivity. I had often reassured him that it was merely a passing inconvenience to be endured. Much like his sour mood.

"Holmes, this is merely a fallow patch," I replied. "You have been through them before and will no doubt do so again. In fact, it has only been... what? Two weeks since the conclusion of our last case?"

"Long enough for the ink to dry on your latest tawdry narrative."

"Holmes!" I rose sharply to my feet and was about to slam down my copy of *The Times* to punctuate my displeasure when I thought better of it. There was enough petulant behaviour in the room already. "You are my dearest friend, but there are occasions, such as this, when I find your company difficult to endure."

Holmes folded his arms and turned to face the window.

"Surely the origin of that must lie with your friend Stamford for introducing us in the first place."

I snatched my overcoat from the stand and proceeded to the door. "I am going for a walk. Some time apart may benefit us both."

Without turning, Holmes gave a faint, dismissive wave.

"Oh, and when you pass Inspector Baynes of the Surrey Constabulary on the stair please tell him to come straight in, there's no need to knock."

"Inspector Baynes?"

"Of the Surrey Constabulary, yes. You'll recall his most erudite handling of the incident at Wisteria Lodge?"

"Certainly. But how do you know he's here? I didn't hear the bell."

Holmes turned to face me, a dark silhouette backlit by the sharp, winter daylight.

"The good inspector is somewhat on the stout side, therefore his weight upon the stair causes it to creak with a different timbre should you or I or Mrs Hudson bring pressure to bear." He crossed to the fireplace and selected a long-stemmed pipe from the rack on the mantel. "Also, he pauses on every fifth stair to catch his breath, suggesting he is in ill health, although nothing more serious than a head cold."

I was readily aware of Holmes's methods but even I was briefly confounded by this deduction.

"You saw him out of the window didn't you? He was arriving as Mrs Hudson was leaving to visit her friend in Worthing, ergo no door bell?"

Holmes gave a flicker of a smile but I sensed something else behind it, a suggestion of discomfort. He studied the pipe as if puzzled by its presence. He placed it back in the rack and elected to take a cigarette instead. His hands were trembling. Holmes has often said it is the observation of trifles that are the most revealing.

"Holmes, are you quite alright?"

"Clearly I am not, or you would not be asking such a question."

"Then what is it that troubles you? I am both your friend and physician, remember?"

He lit the cigarette and drew deeply upon it before slowly exhaling a roiling cloud of grey smoke. The tension that hung about him seemed to dissipate along with it.

"Sleep, Watson, sleep. It and I have never been on the best of terms, but these past few nights my sleep has been sorely tested. I awake in the morning... exhausted."

Before I could answer there was a knock at the door.

"Come in Inspector Baynes," said Holmes. "The door is open. There is no need to stand on ceremony."

"Ah, Mr Holmes, Dr Watson. A very good morning to you both!"

Baynes had changed little since we met the year before. A short, solidly built fellow with a slight puffiness to his features and a red bloom to his cheeks. His frame suggested a family heritage of stout yeoman stock, of honest toil working on the land. His eyes, however, were bright, keen and ever watchful.

It was during the case of Wisteria Lodge, of the murder of Aloysius Garcia and the uncovering of the vile Central American despot Don Juan Murillo – "the Tiger of San Pedro" – that his talents came to the fore. Eschewing Holmes's offer of aid, he ploughed his own course, revealing both murderer and motive at the same time as my friend. I distinctly recall him praising Baynes's exceptional abilities. "You will rise high in your profession," Holmes had declared.

And now Baynes was here in Baker Street and, after sneezing explosively into his handkerchief, was clearly full of cold.

"Forgive me gentlemen. It sounds far worse than it feels. Although I shall endeavour to keep my distance for fear of spreading same."

"Will you take a brandy?" I offered.

"Thank you, no, Doctor. This is but a sniffling trifle; it will work its own way clear in due course. I am not a great imbiber, and I fear a glass of spirits would dull my senses even more."

"Then pray take seat," replied Holmes. "It is the least we can offer."

"That I will, Mr Holmes. Thank you."

I took Baynes's heavy overcoat and wide-brimmed felt hat – the same, I noted, that he had been wearing when we first met. He seated himself at the dining table and laid a large leather satchel before him. Holmes was clearly intrigued.

"Am I correct in assuming this is not a social call, Inspector?"

"I wish I could say otherwise Mr Holmes but no, it is not. It is more by way of a consultation."

"We are all ears," Holmes replied.

The inspector unfastened the satchel and withdrew a thick cardboard envelope. From this he took six large photographs and laid them on the table.

"Now, gentlemen," he said, wheezing slightly. "Tell me what you make of these."

The images were of a corpse, the same one in each but viewed from a different angle and distance, to take in not only the form but also the situation in which it was lying. It was male, judging by the clothes, but the body itself had been denuded of all the soft tissue. There remained only a few shreds of matter and wisps of hair clinging to the bones.

Holmes descended upon the photographs, his face inches from the nearest as he scrutinised it with his magnifying glass.

"It's the body of a man in the final stages of decay," I said. "Although after exposure to the elements, it's impossible to adequately gauge the time of death."

"Indeed," Holmes said. "This is all that remains after the wildlife and water have done their work."

"Water?" I queried.

"He is lying in a reed bed, yet the earth around him is dry and cracked. This area was once marshland but has recently been drained for agricultural use?"

"You're not wrong there, Mr Holmes. It is a small fenland, just south of the Thames, near Mortlake. The farmer was clearing it when he discovered the body."

"I cannot discern any broken bones nor trauma to the skull. Of course there may well have been foul play, but the march of time has trampled over a good deal of the evidence."

"That it has, Mr Holmes," replied Baynes. "However, the fellow's pocket watch and wallet were found upon his person."

"So we can rule out robbery," I added.

"Ah, Watson," Holmes sighed, "there are more reasons to murder a man than merely for the contents of his pockets. But tell me, Inspector, is it now customary for the Surrey Constabulary to photograph crime scenes such as this? If so, it shows great foresight, as it has only recently become common practice here in London."

"Sadly not. But, given the delicate condition of the body, I recruited a local photographer to record any evidence in situ before moving it compromised the remains."

"Ha! Splendid!" Holmes exclaimed. "I have said it before and will say so again, your talents are wasted in your little corner, Inspector."

"You are very generous, Mr Holmes."

"That's as maybe," replied Holmes, a hard edge creeping into his voice. "But perhaps you might tell us the real reason for your visit so that we might end this charade?"

Baynes's genial manner faltered for a moment. "You are quite right: I have not been fair in this matter, but it was not meant with any trickery or malice in mind." He took a second, smaller envelope from the satchel. Inside was a delicate sheet of tea-coloured paper.

"I simply wished to glean your reading of the situation without it first being coloured by what I have here."

The document was rippled and brittle, rather like a dried leaf. It had been wet at some point, causing whatever had been written on it to bleed almost beyond recognition. The printed heading though was unmistakable.

"This is headed notepaper from the British Museum?"

"That it is, Doctor. Now do you see anything else?"

I studied the abstraction of smears but was able to discern only a vague swirl or loop of the occasional letter. It took me a minute or so to see past the chaos and interpret these enigmatic hieroglyphics.

"Good lord, it's an address! It says '221B Baker Street'!"

"And that's not all," Baynes added. "I have been able to decipher a number of other words and a name, a Professor Mori –"

"Moriarty!" I exclaimed.

"No, Watson, it is not he. Nor is it wise to jump to conclusions however accommodating the evidence." Holmes stood, staring at the letter as he contemplated the connection.

"The name is Professor Mortimer Shawcross, the associate head of the department of Anglo-Saxon history at the British Museum and the previous resident of 221B. Almost fifteen years ago now, he suffered a sudden and violent breakdown and has been a resident at The Briars, a private asylum, ever since."

"You've beaten me to it, Mr Holmes." Baynes chuckled. "Thanks to this letter I traced the fellow in the field back to the museum where he was identified as one Peter Allenby, a student and assistant of the professor. They were working on an archaeological excavation in the spring of 1881, not far from where the body was found in fact."

"And shortly afterwards Shawcross had his breakdown and Allenby disappeared."

"It would seem so," the inspector replied. "It was reported that the professor was arrested for indiscriminately attacking a number of people."

"What on Earth happened?" I asked.

"He ran riot in the street late one night, brandishing the still quite deadly remains of a Viking sword," Holmes replied. "He killed three people and injured five more before he was apprehended."

"Do you think he murdered Peter Allenby?"

"It's doubtful," said Baynes. "The professor had returned to Baker Street and left Allenby in charge of the dig site for a few days. Then one day the boy was just gone."

"Closely followed by Professor Shawcross's mental collapse. I doubt very much that it was a coincidence," remarked Holmes.

"Holmes, how long have you known about this?" I asked.

"Since our mutual acquaintance Stamford first informed me that these rooms had become available. He knew some might find it ghoulish to take them on but that I was not so disposed," he replied.

"However, it would have been churlish to simply accept them sight unseen, plus having read of the professor's story in the newspaper I confess to a degree of professional curiosity."

"You knew!" I exclaimed. "You knew all of this right from the very start? Why didn't you tell me?"

"Because it didn't seem relevant." Holmes seemed genuinely bemused. "Besides, I was aware that your battle scars were more than just physical. I did not wish to burden you further."

"How considerate!" I snapped. "And of course it had nothing to do with not wishing to scare me off from sharing the cost of the rooms with you?"

"It was... a consideration," said Holmes, a faint sheepishness creeping into his tone.

"And Mrs Hudson?"

"I counselled her to say nothing to you either, to spare your nerves. She was most sympathetic."

"I see." I felt angry, embarrassed and indignant, but I knew these feelings would achieve little, the injury having been inflicted over a decade earlier.

"What is to be done now?" I said. "With regards the case of the late Peter Allenby, I mean."

"There is only one course of action as far as I can see," remarked Holmes. "We must go and pay Professor Shawcross a visit."

* * *

Located between the cathedral city of Hereford and the village of Stretton Sugwas, just north of the River Wye, The Briars was formerly a country manor house now converted into a mental institution catering for patients whose families were of no small wealth and status. The ancient wall encircling the grounds, a sturdy bastion from the days of the Civil War, had been substantially strengthened and topped with iron spikes. At the main gate, the guards, while being smartly uniformed, would not have looked out of place at a Shoreditch bareknuckle bout.

Upon reaching the entrance, the director, an anxious-looking American by the name of Dr East, was waiting for us. Short, slightly built, with a shock of sandy-coloured hair and round, wire-rimmed glasses, he gave the impression of a small mammal, ever-conscious of the lethal swoop of a hawk.

"Mr Sherlock Holmes?" he enquired in a soft, clipped tone.

"I am he," declared Holmes, stepping down from the cab. "And this is my colleague Dr Watson and the inestimable Inspector Baynes."

"Yes," said East, somewhat disdainfully. "Your brother's telegram said to expect you. I am not comfortable with this," he continued. "Not at all! The families of our residents expect the utmost discretion and that does not include detectives, consulting or otherwise, being let loose in these halls."

"You may have no fear of that, Doctor," said Baynes, his cold making his voice course and rattling. "We are not seeking to roam unfettered. We only wish a few words with Professor Shawcross and we'll be on our way."

We began to make our way up the steps when East

purposefully put himself between us and the building.

"About that," East continued. "You are aware that given his condition, whatever the professor might disclose, it cannot in any way, shape or form be construed as an admission of guilt or used as evidence of any kind?"

"Yes, of course!" exclaimed Holmes and, pointing his cane forwards like a divining rod, marched boldly inside the building. "Your secrets are safe with us."

East scurried after him. "This way, gentlemen," said the flustered physician, leading us down a wide, wood-panelled corridor.

I quickly stepped into pace alongside Holmes. "I didn't know Mycroft sent a telegram?"

"He didn't," he replied, flashing a quick smile. "But I dare say he would've done if I'd asked. Sometimes the mere mention of his name is enough to open doors."

I stifled a burst of laughter, prompting East to cast me a scowl over this shoulder.

"Holmes," I began, "I'm sorry about what happened earlier. Whether rightly or wrongly, I took offence at an ages-old incident without taking into consideration how much richer my life has been for knowing you."

"The feeling is mutual," Holmes replied. "After all, I've done considerably worse things to you and we have still remained civil."

"Such as?"

"Letting you think I'd died and returning out of the blue some years later?"

"There is that."

We followed Dr East down one corridor after another, passing several stern-faced members of staff clad in spotless white uniforms. I noticed a brief flicker of curiosity as they caught sight of us. It appeared that visitors were not a common occurrence.

East asked us to wait as he went to speak to an attendant leaving one of the rooms. There was a sign baring Professor Shawcross's name on the door.

"This is a house of secrets and no mistake," said Baynes. "And that young fellow is the keeper of the keys."

"You suspect something is askance, Inspector?"

"Nothing I can put my finger on, but I have heard of more than one case where an elderly or infirm relative has been committed in order to free up an inheritance. A place like this with its locks and whispers could well facilitate such a practice."

Dr East returned to us, smiling. I did not take that as a good sign.

"My apologies, gentlemen, but Professor Shawcross has been given his medication a little early today. I afraid he won't be in a fit condition to answer any questions."

Holmes gave the doctor a thin, humourless smile. "That is indeed inconvenient. Tell me, Doctor, how long is it before the medication takes full effect?"

"Ten… perhaps fifteen minutes given he's just eaten." East replied with some caution.

"And it was administered when?"

"No more than five minutes ago."

I could sense East's growing agitation.

"Then we may proceed as planned. We need only five minutes of his time and we shall be on our way." Holmes walked briskly past the bemused attendant. "Come gentlemen, *tempus fugit*."

He ushered me and Baynes inside before turning to block East's admission.

"I really should be in attendance…"

"There's no need. We would hate to be a drain upon your time, and Dr Watson is a most eminent physician. If we encounter any problems, you and your staff are just on the other side of this door."

Holmes stepped inside.

"I shall be sure to tell my brother of your most obliging cooperation. I'm certain he will be interested to know how well this institution is being managed."

Holmes shut the door and permitted himself a short sigh of relief. "That will have given him something to think about," he remarked. "If the good inspector is correct, the last thing Dr East will want is the authorities taking an interest in this place. Now, we have little time and much to do!"

The room was cordoned off down one side by steel bars running floor to ceiling. Beyond this artificial annex there was what appeared to be a very compact yet comfortable bachelor's apartment.

On our side was a desk bearing a pair of white enamel surgical dishes. One contained the remains of a snapped glass vial and a spent syringe while the other had several more but unopened. I picked up the broken vial.

"Holmes, we may have less time than you imagine. This is a potent sedative. It has even been proscribed in some hospitals for its potentially deleterious effects. They clearly intended to have the professor too incapacitated to speak to us."

"Thank you, Watson. Nevertheless, we must do what we can."

"Hello? Can I help you?" Professor Shawcross, who had been reading in an armchair, rose to greet us. He was easily six feet tall and broad across the shoulders. He'd possibly been an athlete in his youth, a rower perhaps? His hair was thinning but close cut at the sides and back. His cheeks were heavily pock-marked, suggesting a brush with the measles or chicken-pox.

"Professor Shawcross, my name is Sherlock Holmes. This is Dr Watson and Inspector Baynes of the Surry Constabulary."

"Surrey…" Shawcross interceded. "You've found Peter?"

"Yes, sir, two days ago," replied Baynes. "We found his body just outside Mortlake."

"I didn't kill him, you know."

"Yes, sir," said Baynes. "It's looking more like an accidental death. That area can be marshy and treacherous, especially at night. The ground may seem firm enough but it's easy to put a foot wrong. He wouldn't be the first poor soul to lose his life in such circumstances."

Shawcross fixed the inspector with an intense stare. "I said I did not kill him, but that does not mean it was an accident. He played the tune and paid the piper… with his life. As we all must in our turn."

"And the piper is?" enquired Holmes.

"Why, death, of course." Shawcross blinked and looked around perplexed, as if rousing from a fugue state. "Please excuse me. My medicine is taking its toll. I'm afraid I will shortly be of scant use. What is it you wish to know?"

"Everything. Omit nothing, no matter how trivial," said Holmes.

"Yes, of course, it would be my pleasure," replied Shawcross, lowering himself into the armchair again. "So, where to begin?"

"Perhaps with the excavation?" prompted Holmes.

"Quite so. As you may or may not know, I was formerly Associate Head of the department of Anglo-Saxon history at the British Museum. In March of 1881, I and several of my associates commenced an archaeological dig close to the village of Mortlake. You see, in the ninth century, England was sorely afflicted by attacks from Scandinavian Vikings. Surrey's inland position saw it go largely unmolested until a large invasion force of Danes, some ten thousand strong, made their way up the Thames. They had already sacked Canterbury, then London, and defeated King Beorhtwulf of Mercia in battle. The West Saxon army led by King Aethelwulf rose to meet them, but the odds did not bode well. This was a hardened, battle-seasoned foe they faced."

"And what happened?" asked Baynes, obviously intrigued.

"The Danes were defeated at the Battle of Aclea. Routed, slaughtered. Thousands of the fiercest warriors the world had ever seen."

"How's that possible?" I asked.

"Perhaps a combination of tactics and knowledge of the terrain?" said Holmes.

"Or something else?" added Shawcross. "Legend has it that before the battle King Aethelwulf sought the council of a tribe of cunning women. Witches, shamans, call them what you will. Their arcane practices were being scoured from the land by the one true god, but the King offered them amnesty if they would aide him in his darkest hour. And aid him they did. They summoned the angel of death itself to walk in the vanguard, playing a pipe whittled from the bones of the first human. The King's men were bade to avert their faces and stopper their ears so as not to see or hear it."

I was watching Shawcross closely now. His face was beaded with sweat. Despite the sedative's soporific effect, the professor showed no signs of succumbing. Quite the opposite in fact.

"It's said the Danes gave the piper no mind at first, but when its tune reached them, they froze, rigid with terror. When they then set eyes upon the darkness of the angel's form, it swallowed their gaze and showed them the yawning chasm of eternity that existed after life. There was no Heaven, no Valhalla. There was nothing but the endless void, where a second would last an eternity. Some of them ran, mad. Others remained in shock, even as the king's men fell upon them, butchering them all. That is how the day was won."

"But it's a story, surely?" I said. "Perhaps with a grain of truth at its core, but a story nevertheless."

"I thought so too," Shawcross replied. "That is why I began the dig at the site of King Aethelwulf's muster camp. It was a disappointing dig, yielding nothing of great note. Coins, combs and brooch pins, plenty of broken pottery and several untouched jars of wheat and rye grain."

"So you returned to London and left Peter Allenby at the site?" said Holmes.

"I had business at the museum. I was only back a day or two when Peter's telegram arrived."

"He'd found something?"

"He found *it* – the piper's flute! It had been wrapped in doe skin and buried deep inside one of the grain jars. I was all set to return when a parcel arrived the next morning. It was the flute itself; Peter had sent it to me."

"That's not customary, is it?" Holmes asked.

"Not at all, but he knew how anxious I would be to see it. I imagine he thought he was helping. I telegraphed him to say it had arrived, but, well, events took another turn as I'm sure you're aware."

"Yes, well, I think we've heard enough for now," I suggested. "We don't need to pursue this any further. You should rest."

"There's time for one more question, surely?" said Holmes.

"Holmes, this man's mind is a fragile thing!" I said in terse whisper. "You cannot simply push a stick into it and stir it up as if it were an anthill!"

"It's alright, Doctor, it's no bother." Shawcross was on his feet, standing straight and tall, his arms by his side. His face was sheened with sweat and something else, a calm beneficence that sent me cold. I knew then, without a shadow of a doubt, that Professor Mortimer Shawcross was quite insane.

"The flute was an extraordinary object. It was indeed a human tibia with faint, almost imperceptible, ridges engraved upon its surface. An elaborate scrimshaw of the most beauteous and obscene images I had ever seen. I put it to my lips and played it. It seemed the right thing to do. It gave a flat, dull tone and proved to be something of an anti-climax. However, I was soon to discover that I couldn't have been more wrong in my assumption."

Shawcross held out his hands.

"I studied my hands as they held the flute. I fell into them, past them. I rushed headlong beyond tissue and bone, soaring past atoms and the spaces in between the spaces until there was naught but void."

He looked up at us and I could see tears streaming down his cheek. His face was a picture of saintly elation.

"I lifted my head and did the same. Lath and plaster, brick and sky were stripped away as my mind raced. Planets, suns and stars sped past me, the whorl of galaxies, the very crucible of creation, until again there was an infinite absence. But where was God in all of this? Then it struck me: God was the void, everywhere and nowhere."

Shawcross was face-to-face with us now, only the bars keeping us apart.

"We are born from nothing and return to nothing. It is life that is the abomination, an unnecessary punctuation. Death is the release, which unshackles us from the flesh."

"So you took up a sword and became death?" said Holmes.

"No… but I am its prophet. It is my crusade to relieve mankind of the burden of its mortality."

"Mr Holmes!"

Dr East suddenly appeared, backed by a trio of burly guards. He brandished a telegram in Holmes's face.

"This is not from your brother! You are not the only one with influence and friends in high places. It did not take much digging to discern the truth!"

"You really should not have gone to all that trouble," Holmes quipped. "We were just leaving."

"I guarantee it. Escort them off the premises."

We were pressed sharply towards the door when Holmes called back. "Professor, where is the flute now?"

"Safe, Mr Holmes. As it was below, so it is now above. It lies in Hell with an eye on Heaven."

"Get them out!" shrieked East. And that was that.

* * *

The train journey home was a grim affair. The weather was wretched and the carriage an icebox. Baynes was wrestling with his cold, which seemed to have gotten steadily worse. Holmes's lack of sleep had added to his irritability, while my head was pounding from trying to make sense of what we'd heard thus far.

"I'm no psychiatrist, but Professor Shawcross is clearly suffering from some form of megalomania."

"Yet his friends and colleagues at the British Museum said he was right as rain, right up until he went off the rails that is," Baynes replied.

"So they say," added Holmes. He was slumped in the corner, cocooned in his overcoat and scarf.

"Academics close ranks like any other senior profession, to preserve the solemn sanctity of their trade, yet something pushed Professor Shawcross over the edge just as surely as something else drove Peter Allenby into that marsh."

"You don't think it was an accident?" I said.

"The young man knew his occupation. He also knew the area and would mostly likely know the condition of the soil. I doubt he would simply wander blindly into the marsh."

"So, we're still none the wiser?"

"Not quite; there's one thing we're certain of."

"What's that?" I asked.

"That there's more to know," Holmes said.

In Mrs Hudson's absence 221B Baker Street was dark and cold. We remained swaddled in our coats as I set a fire in the grate and we gradually thawed out. Hot brandies were the order of the day, and this time the inspector did not refuse. Holmes was more animated than he had been on the train, pacing the room, before pausing periodically to rap on the floor with the tip of his cane.

"Holmes is that din really necessary?"

"I don't know yet," was his cryptic reply.

"You think it's still here, don't you?" rumbled Baynes. "Under the floorboards, perhaps?"

"So that's why all the tapping," I said. "You did the same thing in the case of the Red-Headed League when you detected the tunnel to the bank under the street!"

"The flute was never committed to evidence when Professor Shawcross was arrested, and it would go against his very nature, however deranged, to simply discard it."

"Or it may never have existed at all," I suggested. "There were only two witnesses to have seen it. One is dead and the other mad."

"That is also a possibility, thank you, Doctor."

"Also, if it were here don't you think we would have found it by now?"

"Only if we knew to look for something concealed, which we did not until today."

"Good lord, I think I've fathomed it!" Baynes sat forward and put his brandy on the table.

"Inspector?"

"I know where the flute is! The professor told us himself: 'As it was below, so it is now above'. It was buried before, concealed below ground. But these rooms are above ground, so where would you bury it?"

"Beneath the floorboards?" I offered.

"A valid suggestion Doctor, but too obvious. The key is the second part: 'It lies in Hell with an eye on Heaven'. Fire and the sky. Where do we find both in here?"

Holmes clapped his hands with a loud report. "Hah! A fireplace! A chimney!"

"A chimney indeed. The fire is a metaphor for Hell, and the eye on Heaven is the top of the chimney stack."

"Might I suggest we check the other rooms first?" I said. "There are no fires lit in them and I am loathe to douse this one and return to our frozen state simply on a speculation. If the flute is there, it has waited ten years to be discovered. A few more hours will make little difference."

"Duly noted. You are indeed on fine form today, Watson."

I debated whether to feel praised or patronised and chose the former as the less contentious option.

We began in Holmes's room. Baynes stayed in the sitting room by the fire, his health not inclining him to such exertion. Holmes knelt beside the cold grate and commenced tapping a half crown on the brick lining of the chimney.

"We are indebted to Mrs Hudson for having the chimneys swept only last week," he said. "It at least gives us a clean field of play." Each knock was met with a dense, dull response, all bar one. "There's a void behind here." Holmes tapped again to be sure. "Yes, definitely. I need tools."

Moments later he was gingerly scraping away the crumbling mortar before finally easing the brick free. "There's something inside," he whispered. He reached in and gently withdrew a man's shirt, bundled and filthy. Rolled within was a fold of ancient deerskin, and inside that lay the flute. A miasma of soot and fine dust drifted up from it that had me coughing.

There was no mistaking it as anything but a human tibia that had been skilfully shaped and polished with eight holes drilled along its length. As the professor had noted, it was decorated with scenes and symbols I will not utter here.

Holmes sat back on the floor, admiring the relic.

"We have it, Watson. We have it!"

The fire had done its work and the sitting room was like an oven. So much so I was obliged to loosen my collar. Between it and the brandy, I was feeling uncommonly warm.

The inspector, an empty glass before him, had also succumbed. He had keeled sideways in the armchair and was snoring robustly. I moved to wake him.

"Let him rest, Watson," said Holmes. "The fellow has done immense service today. He's more than earned a moment of repose." He laid the flute on the dining table. "I'll warrant that this is your grain of truth behind the professor's story."

"How so?"

"You know my methods of analysis. They are based on data and observation. Yet to some they seem miraculous. Likewise, if you took the science of today back two hundred years it would appear to be magic."

"Or witchcraft?"

"Precisely! Not consorting with dark forces, but a combination of stage magic and ancient herbal healing all wrapped in a theatrical mystique. Now imagine a figure clad as death itself walking ahead of the king's army. Would that not put fear in the enemy?"

I rubbed my temples with my fingertips. My head did

not so much ache as throb. A deep roaring pounded in my ears. I could hear my heartbeat booming like a kettledrum.

"The illusion would only last as long as it took to skewer the mummer with an arrow," I pointed out.

"But what if the Danes had been subject to some form of hallucinogenic? Say, a powder burnt in a firebrand? That is why the king's men were told to avert their faces, in order to avoid breathing it in! Mystics of the time often partook of hallucinogen mushrooms to expand their consciousness."

I could barely hear Holmes now, the agonising thrumming in my head drowning out all other sound. I clawed at my collar, my body burning from within. Everything was too bright. Daggers of light seared my eyes. I pushed the heel of my hands into them, but it did no good.

"Watson!"

I heard a faint, familiar voice, distant and echoing.

"Watson, you're too close to the fire! The fire!"

"FIRE!"

I looked up to see Sergeant Green barking orders to the riflemen at his side, followed by a gusto volley that cut down the screaming ranks of oncoming Afridi warriors.

I lay slumped against a dead horse, my shoulder coursing blood. There were no hands to help me; all were set fighting the foe. I clamped my palm against the wound, blood pulsing between my fingers.

I felt lightheaded, adrift, my soul detaching from the anchor of my body. I looked out over the bodies of my brothers in arms, the 66th Berkshires, red on red in the Afghan soil. Soon we would all come to dust, far from home and forgotten.

Something caught my eye – a black flag fluttering over the field. No, not a flag, a form, a figure! It had a human shape but was featureless, as smooth as oil, like a sheet draped over a cadaver. The vague geography of a body, but that was all. It drifted idly over the fallen, the tips of its toes lightly brushing their bodies as it passed. Raised to its lips was the flute, although I heard no tune above the din of war. Perhaps that was its music?

I drew a breath.

It stopped playing and slowly turned to face me. Its form was a fathomless gateway, unending, eternal. It studied me for a second, then its blank black features tightened, taking on shape and aspect. Its forehead was high and proud, its cheeks scarred and puckered. It smiled at me.

Frantically I looked around for a weapon. A revolver lay close by, gripped in the hand of the horse's dead rider. I groaned between gritted teeth as I dragged myself over to it.

The figure glided unhurriedly over to me as I desperately prised the pistol loose. The black being tipped forwards and hovered parallel to my prone form. I attempted to raise the revolver to fire but it pinned my arms to the ground, the nail of its one hand piercing my flesh.

I screamed as the cold overtook me.

I screamed as the darkness descended.

And then I could scream no more.

I awoke in my bed, aching and thirsty. My throat was so dry I could scarcely make a sound. I rubbed my chin and raked at several days' worth of growth. How long had I been asleep? I looked over and saw a haggard-looking Holmes in the chair opposite. As I stirred, his eyes flickered open.

"Holmes?"

"Watson, my dear fellow! How do you feel?"

I pushed myself upright, my joints groaning in protest. "As if I've been given a good hiding. What in God's name happened to me?"

Holmes pulled up the pillows to support my back. "We have both been stricken with a form of ergot poisoning."

"Ergot poisoning?"

"A particular mould that grows on grain, usually rye."

"Yes, I've heard of it. It happens when the grains are stored in damp conditions. It has some very unpleasant symptoms: mania, delirium, paranoia."

"As you have experienced. As we both have."

"It was that blessed flute, wasn't it! Shawcross said it had been stored in a jar filled with grain. It must have been contaminated somehow."

"That is my conclusion also. I found fine particles inside the doe skin wrappings and the flute itself. When we took it out of the chimney and unwrapped it we were exposed."

"What about Inspector Baynes?"

"He was in the other room. Also his heavy cold constricted his airways so he was unable to inhale the contaminant, and a good job too. He saved our lives."

"How's that?"

"You had a violent hallucination. You almost staggered into the fire, and when I attempted to restrain you, you reached for your revolver."

"Good lord!"

"Fortunately Baynes had taken the syringes and vials of sedative from The Briars to have them analysed. He was obliged to use one on you."

"I think I felt it." I pushed up my sleeve and saw a yellowing bruise on my arm. "His technique left something to be desired, but at least he got the job done. What happened to you?"

"The same, but considerably less dramatic. It appears I had already been subject to ergot poisoning but in a much milder form. Hence my recent, foul disposition. When Mrs Hudson had the chimney swept in my room, it must have dislodged the brick the flute was hidden behind and released a few particles into the atmosphere. By some good fortune, I did not inhale a great deal of the particulate matter from the flute either. I had enough time to research our condition before I began to feel the effects myself."

"We should have both been in hospital!" I exclaimed.

"There was no need. The hospital came to us," Holmes replied. "Baynes contacted Mycroft who sent the best doctors and nurses the British government can call upon. They have been ministering to us for the past three days. In fact, they left only a few hours ago."

"The same must have happened to Professor Shawcross and Peter Allenby," I noted. "Except they received significantly stronger doses."

"Potent enough to break Shawcross's mind and send Allenby, pursued by phantasms, to his doom in the marsh. It is no wonder that in the Middle Ages those afflicted were thought bewitched or possessed by demons."

"And what of Baynes?" I asked.

Holmes grinned. "Come with me."

Holmes helped me out of bed and, like a pair of geriatrics, we made our way into the next room. There, asleep on the settee and snoring like a freight train, was Inspector Baynes.

"Mycroft said he refused to leave. He wished to stand watch until we were well. He is an extraordinary individual, don't you think?" said Holmes.

"It takes one to know one," I replied.

"With a singular exception," added Holmes.

"What's that?"

"He does not have the benefit of a noble Boswell, as I do."

NOR HELL A FURY

Cavan Scott

Irene Adler is an enigma. Like Moriarty, she makes only one appearance in the canon, but her impact in the Sherlockian universe is incalculable – mainly due to the title that she is granted by the Detective himself. To Holmes, we learn, she is always *the* woman. Holmes feels no passion for the former opera singer, only professional respect. She is wily and shrewd, more than capable of protecting herself. Holmes's biographer rather unfairly declares that Adler is of "dubious and questionable memory", even though she does little to deserve such a slur. Yes, she has in her possession a compromising photograph of the King of Bohemia, which she intends to use to ruin the indiscrete royal. But do we hear this from her own lips? No, the allegation comes from the king, and only after he has ransacked her house and attempted to steal her luggage! Holmes's own investigations only bring to light that Adler lives a quiet life, is never out late and has but one gentleman caller, whom she proceeds to marry. If anything, it is the King who behaves in a dubious manner, not to mention a certain detective who employs a series of disguises to entrap the lady.

Perhaps this is the real reason that Sherlock Holmes requests a photo of Adler as his reward at the end of the sorry affair. It is a reminder that not all of the detective's quarries are as guilty as charged...

—Cavan Scott

The last person I wanted to see was Sherlock Holmes. I had made it perfectly clear in my letter to John Watson. Come alone, and tell no one the reason for your visit to Paris. Especially not him. Not Holmes.

And yet here he was, strolling through the door of the Café Verlet. I should have left there and then, head held high – but Watson would have simply come after me, the quintessential gentleman, so gallant, so brave, always ready to leap to the aid of a damsel in distress.

It was what had brought him here, after all. Racing to my aid across the Channel, with Holmes by his side.

Why was I surprised?

I rose, extending a hand that Watson took gladly, his lips brushing against my fingers.

"Mrs Langtry."

"Dr Watson," I responded, attempting to keep the tremor from my voice as I turned to acknowledge his constant companion. "Mr Holmes."

Holmes returned the greeting with a curt bow. How little the man had changed in the years since we'd last laid eyes on each other. As tall and gaunt as ever, his hair resolutely dark, although a few flecks of grey dotted those monumental eyebrows. It was curious that the brows never made their way into Mr Paget's illustrations. Perhaps the editor of *The Strand* had insisted on a more noble aspect for his hero. Give the people what they want, and all that.

I sat, indicating for Holmes and Watson to do likewise. Within seconds, a waiter had appeared at our table and orders were taken, delaying Watson's inevitable apology.

"Mrs Langtry, I realise that you specifically asked for me to come alone—"

"And yet you have brought company," I interrupted, turning to regard the great detective of Baker Street.

Holmes smiled sincerely. "You must not blame the doctor."

"Is that so?"

"Watson is incapable of keeping a secret, especially from me. From the moment he opened the letter, I realised that something was afoot. First, there was the look of surprise on his face, and then the ridiculous attempt to appear nonchalant as he continued to read."

"Really, Holmes," the affronted doctor complained.

"Well, if you will leave the envelope on the arm of your chair, where I could easily make out the handwriting…" Holmes returned his gaze to me. "Naturally, when Watson announced that he was leaving for the continent—"

"You insisted on accompanying him."

Holmes nodded, a genuine smile on those thin lips.

I sat back, regarding them both.

"Mrs Langtry." I laughed, as if rolling my own name around my mouth. "I half expected you to address me as Mrs Norton, or Miss Adler, for that matter."

Watson granted himself a chuckle, although I couldn't tell if it was formed of amusement, or acute embarrassment. "You read my account, then."

"Of course. It's not every day a girl finds herself immortalised, even under an alias."

"One has to protect the innocent."

"And the guilty?"

Holmes laughed heartily, as colour rushed to his Boswell's already ruddy cheeks.

"Mrs Langtry," said the detective, "tempting though it is, I'm sure you didn't summon us all this way to taunt Watson over his literary foibles."

"I didn't summon *you* at all."

"Touché."

Our verbal sparring was interrupted by the waiter as he delivered the gentlemen's orders. Holmes's eyes never left me as the over-attentive Frenchman fussed at our table. Sweat prickled on my neck.

After what seemed like an eternity, we were again left to our own devices. Holmes waited expectantly as I turned to his biographer.

"I am grateful that you would come all this way, Doctor. I admit I had little idea who else to turn to. My letter must have come as something of a surprise."

"I cannot pretend that it did not."

I nodded. "I am a proud woman, and not accustomed to asking for help, from anyone."

Before I could utter another word, Holmes took control of the conversation once again.

"It concerns your husband, Robert Langtry," Holmes interjected, drawing a rebuke from his companion.

"Holmes, really. Let the lady speak."

The detective inclined his head in reluctant apology.

"It is that obvious?" I inquired.

"A lady writes to a man with whom she has had no contact for over a decade. She offers to pay for his transport, insisting that he tells no one his destination. Then, when they finally meet, she spends the entire time playing with the wedding band on her finger."

I glanced down to see that, as always, the man was correct. I clasped my hands together.

Holmes continued, reeling off his theories as if they should be obvious to all. "Her marriage is therefore very much at the forefront of her mind."

"Could it be that she is in trouble herself?" I asked.

This he considered, before rejecting it completely. "Possibly, although if that was the case, why meet in public, choosing a table so near the window? No, she is not concerned for herself, but for the man she loves."

The detective sat back, so confident in his own abilities that he had no need to inquire if his supposition was correct. I burned beneath his gaze, tears welling in my eyes.

"You are correct, of course," I eventually conceded, the mere mention of my beloved's name catching in my throat. "Robert has… not been himself of late." I reached for my bag as the first tear fell. Dr Watson produced a handkerchief quicker than I could find my own. Of course he did.

Offering thanks, I dabbed at my face before continuing my tale.

"After leaving London, Robert and I travelled for a while, before settling here in Paris. Robert established a practice and we started making friends. Good friends. It was everything we'd always wanted." My voice failed me again. "Almost."

"Almost?" Watson echoed.

I offered the doctor's handkerchief back to him, but he waved it away. I folded the cloth and placed it in my bag, knowing all too well that both men's eyes were still on me.

"While Robert and I could build a home," I continued softly, "it soon became obvious that we could not build a family."

Watson's mouth dropped open at my honesty.

"My dear, I'm so sorry…" he began, somewhat flustered that the conversation had taken such a personal turn.

"At first, Robert hid his disappointment, insisting that we had each other, which was all that mattered.

"And yet I know it burned away at him. Our friends would regale him with stories about their children and his face would darken, a shadow that came to consume him over time. He starting drinking heavily, staying out to all hours. He said it was on business, but a wife knows when she is hearing lies." The words stung even as I spoke them. "It is all too easy to fall into the wrong crowd in Paris, gentlemen."

"And, once you fall, all too difficult to claw yourself back out again, I would think," Watson offered.

I nodded, giving the doctor a grateful smile. "He kept up appearances, of course. I was dressed in the latest fashions, we were seen at the right events, and yet…"

"Yes?"

"Things would disappear from the house. Trinkets at first, but then paintings, the miniatures he had begun to collect when the practice had started to do well. He claimed he was bored of them, and yet no replacements took their place. And then I realised that his mother's jewels were missing."

"He was gambling?" Watson asked, the look of compassion in his eyes almost too much to bear.

Again I nodded, the sounds of the café filling the silence around our table: the clatter of china, the buzz of mid-morning conversation.

Finally, Holmes delivered another painfully direct question.

"Where is your husband now?"

I swallowed, struggling to maintain my composure. "I do not know," I told him, the merest shake of my head sending fresh tears spilling down my cheeks.

"A week ago, Robert went out to work and never returned. No one has seen him since. People have been very kind, but I know what they are thinking. You should have seen him, Mr Holmes, that morning. He wasn't the man I married with you standing behind us, stinking of shag tobacco in your ridiculous disguise."

A flicker of recollection crossed Holmes's narrow features, the ghost of a smile playing on his lips.

"He was as pale as I had ever seen him," I continued, "his hands shaking as he picked up his case. He didn't even say goodbye, but rushed out of the front door, slamming it behind him in his haste."

"And when Mr Langtry failed to return home..." Watson began, obviously choosing his words carefully, so not to upset me further, "did you–"

"Did I find anything else missing?"

Watson nodded, looking embarrassed that he would even have to ask.

I sat up straight, determined not to play the helpless woman any more. "As you know, Doctor, I have lived an interesting life. I am not proud of everything I have done, but I stand by the decisions I have made."

"Decisions that have made foes along the way," Holmes reminded me. "Fortunately, you have taken out certain... insurances."

"I have articles that assure my safety, yes. As long as they are in my possession, then the individuals I have wronged will leave me alone–"

"In fear of you going to the press."

"Or going to other interested parties. You may not approve, but it has served me well. I have never demanded so much as a penny for my silence, never acting in spite or retaliation."

"Very… honourable," Watson muttered with little in the way of commitment, but I didn't care a jot what he thought of me. It wasn't as if the man hadn't made his mind up about my "dubious and questionable memory" long ago.

"These articles," Holmes inquired, "your husband was aware of them?"

I nodded. "Of course. I kept nothing from him."

"Which must have been all the more galling when you discovered that he had absconded with them."

It was not a question.

"My husband was… *is* a loyal and loving man, Mr Holmes. Whatever he has done, Robert would never knowingly place me at risk. Wherever he is, I am sure that he believes he is doing the right thing—"

"But has no idea what dangers await him."

"The reason I approached Dr Watson rather than yourself is that I fear for my husband's life."

"My presence would have been more conspicuous."

"Which is why I now regret my choice of this café for exactly the reasons you suggest. We *can* easily be seen from the street. Meeting Dr Watson in such a place is one thing…" I turned to the medical man. "Your appearance is somewhat nondescript, after all, Doctor."

Watson did his best not to look insulted.

"Whereas Mr Holmes bears one of the most recognisable profiles in all of Europe, thanks to your stories."

"You fear my presence can only spell more trouble for your husband, wherever he is." The detective considered my words, before delivering his verdict. "Mrs Langtry, I apologise that I foisted myself on the good doctor. Tell me, have you any idea of the establishments that your husband frequented in the weeks leading up to his disappearance? You say he had been drinking and gambling."

I nodded, opening my purse once again. "I found these," I said, drawing out two dog-eared books of matches. Holmes reached for them, turning them over in his long fingers to read the garish legend emblazoned across the cover.

"*Le Cabaret de L'Enfer.*"

I let my distaste show on my face. "It is a nightclub on the Boulevard de Clichy."

Holmes looked up from the matches. "Near Place Pigalle? The wrong crowd indeed."

"Have you visited this… cabaret?" Watson chimed in. "To ask if anyone has seen him?"

"Watson, the cabarets of La Pigalle are not places for ladies of good character." The doctor soon gathered Holmes's meaning. "Nor could Mrs Langtry request that any of her husband's friends or colleagues investigate on her behalf."

I shook my head. "For its bohemian splendour, Paris is more conservative than Monsieur du Maurier would have you believe. Having survived one scandal in Bohemia, I am eager to avoid another."

Holmes rewarded me with another tight smile. "Watson, you will go to *Le Cabaret de L'Enfer,*" he commanded.

"Of course," the doctor agreed, ever the faithful bloodhound. "I'll make enquiries, see when your husband was last seen, that kind of thing."

"If you are sure," I said. "*Le Cabaret* is rather… theatrical."

"Watson's a man of the world," Holmes insisted. "Not

much shocks him, isn't that right?"

The doctor chuckled, although I could see the trepidation in his eyes.

"And what of you, Mr Holmes?" I inquired.

"I shall return to our hotel," he replied, drawing a look of dismay from Watson. "As you quite correctly surmise, my presence would draw too much attention. As always, I can rely on Watson to be my eyes and ears."

Holmes rose to his feet, reaching for my hand. I had thought that he was a man who balked from human contact – and yet, he bowed and kissed my hand, with such gentleness that I almost caught my breath.

"Au revoir, dear lady. Please be assured that we will do everything within our power to reunite you with your husband."

With that, my saviours departed, leaving me alone at my table. The door to the café closed, and I released the breath I had barely been aware I was holding.

Perhaps everything would be as it should be, after all.

That evening, the streets of Montmartre were heaving from the moment the sun dipped below the horizon. You could almost taste the anticipation in the air. The brave and foolish descended onto the narrow roads, wondering what adventures the night would bring.

No one gave me a second look, sitting outside a pleasantly shabby bistro, smoking a cigarette, a newspaper laid in front of me as I waited, just another soul wiling away the hours until the revels began.

I saw him at once, parading down the road, back ramrod straight, looking neither left nor right, no doubt in case he caught the eye of devils proffering temptations of both body and soul. I couldn't help but laugh. John Watson, the Englishman abroad, desperately trying to look as though he owned the place, even though he was so very far from home. I extinguished my cigarette and rose as he approached.

"Dr Watson?"

He started, caught between stopping to see who had called his name and fleeing in panic.

"I'm sorry, I…"

His voice trailed off as realisation dawned, his eyes growing wide as they took me in from head to foot. "Good lord!"

The doctor took a step closer, dropping his voice so only I could hear. "Mrs Langtry?"

I thrust out my hand, only increasing his bewilderment. Out of habit, he took it, and I shook his sweating hand vigorously.

"That's it," said I, my voice a good octave lower than normal. "Just two old friends meeting in the street. Nothing out of the ordinary."

"I– I wouldn't say that," he stammered, struggling to find the words.

I released his hand, and brushed an imaginary piece of fluff from my sleeve. "I must admit that I'm out of practice, but it's gratifying to know that I can still fool you as I did Mr Holmes on the steps of Baker Street."

Watson was still staring open-mouthed at my attire, from the top hat perched atop a masculine wig to my sharply pressed trousers. "As Mr Holmes suggested, ladies of good character would never frequent *Le Cabaret de L'Enfer*, but as for gentlemen? Well, the same standards never apply, do they not?"

"Surely you don't intend to come in with me?"

"I certainly do. I admit, I wouldn't venture through the gates of hell on my own, but by your side, I fear no ill."

"Shall we then?" the good Doctor asked, wisely deciding that the argument was lost.

I took one last sip from the cup of coffee I had been nursing and, leaving my paper on the table, led Watson down the street. "I thought you'd never ask."

Dr Watson's expression on finally seeing our destination was a delight to behold. If the sight of a woman in man's clothing had been enough to rock his world to its very foundations, nothing could prepare him from the entrance of *Le Cabaret de L'Enfer*. The exterior been fashioned to resemble molten lava, the upper reaches of the building adorned by hideous statues of naked men and women writhing in agony and ecstasy. The door to the nightclub was surrounded by a gigantic carved face of Lucifer himself, crimson eyes blazing with hellfire. You entered by means of a gaping, fanged maw, the doorman dressed as a horned imp, complete with cape and pitchfork.

"Dear God," Watson muttered, appalled at the sight.

"There is little of the Almighty beyond those doors, Doctor," I promised. "At least, that's what the customers hope and pray."

"And your husband came *here*, to such a den of iniquity?" he marvelled, staring at me with judgement in his eyes.

I let my pain show in my face. "Yes," I said quietly.

Realising his insensitivity, the doctor placed a comforting hand on my arm. "I'm sorry. I realise this must be difficult. If you wouldn't rather—"

"No," I said abruptly, before he could send me home. "I've come this far and need to know if Robert was here."

The doctor took a deep breath, and looking as if he was about to offer me his arm, thankfully stopping himself at the last moment.

"Shall we?" he said, covering his embarrassment.

I punched him manfully in the arm. "Whatever you say, *old man.*"

Watson laughed, playing along at last, and we approached the astonishing facade. All at once, the impish doorman danced a jig and hooted in merriment. "A-ha," he shouted out to us in his native French, "still they come, the lost and bedevilled. Oh, how they shall roast."

To his credit, Watson didn't hesitate. He marched up to the red-faced fellow and, with surprising mastery of the imp's own tongue, demanded entrance. The doorman bowed dramatically. "Of course, foolish mortal, we welcome all sinners here." With a flourish, the gaudy fellow opened the heavy wooden doors and stepped aside. "Enter and be damned. The Evil One awaits."

Showing more humour than I expected, Watson rubbed his hands together as he crossed the threshold. "Well, I hope he's stoked the fire. It's been positively freezing all day." The doorman brayed a peel of frenzied laughter, slamming the door behind us.

We found ourselves in a sloping corridor, decorated to resemble the Devil's gullet and lined by glowing grates that belched thick smoke.

"Charming," Watson commented, coughing into his gloved hand. "I'm surprised they don't open a concern in the West End."

"It's only a matter of time," I replied, taking the lead and walking towards a door at the end of the uncanny passage. The music that spilled through the gaudily painted wood was unmistakable: the second act of Berlioz's *La damnation de Faust*. Robert and I had seen it performed at the Opéra de Monte-Carlo in '93 and I was glad that I could blame the smoke for the tears that once again troubled my eyes.

A narrow window slid open in the door, a ghastly face appearing in the gap. Spotting us, this keeper of the inner sanctum let out a howl of pleasure and, throwing open the door, beckoned us in.

"More fuel for the fire – welcome, welcome."

If Watson had balked at his first sight of the club, one glance at this fellow almost had him running for the hills. Unlike the imp on the street outside, the master of ceremonies wore no cloak. In fact, he wore little at all, his corpulent frame naked, save for a loincloth to protect what little was left of his dignity. Every inch of his flesh was daubed red, although rivulets of sweat had carved obscene paths through the greasepaint. Beady bloodshot eyes were caked in thickly applied mascara that ran down prodigious jowls, while his hairless mound of a head was adorned by a pair of wooden antlers, around which some creative soul had twisted velvet snakes of multiple colours.

On seeing Watson's obvious discomfort, the grotesque slapped his immense belly and squealed with shrill laughter, beckoning us towards a table in the corner of the stifling room. He was still giggling inanely as he pranced away, leaving Watson gazing around in horror and bewilderment. The low ceiling was covered in a mass of writhing wax bodies, tormented by demonic effigies that seemed almost alive in the flickering light of the torches that smouldered on the walls. Vapours rose from the floor, bringing with them the unsettling odour of brimstone and sulphur, while, suspended in an oversized cauldron at the far end of the room, five wailing musicians launched into a raucous rendition of Saint-Saëns' *Danse Macabre*. The audience whooped and applauded, as photographers in scarlet dinner jackets and carnival masks chronicled the chthonian gaiety, their flash powder only adding to the disorientating atmosphere.

Watson produced another handkerchief, but this time employed it by dabbing the sweat from his brow. Conspiratorially, he leant forward to make himself heard over the infernal strings and braying laughter of our fellow patrons. Any bravado the doctor had displayed at the gates of hell was now gone, replaced by the near panic of a man who finds himself severely out of his depth.

"My dear," he stammered, his breath warm against my cheek. "Perhaps this was not such a good idea. Such a place…"

"Mere histrionics, nothing more," I replied, turning so his face was inches from my own. "But, you can see why I would worry that Robert would choose to come here."

His eyes swept across the bawdy tableau, the revellers throwing caution and decency to the wind, urged on by scantily-clad waitresses who supplied tray after tray of potent libations in phosphorescent glasses.

Such a nymph soon approached our table, wickedly offering to deliver any pleasure from the nine circles of hell. Watson looked as if he was about to fall from his chair until I advised the poor doctor that she meant drinks, nothing more.

"Oh, t-that's all right then," he spluttered in English, before reverting to French to order two coffees.

"Coffees?" our serving girl parroted, with a look that suggested that she was about to mercilessly mock the doctor to an inch of his life, or have him ejected on the spot for wanton conventionality.

I jumped in, winking at the young nymph. "And make sure there's a shot of cognac in both of those, eh?"

The waitress smiled in return. "Two seething bumpers of molten sin with a dash of brimstone intensifier coming right up."

As she turned to leave, Watson called after her.

"Is there anything else I can get you, sinner?" she asked, with a look that could instantly condemn any man's soul to eternal damnation.

"We're looking for a friend of ours, who came here."

For the first time since her arrival, the imp's outrageous act faltered, her large eyes darting between us. "Hell asks no questions," she replied, with just enough steel in her sing-song voice to warn that the conversation was at an end. Watson was having none of it however, and pushed home his point. "His name is Robert Langtry. We know he came here. We just wish to know that he is safe."

The waitress shot a look over at the portly master of ceremonies, who stomped over, his earlier jocularity a mere memory. "Is there a problem here?" he asked, glaring at us both.

Watson raised a placating hand. "We were merely asking after a friend of ours who we know frequented your… charming establishment a number of times."

The man's glower intensified. "Demons tell no tales. I suggest that you take the hint, *sir*. Otherwise, you could find yourself burned for re–"

A crash from a nearby table cut the obvious threat short.

One of our neighbours, a tall man in fine evening dress, but more than a little worse for wear, had tumbled from his stool, taking a tray of lightly glowing glasses with him.

"*Excuse me*," the drunk slurred in broken French, his thick beard matted with wine and God knows what else. "Here, I'll help."

"No need," the master of ceremonies insisted, helping the inebriated idiot to his feet as an army of nymphs appeared from nowhere to sweep up the broken glass. "Perhaps you have had enough hellfire for one night, proud sinner."

The drunkard laughed off the suggestion. "Nonsense," he drawled, producing a wallet stuffed with banknotes. "I'm happy to pay for my transgressions." He threw his arms out in an expansive gesture that would have struck me in the face if I hadn't ducked at the last moment. "For *everyone's* transgressions!"

His greedy eyes spying the small fortune in the man's wallet, the master of ceremonies guided the poor fellow back onto his stool. "Then your sins are forgiven, monsieur. May I suggest you commit some new ones!"

He clicked his podgy fingers, calling for a waitress to take more of the inebriate's money, before departing, firing a warning glance at Watson as he passed.

I put my hand on Watson's arm. "That was close. I thought we were done for."

The doctor nodded. "Maybe we should tread more carefully, if you're sure you want to stay?"

I had no chance to answer before our waitress returned, carrying two steaming cups. She stepped between us, leaning across to place them on the table in front of Watson. As the doctor went to pay, she hissed in his ear.

"I've seen your friend."

He shot me a look before replying. "You have?"

The girl nodded, proceeding to describe Robert to perfection, from his neatly parted auburn hair to eyes the colour of sapphires. Watson glanced in my direction once again, and I nodded sharply, confirming that the description matched that of my husband.

The girl hovered at Watson's elbow, checking that the master of ceremonies wasn't watching, before continuing. "He came in last week, in a worse state than ever, demanding to use some of the cabaret's, well, more… esoteric services."

"Whatever do you mean?" I asked.

She replied with a question of her own. "Have you heard of the Devil's Closet?"

I shook my head.

"You see that curtain?" she said, indicating a heavy maroon cloth that hung at the back of the room. "Beyond that is a pit covered by a heavy wooden trapdoor. Customers pay to be locked inside, as if they are being buried alive."

"Why on Earth would they do such a thing?" Watson asked in wonderment.

"Hell asks no questions," I reminded him.

The waitress shrugged. "Sometimes they are alone—"

"But not always?" I enquired. "What about Robert?"

"He was alone. I didn't see him go into the pit myself, but passed his request onto the master of ceremonies."

"Our delightful friend with an aversion to clothing?" Watson inquired.

The girl gave another nervous glance in the man's direction. "He only allows customers to be locked in for short periods of time."

"Why?"

"I don't know. A danger of suffocation, maybe?"

My stomach churned as I watched Watson's face. The man was forming a plan even as the girl spoke. "All part of the deprived thrill, I suppose," he commented, rubbing his chin as he came to a decision. "Could you get us into the pit?"

The girl looked uncertain and so Watson added the clincher: "We'll pay, of course!"

"I can ask, if you promise not to make any more trouble."

"You have my word."

She nodded and left our table, distracted on her way to the master of ceremonies by the drunk who, incredibly, was already ordering another round of drinks.

"What are you *thinking*?" I whispered, as soon as she was out of earshot.

He pulled me closer. "If your husband was here, and paid to enter that pit, then perhaps there will be something that will give us a clue to his whereabouts."

"You're joking?" I gasped. "You want us to actually get into the thing?"

"If there's something there, no matter how small, it might be just what Holmes needs. While I would never pretend to share his talents, I can describe a scene as well as the next man, maybe even better."

"Even if the next man is a woman?" I joked, trying to alleviate my own misgivings.

"We must record everything we see, no matter how insignificant. Holmes can see things that others—"

He broke off as the waitress returned to our table. "Two hundred francs," she reported flatly. Beside me Watson swallowed and reluctantly drew out his wallet.

* * *

The moment came just twenty minutes later. The master of ceremonies danced to the front of the stage and made a great show of poking the musicians with a pitchfork before addressing the crowd.

"Prostrate yourself, sinners," he squealed, "before the angel of the bottomless pit, the father of lies and the King of Tyre. Behold, our Lord Satan!"

With a crash of symbols, and a puff of billowing smoke, a mountain of a man strode onto the stage, resplendent in a swirling blood red robe and brandishing a wicked-looking sword. His moustache was waxed into rakish points, while pointed teeth gleamed in a wolfish smile.

"Who summons me?" Satan demanded, the master of ceremonies prostrating himself. "Who invites judgement for all eternity?"

All the time, the photographers' cameras flashed, dazzling us all, as our waitress returned, indicating that it was time. As the pantomime played out in front of the corybantic assembly, we were led to the back of the room, narrowly missing a collision with the bearded drunk who once again fought to stay on his stool.

The serving girl held aside the curtain and we entered a gloomy antechamber, packed full of crates and bottles. The place was filthy, from grime-covered floors to the cracked window-panes of a side door that led to who knew where. I brought my hand to my nose, the fetid stink of stale beer and rat droppings threatening to overwhelm me.

"Good lord," Watson exclaimed, sharing my disgust. "Two hundred francs for this?"

"No," the girl said, walking towards a trapdoor in the floor, and struggling with its large iron ring. "Two hundred francs for *this*!"

"Allow me," Watson said, springing forward. The girl protested, but soon stepped back to allow the doctor to haul the trapdoor open.

To the sound of the performance in the next room, we peered down into the abyss beneath our feet. Watson found an old lantern on a nearby shelf and lit it, swinging the light over the pit to reveal a short ladder, rough brick walls and a grime-covered floor at the bottom.

"And people find this pleasurable?"

"You saw the scum this place attracts, Doctor," I replied, the waitress stiffening beside me. "No offence meant."

"None taken," she insisted, "but now I must ask you to descend into the pit, and I will close you in."

"That won't be necessary," Watson said hurriedly. "You can go about your business, my dear, and leave us to ours."

The serving girl looked unsure. "But I am supposed to seal you in myself–"

I reached into my jacket pocket to retrieve my wallet, producing a generous note, which I pushed into the girl's hand. "We won't be, if you keep watch."

She looked back at Watson, lowering the lantern down into the darkness, and nervously made her decision. "Very well – but you only have ten minutes, while the show is underway. After it is finished, someone is bound to check."

"Then we'd better hurry," Watson prompted and, giving him one last worried glance, the girl slipped back into the drinking hall.

I turned and crouched beside the pit. "So, what are we looking for?"

"*We're* not looking for anything," Watson said, passing me the lantern. "I'm not about to allow a lady to put herself through such an ordeal, no matter how she's dressed."

I argued, but the doctor was having nothing of it. He stood, removing his jacket and placing it on a pile of crates. Rolling up his shirtsleeves, he made his way around to the ladder.

"I shall enter the pit, while you hold the light over my head. There looks to be rubbish on the floor down there. If your husband were here, he might have dropped something – a ticket or some such. If there's something that can help Holmes I'll find it." He paused, steeling himself. "Right, let's get this over with."

Carefully, Watson swung himself onto the ladder and climbed down into the pit. Beyond the curtain, the crowd cheered – Satan's act reaching its climax.

"A little more light, if you please," Watson called up, choking on the dust that had been disturbed by his descent.

"Are you all right?"

"Never better," he said, as if this was an everyday occurrence. "That's it. Keep the lantern steady."

"Can you see anything?"

Watson crouched on his haunches, running his hand over the grime-covered floor.

"Nothing yet, which in itself is curious. If someone had recently been down here, you would expect this grime to have been disturbed."

I pointed down at the far corner of the pit. "What about that?"

"What?"

"I saw something glint in the light."

"Really?" Watson exclaimed, turning in the tight space. As soon as his back was towards me, I placed the lantern on the edge of the pit, leaning down to grab the ladder. As smoothly as I could, I pulled it up from the hole in the ground.

Feeling movement behind him, Watson turned, staring up in confusion.

"What are you doing?"

My only reply was to place the ladder against the wall and retrieve the doctor's jacket. I tossed the garment down into the pit and crossed to the trapdoor, heaving it shut with all my might.

"Mrs Langtry!"

The trapdoor was heavier than it looked. No wonder the waitress had struggled, but I had come too far to be confounded now.

Grunting with the exertion, I slammed the door shut, sealing Watson inside. I froze for a moment, convinced that the crash would have been heard in the drinking hall, but the music from the band blared on, and no one rushed to see what had occurred.

Of the doctor, there was barely a sound, the thick trapdoor muffling his cries for help. No one would find him here, not until I was long gone.

Stepping over the wooden lid, I put the lantern back where he had found it and extinguished the flame. The room was plunged into blackness, but I had already committed the route to memory. I was out of the side door and into the service corridor beyond within seconds, hurrying towards the back entrance that I had arranged to remain unlocked. I stepped out into a moonlit alley and was away, leaving John Watson to pay for his sins once and for all.

Back at my lodgings, time was of the essence. The train was leaving within the hour, but that would be ample time. It wasn't as if I had much to take with me, not any more.

I had packed, ready to leave, long before meeting Holmes and Watson that morning. All that remained was for me to cast off my disguise.

I made for the dressing table, intending to remove the damned wig that threatened to itch my scalp red raw, when there came a knock at the door, two sharp raps.

"Who is it?" I asked. There was no answer, save for another dreadful knock.

"Give me a minute!"

There was nowhere to run. The room's small window led only to a three-storey drop, and certain injury. Out of options, I pulled open the front door.

The drunk from *Le Cabaret de L'Enfer* stood in the corridor outside, his face no longer merry, his eyes focused and cold.

Behind him, glaring over the fellow's narrow shoulder, stood the Banquo at my feast – John Watson.

"May we come in?" said Sherlock Holmes, not waiting for an invitation. He stepped over the threshold, already removing his false beard, which he discarded on the bed.

I wanted to slump to the floor, but forced myself to stand, tight-lipped. Holmes would have to break the silence; he would have to speak, not I.

Watson followed the detective into my room, and closed the door behind them.

When Holmes finally spoke there was no kindness in that strident voice of his, no pity. He laid out the facts as if giving evidence at a trial.

"Your husband is dead," he began, his words like barbs. "That much was easy enough to ascertain from a simple visit to his practice. Robert Langtry's name has already been painted from the sign. But how did he die? A visit to the local newspaper revealed that, according to the public record, Mr Langtry had been murdered three months ago during a burglary at his home, along with his maid and footman. As for his grieving widow, well, she is still missing, presumed dead."

I sank on to the edge of the bed, the weight of the last three months too much to bear.

"Dead, or in fear of her life? Which is it?"

There was no point lying, not any more. Not to him.

"They were agents of the Tsar, sent to retrieve the… evidence I held concerning his family."

"The photo of you and Grand Duke Paul Alexandrovich of Russia."

I allowed myself a bitter smile at Watson. "How clever of Dr Watson to protect us all with pseudonyms. The King of Bohemia. Irene Adler. Godfrey Norton. No one would ever know the true identities of the characters he splashed across the pages of *The Strand*. Or at least that's what you obviously hoped."

"They worked out who you were," Watson intoned.

"No," I replied, quietly. "They worked out who *he* was."

"Who?"

"Who do you think?" I spat in fury, jumping back to my feet. "Your oh-so-dramatic visitor with his mask and his barrel chest and, what was it? Oh, yes – 'the limbs of a Hercules'. Well, it appears that your Hercules is as unlucky in love today as he was then, and has found himself in the middle of another scandal. The vultures are circling and have seen beyond the smoke and mirrors. Once they had realised the true identity of your King of Bohemia, it didn't take them long to work out which prima donna had so vexed him in London, the woman who still held proof of his past indiscretions."

Watson's face was pale, smudged only with the grime of his subterranean prison. "Evidence that could be used against him."

"The last thing that Nicholas wanted was for his brother's sins to be found out all over again and so the photograph that had kept me safe for so many years became my death sentence."

"Or rather that of Robert Langtry," said Sherlock Holmes.

The memory of that fateful night brought tears to my eyes. "They came to our house, demanding the photograph. They had already killed poor Cammi."

"Your maid."

"Robert tried to protect me, only to receive a knife to the stomach. They already had the photograph. There was no need for him to die."

"You escaped."

"Evidently. Our footman – Pierre – tackled my husband's murderer, and in the confusion I managed to slip away. I ran from the house, from everything I owned. I had nowhere to go, no friends I could turn to. Do you think the Tsar's agents would let me live, after what I had witnessed?"

"So you lost yourself in Paris, returning to the stage, rebuilding your life."

I threw my hands wide and turned on my heels. "And here it is, my new nest."

Holmes didn't pass comment, but reeled off what I already knew, ever the showman. "The apparently fine clothes you wore this morning were as false as the name Watson gave you all those years ago, costume reproductions designed to fool an audience from the stage."

"Or a doctor," I added, with little humour.

"And when I kissed your hand, there was a distinctive odour, barely disguised by inexpensive soap and cheap perfume: sulphur, used to create the allusion of walking through a volcano."

"Or an inferno," Watson added with a grimace.

"The reason you dressed yourself as a man tonight is that you are known at *Le Cabaret de L'Enfer*, not as a customer, but a member of staff, perhaps one of the musicians who play from within the cauldron. There are usually six from what I can gather, although tonight there were only five. That's where you discovered the pit. No one pays to be buried alive at the back of the cabaret. That was a fiction, designed to reel Watson in, appealing to his more melodramatic tendencies. His early grave was nothing more than a little used storage area, not opened from one year to the next."

Watson's eyes bored into me, bristling with recrimination. "I may never have been found. If Holmes hadn't forced his way past the curtain…"

"Needless to say that the infernal masters of the cabaret are keen to keep the entire sorry affair out of the public eye."

"Until Dr Watson writes an account of it…" I sneered.

"As for your accomplice," Holmes continued, ignoring my interruption, "the obliging nymph who just so happened to remember Robert Langtry, she has vanished into the ether."

"No doubt assisted by the two hundred francs purloined from my wallet," Watson added.

"Not stolen," I reminded him. "You gave it gladly."

"To help you!"

"Instead you have helped her escape a life in the Pigalle,

and for that I am grateful. At least something good has come of this evening."

"Quite so," agreed Holmes.

I looked the detective in the eye. "And what of me?"

Holmes walked over to my mirror to remove the last scraps of his make-up. "From the ticket on your dressing table, you are preparing your own escape, although the chances of you now catching the last train to Vienna are minimal."

"Because you intend to turn me over to the police?"

Holmes turned to face me. "Because you will never make it to the railway station in time, that is all."

Holmes strolled across the room with such confidence that I wanted to scream. He opened the door and indicated for his companion to take his leave. Watson walked out without so much as a backwards glance.

Before he followed his friend out into the corridor, Holmes paused, turning to face me. "Mrs Langtry, you sought to take revenge on the man you believe ruined your life. You lured him to the City of Lights with the intention of leaving him to rot in the dark. I for one am grateful that I was on hand to ensure his safety. I bear you no malice, and hope you can indeed rebuild your life."

The man's hubris made me sick to my stomach. "How gracious of you."

"But know this: move against Watson again, and I will move against you. Yesterday, I was your admirer. Today, I am your enemy."

With that, Sherlock Holmes closed the door behind him.

* * *

A chill wind blew along the banks of the Seine the following morning. As Holmes had predicted, I had missed my train. There would be others, of course, but for now I was content to sit, gazing over at the great cathedral of Notre Dame, wondering what might have been.

Would I really have gone through with it? Would I have let a man die in that pit? I told myself not, that I would have sent word when I was away. The police would have raided the cabaret and found Watson, despairing but unhurt. It would have been hard to keep such an occurrence out of the papers, the good doctor finding himself in the middle of a scandal of his own making, indirectly at least.

I watched the gulls whirl in the sky above the ancient buttresses, convincing myself that yes, that's exactly what I would have done.

And Holmes was right. Now I had to start again, to build another nest, far away, where no one would find me again. It was time to take another name.

The gulls shrieked, twisting in the air before swooping away. I watched them go, barely noticing the man who came to sit alongside me on the bench. He regarded the cathedral for a moment, before rising to walk back the way he came. I waited, counting to ten, before dropping my gloved hand down to the envelope he had left behind.

Opening the flap, I removed the photographs that I had ordered – Dr John Watson sat in the bowels of the cabaret, his hand on the arm of a handsome young man, their faces surprisingly close, lips inches away from each other. Then there were the images of the good doctor handing over a wad of notes to a scantily clad girl. You couldn't see her face, but Watson's profile was clear for all to see.

Certain editors on Fleet Street would pay good money for

such shots. Think of the papers they would sell. Think of the headlines. Give the people what they want, and all that.

My words of yesterday came back unbidden.

I have never demanded so much as a penny for my silence, never acting in spite or retaliation.

I slipped the photographs safely back into the envelope and smiled. If I sent them, I would not ask for recompense. Instead, copies would land anonymously on every news desk in the land.

If I sent them.

I rose from the bench and strolled along the banks of the river. Interesting times lay ahead for Dr Watson, and I wished him well.

After all, whatever threats Sherlock Holmes made, to me, John Watson would always be *the* man.

THE CASE OF THE
HAPHAZARD MARKSMAN

Andrew Lane

Langdale Pike never appears in the canon, although he is mentioned in "The Adventure of the Three Gables". He is described as being "strange" and "languid" (a condition I have aspired to ever since I was a teenager) and he apparently makes a living as a gossip columnist. He does actually turn up in the 1980s TV adaptation starring Jeremy Brett as Holmes, played memorably by the excellent Peter Wyngarde. It is Wyngarde who I imagined when I was writing this story.

—Andrew Lane

My name is Langdale Pike. You have probably heard of me. In fact, I would be surprised if you had not. I write what are popularly known as "gossip columns" for several of the more popular newspapers and magazines available in this, the greatest city in the greatest nation of the world. From the centre of my web of information I pick up on the slightest of vibrations in strands that extend into the servants' quarters of every large house, into the snugs and taprooms of every tavern and bar, into the fronts-of-house of every theatre and music hall of note and into the comfortable seating of every café and coffee house. Or, to put it more prosaically, from my preferred window seat in my club in St. James's I have a network of runners who perpetually shuttle snippets of information from maids, footmen, attendants and serving girls into my hands and, subsequently, small sums of money from me back to them. There is no assignation, no affair, no gambling debt and no underhand activity of which I am ignorant – if, that is, the public would find it titillating. If not, you need have no fear. If your fumbled indiscretion with your wife's sister or your surreptitious channelling of church funds into your own pocket would not sell a few more newspapers were it to be reported in the press then, rest assured, I am not interested. Go, as they say, and sin in peace.

Gossip is, I am convinced, one of the basic drives of

humanity. Without gossip what would we have to talk about over the garden wall or across the dinner table? Only the weather, and given London's dismal record in that regard the conversation would soon peter out. We all have a burning desire to know what members of the aristocracy, royalty, the Church and the House of Commons get up to behind closed doors. I am merely fulfilling a public service by collating and disseminating these details.

Contrary to certain canards that have been spread around about me recently, I do not, I promise you, blackmail people using the information I have about them. Blackmail is an appalling crime, and I am a law-abiding citizen. I have never taken a single shilling to suppress details of a scandal, but I have taken many shillings in the service of getting those details in front of a voracious public. These wicked slurs have, I am sure, been spread by some who have been hurt by the – to them, uncomfortable – truths I tell in print. I understand that their marriages may have been destroyed and that they may be facing financial ruin, but to them I would say that their travails are a result of their own peccadilloes. If they had not lapsed, they would not have lost so much.

Not only do I not profit from the vile trade of blackmail: my services are, in fact, taken advantage of by various guardians of law and order in London – the police, and the increasing number of consulting detectives setting up shop in Paddington and Pimlico. It is often crucial to their investigations to know that this suspect has been having a torrid love affair with that maid and that his recently murdered wife had, just prior to her death, discovered them locked in an amorous embrace. In the interests of telling the complete truth I have also, I admit, been approached by those who labour at the other end of the spectrum of legality. They, of course, do not share my repugnance at blackmail. I try my best not to get involved with these insalubrious characters. We have something of an armed standoff – I know the details of their dirty little schemes and could expose them to the police if I so chose. In fact, I have collections of information lodged with several solicitors scattered around London like so many infernal devices. If anything were to happen to me then that information would be released, and for a while the streets would be a great deal cleaner. But only for a while.

The only exception I make in this regard is a certain, shall we say, academic gentleman who occasionally seeks out my services. He is the kind of man whose mild requests have the force of barked orders, and unpleasant things happen to those who ignore those requests. Fortunately, he regards blackmail as trivial and beneath his intellect. The information with which I provide him is used in other ways that I rarely get to see. He also invites me for lunch every now and then at his club. He is a surprisingly pleasant conversationalist.

Talking of this gentleman brings me in a circle, back to the consulting detectives who seek me out and pay me for information. One in particular – a Mr Sherlock Holmes – frequently takes advantage of my services. He does not approve of me, but I am well past the time in my life when I require anybody's approval. He finds me useful, however, and it does amuse me to see the daemons of his practical side fighting with the angels of his better nature. The poor man does suffer so.

I keep up to date with the cases undertaken by Mr Holmes by reading the accounts written by his fellow lodger and amanuensis, Dr John Watson. Often I can see within those accounts elements that I provided to Holmes but that he has, I presume, failed to explain properly to Dr Watson – preferring instead to take the credit for discovering them himself. And, who, frankly, can blame him? I trust, by the way, that Dr Watson's skills as a physician exceed those he displays as a writer of prose. Or perhaps I am just irritated by the way his lumpen phraseology seems to catch the public imagination. Those of us who make a professional living from journalism tend to look darkly upon the fortunate amateur.

Perhaps that is why I have turned my attention now to writing up one of the times when Holmes required my assistance – and, as it turned out, for more than just information. This was during one of the periods when Watson was living separately from Holmes, thanks to a recent marriage. It was his third, I believe. Holmes seemed to have a blind spot where Watson was concerned: the man was a serial womaniser with a serious gambling problem, but Holmes never criticised him for this, as far as I know. He certainly had enough reason: Watson was always criticising Holmes for his dalliance with the needle.

At the time this particular case came to my attention Watson was out of London – holidaying in Eastbourne with his new wife. I already had a thin file on her, but I saw no need to spoil the good doctor's marital bliss by telling him anything of his wife's rather colourful past. Perhaps he already knew. At any rate, it was early one morning at my club when Holmes appeared, accompanied by a footman and a young woman who looked as if she had been crying for some time.

I nodded to the footman, and as he withdrew I gestured to my visitors to sit down.

"Mr Holmes," I said, "it has been too long."

"Not long enough for me, Pike," he rejoined. "I apologise, by the way, for the timing of my visit. I know that the hours you keep tend to run completely counter to the hours of the civilised world."

"And I know that you keep whatever hours you choose, without recourse to looking at any clock," I responded. "We are both as bad as each other."

"Certainly not," he snapped. He had thrown himself into a chair when he arrived, but now he drew himself up and nodded his head towards the lady with whom he had entered. "This is Miss Molly Morris," he said. "Miss Morris has consulted me on a problem, and I find I am in the regrettable situation of requiring your unique brand of assistance."

I gazed at Miss Morris, who was wiping her eyes with a lace handkerchief. She was dressed quite cheaply, but well. I would have put her down as an assistant in a haberdasher's shop, rather than one of those women often and confusingly described as being "no better than they should be", and I am rarely wrong on these matters.

Holmes continued: "Miss Morris's fiancé was killed several days ago in the Vauxhall Pleasure Gardens, down near the Embankment. The exact nature of his death is odd; odder still has been the reaction of the police."

"He was shot," she interjected forcefully. "My family has worked in fairgrounds for generations, and I've seen shooting galleries. I know what a rifle shot sounds like. Gordon was standing in front of me, just opening his mouth to say something, when he was shot in the chest. He clutched at the wound, and keeled over."

"I'm terribly sorry for your loss," I said, leaning forward

and patting her hand. "I fear that Mr Holmes may have misled you, however. I know he disapproves of the way I make my living, but I do not, I assure you, either commission shootings or know anyone who carries them out. Nasty, unpleasant, noisy things."

"You make your living by making other people unhappy," Holmes snapped. "Nevertheless, I am aware that you have a finely tuned ear for gossip and innuendo. Miss Morris's fiancé is of, shall we say, a higher social station than she. I would like to know whether there is any family feud, any argument over a legacy, any dubious business arrangements, or any other reason why young Mr Gordon Drake might have been shot."

"Drake is a common name," I pointed out.

"Indeed. But this particular family have been involved in maritime insurance for generations."

"Ah – the Cheyne Walk Drakes, with offices in Fenchurch Street and Deptford." I nodded. "I have indeed heard of them, but not in any way that would help in your investigation. There is, as far as I am aware, no hint of scandal in that family." I smiled at Holmes. "I would consider them to be consumers of the work I do, rather than the fuel for it."

"The police tried to tell me he was stabbed," Miss Morris interjected. "They told me that some mugger tried to take his wallet, and that when he resisted was knifed through the heart, but that's just not so."

I patted her hand again – I wasn't sure if I was helping, but I had to do something. "Perhaps his family were unhappy at the impending marriage," I said, "and they were trying to kill you, but missed. Had you thought about that possibility?"

Miss Morris looked at me in shock, then buried her face

in her handkerchief and descended into a peal of sobs.

Holmes gazed at me sternly. "I have made investigations," he announced, "and I am quite certain that Mr Drake's family were happy that he was happy, and that they had taken Miss Morris to their bosom." He held up a hand. "And, before you attempt to suggest that someone in Miss Morris's family – perhaps a funfair shooting booth operator – was the guiding intelligence behind the shot, I have found only happiness in the extended Morris clan at the forthcoming nuptials."

"No jealous paramours?" I inquired.

"Gordon was my first beau," Miss Morris stated, cheeks still damp from her tears. I glanced at Holmes, and he nodded in agreement.

"I wish I could be of more help," I said. "The trouble is that I know nothing." I couldn't let the opportunity to bait Holmes a morsel pass. "And, as you well know, Holmes, I'm not the kind of journalist who would just make something up. All my stories are based on verifiable facts."

He raised an eyebrow, but made no response. Instead he stood up. "Watson has kindly offered to travel up to London and consult on Mr Drake's –" he paused, "– physical state in the pathology lab at Scotland Yard. I have to meet him shortly." He turned to Miss Drake. "I shall call a cab for you, and I shall report if I make any progress." Glancing at me he added, "As for you, Pike, shall I slip you a shilling now or merely settle your bar bill on the way out?"

"Neither," I said, surprising myself as much as him. "Take me with you to see Dr Watson, if you wish to recompense me."

He fixed me with a gimlet eye. "Why would you want me to do that?"

I shrugged. "Boredom. That, and a feeling that there might be something in this case of interest to me."

"Very well," he said, "but do not get in the way."

Holmes escorted Miss Morris to the door of the club while I collected my various notebooks and pens together and put them carefully in the shoulder bag I habitually carried with me. Men, I have noticed, have much less latitude than women when it comes to personal items. They have both clutches and handbags to choose from when carrying their personal items, whereas we have to make do with briefcases and, in extremis, carpet bags. It seems unfair on the male sex, so I instructed a man who works in leather in the back streets around Charing Cross to construct a square bag for me into which I can fit everything than I need and that I can then sling over my shoulder with a strap. It attracts a certain amount of attention when I am out. Jealousy, I expect. Some men are undoubtedly ahead of their time. Still, Oscar Wilde has complimented me on it, so I know I am on safe ground.

I met Holmes outside the club and we walked the fifteen minutes or so along the Embankment until we reached Scotland Yard. He was recognised by the constable on the door and waved through. My experiences of police stations have not been comfortable, and so I was nervous as he led the way towards the stairs and then down into the basement. For an uncomfortable moment I thought we were heading for the cells, but in fact he took me to a large room with several long, rectangular windows along the top of one wall through which, if I strained, I could see the feet of people walking past. The walls were lined with shelves containing all manner of unpleasant surgical instruments and anatomical specimens in glass jars. Three metal tables had been placed side by side in the centre of the room, with gaps between them large enough for two people to pass, side by side. The floor was tiled in white, and several drains had been sunk into it. The purpose of the drains became unpleasantly clear when I realised that the body of a naked man was lying face-up on one of the tables. No cloth or towel covered his modesty. He was, I should make clear, completely dead. It was not that kind of establishment.

The room was filled with a strong smell of carbolic acid and formaldehyde. I took my lavender-scented handkerchief from my pocket and bundled it up beneath my nose. It did not help much.

Dr Watson was standing over the body, examining it intently and professionally. I do not believe I have described him before, and he has never described himself, so let me make the first attempt – he is a man of slightly less than average height, with a rugby player's physique and a well-kept and luxuriant moustache. His hair is generally brushed back from his forehead, but often flops forwards. It is clear why he is so fortunate with the fair sex. Looking at him now I noticed that his sleeves were rolled up and secured with flexible metal bands and he was wearing a waxed green apron to protect his shirt and trousers from what I shall delicately refer to as the "bodily fluids" of the man on the table.

"Ah, Holmes!" he exclaimed, looking up. His attention moved to me. "And – yes, it's Mr Pike, is not it? Langdale Pike. What are you doing here?" He moved his gaze back to Holmes. "What is he doing here?"

"Mr Pike is joining me on this case," Holmes said, his gaze fixed upon the body. "Given that you can only spare a few hours of your precious time, and given also that Mr Pike knows more about the hidden secrets of the average Londoner than most people, it seemed logical so to do. Now, what can you tell me about this gentleman?'"

As Watson pointed at an obvious chest wound, which he appeared to have methodically enlarged with a scalpel, I found myself feeling a strange mixture of interest and revulsion. The body – which I presumed to be the unfortunate fiancé, Mr Drake – was of a young man, in his early twenties I would estimate. His hair was blond and rather long, and his body shape – wide shoulders and narrow hips – suggested to me a swimmer, rather than the rugby player that Watson resembled. His eyes were mercifully closed. His skin was white on top, but this faded into a maroon colour for a distance of about two inches from the surface of the table. It was the kind of effect one would obtain if he had been lying in a pool of purple ink for a while, although I could not imagine why anyone would have done that.

Dr Watson noticed my queasy interest. "You've noticed how the blood settles in the body under the influence of gravity in the absence of pressure from a heartbeat," he said, straightening up.

"In that case," I observed, "I shall endeavour to keep my heart beating for as long as possible. It is a faintly ridiculous look, and I have no intention of indulging in it myself."

Holmes was still looking at the chest wound, which resembled a flower constructed from dark red meat. Watson turned to join him. "A bullet has obviously entered the body here, and travelled onwards through the heart," he said.

"The death of this man was almost certainly intentional,

then," Holmes mused. "If the shooter had been aiming at someone else in the crowd then it is extremely unlikely that he would have so accurately hit this man's heart."

"I have found a corresponding entrance wound in his back, just to the right of his left scapula." Watson slid his hands beneath the body and turned it half-over. "Here, take a look."

Holmes bent over eagerly. I stepped back. This was not the kind of thing I had anticipated to be doing that day. Or, indeed, any day.

"The exit wound is lower than the entrance wound," Holmes observed. "The shot must have come from above."

"Indeed," Watson said. "That was my assumption also."

"Assume nothing," Holmes snapped. "It is a valid deduction based on evidence to hand." He straightened up. "Did you recover the bullet?"

Watson nodded. Letting the body fall back to the table with a flabby thump reminiscent of a large fish hitting a fishmonger's slab, he crossed to a table at the side of the room and picked up a glass vial. Inside was a twisted piece of metal: brass or copper, I estimated, based upon the colour.

"Quite a soft one," he observed. "Designed to deform as it travelled through the body. Its velocity had slowed so much that it was caught by the man's cigarette case. Its diameter is slightly less than half an inch, which suggests that the weapon that shot it was a Martini–Henry rifle or something similar. It's certainly bigger than the .303 rounds fired by the Martini–Enfield or Lee–Enfield rifles."

"That would certainly have the range," Holmes mused. "The Martini–Henry is sighted to 1,800 yards." He nodded decisively. "Very well: are there any other points of interest to which you would draw my attention?"

Watson shrugged. "The state of the body is similar to half a hundred I saw in Afghanistan." He clapped his hands and then started to pull off his apron. "Now, if you will excuse me, I have a holiday to return to."

"Would it have been a difficult shot, in your estimation?"

Watson was, by now, rolling his shirtsleeves down and fastening his cufflinks. "Not if the shooter was a practised hunter – big game in India or deer on the Scottish Highlands, it makes little difference."

"Distance?"

"A shot like this, taken with a standard rifle by an experienced marksman, could be accomplished accurately – by which I mean within an inch of the aim point – over, perhaps, five hundred yards."

Holmes glanced over at me. "I do not suppose that you recognise this man from any of your… regular haunts?" he inquired.

I shook my head. "Absolutely not. I would have remembered such a noble brow, and such a fine head of hair. And, of course, those muscular shoulders."

"Indeed."

By now Watson had pulled his jacket on, picked up his bowler hat and his medical bag, and was heading for the door. He turned, in the doorway, as if expecting Holmes to say something – "Goodbye", perhaps, or "Thank you!" – but his friend was frowning and looking at the floor. Instead, I waved at the good doctor, and he left with a scowl on his face.

"We must go to the Vauxhall Pleasure Gardens." Holmes said. "I need to see the scene of the crime."

We left the unfriendly edifice of Great Scotland Yard behind us and Holmes hailed a cab to take us to Vauxhall.

It was late afternoon, and as the sun began to dip behind the roofs of the buildings, I drew my coat closer around me.

Characteristically, Holmes did not seem to feel the cold. He did not, I had noticed, seem to feel much of anything. I envied him that. I felt too much of everything – my mind is vulnerable to insults and slights that the average man would shrug off, and my skin sometimes feels as if it has been sanded down to a tenth of its previous thickness. I had to try five different laundries before finding one that uses just enough starch to keep my collars and cuffs stiff but not so much that it makes me come out in a rash.

We left the cab at the corner of the Vauxhall Pleasure Gardens, and entered via a gap in the low stone wall and tall hedges that surrounded the area. Lanterns had already been lit and were hanging from posts, and there were enough people promenading along the paths and sitting or lying around blankets and picnic hampers on the grass that it was beginning to look crowded. A band was playing off to our right, and a puppet show was taking place in a booth to our left. I had seen similar scenes many times over the past few years – carefree Londoners enjoying their free time. It made me wistful. I wish I could join in, but I am not a gregarious man.

A young lad in a cloth cap passed by. He winked at me. I was about to wink back when I remembered that I was on what I can only describe as "duty". With a tinge of sadness in my heart, I looked away.

Holmes pulled a folded sheet of paper from his pocket. Unfolding it, he glanced at the illustration upon its surface. He glanced around.

"According to this picture, which I had Miss Morris draw for me, she and her fiancé were standing about a hundred yards away from here, in this direction."

He set out in a straight line across the grass, nearly stepping on plates of food or knocking over bottles as he went. A chorus of complaints rose in his wake. Instead of following and apologising – which I suspect Dr Watson would have done – I diverted around the edge of the grass until he stopped, and then found a path to him that offended the least number of people. I have no problem with offending people, by the way – I merely prefer to do it at long range, in print, and to get paid for it.

"This is the spot, as near as I can tell," he said, looking around. We were over towards the edge of the grassy area, near to the bushes that marked one of the Pleasure Gardens' borders. "Miss Morris stated that her fiancé was facing her, and she was facing away from the bushes. She said that she remembered seeing that church steeple –" he pointed into the distance "– directly behind his head. Now, you shall be Miss Morris and I shall be her fiancé."

"I would not have it any other way," I murmured as he grabbed me by the shoulders and positioned me. He was a tall man – taller than Miss Morris's fiancé – and so I could not see the church spire behind his head, but I found that if I moved my own head then I could spy it over his shoulder.

Holmes pointed over my own shoulder. "Based on the downwards trajectory of the bullet, the shot can only have come from the roof of that building."

I turned to see where he was pointing. Over the hedges I could see the top of a brown stone building with thick sills above narrow windows. They made the building look as if it was frowning heavily. "We need to gain access to that roof, in case the shooter has left any evidence behind."

"You do that," I said, catching sight of one of the

Garden's attendants, obvious in his striped shirt and cap. "I shall go and question the natives."

Holmes bounded off without a backward glance, while I raised a hand to attract the attendant.

"Can I help you, sir?" he asked, approaching. "Directions to various entertainments or cafes, perhaps, or just a potted history of the gardens themselves and the famous people who have visited in the past and continue to do so?"

"Perhaps another time," I rejoined. "I am assisting the police with their investigations into the recent death of a young man." I felt no guilt at saying I was assisting the police – I was assisting a man who was assisting the police, and that seemed good enough. I once danced with a man who'd danced with a girl who'd danced with the Prince of Wales, which leads me to tell people that I got close to dancing with the Prince of Wales – it is a similar situation.

He winced. "Ah, yes. We have been instructed not to talk about that, sir. Bad for publicity, if you see what I mean. I believe the owners of the gardens have impressed upon the owners of the city's newspapers that their regular advertisements would be stopped if the newspapers carried anything more that a cursory report. People would not like to go to a place where someone has recently died."

"Oh, I don't know," I said. "The general public, in my estimation, have a vein of morbid curiosity running through them like the letters in a stick of Blackpool rock." I slipped a coin into his hand with a well-practised motion. I suspect I could be a theatrical magician and prestidigitator with little or no practice. "Was this where it happened?"

"It was, sir," he said, slipping the coin into his pocket with a similarly smooth motion. Perhaps we should form a double act. "The young man was just over there, on that patch of grass. Some say that he was shot. With a bullet! Others say he was stabbed, or suffered a sudden haemorrhage."

"Indeed. And if a gun was fired, did you see where the shot might have come from?"

He shook his head. "There was nobody around holding a gun, and nobody did a runner."

"Thank you," I said, and started to turn away.

Perhaps he did not think he'd given me enough value for my money, because he added: "Of course, if the man was shot then another two feet to the left and it would have been a greater tragedy. Not that this was not a tragedy, but the Earl of Montcreif was standing just beside the young man."

"Oh, was he?" I asked. That was, indeed, worth the money. "And what did he do?"

"Like everyone else, sir, he legged it."

"As one would," I observed.

I waited, watching the crowd and thinking, until Holmes returned.

"Some scratches on the stonework," he said, his face contorted into a frown, "and some scuffing in the moss suggestive of footprints, but nothing I could use to make an identification or further the investigation."

"I have found out something rather interesting," I said.

He raised an eyebrow. "Indeed?"

"You can remove that sarcastic tone from your voice. I have an intellect, you know, even if I use it in ways you disapprove of."

He smiled slightly. "I apologise if I gave offence. I am too used to being with Watson. You do have a fine mind, Mr Pike, otherwise I would not have let you join me on this investigation. And as for disapproving of what use you make of it… well, on the list of people in London whom I disapprove of, your name appears far down the list."

"I shall take what crumbs of comfort I can from that," I said. "What I discovered is that the Earl of Montcreif was also in the Vauxhall Pleasure Gardens at the time the fatal shot was fired, and was standing very close to Mr Drake."

Holmes shook his head. "I have already established to my own satisfaction, based on the accuracy of the shot, that Mr Drake was the intended victim. This was not an accidental shooting, with the shooter firing at the Earl of Montcreif and missing."

"I would agree with you," I said, "except that I happen to know that the earl's valet took several items of jewellery belonging to his master to a pawnbroker's in Mayfair yesterday morning. The cash value was in the order of ten thousand pounds."

"And how do you know this?"

"I have my sources. Knowing when the gentry are short of cash or in need money in a hurry has led to a number of my columns."

He stared at me fixedly, but I could see that his mind was elsewhere. "There is no connection that I am aware of between the Earl of Montcreif and the unfortunate Mr Drake, although now that I have been made aware of this information I will need to check. I cannot believe that the earl would have paid for Mr Drake to be shot and then stood beside him – he would have been far better off establishing an alibi some distance away." He raised his head and gazed upwards, eyes half-closed, seeking inspiration. "Does the Earl of Montcreif have any, let us say, 'habits' that would require him to spend a great deal of money in a surreptitious and rapid way?"

"If you are asking whether he has a mistress, frequents *les grandes horizontales* or gambles excessively then the answer is 'no'. The earl is one of the straightest members of the nobility that I have ever encountered. There is not one whiff of scandal about him."

He nodded. "Very well – I shall make inquiries of my own. I suggest you return to your club and await my instructions."

He turned and strode off, leaving me seething with anger. "Instructions", indeed! What was I – his lapdog?

I did indeed return to my club. It was night by then, and so I ate a small plate of turbot and new potatoes, drank half a bottle of Bollinger Blanc de Noirs and settled down to make notes on my next set of columns.

It was after midnight when a small child in ragged clothes appeared at my side.

"Does your mother know you are out and about at this time of night?" I inquired.

"I do not know where she is," he rejoined, "so I do not think she knows where I am."

"A fair point well made," I said. "How did you get in here?"

"Through the cloakroom window."

"How very enterprising. I presume that you have a message for me from Mr Holmes?"

His eyes widened. "You as bright as 'e is, then? Cor!"

I sighed. "What is the message?"

He handed over a dirty scrap of paper. I doubt that Holmes would have let it go in that state; I can only assume that its passage from him to me in the pocket of this ragamuffin had caused its fall from grace.

He kept his empty hand extended. I waited with an

eyebrow raised, but he obviously was not going to feel any embarrassment, so eventually I gave him a half-shilling.

"Thanks, mister," he said with a smile that would have been dazzling if he had not lost most of his teeth. A moment later he was gone.

I queasily unfolded the paper. It said, in Holmes's characteristic scrawl:

Have any of the following moved large sums of cash in the past few months?

There followed a list of names, some of whom I recognised as being members of high society and the nobility. By sending a footman to retrieve the club's copy of *Who's Who* from the library, I discovered that the remaining ones were largely industrialists and financiers, many of them ennobled or otherwise decorated by our gracious sovereign.

I know that Holmes keeps many files in Baker Street containing information on the criminal underclass (and, indeed, overclass, given that illegal and immoral behaviour spans all levels of society to my certain knowledge). I have my own files, but I keep them in my head. That way they cannot be stolen. Closing my eyes, I walked through the house in which I was born and lived for the first twenty years of my life. In this still-vivid memory I place different facts that I wish to remember in particular places in that imaginary house. I have found that it makes it easier to recall all of the details relating to, for instance, Lord Cathcart if I place them all in a cart, just outside the kitchen door, where the cat used to sun itself in the afternoons. Cat-cart, do you see?

By traversing my imaginary house, I retrieved details of the lives of all the names I knew on the list. A flurry of telegrams sent by another of the club's footmen to my various agents and informants around this fair city elicited, within a few hours, answers on the names that I did not know.

The sun was shining over the top of the building opposite, casting an unwelcome roseate glow into the club's writing room, when I was able to pen a simple telegram to Holmes:

```
. All of them on which I have been able
  to find information have recently taken
  out bank loans, pawned possessions or made
  large withdrawals from their accounts.
```

I could just have said "All of them", or even just "All" in order to save money, but I knew that Holmes would appreciate accuracy over brevity and I have, sadly, always managed to use a hundred words where ten would have done. Well, I say "sadly", but when one is paid by the word then one quickly learns to describe things as completely and redundantly as possible. Even simple words like "a" or "the" are cash in the bank, and they are far easier and quicker to write than a word such as "farinaceous".

I looked at the clock; it was half-past nine in the morning. Assuming it would take an hour for the telegram to get to Baker Street, and that he lived twenty minutes away by cab, I expected to hear from Holmes, or even see him in person, by eleven o'clock at the very latest. Perhaps I was being grandiose (something to which I admit I am prone) but I felt that I had provided him with interesting, if not crucial, intelligence.

It was one minute to eleven when Holmes strode into the

club and up to where I was sitting, eating a madeleine cake and sipping at a small, dry sherry. To clarify: it was I who was eating the cake and drinking the sherry, not him. I'm not sure I can ever remember seeing Holmes take sustenance.

"We do not have much time," he snapped.

"Speak for yourself," I said, taking a rebellious sip from my glass. "Sit down and tell me what you have discovered. If I am to go anywhere with you then it will be in full possession of the facts, not blindly like poor Dr Watson."

With poor grace he flung himself into a chair. "Two lines of investigation have intersected," he said. "Firstly, I have discovered that over the past six months there have been a spate of murders in the capital in which there has been no clear motive and no obvious suspects. All of the deaths occurred in public places, and all were shootings, apparently from a distance."

"Intriguing," I said, and indeed it was. "However, given that I know you habitually scour the newspapers for intriguing or eccentric events, and given also that certain sergeants and inspectors within the Metropolitan Police appear to have hansom cabs on standby so that they can easily consult you when they have reached their intellectual limits, which seems to happen with monotonous regularity, I am forced to wonder how this list of mysterious murders has escaped your attention."

He scowled. "Partly I am to blame for that – I have, until a few days ago, been investigating a case with international ramifications that has quite taken up my attention, involving the Archbishop of Canterbury and a basket of hallucinogenic mushrooms. Also, the police have been conspiring with the owners of the various public spaces to keep the information out of the newspapers. The police

– or, rather, their government masters – fear widespread panic at the thought of a random marksman at loose in the capital; the owners of the public spaces – which include parks, theatres and funfairs – also fear a sharp drop in their revenues. While a small unit within Scotland Yard has been tasked with urgently finding this sharpshooter, efforts have been made to suppress any mentions in the newspapers and to class the deaths in other ways – stabbings, muggings and the like – and to dissuade the families of the victims from saying anything. I have also sensed, but have no proof, that bribes have been paid in order to suppress the facts. The police did not consult me for the simple reason that they were forbidden from discussing the details of the case with anybody outside the Yard. For the past few hours, I feel as if I have been navigating my way through a fog that deliberately shifts in order to confound my navigation!"

I nodded, remembering my discussion with the attendant in the Vauxhall Pleasure Gardens. "You mentioned two lines of investigation. What was the other one?"

"It was the one provoked by your own fact-gathering activities. You recall I sent you a list of names of rich and influential personages?"

"Indeed."

"Each name on that list has recently paid over a large sum of money to some unidentified person or organisation."

"I know," I said. "I told you that."

"What you had no way of knowing was that each of those names was standing near to one of the unfortunate victims of the shootings at the exact time they were shot."

Holmes sat bolt upright, fixing me with his challenging gaze. I felt an unaccustomed sense of burning excitement flowing through my veins. "So, what you are suggesting,

I presume, is that the shootings were a combination of demonstration and warning," I said. "I would say that the poor victims had been chosen at random, but that is not true. They were chosen because they were standing near a rich personage, and who would shortly afterwards receive a blackmail demand – 'Pay us £5,000 or you will be next – and we have shown that we have the capability and the intent'!"

"Exactly." He shook his head in grudging admiration. I could see a half-smile on his face. "The problem with classic blackmail, of course, is that if a potential victim refuses to pay then there is precious little reason to go ahead and publish the incriminating material. The potential victim will certainly not pay after the event, so the action makes no profit while exposing the erstwhile blackmailer to risk. The only two reasons to go ahead are to take revenge on the potential victim for failing to co-operate and to provide an example for the next victim. This scheme, by contrast, warns the target in advance of what will happen to them if they do not pay."

"How ingenious," I said.

"Oh," Holmes added, "and you were mistaken. In at least some cases the victims were forewarned. I deduce that this was to deliberately 'soften them up', as the phrase goes, and also to potentially avoid a needless shooting if they paid up promptly. However, knowing the blackmailer's modus operandus gives us our chance to capture the villains behind this callous scheme."

"How so?" I asked, realising as I did so that I was falling into the same role that Dr Watson played in this relationship – asking questions and making admiring statements.

"I had been wondering exactly how and why the blackmail victims were chosen. I deduced, in the end, that they were selected after their names appeared in one of the very newspapers for which you write your shoddy little columns."

"Have a care, Holmes," I murmured.

"In each case, the names of the blackmail victims appeared on the front page exactly five days before the deaths of the bystanders occurred. Inevitably, the appearance of the name was connected to some mention of their wealth or importance."

"And so you have deduced the next potential blackmail victim," I said.

"I have," Holmes said. "It is –"

"– The Right Honourable Quentin Furnell," I said.

Holmes gazed at me for a long moment. I think – I hope – he was surprised, although his expression rarely gives anything away. "You obviously recall that his name was on the front page in regard to a question raised over the large number of shares he has in a coalmining company whose business affairs he recently defended in Parliament," he said eventually.

"And I also happen to know, based on the research I do for my 'shoddy little columns', that he will be attending a charity benefit at the Prince's Theatre tonight. Given the five-day gap between the appearance of his name and the event, the conclusion seems obvious."

"Can you obtain a ticket for me to this benefit?" Holmes asked. "I could ask my brother, but he would only tell me to stay out of the affair and pass my conclusions to the proper authorities."

"Which raises the obvious question – why don't you?"

He leaned back in the chair and put on an air of casual disinterest. "If I were the person who might end up in the sights of the blackmailing marksman," he said, "I would prefer to think that my survival lay in the hands of Sherlock Holmes, not the Metropolitan Police."

"Also," I ventured, "despite Dr Watson's curious belief that you care little for money, and undertake these cases for sport, in fact you are running a business, and if you can demonstrate to the Right Honourable Quentin Furnell that you have saved him from attempted blackmail then he might well divert a fraction of the money he would have spent on paying the blackmailer to your account. Better that than the Police Benevolent Fund."

"Watson is curiously naïve about the way the world works," he said softly, "and besides, I have found it best not to mention money too often in his presence. He has –"

"Issues to do with horses," I murmured. "I quite understand."

"And I am sure I can count on your discretion in this case," he added.

"Mr Holmes, you of all people should know that I have no discretion. It is how I earn the money that keeps me in cake and sherry. In this case, however, I am pleased to make an exception." I thought for a moment. "Yes, I could obtain tickets for both of us, but alas they would not be near the Right Honourable Quentin Furnell, and thus we might be too far away to save the innocent victim. We would need to be close to Furnell, which means that we might have to take him into our confidence."

"A fair point." He grimaced. "As a rule, I am generally not in favour of telling those involved too much, but in this case it might be wise."

And so it was that, several hours later, I found myself in the front row of the Circle of the Prince's Theatre. Tragically, I was not wearing my finest evening dress – the one that has been known to make grown men weep with the extravagance of its material and the skill and daring of its cut. Neither was I wearing the deep violet cummerbund and bowtie that set it off so beautifully. Sadly, neither of those items were baggy enough to cover up the undergarment of varnished leather and multiple layers of silk that I was wearing underneath, which is why I was wearing a cheap ensemble of the kind that I would normally not have been seen dead in – an unfortunate phrase, I know, but it seems apposite. Following my intervention, Holmes had thrown himself wholeheartedly into a plan to catch the killer in the act without risking the life of a member of the public. With the baffled collaboration of the Right Honourable Gentleman in question, several of his party, including his stately wife and almost equally stately daughter, were dropped from the trip to the theatre, leaving several empty seats, while the occupied seats around him were filled with other agents and associates of Holmes wearing protection that would apparently be proof against bullets of the calibre used. I, sadly, was one of those associates, which meant I was sitting there sweating and looking almost as large as the Right Honourable Gentleman's wife would have done.

"My research indicates that the marksman invariably shoots someone within six feet of his blackmail target," Holmes assured me, "and one who is not related or known to the target. All of the seats within that range are occupied by my people. There is no risk to anyone else in the theatre."

"If you are right," I pointed out.

He looked at me as if he did not understand my words. "Of course I am right," he said.

"I cannot help noticing that the protection is confined to my torso, leaving my head and limbs exposed."

"The marksman has, to date, always shot the body rather than the head. The body is a larger target, of course, but there may also be an intention to make it less obvious that something has happened. With a bullet to the body, the victim slumps or falls, and that might be blamed on all manner of things. With a shot to the head the effects are… let us say… considerably less ambiguous."

The performance was a collation of short scenes from Shakespeare, Marlowe and Johnson, interspersed with sonnets set to music by various well-known composers. It was not really my cup of tea. I spent much of the first half surreptitiously gazing around the theatre looking for the marksman, knowing that Holmes would be restlessly exploring the front and rear of house.

And all the time I was anticipating the impact of a bullet to my chest or, worse, to my head. I was sure I could trust Holmes's deductive powers, but it was not him the killer was aiming at.

Two seats to my right, Quentin Furnell was looking distinctly sick. He kept sipping from a hip flask; I thought I could smell brandy. I noted that down for future use.

It was during a dramatic interpretation of the storm scene from *King Lear* that I noticed something amiss. To each side of the stage and further back, above the second box on either side, incandescent electrical spotlights were being controlled by men in hanging chairs. They were dressed entirely in black, so as not to distract the audience from events occurring on stage, but that process seemed to be breaking down on my right, where one of the spotlight operators was engaging in a tussle with a man who had apparently climbed down from the upper circle and clambered across to the spotlight. The tussle was causing the light to swing wildly around. I realised two things simultaneously: the man who had clambered down from the Upper Circle and instigated the fight was Holmes; and the man he was fighting with was clutching what appeared to be a rifle.

The audience had noticed something amiss by now. Some were leaving their seats, but others were craning their necks to get a better view. On stage poor Lear and his Fool were stuttering to a halt.

I saw Holmes swing his fist. The black-clad murderer and blackmailer ducked and twisted, trying to send Holmes falling to his death. The wildly swinging spotlight suddenly played across my face, blinding me momentarily. I heard several shots – the struggle between the two men had probably caused the marksman's finger to inadvertently tighten on the trigger. I presumed that his plan had been to use the sound of the theatrical thunder to cover the noise of his shot. By the time my vision cleared the audience was panicking, and the marksman had Holmes's throat in one hand while his other hand was still clutching the rifle. Quentin Furnell had sprung from his seat and was struggling along the row away from me and towards the nearest aisle.

The marksman swung the rifle and caught Holmes in the face. As Holmes automatically raised his free hand to protect himself the marksman swung the weapon around, aiming straight at Furnell's chest.

"Down!" I screamed at Furnell, abandoning, for the sake of brevity, "Mr Furnell", which is the *Debrett's* approved form of address for a Privy Councillor. I dived towards him and pushed him in the middle of his Right Honourable back. He sprawled forwards, pitching into the velvet seats. I looked back up at the suspended fight, just in time to see a flash of light. Something struck me in the centre of my chest, pushing me back. I fell. My chest felt as if a horse had kicked it. I could hardly take a breath, the pain was so intense.

By the time I could pull myself to an upright position, most of the audience had left and the suspended spotlight and seat arrangement was empty. I clutched at my chest, and found a large hole in my starched shirt, a great deal of shredded leather and silk, and a still-hot bullet, but no blood.

I looked around, and found Holmes sitting a few rows behind me.

"I take it that everything has concluded satisfactorily?" I asked.

"The blackmailer is in custody," he said, "and, thanks to your actions, the Right Honourable Quentin Furnell is alive and well." He stared at me, and there was a curious expression on his face. "I sometimes need reminding," he said, "that events do not always follow their predicted course. Random incidents, such as the inopportune and unintended tightening of a finger upon a trigger, can sometimes lead to unanticipated but tragic outcomes that logic can neither foresee nor prevent. I have learned something today, and for that – and your invaluable help – I thank you."

I thought about some of the things I had seen as I had looked around the audience earlier – several well-known people together in boxes who should not have been seen together at all, and people with their wives or husbands beside them who had nevertheless been casting loving glances at others nearby. I had made copious notes – mentally, of course – and I could already anticipate a series of columns appearing in the newspapers in the near future.

"Glad to help, Mr Holmes," I said. "Glad to help."

THE PRESBURY PAPERS

Jonathan Barnes

I've always been fascinated by **Professor Presbury** – that murky figure at the heart of Doyle's late addition to the canon, "The Adventure of the Creeping Man" (1923). It's an often-overlooked case for Sherlock Holmes, as notable as much for what is not stated as for that which is set out plainly by the author. Writing in *The Times Literary Supplement* in 2010, I suggested that the piece is "a sour parable about the endurance of lust" and that, upon finishing the tale, "the feeling persists that there is something in the narrative – hidden, submerged – which the reader is not permitted to comprehend but which forms the source of its power".

What a terrific opportunity it was, when I was asked last year to contribute a story to the current volume, to go back into that adventure and to tease out some of its subtext, to dive down towards that which is submerged and bring it up into the light. I've often wondered what became of the Professor and have speculated as to where his dark desires might have led him. Holmes, after all, once said of his opponent that, "when one tries to rise above Nature one is liable to fall below it". I couldn't help but ask if, having experienced animal passion, the old man could really have walked away from it. Any time spent in seclusion and disgrace, I reasoned, would surely be only temporary. My story imagines the end of such an exile – as well as its final, tragic consequences.

—Jonathan Barnes

From Callitrix, *the journal of Sapperson College, Cambridge, Michaelmas Term, 1904*

VALE PRESBURY

The college bade a reluctant if heartfelt farewell this term to one of its noblest and most accomplished sons. Professor C.R.H. Presbury, whose fame as an authority in the field of physiology burst long ago the banks of academe to become a national byword for intellectual rigour and clinical expertise, has chosen retirement following a recent, regrettable period of ill health.

His departure was marked by a brief ceremony, which was attended in considerable number by students and fellows and by sundry others whose lives have been enriched through interchanges of various kinds with the professor.

Presbury himself, a notably frailer figure than he who once bestrode the lecture hall, gave a warm speech in which he thanked the college authorities for their exemplary treatment of him in what he called "trying circumstances". He also regretted deeply the absence of his daughter and her husband (who were, he said, now resident in the Americas) and declared his intention to leave the university town in favour of a small fenland village where he meant to live out his widower days in "contemplation of the highest of life's callings". It needs hardly to be said that he shall be missed greatly by all who knew him.

From An Almanac of the Towns, Villages and Hamlets of the East of England *(1908 edition)*

The overwhelming impression which is acquired during a visit to the village of SEATON LEIGH is one of stark inhospitality. Although not without elements of the quaint and picturesque – its inn, The Upright Badger being, for example, unexpectedly well-stocked and well-appointed – the place boasts a largely taciturn community and a flat fenland landscape. Lone and level fields extend in every direction, studded occasionally by severe dark hedgerows and glowering patches of woodland. There is little to divert that curious traveller who comes in search of the aesthetically pleasing (far better for our wayfarer to journey instead to the nearby homesteads of Baker's Drive or Graverton) and nothing at all to suggest why, if one were not born to this cold agrarian realm, one should ever choose to make a life for oneself here.

Nonetheless, and against all odds, the village boasts a celebrated resident. Professor C.R.H. Presbury, the once-noted university physiologist, dwells in what was formerly a coaching inn, leading, it is said, an intensely private retirement and taking no part in the business of Seaton Leigh.

I do believe, however, that, during my visitation, I glimpsed him: a tall, defiant figure, stalking into the woods to take his evening constitutional, moving with determined but unfathomable purpose, like some weirdly animate scarecrow.

An extract from the private correspondence between Mr E.S. Foote, proprietor of the Epicurean Bookshop, and Professor C.R.H. Presbury (ret'd)

24th October 1911

Dear Professor,

It is my honour and privilege to enclose within this parcel those curious and singular books that you requested in your last communication, namely:

(i) The Secret Life of a Ballerina

(ii) A Schoolgirl's Education

(iii) Confessions of a Flagellant

(iv) Further Memoirs of a Courtesan

(v) A Discourse on the Worship of Priapus

I trust that these volumes shall educate and enchant in equal measure. Should you require further additions to your library, pray do not hesitate to renew our correspondence. Until that time, I would remind you respectfully of the ceaseless necessity of discretion and tact.

I remain, sir, your most humble servant,

E S Foote

Telegram

```
Sent: 3rd January 1913
From: Scheherazade
To: Panjandrum


Subject located. Extraction begun. Expect
further word soon.
```

From the private journal of Professor C.R.H. Presbury

4th January 1913

More than a decade has passed since last I set pen to paper in this fashion. That was at a time before the delightful – if ultimately faithless – Miss Morphy came first within my purview, before the gentleman from Prague provided the chief instrument of my downfall, before the advent in my rich existence of that professional busybody Mr Sherlock Holmes and before the ignominious end of a career which cannot be characterised as having been anything other than amongst the very first rank. My life since those unhappy days, which saw the cessation of my engagement and the severing of all professional and personal ties of any significance, has been spent in quiet contemplation and solitary philosophical enquiry. I have been – let us not be circumspect – a long time indeed in the wilderness.

What, then, has occasioned my return to this journal, its pages, like the skin of its author, thin, worn and showing advanced signs of age? What has made me write once more of myself?

The answer is this: that an event has woken parts of my character that I had thought to have been forever buried, that the sight of a new face and the speaking of certain words has breathed again on embers in me and coaxed back into full flame the fires of an appetite which I have endeavoured in this long hermitage of mine to curb, to suppress and to cast aside.

It began this morning with a knock upon my study door. I was engaged in the perusal and study of certain antiquarian texts and, being cognisant of their fragility as well as their extreme rarity, I was careful to stow them away in the safest drawer of my desk before answering the bid for my attention with a sturdy "halloa!" It was, of course, Mrs Scott, my redoubtable, boot-faced housekeeper and maid of all work, the only representative of her sex nowadays with whom I pass any words of substance.

Her face was arranged so as to suggest an emotion of which I would not hitherto have thought her capable, namely a crude species of curiosity.

"Mrs Scott? What occasions this interruption?"

"You have a visitor, sir," said she, her rustic origins evident in every elongated syllable. "A fine young woman."

Even at these rare words I fancy that something shifted within me, that some new chain was forged.

"Did she give her name?"

In the manner of an angler presenting some oversized prize, Mrs Scott, with a decided flourish, produced a white business card. "See here." And she passed the thing, with an odd admixture of wariness and pride, to me.

I looked down with considerable interest, callers of any kind being a rarity and those of this stranger's sex and age unprecedented, and I saw written there four words.

The first, evidently the caller's name, in bold type and gothic calligraphy, read:

Scheherazade

Underneath, in more modern print, ran the legend:

TELLER OF TALES

"How very intriguing," I said. "Now, really I think it is high time that you showed this singular young lady in, Mrs Scott. Don't you?"

Given the consequences of so long and enforced a solitude, my imagination had, naturally enough, begun by this time to adopt the most fantastic postures. My breathing quickened and a raft of the most vivid and diverting imagery rose up before me. Those moments in which I was left alone in the study as Mrs Scott bustled in the hallways beyond were especially interminable.

Nonetheless (and how I find my hand a-trembling as I consign these thoughts to this secret depository) their sequel was to surpass even the most idealistic of my fancies. For, a minute or so later, the housekeeper returned and in her wake was a young woman of the rarest and most striking aspect, brunette, not more than five and twenty and in possession of a truly wonderful silhouette.

Her gaze met mine without the least sign of nervousness. She was dressed in a demure, even a somewhat antiquated fashion and her voice was gentle yet determined.

"Professor Presbury, I presume?"

I peeled back my lips. "I am most certainly he. To whatever do I owe this pleasure? Are we acquainted?"

That dear lady shook her noble head. There was

something sweetly feline in the gesture. "I fear I have not until today had the pleasure of making your acquaintance in person. Although, of course, I feel that I know you through your work, so much of which I have read with the keenest interest."

I waved away this compliment casually enough, although I admit that at the declaration I felt a distinct spasm of delight.

"Yet I do believe," she murmured, something quietly imploring now in her big hazel eyes, "that you once knew my late father."

"I may well have done," I said. "Now what was that good man's name?"

"Lowenstein," she replied and showed me her sharp white teeth.

"Mrs Scott," I said to that stout creature who had, throughout this conversation, lingered by the door. "Would you be so kind as to fetch Miss Lowenstein a pot of tea? Perhaps the walnut cake also? For this is somewhat in the spirit of a reunion, and we should mark it with all good things."

The domestic nodded gruffly. Miss Lowenstein seemed delighted. "I do so love walnut cake."

"Happy," I said. "I am happy to oblige."

"And yet?"

"Yes, Miss Lowenstein?"

"Today is not meant merely as a means by which we might revisit the past."

"No?"

"No indeed, Professor. For I have come here in large part for a single reason – to put to you a most remarkable proposition."

And so we sat and we took tea together and Miss

Scheherazade Lowenstein put to me that proposal at which she had hinted. It is born, I think, at least in part from guilt at the role that her departed father played, however indirect and unwitting, in my fall from grace. It is, she says, loyalty that drives her, loyalty to her parent's memory as well as a desire to restore honour to a family name, which is at present mired in disrepute. So she has sought me out to set things right. I have, after only the most perfunctory of protests, acceded to her request and I am, in two days time, to go to London where I shall be put up in the Bostonian Hotel in Bloomsbury and from where, Miss Lowenstein assures me, all that has been taken from me shall be once again restored.

More than that – the specifics of what is to pass between us – I shall not write here. To do so would be to subject them to the cold and unforgiving light of reality whereas at present they have still in my mind the qualities of phantasy and delight. Yes, they have about them the sense of some strange and wonderful dream, which has lingered long into the waking hours.

Telegram

    Sent: 4th January 1913
    From: Panjandrum
    To: Scheherazade

    Proposition accepted and subject gladly
    lulled. Suite in the Bostonian to be
    prepared for 6th January.

Telegram

```
Sent: 4th January 1913
From: Scheherazade
To: Panjandrum
```

```
Congratulations. You are indeed a patriot.
Report to me again in London.
```

From the private journal of Professor C.R.H. Presbury

5th January 1913

I have spent today in preparation, not only of the practical kind – baggage to be packed; Mrs Scott to be informed and appraised of my imminent absence; arrangements to be set in motion for the temporary shutting up of the house – but also of an emotional, one might almost say spiritual, sort.

There are parts of my soul that have long been left unvisited and it was to those that I tended this afternoon. Shortly before dusk I took a walk, as I have so often before, into those patches of woodland which abut this little village and there I took a moment to stand alone, to collect my thoughts, to reflect upon the errors of my personal history and – I do not flinch from such an admission – for the first time in far too many years, to pray. For an instant or two, I was lost in the gathering evening to something far greater than myself.

Then I awakened from my reverie, turned and hurried back to my isolated little home. Such higher thoughts I leave here in the fens. In London I shall be all of the body – a corporeal and not a sacred being, devoted no longer to penitence but rather, I fancy, to the furtherance of sin.

6th January 1913

I write these words upon the train to the metropolis, the details of my long exile fading already into disagreeable memory. I think now only of what is ahead of me: of the Bostonian Hotel, of the rich and subtle pleasures of the city, of my particular appetites – for too long in abeyance – and of Miss Lowenstein's white beguiling smile.

Telegram

```
Sent: 6th January 1913
From: Scheherazade
To: Panjandrum

Subject arrived safely. Eager to commence
first stage. Cannot recall an easier
corruption. Request, as discussed,
immediate release of funds.
```

Telegram

```
Sent: 6th January 1913
From: Panjandrum
To: Scheherazade

Request accepted. Funds to be delivered
in customary fashion. Thoughts of all the
Service are with you.
```

Telegram

```
Sent: 7th January 1913
From: Scheherazade
To: Panjandrum
```

We have him. Ready to begin second stage.

From the private journal of Professor C.R.H. Presbury

9th January 1913

You will forgive my absence from these pages in recent days. I have been engaged in alternative pursuits. I dare not provide complete details of my excursions even here. Let it suffice to report that the pleasure gardens of London are aptly named, that the diversions of Bloomsbury are various and plentiful, and that there is in this mighty capital no hunger that might not be anticipated, that might not be met with expertise and surpassed. To this I must add that Miss Lowenstein has proved to be an excellent and knowledgeable guide. It is difficult to imagine any father having been precisely proud of such a daughter but it is surely to be hoped that he might at least have respected her comfortable acceptance of her nature.

The two days that I have spent here, in this marvellous hotel, have been unusually pleasant ones, unparalleled in the great majority of my adult life. Yet I am no longer a young man. I have not the vigour of my former days. I grow tired and I grow stale and I recollect the words of the Bard when he wrote of that rambunctious trickster that desire should so many years outlive performance. I had accepted the truth of the matter – that this delightful and unexpected sojourn had come to its natural conclusion, that my spirits were truly spent and that I would shortly have to contemplate a return to Cambridgeshire. Certainly, I considered any debt that might have been owed to me by the Family Lowenstein to have been paid in full and with considerable interest.

It was with no small quantity of surprise, then, that I woke from a stupor this afternoon to discover that notable lady sitting at the foot of my bed with a small wooden box before her. I struggled upright and asked Scheherazade what it was that had brought her to my chamber in so unorthodox a fashion.

Her reply, at first, was perhaps a little cryptic. "I see you," she said. "And I know you also."

"Whatever do you mean by that, my dear?"

"Only this: that you wish, do you not, to stay? Here in Bloomsbury? That there are depths for you to plumb? Blank spaces on the map still to be charted? Fabulous, fertile islands to be colonised and made your own?"

I swallowed deep and hard at this but made the inevitable protestation. "I am old, my dear, simply too old and too weak."

"Truly," she said, "it is not so. You are familiar, I know, with the contents of this box?"

I craned my neck forward to see what lay within, although I do believe I already knew what I would find there.

A set of full phials. A hypodermic already prepared.

The lady's voice was gentle but firm. "I have continued my father's work. The serum has been intensified and improved. You would surely appreciate the artistry of the thing. You will reap – oh, shall you reap – such benefits."

"The side effects," I stuttered. "The things before, the things it made me do…"

"All gone now. It has been improved upon. There is nothing that this could make you do that you did not wish to do. The serum would be to you a tyrant no longer but rather a most willing and most biddable accomplice."

"I… dare not…"

"You?" Scheherazade opened her eyes improbably wide, in near-pantomimic shock. "How could you of all people use such a word? I thought you fearless, Professor. Fearless!"

I bowed my head to demonstrate that I felt appropriately shamed.

"Please," she said. "This is my present to you. My final gift. And so I ask once more, Professor Presbury, sir, will you take this serum?"

And, of course, I nodded and I said that I would, and I reached out for the tools of vigour and strength and newfound youth. And I have begun – so I happily suppose – the final tranche of this, my most pleasurable damnation.

Telegram


```
Sent: 9th January 1913
From: Scheherazade
To: Panjandrum


Study proceeds apace. Subject a willing
participant. Earliest results expected
within hours.
```

From the Pall Mall Gazette, *10th January 1913*

A CURIOUS DISTURBANCE
ON DEAN STREET

It is often said, at least by certain worthies, that it is the youth of our present time to whom we must look for demonstrations of dissolute and impious behaviour. The events that took place last night towards the southernmost end of Dean Street would seem to stand in ironical rebuke of so conventional a suggestion.

Shortly after midnight besides a nest of lodging-houses of the most disagreeable sort, a minor conflagration was seen to begin, as well as a great deal of commotion. In particular, a flurry of coarse and violent language was heard from he who was subsequently found to be the source of the blaze, a gentleman who was also in pursuit of a very young woman, busily engaged in chasing her along the avenue. The scene was said to resemble some antique woodcutting or portrait from some latter-day Rake's Progress.

Bystanders reported this noisy malefactor to be crouched over and almost barking in the manner of an animal. It was to considerable surprise, when the culprit was eventually run to ground, that the gentleman in question was discovered to be aged indeed, more than seventy and at least the threefold senior of his young quarry. Police were summoned (here we may imagine the disquiet of several present) and the amateur arsonist arrested. In such unexpected ways are the commonplace assumptions of our society upended and overturned.

Telegram

```
Sent: 10th January 1913
From: Panjandrum
To: Detective Inspector Arnold Blakely,
Scotland Yard


Understand you have our man Presbury in
custody. Professor part of larger design.
Please release forthwith without charge.
Your brother on the square, Panjandrum
```

Correspondence of the Bostonian Hotel

12th January 1913

Dear Professor Presbury,

I regret to inform you that certain recent conduct upon your part has been brought to our attention and that, in consequence, we must request your departure from this establishment by six o'clock tomorrow. You will understand that we have the reputation of this hotel to consider at all times and we cannot be seen to indulge or tolerate (let alone condone) such behaviour.

I understand, sir that you were once a gentleman and so I should be most grateful for your total and discreet acquiescence in this matter.

Yours, with regret,
I.A. Richards, Manager

From the private journal of Professor C.R.H. Presbury

13th January 1913
There is much of the past few days which is now to me both murky and obscure. There are in that time elements which possess a quality of the oneiric, and others which I believe I can see in the crisp, cold light of day, to have been largely shameful. There is much that I have no desire to record here. That peculiar and unexpected incident which has just occurred, however, I surely have no choice but to set down.

Following a most unsatisfactory interview with the wearingly small-minded manager of this otherwise pleasant hotel in which he refused altogether to weaken his resolve or to consider any alternative course of action than that to which he is committed, I returned to my room in order to pack together my belongings and so prepare for my departure.

When I opened the door, however, it was to discover within a gentleman sat upon a chair, observing my entry with a look of something like watchful disapproval. We had met on only a handful of occasions, a decade past, during a period of my life much befogged and dimmed, yet did I recognise him at once, for this man's fame precedes him as a mourner goes before a hearse.

As I crossed the floor he rose to his feet and extended his right hand. With his left, he smoothed his moustache, a brisk gesture which nonetheless, at least to the trained eye, betokened anxiety and even mild disquiet.

"Dr Watson?" I said. "To what do I owe this pleasure?"

"You remember me, then?" His voice was full of that bullish determination to state the obvious which typifies the military mind.

"How could I not?" I replied. "After you and Mr Holmes took so great and uninvited an interest in my affairs?"

"A wholly neutral observer," began the doctor, "might rather be inclined to suggest that the encounter to which you allude ended with our saving your life."

"That may be so," I replied with a forbearance that was, I think, something of a marvel. "Yet our acquaintanceship was a fleeting thing. Might I ask how you have found me and what is the nature of your business here?"

"Locating you, Professor, has not been difficult. One had merely to follow the trail of destruction that you have left in your wake. And as for the nature of my business, let me be quite clear. It is an intervention born of concern and of fellow human feeling. I have come here today to deliver a warning."

At these words I felt a distinct surge of anger. "Whatever do you mean by such impertinence? Whatever is this absurd warning of yours?"

"I should close the door, Professor," said he, "and sit before me. We do not have much time and the words I have to say to you now are of the most sensitive and significant kind. Indeed, if you pay proper heed to them, they will yet save your life."

"Do you take me for a fool, sir?" I began and felt myself ready to tumble again into a paroxysm of righteous rage.

Yet Watson interrupted – "Professor!" – and I saw in his eyes not only absolute sincerity but also (and it was this which persuaded me to stay my words and, almost meekly, obey) something very close to fear.

So it was that I found myself doing as I had been asked and sitting opposite this unwanted visitor as that old storyteller began to speak.

"Let it first be noted that I am here today not on my own behalf but as an emissary from Mr Holmes."

"Sherlock Holmes," I breathed, perhaps more in the manner of a villain from the popular stage than I had intended. "It was my understanding that that jackanapes – that meddler-in-chief – had retired. That he drowses now by some Sussex fireside."

"Your understanding, at least in regards to my friend's retirement, is correct. Nonetheless…" At this, a smile of an uncharacteristically knowing, even sly, nature crossed my visitor's face. "It is not Mr Sherlock Holmes who has sent me to speak to you today."

"No?"

"Rather, I am present on behalf of an equally noble man: Mr Mycroft Holmes."

I rummaged for a moment through that portion of my mental apparatus that is devoted to trivia before retrieving the necessary fragment of data. "The elder brother, yes? He who is reputed to dwell in the upper reaches of government?"

"Quite so," said Watson. "Though I fear he is not now nearly as close to the centre of things as once he was. We are none of us – are we – quite as at home in this new century as we were in the last? We are all of us, I think, essentially Victorian."

"On the contrary," I said, adopting a pleasingly lofty tone such as I had for many years deployed in the faces of students too unwavering in their convictions, "it is my greatest regret that I was not born very much later. This new age of abandon suits me so very much more nicely than did those stultifying decades in which you thrived."

"I confess myself surprised, sir, given the unmanly

excesses of your biography, that the simple accident of your birthday should prove now to be the greatest of your regrets."

I glared. "You spoke, I believe, of a warning."

"I did."

"Then pray deliver it. My courtesy is not without limit."

My guest looked at this as though he intended to issue a rejoinder. In the event, he contented himself with the following, rather lugubrious words: "Mycroft cannot be seen to act in this matter. Therefore he must do so at one remove."

"You are his cat's paw?"

"Surely something a trifle more benign than that. Nonetheless he wished me to convey to you the extreme danger of your predicament."

"I am in no danger, sir. My situation is surely the reverse of that state."

"Professor, nothing is what it seems. The lady whom you know as Lowenstein has no true claim upon the name. Rather she is an agent of the War Office. She is employed as a singular agent for those extraordinary projects which have, given the present European situation, been granted tacit authority."

I shook my head at the absurdity of it all. "You have spent too long in the pages of your own books. Such things do not happen in real life. Why should the lady lie to me in so bald a fashion? What possible interest would that office have in me? Besides, I find your pessimism concerning our continental relations to be positively dispiriting."

"As matters stand, sir, there would seem to be little alternative to conflict before long. And as to the matter of the War Office's interest in you – an office, might I add, against whose methods Mycroft stands vehemently opposed – why, surely that is obvious."

"It is not obvious to me."

"The serum, Professor. The serum! Do you not see its potential?"

"For the lending of additional vigour, perhaps, in elder males…"

"No, sir! Do you not see its possible military application?"

I gaped at the man for this wild flight of fancy. Yet was he persistent.

"Do you not see? They are experimenting upon you! They are testing your endurance, testing the effects of this new substance upon the only man in Europe to have regularly imbibed the drug. Imagine it, Professor. Imagine the scene. Battlefields swarming with soldiers who are more than human. More feral, more savage, more lethal than their Teutonic counterparts. Legions, sir! Legions upon legions of creeping men!"

With this barrage of lurid melodrama, the doctor had at last gone too far. I rose to my feet and said, with all necessary sombreness: "this, sir, is now intolerable. You do me and Miss Lowenstein a grave disservice."

"Professor, I speak only the truth."

"You speak slander and, I fancy, something very near to treason. Now, you have delivered your warning. I should ask you now to leave. Under normal circumstances I would request also that you bear my felicitations to your master, Mr Mycroft Holmes, yet so unworthy has been your conduct and so vile have been your insinuations, I cannot find it in my heart to do so. Dr Watson, sir, it is high time for you to depart."

The old doctor stood up, looked sorrowfully at me,

smoothed his moustache once again in that distinctive gesture and walked, slowly and wordlessly, towards the door. Once there, he turned back.

"As a scientist, Professor, you will know well what the next and final stage of their unnatural experiment will surely be."

"And what, sir, is that?"

"They will test a thing to its very limits. To the point of its destruction. And beyond."

I scowled in disbelief at the continuance of such folly.

"Good day, Professor Presbury. I should recommend immediate flight yet I fear you are now deaf to reason. Instead, I shall have to content myself merely by wishing you the very best of luck."

And then he turned once more and he was gone, back to his dreams of the past, to wish himself resident again in that vanished epoch of gaslight and hansom cab.

Although certain of his more pungent fantasies have, naturally enough, lingered in my imagination, I have pushed the great majority of them aside. For I am quite certain that there can be no truth in any of it. Indeed, I am to see Scheherazade later today and to her I shall say nothing at all of this queer visitation. She will, I am certain, secure for me alternative accommodation and she has promised to take me once again upon the town. That she will have supplies about her person is to be expected.

Only pleasure lies before me now. I cannot – I will not – believe anything else. The story of the rest of my life will be one of pleasure and delight, of excess and of deep, dark, trembling joy.

From The Pall Mall Gazette, *27th January 1913*

A GRISLY DISCOVERY;
CIRCUS OWNERS QUESTIONED

It is a tragic fact that such discoveries as the one that was made in the early hours of this morning by the banks of the Thames in the vicinity of Waterloo are commonplace. A body was found, which appeared at first sight to be that of an elderly gentleman – another victim, it was thought, of old age, want, despair and that illusory comfort which is surely suggested to the desperate by the deep cold waters of our great river. Further inspection, however, revealed a more curious element to this seemingly well-worn tale.

The deceased was profoundly deformed, bent almost double even in death and possessing great and unnatural quantities of hair, as of those sported by certain simian denizens of the animal kingdom. That there is something freakish and abnormal in the business surely lies beyond all reasonable doubt, and the discovery of this ill-fated "Monkey Man" has already excited all manner of speculation.

Detective Inspector Arnold Blakeley, who is investigating the mystery on behalf of Scotland Yard, professed to this correspondent that his investigation is in its earliest stages. He considers the likeliest suspects to be found in the worlds of the circus and the carnival. It is in these disreputable quarters, he says, that all his energies shall be expended and he is confident that a plausible solution shall in time emerge.

Telegram

```
Sent: 30th January 1913
From: Mycroft Holmes
To: Panjandrum
```

Noted with interest thorough failure of your Presbury project. I expect to learn shortly of its total cessation.

Telegram

```
Sent: 30th January 1913
From: Panjandrum
To: Mycroft Holmes
```

Expectation unfounded. New alternatives soon to be explored. Suggest you consider retirement at earliest possible opportunity.

Telegram

```
Sent: 30th January 1913
From: Mycroft Holmes
To: Panjandrum
```

Retirement impossible while such men as you defame good name of Empire.

Telegram

Sent: 30th January 1913
From: Panjandrum
To: Mycroft Holmes

Not defamation; rather necessary protection. Project ongoing. Will brook no opposition.

Telegram

Sent: 30th January 1913
From: Mycroft Holmes
To: Panjandrum

Useful phrase, much used by younger brother: Game is afoot.

A FLASH IN THE PAN

William Meikle

Shinwell "Porky" Johnson is a former criminal who appears in "The Adventure of the Illustrious Client", in which he protects Kitty from Baron Grüner's henchmen and provides Holmes information on the best way to get into Grüner's secure residence. He is muscle for hire, and when I was asked to write for this anthology, the image of him standing at the door of a music hall as Holmes and Watson ascended the steps came to me almost immediately – from there the story came to me all at once, and I had a lot of fun writing it.

—William Meikle

They call me Porky Shinwell around town on account of me carrying a bit too much meat on my bones – at least most people do. But there is one gentleman that doesn't – one that has always treated me as if I mattered, and I shall never forget that kindness.

I was at the door, making sure no undesirables got inside, and it had been a while since I had seen him, so I almost didn't recognise him in his tall hat and frock coat. I had only ever met him on the job before, but it was him right enough – Mr Sherlock Holmes himself, coming up the steps to the Gaiety Theatre for the evening show, with the doctor at his side.

"Mr Johnson," he said. "It is good to see you in gainful employment for a change. And I note you have been following Watson's advice. A bit more lime in the mixture though – you will see better colour in your gums."

Holmes was the main reason I decided to go straight several years back. Having seen how he could just look at a man and see the history of his misdeeds writ large, I knew that I would never feel safe on a job after that – the old nerves would not take it. And here he was, at it again – how in blazes he could tell from where he was stood what manner of antiscorbutic I had been using for the scurvy I shall never know. But, damn him to hell, he was right. Mr Sherlock Holmes is always right, even when you think he is wrong.

I expected that to be the end of it, for we were in a public place and neither of us was overly keen to draw attention to any relationship between us, wishing to stay on opposite sides of the fence as it were. So Holmes surprised me when he leaned closer and, under the guise of passing me a tip, whispered in my ear.

"Keep an eye open, Shinwell. There are dark deeds afoot here tonight, and I might have need of you before the show is over."

He said nothing more, and was off and away into the foyer before I even thought of a question. Besides, there was little enough I could do at that moment – I had to watch the door, let the gentry in and keep the rabble out until the show began. So it was that it was nearly twenty minutes later before I retired to the foyer and shut the house doors behind me. As Holmes had asked, I kept my eyes peeled, but for the life of me I could not see what had drawn him here; I did not have him pegged as a man to enjoy the musical frivolities of *The Spring Chicken*. I had seen no one pass me whom I would consider capable of what Holmes had called "dark deeds", but both Holmes and I knew from our respective backgrounds that appearances could be most deceptive.

I did a tour of the foyer and saw nothing out of the ordinary, then went inside to stand at the back of the house. Up on stage Gertie Millar had them eating out of her hand as usual, but Holmes seemed to be the only one immune to her charms. I spotted him in a box near the stage on the right hand side, and he wasn't watching Gertie at all – his complete attention was on a box directly opposite him.

I followed his gaze. There were two gentlemen in the box, and both had their opera glasses fixed firmly on Gertie. I didn't recognise either of the men – out of my league if you catch my drift, all starched shirts and oiled hair – but if Holmes was watching them that closely, I decided I had better do the same. When Gertie's big song came to an end, one of the toffs left his seat before the applause died down. I made sure my blackjack was snug in my hand and hurried round the stairs to that side of the house. I was just in time to see the toff reach the stage door. Sleepy Jack was manning that one – or so I thought – but the man opened it and went through without stopping. I saw why seconds later when I reached the door myself. Jack was sleepy all right, addled with what smelled like cheap gin, slumped against the wall. I suspect he'd been bribed, but I had no time to cogitate, for the toff was already walking away, past the wings and towards the dressing rooms at the rear. Given the ferocity of his gaze when he'd been eyeing Gertie just minutes before, I was starting to fear for the singer's wellbeing.

I was almost running by the time I got to her dressing room. I burst in, blackjack in hand and immediately realised I had made a damn fool of myself – and not for the first time either. Our Gertie was a married woman. I knew her husband well, and the man she was wrapped around wasn't him, but was indeed my mystery toff.

Luckily they were too involved in the kiss to even take note of me so I was able to back out without any fuss, only to almost bundle into Holmes and Dr Watson who were coming along from the other direction.

"Did you see him, man?" Holmes said.

"He's in there with Gertie, Mr Holmes."

Holmes pushed past me, intent on heading along the corridor back to the main house. "Not the duke, you idiot. The other one."

The amorous couple had finally noticed that something was amiss, and the door opened behind me. The toff stood there, looking slightly dishevelled and more than a tad embarrassed. A look of disgust crossed Holmes's face.

"I would stay where you are, sir," Holmes said to the man. "You have exposed your infidelity far enough for one night."

Gertie was standing behind the toff, and she didn't look in the slightest bit mortified by the situation.

"One minute, Miss Millar," someone called.

Gertie pushed past me, heading for the stage. The toff made to follow, but Holmes pushed him back inside the room.

"Not you, sir. I shall have questions for you anon. Shinwell? Can I prevail on you to ensure that this gentleman does not leave the room?"

I smiled – the toff did not like that one bit – and nodded. Holmes and Watson left quickly, following Gertie up towards the wings. The toff looked like he might try to pass me, but I slapped my blackjack into my left palm, and just the sound of the thud it made was enough to quiet him. He went back into the dressing room and made quite an act of lighting a cigarette and feigning nonchalance, but I saw the tremor in his fingers clearly enough – he wasn't going anywhere as long as I was at the door.

He was still smoking when Holmes and Watson returned.

"As I expected," Holmes said. "He fled as soon as he got his picture of the duke going through the stage door. I found this by his chair in the box." He poured a fine powder from a paper cone into a glass vial and handed it to Watson. "He used this for the flash gun. Magnesium powder and potassium chlorate if I'm not mistaken, Watson. If I can identify the ratio of the mix back in Baker Street, we may be able to trace the supplier, and thence our man. Remember, do not let it get wet – or at least, if it does, do not let it near your matches. We would not want an explosion in your pocket. And there'll be a camera somewhere to be found too, although I expect we shall only uncover that once the film has been removed for developing."

"Powder? Film? What the blazes is going on here?"

The toff had finally realised there was more to this night than a kiss with a pretty woman. Holmes ignored his question and answered with one of his own.

"What can you tell me about your companion in the box this evening?"

"Johnnie? Fine chap – met him last weekend at my club. Rowed for Cambridge, you know?"

"I doubt that very much," Holmes said. "And I suppose he does not have a second name?"

"I never asked. And what bally business is it of yours?"

Holmes smiled thinly.

"Your father made it my business – when he got the first blackmail letter on Monday morning. I expect there will be another tomorrow, after your little fiasco here."

The toff started to spit and bluster, but it seemed that Mr Holmes had already done with him, and the three of us walked away, leaving the toff shouting some rather ungentlemanly curses at our backs.

"Would you mind telling me what's going on here, Mr Holmes?" I said when we got back to the stage door. Sleepy Jack was still out, snoring soundly.

"I am after a blackmailer, Shinwell. A nasty cove. I believe this is at least his third such case of extortion, and he is developing a taste for it. He targets young gentlemen with more money than sense. And, as you know, in this town that gives him plenty of custom. Our young duke back there has not been circumspect about his affair with Miss Millar − and that has been his undoing."

"This blackmailing chap − you do not have a name?"

"Not yet. I was hoping you might be able to help with that. It is provident that you are here tonight, and I shall not look askance at such good fortune."

"Anything I can do to help, Mr Holmes − you know that."

"Good man − put out the word in the usual places − I am looking for someone, not from money himself, who has come into more of it than he knows what to do with. He might be spending a lot more than his usual means, and that might have caught the attention of one of your acquaintances."

I laughed.

"That it might, Mr Holmes − it might even have caught my attention, once upon a time."

There being a degree of urgency inherent in Mr Holmes's request for help, I started that very night, after I got the crowd − including a very sheepish-looking duke − out onto the street and closed the doors of the theatre. Gertie wanted to go for a drink − eager to chase more young dukes no doubt − and some of the cast and crew agreed to accompany her, but I declined. She was heading uptown, whereas I was intending to travel in an altogether different direction.

But my first job was to get Sleepy Jack upright. I should have torn his ear off and tossed him out, but we go back a long way, Jack and I, and if the job, even menial as it was, was taken from him, the bottle would have him within days. He was too good a man to lose like that. I walked him up and down Aldwych until he was nearly sober.

"Who gave you the gin, Jack?" I asked when he was able to talk clearly.

"Some posh lad," Jack said. "A bottle if I looked the other way."

I described the young duke, but Jack shook his head.

"No – this lad had blond hair. Blue eyes, big nose and an old scar – here," he ran a finger from the corner of his left eye down his cheek.

I thanked Jack and sent him on his way. I had somewhere to start.

I headed east to try to find someone who could tell me more. I'd been in most of the public houses the length of the Strand and Fleet Street and was in the Black Friar at the north side of Blackfriars bridge before I got the first whiff of our man. It was Blackie Collins who put me on the right trail. Blackie is a pickpocket – one of the best. He can have your wallet away from an inside pocket as nice as ninepence and you'll never be the wiser. He was working the taproom when he saw me, and came to join me in a corner when I bought two pints of porter. I saw him take a pocket watch and a purse on the way over – Blackie never stopped working and I made sure my own wallet was tucked well away before I let him close to me.

In the end it cost me eight pints – four each – but it was worth it, for I left Blackie with my wallet still in my pocket and a name.

* * *

"James Mackie, from Edinburgh," I said to Mr Holmes. It was early morning but he did not look like he'd had any more sleep than I had. He was still in his eveningwear from the night before, even as his landlady arrived with a spot of breakfast that I took to most eagerly.

"Is the name all you have?" Holmes said. He did not so much as look at the toast and eggs, but instead lit up a pipe.

"That, and the fact he lives somewhere around Russell Square these days," I replied. "I can do some more asking around this evening after the show if you'd like."

Holmes smiled. "I think I can get an answer rather sooner."

He opened the window and whistled loudly. Within a minute there came the sound of many footsteps clattering up and down the stairs, accompanied by Mrs Hudson's shouting.

Half a dozen street urchins burst into the room and gathered around Holmes while more continued to cause havoc out on the landing. At least the ones gathered in our sitting room seemed able to behave themselves, although that probably had something to do with Holmes's supply of small denomination coinage.

"Now lads, you know what to do? Russell Square. James Mackie." Holmes said. "First one to find him gets a florin."

The boys departed in a rush of thudding feet, leaving only a smell that even the open windows didn't quite dispel. Holmes seemed quite satisfied.

"I have deployed my scouts, Shinwell. Those lads know the streets far better than any of Lestrade's men and at least as well as your own contacts," he said. "If our man surfaces, then they will find him."

And with that, Holmes seemed to have satisfied himself that as much as could be done was being done, and now he joined me at the breakfast table. The doctor arrived as I was on my second round of toast, and made a bit of a fuss checking my teeth and gums before he too joined us. I knew any camaraderie was only momentary, but for that short time I quite felt that I had indeed risen above my station – and for that, too, I have Mr Holmes to thank.

It could not last of course, and just as we were finishing breakfast I heard a pounding at the front door. Mrs Hudson showed a red-faced boy upstairs and into the sitting room, where Holmes had him stand by the fireplace for questioning.

"I done found 'im, Mr Holmes," the lad said, even before Holmes could speak. He was out of breath, and smelled rather ripe – so much so that Mrs Hudson made a point of opening all the windows before she retired swiftly to the cleaner air in her domain below us.

If Holmes noticed the smell, he did not show it – the lad had his full attention. He took a florin from his waistcoat pocket and showed it to the boy, who made a grab for it, but was too slow to beat Holmes's reflexes as the coin was made to vanish again.

"The story first," Holmes said.

"After you described the geezer you was after, George and Ratty and the others went off to the houses on the south of Russell Square, but me and Tom, we decided that we'd have more luck trying where they weren't, if you catch my drift? So we went round to the big hotel. Nearly got pinched by the doormen a coupla times too. We had to do a bit of duckin' and divin', I can tell you – Tom was fed to the back teeth. And right then, right when Tom was ready to jack it all in – that's when I saw 'im – your cove, Mr Holmes. Just sitting there in the reading room – white hair and a big scar down his cheek, just like you said."

Holmes sighed and waved the florin in front of the lad's nose again.

"Try to keep this as brief as possible, there's a good boy. And where might this have been, Stevenson?"

"I done told you already, sir — the big old place on the square with the columns and statues and such like."

"The Hotel Russell?"

"That's the one. He were just sitting there reading. I left Tom watching 'im, and ran right back here."

Holmes passed the lad the florin.

"Mind to share it with Tom — if you do not, I shall hear of it."

"Will do, sir. I'll head back there now — just to make sure your man's still there."

The boy left at as fast a run as he had arrived.

Holmes immediately made for his coat and walking stick. Watson rose to join him, but I was unsure whether I was invited. Holmes soon put me to rights.

"Do join us, Shinwell. He disrupted you at your place of work last night — perhaps you should return the favour today."

Two minutes later the three of us were in a hansom on our way to Russell Square.

I know the Russell well from the old days. Toffs leave all kinds of things in hotel rooms that they would not leave lying around in their homes — don't ask me why, that is just the way it is — and it is easy pickings for chaps like me, or it was, back then. Rory Calquoun on the desk raised an eyebrow when he saw me with Holmes and Watson — back in the day he would have taken a couple of shillings off me and looked the other way for an hour. Today he made half a crown vanish into his waistcoat pocket when Holmes passed it over the counter and asked where Mackie could be found.

"Top floor," he said. "Room 414 – he went up just five minutes ago."

Holmes thanked Calquoun and took the stairs two at a time. I was quite out of puff by the time we reached the top, having carried twice the weight of the other two all the way up, so I was a few yards behind Holmes when he rapped on the door. A thin, blond chap opened it, and I recognised him immediately even before I got close enough to see the scar – he had been the one sitting next to the duke in the box last night – and he did not seem in the least bit surprised to see Holmes.

"After last night's performance I have been expecting you, gentlemen. Come in and let us have a drink like civilised chaps."

"There is little that is civilised about your behaviour, sir," Holmes said as he followed him into the suite. The man, Mackie, merely smiled and waved a hand around, as if showing off the opulence and splendour that his endeavours had brought him. As I looked around I realised I had been in these rooms before too – a Russian gentleman had them then, and I had relieved him of thirty pieces of gold coin. I also knew that my knowledge gave me an advantage here that Holmes did not have. I made a bit more of my condition than I needed to, making a great show of being breathless and in dire need of water. Mackie was taking little note of me anyway, having his full attention on Holmes.

"You have nothing on me, Mr Holmes – and we both

know it. It is not illegal to take photographs and none of my – shall we call them – customers will say anything against me to the authorities."

"I might not have you to rights, yet," Holmes replied. "I merely wanted you to know that I know – and that I shall be watching you closely."

I missed the rest of the conversation – I was already off and away down the internal corridor of the suite. I found the bathroom, and a glass of water, which I carried with me for appearances' sake should I be caught while casing the rest of the rooms.

At first I thought I was going to be out of luck – there were only clothes in the bedroom wardrobe – top quality though. But the second bedroom was where the real find was – the room had been made over into a small photography studio. I didn't know what half the stuff was or what it was used for, but I recognised the flash powder right enough and remembered what Mr Holmes had said about it. I did what needed to be done and left quietly, putting the empty water glass on a sideboard before rejoining Holmes, Mackie and Watson in the main room.

Holmes and Mackie were still facing off to each other, but they were now sitting in armchairs and smoking cigarettes. I poured myself a Scotch – nobody seemed to be offering to do it for me, but nobody stopped me either – and joined Watson on the Chesterfield sofa. It all seemed a mite too civilised for my liking – I would have preferred to bust the villain's head and have done with it – I suppose that is just another difference between Mr Holmes and myself, but I can't say it's one I am overly jealous of.

To be fair to him, Mr Holmes did not seem to be enjoying the verbal fencing, and his contempt for the Scotsman was writ large on his face as he listened.

"You cannot deny that I am only ushering in what we all know is in our future, Mr Holmes. The great unwashed do so love their tittle-tattle – gossip about their betters is the only thing that keeps them from despair. Who am I to deny them those pleasures if I am not to be paid to keep them to myself?"

"You talk far too blithely of despair for a man with so few moral scruples," Holmes said. "I know it was you last night in the box, for I can see the magnesium powder in your hair where it has not been completely brushed out, and that scar on your cheek can be clearly seen even from the other side of the theatre."

"And I know you saw me," Mackie replied with a smile. "But here we are – and you can still do nothing about it, shackled by your conventions. Besides, even if you did find something against me, it is not as if you yourself are immune to scandal, is it Mr Holmes? There is more than enough in your past to keep your friend Lestrade busy for months should he come to hear of it."

To his credit, Holmes never so much as blinked.

"We are not here to discuss my failings, Mr Mackie – I am all too aware of them. As I have said, I am merely here to let you know that I shall be watching you closely from now on until you make the mistake that allows me to put a stop to you once and for all."

"Watch and learn, Mr Holmes. I have developed a taste for this life, and it is surely preferable to joining my stoker father on the Great Eastern Railway, so do your worst. I intend to be busy here in London for quite some time yet."

And with that we were dismissed. As Holmes rose and walked past me he turned, looked into my eyes and raised an eyebrow, but said nothing. I, however, knew that look of old – he had spotted something, something that he deemed important. He did not speak of it though, not then, nor on the way back to Baker Street, where I took my leave of him and Watson and went down to the theatre to prepare for that evening's show and, hopefully, catch a couple of hours of well-earned sleep.

I heard no more until three nights later, when a street lad – I think he was one that I had seen in Baker Street but I cannot be sure – delivered a note to the stage door.

If you wish to be in at the end of it, meet me at Miss Jane's house in Berwick Street at nine tonight.

It was not signed, but I knew the sender. I left Sleepy Jack in charge of the house – with severe admonishments as to the consequences should he take to the gin again – and made my way across town to Soho.

Everyone in central London knows Miss Jane's, but nobody will admit to ever being there, despite it being packed to the gunwales with lonely gentlemen on any given night. Tonight was no exception – the downstairs hallway was so crowded with well-suited toffs that I had to push through them to make my way inside. Holmes and Watson were there ahead of me, standing at the foot of a flight of stairs.

"The Irregulars followed him," Holmes said. "And they did a fine job of it. He has a new quarry tonight."

Holmes mentioned a name and this time it was my turn

to raise an eyebrow. European royalty, even minor royalty, was indeed a step up for Mackie, and one that would ensure him plenty of those worldly pleasures he seemed to covet should he succeed in his play.

"He has two rooms – His Majesty is in one with the lady, and I believe Mackie is in the other with his camera. Watson will get the prince out without any fuss, and you and I shall beard Mackie in his den. Agreed?"

Both Watson and I nodded, and we made our way upstairs.

Watson seemed concerned. "Even if we catch him in the act, Holmes, there will still be nothing that Lestrade can use for a conviction – not enough in any case."

"At least we will stop him tonight," Holmes said, and he looked at me pointedly in the same manner as before; he knew more than he was saying.

We arrived outside a room on the second landing. It was obvious from the noises from within that His Majesty was enjoying all that the house had to offer.

"On my mark, Watson," Holmes said, leading me to the next door along. We stood there for some seconds.

"Are we waiting for something, Holmes?" I asked, and again I got the raised eyebrow in reply.

"I was rather hoping you would tell *me*, Shinwell," he said.

Luckily, before I had time to think of an answer that would be evasive enough to get past Holmes, the gap at the bottom of the door lit up as a flash went off within. Even as I put a shoulder to the door, I knew we would be too late, for the screams that immediately followed the flash were too high and too wild to come from a man with any hope of living.

The door split under my weight, and revealed the hellish scene inside. Mackie's whole upper torso was aflame, his hair singed off, his skin bubbling and seething under a white fire that burned so hard it hurt the eyes to look at it. By the time we reached him he had already fallen to the floor, and by the time we doused the flames by wrapping him in a rug the man was dead. There was only a smoking ruin where his smug smile had been.

I saw through a connecting door to the room beyond that Watson was already leading the prince away and out of sight of what would soon be many prying eyes.

Holmes looked down at the body and pursed his lips.

"Well, Shinwell, it seems that your ploy worked." He went on, without giving me time to protest my innocence. "I smelled the fixing reagent on you as soon as you came back into the hotel room so I know you found the developing room. And I noted the empty glass on the sideboard as we left. That, and the fact that you were present when I told Watson of the properties of the flash powder, and now the look on your face. I know this is your doing, so there is no sense in you denying it."

"I would not want to deny it, if truth be told, Mr Holmes," I said. "For if anyone deserved it, it is this piece of vermin. But I am happy to pay whatever price you deem necessary."

Holmes smiled thinly.

"It is as much my doing as yours, Shinwell, for I knew it was coming and did nothing to intervene. Just do not tell Watson – he would not understand, and this is one case I would rather never have documented in full."

We left the room together, just as the sound of police whistles pierced the air and Mr Mackie quickly became one of those very stories that he was so keen to see publicised.

THE VANISHING SNAKE

Jeffrey Thomas

My first impulse in selecting a character from the Holmes canon for this volume was to choose a female protagonist, and I quickly settled on **Helen Stoner** from what is said to be Arthur Conan Doyle's favourite Holmes story, "The Adventure of the Speckled Band". I liked that, rather than passively fall victim to her stepfather's plot to murder her, Helen took a proactive route by sneaking off to avail herself of outside resources in the form of Holmes and Watson. I decided on following Helen through a direct sequel, which takes the original story's grotesque gothic vibe a step over the line into horror, and in so doing seeks to address certain biological issues some readers have had with "The Speckled Band". Helen's new adventure also provides Holmes with the inspiration to visit a certain region of Asia, which he is revealed to have done in his back-from-the-dead story, "The Adventure of the Empty House".

—Jeffrey Thomas

"I am sorry to say there is no such snake in existence as a swamp adder, Mr Holmes," I proclaimed upon being let into the sitting room of the Baker Street rooms Sherlock Holmes shared with his companion Dr John Watson, also present.

"Helen Stoner, gentlemen," their landlady Mrs Hudson belatedly introduced me, no doubt thrown a bit by the words of greeting from this unexpected visitor. She departed, and I took a seat by the window.

Mr Holmes certainly did not require her introduction, in any case. Only a few weeks prior, he had saved me from sharing the tragic fate of my twin sister, Julia. Our own stepfather, Dr Grimesby Roylott, had connived to murder us shortly before we could marry, for fear of losing the inheritance he had been given to control upon the death of our mother, so long as her daughters lived under his care. Dr Roylott had been successful in doing away with poor Julia, by introducing a venomous snake into her room, but when he had made an attempt to do the same to me only two years later I had brought my unformed suspicions to Mr Holmes, who had not only uncovered Dr Roylott's plot but, in repelling the serpent, had inadvertently caused it to kill its own master.

Having apparently finished a late breakfast and now enjoying a pipe while slumped back comfortably in his chair, Mr Holmes arched an eyebrow at me, clearly intrigued that his identification of the reptile had been challenged these several weeks after the investigation's conclusion. I have no doubt the observant Mr Holmes took note of my uneasy manner, surely not so different from my greatly troubled demeanour when I had first come to him, much oppressed by strange nocturnal occurrences. I knew too well that my hair was even more shot through with white than before, though I was only thirty-two years of age. Yet with my brutal stepfather deceased, and the snake itself having been captured by Mr Holmes using a noose and locked away inside an iron safe in my stepfather's room, I can well imagine that he wondered what there was to cause me such anxiety.

Mr Holmes said, "You speak with much conviction, Miss Stoner. Might I ask how you arrived at this certainty?"

I replied, "I should like to recount all the events that led to this conclusion, Mr Holmes. Owing to your recent involvement in my situation, I thought you would want to know of the even stranger happenings that have followed in the wake of the former. I am beyond curious to know what you will think of certain elements of these occurrences, which are so uncanny that I fear you will ultimately scoff at them."

Mr Holmes sat up straighter in his chair and said, "It is a rare thing indeed for one of the cases I have undertaken and thought to be thoroughly resolved to not be concluded after all. You have my keenest interest, Miss Stoner. I will withhold my judgement until I have heard all. Please proceed, and leave out no detail of your account."

"Thank you; to the best of my ability I shan't." Here I drew in a long breath to bolster myself. "As you will no doubt recall, Mr Holmes, you and your good friend Dr Watson here kindly saw me into the care of my maiden aunt,

Miss Honoria Westphail, directly after the dreadful events that culminated in my stepfather's death. However, in the absence of any other heir, and though I was not his blood relation, it fell upon me to address matters pertaining to his estate of Stoke Moran, and so I was obliged to return there.

"The coroner had removed my stepfather's body quickly enough, of course, but there remained the business of the snake trapped in the heavy safe. The animal would presumably not suffocate, as my stepfather had kept it in the safe all along, so apparently it was getting sufficient air somehow. The hope was that the snake would starve to death, but then how long would that take? When would it be prudent to open the safe, using the key that stood in the lock, to ascertain whether the snake still posed a threat? These concerns were expressed to me by the police who followed up the business after your involvement.

"Before my return to Stoke Moran I gave my consent to have the safe removed from the house and for the police to deal with it as they would. Upon my arrival back at the old manor house I was visited by one of the constables who had been present when the safe was opened, and I was informed of the result.

"It seems the men who unlocked the safe had improvised weapons at hand, meaning to thrust a sod cutter's spade into the aperture as soon as the door came open and crush the beast immediately, but they were prepared in case it should slip past this blade. Another man had a long, makeshift torch ready, to thrust in the same if need be. A third constable turned the key and at a signal cracked the door open, but before the man with the spade could attack, the man with the torch – who had glimpsed the interior by the light of his fire – begged the other to hold off. A moment later, though the three constables remained tense with caution, the door was hauled fully open.

"The snake that had killed both my sister and stepfather was gone. Or, at least, what remained was less than a carcass. The constable described to me a coil of colourless, dry matter, that when stirred with the spade proved to be comprised of a fluffy white material that broke up like ash. So unsubstantial was this matter that even the merest probing caused it to disintegrate, the ashy remnants so fine that there was ultimately left not even a residue within the safe."

Mr Holmes interrupted, "Were they certain the snake did not slip out through the bottom of the aperture once the door was cracked open, while the men were distracted and confounded by the sight of this pale coil? The glare of the torch itself may have shielded this action. My suspicion is that the dry matter was nothing more than the serpent's molted skin."

"That was my own initial reaction to this account, Mr Holmes, and I suggested the same to this constable, who was in fact he who had wielded the spade. He assured me that with three sets of eyes on the safe the snake could not possibly have slipped past them. And there was no other means of escape from the safe, for, had there been, surely the snake would have made use of it before. Also, he swore he could tell this was not merely a shed skin, for he had found and handled such in his youth. He and the other two could only conclude that the snake had died and become strangely desiccated or mummified due to some property of the sealed safe."

"Unless, of course, another had entered the mansion in your absence and removed the snake, the key, as you say, still slotted in its hole."

"One might readily wonder that, but further events I am to relate will shed a different light on that consideration."

Mr Holmes said, "Forgive my interruption, then. Please continue."

"Well, mysterious though this situation was, I soon turned my attention to the matter that had brought me back to Stoke Moran. My fiancé, Percy Armitage, was dear enough to already be investigating for me a means by which I might sell the estate, as I have no sentimental attachment to it. The house itself, being in such ill repair as you will recall, with the roof of the east wing even having partly collapsed, we thought might best be demolished, but we proposed to leave that decision to whomever proved interested in acquiring the property.

"Meanwhile, with the aid of my stepfather's former housekeeper, Mrs Littledale, I intended to set about packing up the remainder of my belongings to transport back to my aunt's home, along with whatever had belonged to my sister that I might care to retain. As for my stepfather's possessions, I had no desire to own any of it, so poisonous had his memory become to me.

"Mr Armitage had come to meet me upon my return to Stoke Moran, to ensure that I was capable of re-entering the scene of so much horror, but once I had thoroughly reassured him he returned to his home, near Reading, where his occupation made demands on him. I planned to stay only a matter of days at the manor house, but I would be sleeping in my old room, despite the minor repairs that had been begun on it as a ruse to force me to stay in my sister's old room and thereby make me vulnerable to my stepfather's dangerous pet. Mrs Littledale consented to sleep in Julia's room during my stay so that I would not be in the house alone. Though the place repulsed me, rationally I knew the threat had passed. The police had even, at my request, warned off from the property those gypsies whom my stepfather had strangely, given his violent temperament and reclusive nature, permitted and even encouraged to set up their tents on our grounds.

"There was one unresolved and perplexing matter, however, that still caused me a good deal of nervousness, so that I slept at night locked in my room and never ventured from the house after dark. You will remember that in addition to his snake, my stepfather was also in possession of a baboon and a cheetah, which rather than being penned or chained up he allowed to roam freely within the broken-down stone wall surrounding the property, doubtlessly to intimidate and ward off any curious village folk."

Dr Watson spoke up, "Yes, you told us that a correspondent of Dr Roylott's had sent these animals and the snake over from India. Holmes and I, much to our unpleasant surprise, crossed paths with the baboon the night we came to investigate your situation, and once we had hidden ourselves in your room we heard the cheetah sniffing around at the shuttered window."

I said, "The constable I spoke with told me no one in the area had seen either the baboon or cheetah since that night, nor had Mrs Littledale. Only my stepfather had ever cared for them, though I myself had never actually seen him feed them, nor even seen the substantial amounts of food they should require, particularly the cheetah. My fear was that now, starving, they might harm someone, even venture towards the nearby village in the search for food. That no one had seen them suggested three possibilities to me. For one, they may have indeed left the area to seek sustenance. Or else, the gypsies, when they had been shooed off, had taken the beasts with them, for as my stepfather's only friends they may have been more familiar with the animals than I had known. This would explain why the creatures had never attacked the gypsies. The only remaining possibility was that, weakened with hunger, the big monkey and great cat had taken shelter in the dilapidated wing of the house, having entered it through a broken window or even the caved-in roof, and now lay helpless within.

"That first night back I slept poorly, as one might imagine, having suffered wretched dreams about my stepfather's pets trying to claw their way into the house. In the morning, as I was taking my breakfast, a letter came that was addressed to Dr Roylott. I accepted it, and recognised at once that it was from my stepfather's longtime correspondent from India, Mr Edward Thurn. It did not surprise me that Mr Thurn should not yet know of Dr Roylott's passing, but I was surprised to see that the letter bore a return address from Upper Swandam Lane, indicating that my stepfather's old friend was now staying in London. You see, the two had become acquainted during that period in which my stepfather lived in Calcutta, where he had first met my widowed mother and where Julia and I lived until only eight years ago. It was my understanding that Dr Roylott and Mr Thurn had become friends when the latter was a patient of my stepfather, shortly before the time Dr Roylott was convicted of murdering his Indian butler in a fit of rage over some thievery, thus incurring his lengthy prison sentence. It was Mr Thurn who had shipped to Dr Roylott the baboon, cheetah, and the snake you identified as a swamp adder, Mr Holmes.

"I felt it would be a violation against Mr Thurn to read his correspondence, though my stepfather was beyond such consideration and undeserving of it, so I refrained from opening the letter, though I bade its deliverer to remain until I could pen a quick reply. In my message I informed Mr Thurn, without going into all the complex and unsavoury particulars, of his friend's passing. I thought it was the decent thing to do, given that I could hardly imagine he was aware of the use his friend had planned for that venomous serpent. As I was unwilling to preserve any of my stepfather's belongings and wanted to be rid of them, I invited Mr Thurn to come have a look at them and freely take away whatever might strike his fancy. I knew little of Mr Thurn, never having met him in person myself, but my stepfather had said he was a world traveller with an inquisitive mind and hence an avid reader, so I alluded to Dr Roylott's library, which, though it consists of many medical texts, also contains numerous books on very esoteric and outré subjects. I sent my letter, but later in the day regretted somewhat my haste in offering Mr Thurn a look at my stepfather's things before I could consult with my fiancé about their potential value. Chiefly, though, my regret was due to the fact that I did not intend to remain at Stoke Moran for many days and might not still be there should Mr Thurn come visiting from London.

"That night, shortly after Mrs Littledale had retired to my sister's former room and I to mine, a most strange and horrible sound came to us from outside the house. In her terror, which was no doubt exacerbated by the housekeeper having to sleep in the room into which Dr Roylott had introduced his snake to murder poor Julia, Mrs Littledale came pounding on my door looking quite frantic. I felt certain the weird howling cries came from either the baboon or cheetah, though I could not tell which, and I even wondered if the starving cat was attacking the monkey in its desperation. We stood paralysed, listening at the shuttered window of my room until, despite my horror, my curiosity could bear it no longer. I removed the heavy bar that secured the shutters, and cracked them open enough to peek outside.

"It was a clear night with the moon almost full, and the grounds beyond lay silvered with its glow. On the lawn not far beyond my window a strange figure lay writhing and contorting, while arching back its neck and emitting the uncanny cries we had heard. Indistinct as it was, it could only be the baboon. The primate had always been of a darkish brown colour, and I considered that it might only be the moonlight that made the animal's body appear so pale that it almost gave the impression of being faintly luminous. It was also of a ghastly, cadaverous aspect, and I had no doubt the pitiful beast was in the final stage of starvation.

"We watched until the creature gave a last violent convulsion, and its terrible howl tapered away to silence. It lay still, and almost in tears Mrs Littledale begged me to close and bar the window again. We could do no more than leave the creature where it had died until we should summon someone to bear away its body on the morrow.

"Mrs Littledale could not bring herself to return to her room alone, and in my guilt at having insisted she keep me company at Stoke Moran I permitted her to doze in the chair in my room. However, neither of us actually got much sleep for the remainder of that night.

"In the morning I was awakened by a shriek from outside, but this time the cry was human. I went racing from the house in my nightgown to find Mrs Littledale had already dressed and ventured outside to inspect the baboon's corpse. As I came beside her I could readily understand her cry of shock and revulsion.

"The large monkey had decayed to an astonishing degree in a matter of hours, so that all that remained was a husk-like figure fashioned from what looked like the pale grey paper of a wasp's nest. Even as we watched, a mere breeze caused one of its upper limbs to break off and tumble away across the grass like a chunk of ash, breaking up as it went. As we continued to gaze upon it in disbelief the animal's dog-like head caved in, crumbled and disintegrated, until not even its long fangs remained. All was swept up and away in a cloud of fine powder in only the few minutes that we stood watching mesmerised and aghast.

"I was, of course, reminded of what the constable had told me about the remains of the snake that had been revealed inside the safe. What ailment, affliction or poison, I wondered, might cause two such different animals to decompose in so unnatural a way?

"All we could do now was go about our day as we had planned, my most fervent desire being to see myself rid of Stoke Moran soon.

"Later that day my Percy once more travelled to Surrey to discuss with me the progress made on divesting ourselves of Stoke Moran, and we also discussed our plans to move our wedding from May to June because of the strenuous occurrences of late. We thought to enjoy a quiet afternoon together at the estate now that my vile-tempered stepfather no longer dwelt there, but his shadow still lay heavily upon us, all the more so when I related to my fiancé the strange spectacle the housekeeper and I had witnessed the night before and our discovery that very morning. Mr Armitage was at a loss as to any explanation, his only half-heartened suggestion being that someone, perhaps one of the expelled gypsies, had placed a papier-mâché effigy upon the spot where the monkey had perished in the night. I do not think he held any more faith in this theory than I did. In any case, I also told him of my note to Mr Edward Thurn, and my fiancé expressed no regret regarding the offer I had extended, though he was concerned as to whether Mr Thurn truly had been ignorant of Dr Roylott's intentions in wanting that poisonous snake sent to him from India. I assured him I could not conceive of my stepfather confiding in an accomplice when there was no need to do so, and that surely Mr Thurn only believed he was supplementing my eccentric stepfather's existing menagerie.

"Mr Armitage departed in the early evening, leaving me and Mrs Littledale alone at Stoke Moran once more. The night, however, proved uneventful and Mrs Littledale slept in her own room, though I dreamed that the cheetah, bony and ghastly pale, circled the house all night looking for a way in.

"The following day I was sitting on my sister's bed leafing through some of her books and feeling very dispirited by my recollection of the terror and confusion that had preceded her death when Mrs Littledale sought me out to say we had a visitor. When she gave me his name I told her to have him brought to me in one of the seldom-used sitting rooms in the central portion of the mansion. It was none other than Mr Edward Thurn, who greeted me very cordially and took a seat opposite me while Mrs Littledale went to prepare tea. I had previously formed no mental image of the man, but his appearance, except for his shortness of stature, did not surprise me. He was thin but appeared healthy, his age difficult to ascertain – I would say anywhere from late forties to perhaps sixty – his black hair less grey than my own. His face was very brown, leathery, and deeply creased by much exposure to the sun, with exceedingly keen dark eyes couched in fleshy folds. I should think at a distance he might be taken for a man of the Orient. He wore good clothes that had seen better days.

"He said to me, 'I believe I had a presentiment that things were not well with your stepfather, and that was part of my reason for returning to England. I only just arrived several days ago and immediately wrote that letter you received, to let him know. I am terribly sorry to learn of the death of my good friend, Dr Roylott, and I am sorry for your loss as well, Miss Stoner. I know he had acted as a devoted father to you and your twin since you were very small children.'

"Unable to stopper the bitterness that rose to my lips, I replied, 'He never told you of her passing? Small wonder. My twin, Julia, expired two years ago, Mr Thurn. She was murdered by your friend, my devoted stepfather.'

"'What is this you say?' my visitor cried. His expression of surprise and dismay appeared utterly genuine to me.

"'It is a long, strange story,' I forewarned him, and I proceeded to tell it in all its details, naturally including your own involvement, gentlemen. Mr Thurn sat riveted and was plainly disturbed by what I had to report of his long-time friend's murder of my sister, his plot to murder me as well and his own accidental death by the very serpent my guest had shipped from India.

"Mr Thurn turned his face away and said in an odd,

quiet tone, 'But I never actually shipped him that snake. Nor the baboon or cheetah.'

"'You did not?' said I. 'But if not you, then who?'

"He said, 'I am responsible for providing those creatures to him, but not in the way you imagine. It would be very difficult to make you understand, but in all fairness it is my duty to try, after the ordeals you have suffered. Yet first I must explain to some degree about myself.' He turned his eyes back on me, and if they had been of a piercing quality before I nearly squirmed under their gaze now. I trembled at their unnerving intensity and yet, as though hypnotised, I could not look away. There was a quality to them that suggested the man possessed an immense reservoir of internal power. I will stress, however, that this did not strike me necessarily as an evil force, but as a power such as electricity held in reserve.

"Mr Thurn began, 'You may wonder, as I wonder now myself, how Dr Roylott and I could be such close friends, and yet even after all our years of association with him, you and I were blind to the full picture of his nature. We were similar in that we both possessed questing minds and restless spirits that led us to seek fulfilment beyond the conventional precincts of man. That is, of European man. I travelled widely in my restlessness, beginning in my youth, without even quite knowing at first if my quest was a spiritual one. I encountered your stepfather in India, yes, but it was not due to my being a patient of his, as he led you to believe. It was in prison that we met, after he had been convicted of killing his servant. My own crime was of a political nature, but I have more than once run afoul of local law in my travels, since I have often journeyed to places that were prohibited and seen things I was, as an outsider, not meant to see.

"'I was released from prison much before Dr Roylott, and I resumed my travels, going on to the holy temple of Badrinath, taking my cue from the Portuguese Jesuits Andrade and Marques and masquerading as a Hindu on pilgrimage. After some time in that region I travelled on to Tibet, entering it through the Mana Pass in the Himalayas.'"

Here Mr Holmes cut in, "Are you sure this fellow was not deceiving you, Miss Stoner? Tibet has forbidden foreigners from crossing its borders for the past three decades. Violating that ban by entering through such a conspicuous point of ingress as the Mana Pass leaves me suspicious."

I replied, "I can only relate what I was told, Mr Holmes, and he did say that he had been turned back in an earlier attempt. But Mr Thurn informed me, without any apparent boastfulness, that he was masterful at disguise."

"He rather reminds me of you in that regard," Dr Watson said to his friend.

"He also claimed rather provocatively that he had developed the means of going unseen, though he did not elaborate on what he meant by that."

Mr Holmes said, "The thought of his actually succeeding in penetrating Tibet is intriguing. I have long desired to travel there myself, and one day may attempt it. But again I apologise. Please resume your account."

I did so. "Mr Thurn went on with his personal history, saying, 'Though anyone who aids a foreigner who has infiltrated Tibet runs the risk of punishment, including death, I nevertheless met people who, having lived all their lives in so isolated a region, were as fascinated by me as I was by them. I spent two years in Tibet, during which I devoted most of my time to the study of Buddhism. I was fortunate in impressing with my earnestness a *gomchen*, a

Tibetan hermit said to be capable of working wonders, who at great risk accepted me as his secret student. It was he who taught me how to conjure seemingly living entities with my mind.'

"'I do not understand,' I told him.

"He said, 'I warned you that it would be difficult for you to accept. Nevertheless, what I am telling you is the truth. It is possible for one to materialise a form the Tibetans call a *tulpa*, which is a manifestation of thought with the appearance of a living being, brought about through intensely focused concentration. It is an illusion, but not a delusion; a hallucination so convincing that not only does the conjurer himself witness it but, ideally, it would be visible to others as well, this phantom construction as perceptible as an authentic material entity. A *tulpa* might even, ultimately, take on a personality of its own and defy its master's direction, living so to speak as an independent being.'

"'Are you suggesting,' I said, 'that the snake… '

"'Not only the snake,' he answered. 'I manifested the baboon and the cheetah, too, purely through the power of thought. They were not sent physically from India. It was my mind that sent them here at Dr Roylott's behest. During our correspondence after I had left Tibet I told your stepfather of my experiences there and my own success in conjuring *tulpas*, and he was thoroughly intrigued. We devised an experiment: would I be able to manifest a *tulpa* remotely, by transmitting the power of my thoughts to his location in England, with the doctor acting as a sort of receiver to supplement my efforts? Would it be possible to create a *tulpa* through such a joint effort? Oh, of course the conjurations were mostly mine, but your stepfather's belief in my efforts, and his concentration on the subjects we chose as our models, helped enable them to manifest, and after they had done so it was mostly through Dr Roylott's own will that these forms were sustained. With these things, belief is all, a belief more complex than the blind faith of religion, because one is always aware that the object of belief is an illusion.

"'First I created the baboon, based on mental images of creatures I had seen in South Africa. Shortly after, I manifested the cat, patterned after the Asiatic cheetah. It was not until later that Roylott specifically requested a dangerous serpent. I did question why he should want this particular creature, and his response was that it would render our ongoing experiment all the more fascinating. Would a mouse, for instance, seemingly struck by the fangs of this snake believe so in the creature's veracity and its non-existent poison that it would perish as a result? Have you heard of the aborigines of Australia and their bone pointing? How one of them so cursed will die purely from their belief in the magic?'

"'This is preposterous,' I protested. 'This snake drank milk, proving that it required sustenance as a physical creature. It could not have been an illusion. I am not calling you a liar, sir, and I believe at least that you yourself believe in such things, but my stepfather must have acquired actual animals from another source if not from you.'

"'Miss Stoner,' he said, with his black eyes burning into me, 'snakes do not care to drink milk. If your stepfather put a saucer of milk in front of it, it was only a prop to help him continue to think of the snake as an actual creature, and a loyal pet. Summoning a snake by whistling? As a snake does not hear as we do, I am doubtful one might be trained in such a manner. Again, something Roylott did only to convince himself that his snake was real and obedient to him. I hardly believe that an actual snake could climb a bell pull, so as to lower itself to your sister's bed and back again, but this snake did so because your stepfather imagined that it could. In as much as he was able, he was controlling those beasts. Why, I ask you, do you think the baboon and cheetah, which could easily have passed over the wall of your property here, did not do so? And, incidentally, there is no such animal as a swamp adder. Oh, infrequently the African swamp viper may be called that, but its venom is not nearly as toxic as that I imagined for the cobra-like snake I invented for Dr Roylott. Creating an animal that did not truly exist, based on the attributes of a number of snakes, was another aspect of the proposed experiment. I gave it the fanciful name of swamp adder, and it is interesting to learn that the appellation suggested itself spontaneously to the sensitive mind of your friend Mr Holmes.'

"I said, 'But if my stepfather knew all along that the snake was not real, why then did he himself succumb to its bite when it was frightened by Mr Holmes back into Dr Roylott's chamber?'

"Mr Thurn said gravely, 'In order for the snake to successfully kill you, Miss Stoner, at that moment your stepfather believed in its existence with all of his might. Without my level of training, he could not balance his belief with his awareness of the illusion. His instinctual fear of a snake attacking him leant the manifestation potency. No poison entered him. It was his own mind that killed him.'

"'Yet how,' I asked, 'would this have worked on my sister, who never knew it was a snake that attacked her?

She could not die of imagined poisoning if she did not take in the illusion of a snake at more than a glance. She referred to it only as a speckled band.'

"He said, 'Grimesby Roylott was a man of great willpower; it is why our experiment was so successful. His will that your sister should die transmitted itself to her mind, almost in the way of a powerful hypnotic suggestion. It was not the snake that killed her, not even an illusory snake, so much as the sheer malevolent force of his own mind. He had no fear of puncture wounds being found on her flesh, because there would be none. You told me your first impression regarding your sister's demise was that she had died of fear. This was essentially true.

"'Those three animals were extensions of your stepfather's will; that is why they were sustained and were so convincing. And from what I have now learned from you, seeing my complicated old friend in a new light, I suspect it was not only to frighten villagers away from his property that he let the baboon and cheetah roam free, but to frighten you and your sister from venturing outside. To keep you prisoners here. I cannot help but wonder if it was not only the money he would lose once you two should marry that caused him to react in so brutal a manner, but fear that you two, upon going into the world, would inform others of his behaviours.'

"My visitor's speculation caused me great discomfort, and you will forgive me if I do not elaborate," I said, with my eyes averted from Mr Holmes and Dr Watson. I could utter no more on the subject of this personal distress. On the occasion that we had first met I had exposed the marks of Dr Roylott's fingers on the flesh of my wrist, and the great fear of my stepfather I had evinced had likely suggested to Mr Holmes and Dr Watson abuses that, as gentlemen, they had not pressed me to discuss.

I continued with my narrative, "Mr Thurn went on to say, 'Roylott could have had a great mind. He had immense resources of willpower and intensity, but he lacked self-discipline, and now I see how thoroughly he lacked the moral compass as well. Knowing that he had killed a man in uncontrolled fury should have been enough of an indication that he was not a man with whom to share the knowledge I held, but I am too trusting a soul and believe too much in a person seeking betterment. Yet I knew his appetites tended toward the wanton. You told me of the days and even weeks he would spend in the tents of the gypsies he permitted to encamp on this property. I am embarrassed to confess that before I manifested the animals, his first request was for me to conjure a woman for him, which I refused to do.'

"Here, my guest paused and looked away from me as though lost in deep reflection. At last, he directed his eyes back to me.

"He said, 'My blindness, Miss Stoner, and my assistance in your stepfather's plans, however unknowing on my part, shame me beyond words. Would that I had never met him, or, having done so, had never struck up a friendship with him no matter how fascinating a person he was to me, how ardent a believer in the marvels I revealed to him. I cannot undo what I have done, but the least I can do is make certain that the last of the three *tulpas* is destroyed. With your stepfather dead the creatures have lost the force of his will and have, in a way, been starving to death, so the *tulpa* of the cat may have already expired as well, but I must be sure of it. You say you feel the cheetah has taken shelter in a closed-off wing of this house? Please, will you take me there now?'

"And so I did, first fetching the key to the door that closed off the disused wing. I also brought with me a lantern, and as I unlocked the door I whispered to Mr Thurn, 'A portion of the roof has collapsed, and I suspect the cheetah has either crawled in through there or through a broken window, although most of them are boarded up.'

"He said nothing, but merely stood silently and grimly beside me at the threshold as I drew the door open. I felt a terror that the great cat might at that very instant be waiting in the shadows beyond to pounce upon us, but the lamplight only showed us a long hallway stretching off into darkness. Again I whispered, 'The damage to the roof is over the central room. With the door shut and locked it is fortunate that room does not communicate with the rest of the wing.'

"Before I could utter more, my visitor said, 'It is in there. I can sense it. You may close the door now, Miss Stoner, and pray lock it and leave it locked no matter what sounds you may hear from within.'

"As I locked the door, and I will say I was greatly relieved to do so, I asked, 'What do you intend to do now?'

"Said he, 'I will be taking the earliest train back to London.'

"'London?' I exclaimed. 'But you said you meant to deal with this situation somehow, Mr Thurn.'

"He said, 'And so is it my intention, but I must be alone and undisturbed. I created these *tulpas* at a great remove, and at a remove I will destroy the last of them, but it will require the greatest concentration. It is perhaps even more difficult to unmake a *tulpa* than to make one. You see how they persisted even if only in a declining state after the death of your stepfather, though deprived of his belief in them? Even before his death they had taken on life of their own. I must have that life back. It will be no small effort.' Here he affected a smile, but it was a horrid mockery of such an expression. He said, 'To think that I studied and strived all these years, only to create weapons for a murderer.'

"'Is there nothing I can do?' I asked him.

"'If it is possible,' he replied, 'you must focus on the knowledge that this creature is not a flesh and blood entity. It is an illusion, and you would do best to hold onto that thought with all your power, for surely the creature has been feeding off your own belief all this time, as well.'

"Mr Thurn bid me good afternoon then, and the last I saw of him he was walking off in the direction of the Crown Inn, so as to get a dog-cart to take him to Leatherhead, where he would take a train to London.

"You will not be surprised when I say I did not sleep that night as I lay wondering if I had entertained a madman in my home that day. And yet, almost against my will, I could not entirely dismiss what he had told me as absolute fancy. I suppose madmen are earnest in their madness, but this gentleman seemed entirely lucid to me. Looking into his too-keen eyes was much like looking into your own, Mr Holmes.

"In any case, at about half past two in the morning my restlessness caused me at last to rise from my bed, take up my lantern and venture from my chamber, stepping quietly so as not to disturb Mrs Littledale next door. I was drawn to the locked door leading to the abandoned wing of the house. I do not know quite why, but it was as though I had sleepwalked there; that is to say, it did not seem a conscious decision. I feel now that I was acting on an intuition.

"I leaned my head close to the panel but heard nothing

beyond, even when I laid my ear against the wood. One might think I would then have gone back to my bedroom, and yet my compulsion had not been satisfied. I had brought the key with me as before, and again I unlocked the door and opened it while shining my lantern into the dreadful blackness beyond.

"Oh that I had not done so, Mr Holmes, because I will never forget the sight that lay before me. I dare say I would not have needed my lantern to see into that long, dark passage, because the two figures situated in its centre seemed to radiate a soft, pale glow much as though bathed in moonlight. There on the floor of the hallway lay the cheetah, though I would not have recognised it as such had I not known what it was. Otherwise, I might easily have taken it for the skeleton of a large dog, impossibly imbued with life. It lay on its side, so wasted that it was a wonder it was able to raise its head. But its head was indeed raised, as it glared with a palpable malice at the man who stood over it only a few paces away.

"That man was Mr Edward Thurn. I am embarrassed to tell you that he was without clothing, his skin appearing almost radiantly white as I have described. He was returning the animal's gaze, but he had obviously heard me open the door and from the corner of his eye seen the glare of my lantern, for without taking his eyes off the creature he raised his left arm and pointed his finger at me. I understood what he signified by this gesture. He was commanding me to withdraw and close the door. This I did, and when I had turned the key in the lock I backed away from the door with the whole of my body shaking, for I had never in my life witnessed so ghastly a scene but for having watched my dear twin die before my very eyes. I returned to my room then and sat upon my bed, still shaking, until dawn. Only then could I summon the courage to return to the locked door and crack it open sufficiently to peer beyond. This time there was nothing to see but shadows. I experienced another intuition, and that was a certainty that the cheetah was gone forever."

At this point in my narrative Mr Holmes asked, "Might this nocturnal excursion have only been a dream, Miss Stoner? For I am sorry to report that your visitor Edward Thurn is no longer among the living."

"What's this, Holmes?" Dr Watson said, quite surprised.

"Really, Watson," Mr Holmes said to him, "you must pay closer attention to the morning paper." Here he gestured to a folded copy of that morning's *Daily Telegraph* that rested nearby. "I knew the name as soon as you uttered it, Miss Stoner, but I wanted to hear your story in full before I admitted as much. Yet I suspect you are already aware of the man's fate, for you have just now come from the place where he had taken a room in Upper Swandam Lane, have you not?"

"You guess correctly, Mr Holmes," said I.

"I do not guess, Miss Stoner. I deduce. Your breathlessness when you entered this room and your agitated comportment indicated a very recent shock."

"I did not realise his death had already been reported in the paper. This morning when I inquired about Mr Thurn at the address given on the letter he had sent to my stepfather I was told there had been a terrifying cry from his room at about three in the morning, and when the door was finally forced Mr Thurn was found lying dead on the bed, his eyes staring fixedly into nothingness. It was the opinion of those who saw him that his heart had given out."

"The cause given in the paper was apoplexy," Mr Holmes stated. "But surely you see the dilemma here, Miss Stoner. The body of the obscure explorer and world traveller Edward Thurn was discovered at three in the morning, but you claim to have seen him standing in your very home at approximately half past two. It is impossible for him to have arrived back in London in so short a time."

"Precisely, Mr Holmes. It would be an impossibility under natural circumstances."

"Then I will propose supernatural circumstances, in keeping with your account. That it was not actually Mr Thurn you saw, but some projected essence of himself that he sent to deal with that other phantom being."

"Make of it what you will, Mr Holmes. It is all beyond me."

He clicked his pipe stem against his teeth, then pondered aloud, "Of course there is no such thing as a swamp adder. What was I thinking?"

"With all respect to Miss Stoner, whose own trustworthiness I do not doubt," Dr Watson said to his friend, "if one were to entertain for even a moment such outrageous notions, surely a man as hateful as Grimesby Roylott would not be capable of the mental feats this Thurn fellow claimed were required for their collaboration."

Lowering his pipe, Mr Holmes replied, "But Roylott was, in some ways, well suited to such an exercise, being that he felt he answered to no man or God, and that his mental acuity entitled him to power. There is no richer soil for the growth of evil than the supposition that one is superior to one's fellow human beings. Mind, there are those who, being cognisant of their greater-than-average intelligence, will utilise it for the betterment of others as if it were a resource they had received in unfair quantity. But too many hoard their intelligence, and allow it to deform their self-conception into something superhuman, when in fact 'inhuman' would be the better designation. Unfortunately, Roylott was not a singular specimen; this world teems with his ilk."

"True enough," said Dr Watson. "But all that aside, you are the most rational of men, and surely you cannot believe in ghosts and hobgoblins."

"There are more things in heaven and earth, Watson, than are dreamt of in my philosophy. There is only one matter I am certain of."

"And what is that, Holmes?"

"One day, truly, I must travel to Tibet."

I rose from my chair so as to excuse myself, saying, "I am meeting my fiancé soon, Mr Holmes, so I will take my leave. Perhaps, as you muse upon the events I have recounted, you will come to some other explanation that escapes me, and if so I hope you will share it with me. Until that time, I extend to you the same invitation I did to poor Mr Thurn, who I fear may not only have died from the strain of battling his final monster, but may even have hoped to do so, to atone for the sins he felt he had committed."

"You are offering me your stepfather's books, then?" enquired Holmes. "It is kind of you, and, as you mentioned there were some of an esoteric nature, I wonder if they might shed further light on these mysterious events, but I suggest that despite your reluctance to retain any of your stepfather's belongings you keep them and read them yourself, Miss Stoner. You have a sharp and inquisitive mind, and perhaps it is you who will one day better explain to me what transpired at Stoke Moran. And, might I say, I hope your next home proves less haunted."

I reached my hand to the sitting room door. "I repeat that my only hope is to soon put Stoke Moran behind me once and for all. A good day to you, gentlemen."

A FAMILY RESEMBLANCE

Simon Bucher-Jones

Mycroft Holmes, Sherlock's older, and perhaps smarter, brother was introduced to the canon in "The Adventure of the Greek Interpreter" (*The Strand*, 1893, thereafter, *The Memoirs of Sherlock Holmes*). It has long been a regret of mine that no meeting between Mycroft and Professor Moriarty had come to light, and, while this story only supplies this at, as it were, one remove, I trust that this meeting of brothers throws light on the characters and on their respective siblings.

—Simon Bucher-Jones

B eing an account extracted from the Papers of Mycroft Holmes, released under the sixty-year rule and subject to such elisions as have been deemed necessary for National Security. Mycroft appears to have had a near-perfect memory, but he augmented – and perhaps to a degree even produced – this effect, in practice, by writing memoranda of his day's activity each night including a verbatim account of his conversations.

A CONVERSATION
AT THE DIOGENES CLUB

There have been some interesting, though somewhat juvenile to my way of thinking, monographs out of Vienna in the last year[1] – which speak to the central problem of humanity – that is, why it is so difficult for a rational man to deal with those who merely regard themselves as rational.

Take my brother for example. There will be, I am sure, as our knowledge of the mind and body develop beyond that of Aristotle and the Edinburgh school of dissection-inclined materialists, a specific diagnosis that defines a man who oscillates between frantic activity and reptilian

---

[1] This appears to refer to the three papers published in the first half of 1896 by Sigmund Freud.

inaction. If the late Robert Louis Stevenson[2] had been more astute, he might have determined that the divide in man was not good and evil, but energy and lethargy, or extroversion and introspection. An introspective evil is more akin to an introspective good than it is unlike it, and an active force in the world, whether for good or evil, must move in similar ways albeit to different aims.

A rational being, as Hume might define one,[3] determines the modes in which his brain best functions and, having so determined, constructs a mechanism to permit the world to encroach upon that functioning as little as possible, as is commensurate with making a rational supportive contribution to the maintaining of that mechanism. We pay a debt to society, in so much and so far as society is necessary for us, either as a value in itself, or as a means to permit our protection from mere anarchy or worse. Where the mechanism forms a join with the irrational world it may become partly irrational, but that contact should be limited so as to prevent such contamination.

An irrational being, however effective it may be in one or more of its modes, risks everything in tearing itself apart when those modes do not suffice and, by working first in high gear and then in low, is always vulnerable to the specks of grit the world may throw into the delicate cogs of the vulnerable mind. Now I amend my path to

[2] The papers of the late Mycroft Holmes from which this account is derived do not date events. They were originally filed in an order that would have made their timing self evident to their maker. Sadly this arrangement was lost in the Blitz, when some of the papers were destroyed and all were scattered. Robert Louis Stevenson died on 3rd December 1894; this, and the earlier reference to Freud suggests that this account dates from 1897 at the earliest.
[3] Mycroft is perhaps here referring to the definition of rational as opposed to superstitious in Hume's *Of Suicide* unpublished in the philosopher's lifetime except as an anonymous private pamphlet.

minimise such dust, and by preserving the mechanism – under glass as it were – ensure its maximal utility. I wake, dress, attend my office, perform such tasks as are necessary, lunch at my club – whose silence suits the rumination over the morning's data with a view to the creation of the afternoon's synthesis. The daily task successfully dispatched I spend the evenings in equally splendid isolation. After a quiet sojourn once more at the Diogenes, I return to my lodgings – a grace and favour apartment in Admiralty Arch, courtesy of the Foreign Office – perfectly positioned to minimise unnecessary perambulations. I wash, I sleep – rarely dreaming (so far as I can determine) – and I repeat. All is as it should be. A working mind in a working body.

My brother, as you will perhaps have heard, gads about. He wastes time. He has created a useful tool in the Baker Street Irregulars, and yet he cannot bring himself to rely upon them consistently, but must always be running about in this disguise or that. Such tactics are effective no doubt among the unobserving criminal classes, or the Scotland Yarders, and no doubt there is a minor satisfaction in the perpetual surprise of his Boswell, but there came a time when he ran afoul of one of the bigger fish, who was less taken in by the ribbons of weed wrapped around the caddisfly larva and saw it for the plump dragonfly morsel it was in potential. That bigger fish was your brother – oh please don't bother to deny it. I know you have protested the professor's innocence in the newspapers, but between these four walls we both have good reason to look with some alarm at our families' wilder members, have we not?

My brother too is also unafraid to break the law, for a supposedly good cause – a short-sighted moral position which has required me to intervene on his behalf with the authorities more often than I suppose he supposes. Yours did so for reasons of his own, about which I will not speculate.

That my brother does much that is good is undeniable. That he does the most good he could do is hardly likely. If he were to train his mind to wider questions – to address through support of social legislation by the government of the day towards the underlying causes of crime, to watch as I watch for the broader threat, and the less obvious larceny – he would be, in time perhaps, as indispensable as myself. Still, they tell me I shouldn't expect old heads on young shoulders.

What has he been up to lately, you ask? Well, certainly – it is the hour when visitors are permitted to discourse here in the Stranger's Room, and I can perceive you will need time to consider my last chess move. I have no objection to making my observations on my brother more specific.

If you were to believe that the accounts of the ingenious Watson[4] represent the norm or status quo of my brother's activities, rather than a subset selected by their suitability for publication, you might conclude that the cases that come to my brother's attention invariably begin with an impassioned plea from a caller at their Baker Street rooms. Perhaps a masked member of the nobility, or a governess singularly attractive for her class. However, Watson has not given publicity to the fact that Sherlock, like a little dog eager for scraps, has taken to calling monthly on the detectives of the Yard in a carefully timed "wander" through

[4] There is some possibility that this is not a compliment; Mycroft's papers almost never use the term "ingenious" except in the sense it is used in Ambrose Bierce's story "The Ingenious Patriot" (1899) where it signifies a technically adept individual with no grasp of the long-term consequences of his actions. This does not, however, in itself date the action to after 1899, as this usage of the word – which is essentially sarcastic did not originate with Bierce.

their offices that takes in each in turn without permitting the others to observe his interest. Thus he gains an early insight into cases yet to be from his minute observations of their environs and his picking up of casual gossip, to which the common constable is not immune. It is generally at around three-forty or so on the third Wednesday of the month that he calls upon Inspector Lestrade.

The Metropolitan Police detective force has suffered a certain amount of gentle lampooning at the pen of the Good Doctor and his literary agent, but there is no doubt in my mind that they are the best that can be obtained – for the money allocated by a niggardly Treasury. Their offices at New Scotland Yard administer a force that in total amounts now to over thirteen thousand, inclusive of their colleagues who perform the services behind the scenes, without which no substantial organisation can function, and they are no longer the well meaning but ill-organised handful of burly thief-catchers of Rowan and Bayne's day.

What's that? Yes, I agree that it is a slight embarrassment that New Scotland Yard was itself founded upon an unsolved mystery. The torso of the woman dug up in the preparation of the foundations in 1888 has, I must admit, never been identified to a degree that would permit a case to be made in law. However, strictly between ourselves: the disappearance, in July of that year, of the Countess of Strathmore's lady's maid Jane from the Royal Box at the Wimbledon Championship – together with the Strathmore tiara, valued I believe at over seven thousand pounds for the gems alone – did not, I fear, end well for the cat's-paw who allowed herself to be persuaded by the honeyed words of her eventual killer. The theft was a well-planned one involving the distraction of the sporting event in which I believe, if I recall correctly, the thirteenth Earl[5] received a substantial defeat in the mixed doubles at the hands of the Renshaw brothers.[6] I wonder if it was the failure of him and his partner on the lawns or the theft that rankled most when the family sat down to dinner that night. One day the hand of retribution will fall upon the shoulder of the personable Colonel Moran – but forgive me it was not my intent to raise old spectres, and I fear I have allowed myself to be diverted by your remark from the narrative you originally requested. My apologies: I fear even Homer may nod.

On this particular Wednesday, Lestrade was going through reports of the beat officers from the Dulwich area looking for signs of crimes in the making. Indications that known criminals might be congregating, or for unusual spending which might tie any of the men known for such acts to the recent spate of robberies in that part of the city. You can well imagine the sort of thing that an intelligent man can glean from the chaff of the threshing, and Lestrade is by no means unintelligent. That he has not the flashy legerdemain of my brother, nor his accrued collection of bad habits, are both strengths in a man working with a regimented body: the crime solving engine that is the Metropolitan Police.

Knowing that a tool is best used for the types of fastenings with which it is by its forging designed to engage, Lestrade did not attempt to lay before Sherlock any of his diligent work, but immediately handed him the most outré and time-consuming task of the many demanding his attention.

[5] Patrick Bowles-Lyon, thirteenth Earl of Strathmore and Kingshorne.
[6] William Renshaw and Earnest Renshaw defeated the earl and his partner Sir Herbert Wilberforce: 2-6, 1-6, 6-3, 6-4, 6-3.

The Yard does this now at my suggestion, for a study which I am carrying out concerning the management of time has indicated that the solution of a single high profile case, though often of political importance, does not accomplish as much for the general repose and security of society as the countless smaller crimes which can be solved or even averted by the correct placement of resources. As a self-motivated agent, my brother can be deployed at no formal cost, boasting that he never varies his charges except where he defrays them altogether (a claim I do not expect always holds true, if only because he is inclined to discount the odd princely gift from a grateful nobleman or woman). He is – when bored – perfectly happy to be set upon a goal, and will – at his own expense – dig into anything if it be sufficiently interesting.

In this case it was the discovery of the body of Sergeant Major Lewis Rourke, absent without leave for five days from his Barracks – shot, it appeared, repeatedly in the chest, though not with any projectile from a normal rifle, and – this the matter that encouraged Lestrade to pass the case over to my brother – entirely clean shaven, despite his possession before his disappearance of both a large moustache, and formidable sideburns. No doubt this will eventually appear in print under such an attention-grabbing description as "The Adventure of the Shaved Sergeant" or perhaps "The Case of the Curiously Obsessive Murderer", for, while to shoot a man more than once may be prudent, to shoot a single body twenty or thirty times suggests an unusual determination to ensure that the body breathes no more.

To give him his due, Sherlock began sensibly enough, delegating Watson – whose military background and medical acumen enabled him to undertake both tasks – to interview the enlisted men at his Barracks as to the character and history of the deceased, and to review the report of the doctor who had examined the body.

This produced the following information, which I can attest is completely true, so far as it goes: the sergeant major was – at forty-one years of age – an old campaigner and had served in India where his bald pate had been tanned by the Indian sun and his complexion had been given a florid hue that might otherwise have suggested drink. Thereafter he returned to serve as a drill sergeant and instructor of new recruits. He was regarded as being a fair man, not without a certain mawkish sense of humour, though still capable of enforcing discipline. Being himself a strict teetotaller, despite his appearance, he was but little inclined to overlook the minor japes and misdeeds committed by soldiers in their cups. Nevertheless he was well spoken of, and even those members of the regiment who had had occasion to be subject to military discipline under him appeared to have no onus for revenge, nor could a motive for his death easily be ascertained. He had been in fine fettle the day before his disappearance, and one of the gunners recalled that the sergeant had received a private letter, which had appeared, from the manner of its reception, to have conveyed good news.

As to the body itself, aside from the shaving of the moustache and sideburns, it showed no injuries other than the wounds to the chest. This was unusual, because of the many impacts and the exceptional accuracy of the marksmanship. The wounds were shallow indents from small-bore grapeshot of the kind used for the sport of hunting birds, one or even a dozen of which would not have necessarily been fatal to a man but which, impacting in great numbers upon a small part of the sergeant's chest – which had been bared – had produced, cumulatively, a cratered wound from which he had evidently expired, the proximate cause of death being loss of blood.

At this point, if Watson were recounting the tale, there would no doubt be an erroneous theory of his coinage, there to be transcended by Sherlock's own true account of the crime and the apprehending of the villain responsible. As I am standing in for Watson in recounting my brother's exploit, perhaps you would care to supply your own surmise at this juncture?

Ha, you know, that's very Watsonian. You have a surprising talent for mimicry. Your theory is not an impossible one. You suggest, on receiving good news, perhaps of a legacy long wished for but also long pushed to the back of the mind, the sergeant major slipped from his teetotal pedestal – a position occupied most forcefully always by the reformed bibber. Finding him drunk, his men – not wishing him ill, but possessed of that boisterous spirit that can make a man as intolerable in peacetime as he may be invaluable in war – proceeded to shave him, leaving him to wake to the shame of a barefaced hypocrite. So far so good. But how then in this condition would you venture the man came to die? Presumably, you frame it as an accidental demise?

You wonder if I have made any investigation into the forging of birdshot? Obviously it was the first thing to occur to me, as no doubt it was to Sherlock. The round shot is still used in fowling, although before the invention of the rifled barrel and the shell and cartridge it formed the ammunition of our armies as recently as forty years ago.[7] I am sure it will not surprise you that the first suggestions that soldiers might fire anything other than a ball from their firearms was rejected by the British Board of Ordinance in 1826 on the grounds that spherical shot had been good enough for the last three hundred years! Such shot is forged by dropping molten lead through a copper sieve, and, as it falls through the air, it solidifies into a perfect sphere. The fall needed is a considerable one, as the spherical shape is formed by the surface tension of the molten metal, and towers for the purpose of this forging exist at many metal works. As a point of interest there is such a tower,[8] which opened nigh on sixty years ago, at the Lambeth Lead Works between Waterloo and Hungerford Bridges. Well within the distance that a drugged man or a body could be conveyed by hansom cab. As to the method of the inflicting of the singularly uniform and regular injuries then, I fancy we are in agreement.

Your contention then is that his men, in ignorance of the tower's function but aware of it as a landmark, conceived the idea of leaving the freshly shaved Rourke there, with a view to spying upon his awaking in such incongruous environs, bereft of his military moustache. Returning from a carouse to find him dead, as a result of some random accident sending a fusillade of shot down upon him where he lay, the men then panicked and, swearing their cabbie to secrecy, perhaps with bribes, carried the body to the wasteland where it was discovered and there left it – no

[7] While gun barrel rifling began in the sixteenth century in Germany, the end of smoothbore musket usage by the British Army was considerably delayed. The "Brown Bess" musket was in use until 1838, and the percussion-cap musket that replaced it also did not have a rifled barrel and remained in use until 1851.

[8] Designed by David Riddal Roper for Thomas Malby & Co in 1826, the tower was still in use as late as 1949.

doubt quaking in their boots at the thought that this crime might be brought home to them.

So, no doubt, a kind-hearted Watson, inclined always to see the best in mankind, was willing to construe as an accidental result of high-spiritedness what was in actuality one of the vilest and most inhuman crimes to come to my brother's, and hence my, notice.

The fact of the body being exquisitely positioned to receive the fatal shot, with its breast bared, will not admit of accident.

There are many reasons why a man might shave his own face, from vanity to disguise. There are many reasons why a man might shave the face of another man who will go on living, from the obvious one of being employed as a barber, to the japery you wished to suggest to me. But to shave the face of a man only with the intent of killing him thereafter?

Only three theories occurred to my brother. The first, so as to facilitate the substitution of a bearded brother for a clean-shaven one, he quickly discounted. There was no such person in the case. Rourke was well known to many in the area, and both his superior officers and the men under him identified his body, despite the alterations. He had no dependants, was, so far as his men knew, unmarried, and in the event of his death, his goods were to be sold and the monies sent by a firm of lawyers to distant relatives in Ireland. Thus any question of substitution perhaps in pursuit of the suggestive legacy was ruled out.

The second theory I myself favoured for a little while. I do not know if you are aware, but the presence of certain poisons taken over time can be proven by the subjecting of samples of body hair to certain reagents. As the hair grows out from the follicle it forms a record of the chemical composition of its – ah – native soil. Perhaps because of relative rates of growth, while hair abounds on the human body, the analytical technique is most effective when carried out upon the hairs of the head. Rourke's baldness has already been remarked; I confess to wondering then if his beard and sideburns might have been removed in order to render less discoverable a cause of death that owed nothing to the impact of the falling shot. Sherlock also went along this blind alley – though for longer than I, working from pure logic alone. He haunted public houses, and discovered that the teetotal Rourke had, with other members of the Temperance League, lectured and argued with the regular drinkers and the publicans alike. In the process – for Rourke, despite his age and his baldness was in other respects a virile and even an imposing figure – he had conceived a friendship with a member of the Ladies League Against Alcohol, one Margaret Athol, on one occasion violently defending her from the attack of several inebriated young men who had taken drunken offence at her characterisation of their behaviour and determined to live down to the description she gave of it. There was an understanding between them, and while not officially engaged, she had given him a lock of her hair to keep, and he – recently enough for it to be of interest to Sherlock – had provided her with, of all things, a scented pillow favour, stuffed with aromatic herbs and cuttings from his own hair.

Whereas you or I might perhaps have taken the lady into our confidence, given that this was a matter of murder, the vanity of my brother, which knows no bounds of good taste nor any check to his actions, led him to proceed to burglarise the lady's boudoir in order to extract a lover's keepsake which he then went on to render down to its constituent parts and subject to minute chemical analysis.

The spectacle of my brother, diligently teasing apart tufts of a man's whiskers and boiling them in a variety of reagents is, I confess, an amusing one – and I must not let it deflect my mind from the fact that this was – and remains – a very brutal crime. Nevertheless, albeit grimly, I am inclined to smile at the mental image. Even Watson – I have little doubt – must have chided him for this graceless action, the more so because it availed nothing in terms of practical proof.

The theory was sound – something must have caused Rourke to lie unmoving while the hail of shot let out his life, and the absence of wounds at the wrists and ankles spoke against any physical restraint. Although the hair proved nothing either way as to poison, it might have been removed by an extremely careful assassin as a precaution. More likely though it spoke of a poison that required only a single dose, rather than a gradual building up of toxicity in the body. I do not share my brother's interest in the minutia of murder, but any classicist must have been struck by the possibility of hemlock, and Sherlock considered the most likely poisonous agent to be *conium maculatum* – the poison which, in legend at least, was imbibed by Socrates. Hemlock tea can be given as a pleasantly tasting tisane – easily pressed upon a teetotaller. Its action is mild, and its predominant effect short of death is of a complete muscular paralysis. Under its influence, a victim – even if he had not in fact ingested a sufficiency to die – might well prove unable to stir a muscle to save himself from the slow drop, drop, drop of the fatal metal. Though unproven, my brother (and I) considered such a drug to be the likely means by which the victim was rendered helpless.

You're right; I did mention a third theory, other than disguise, or the removal of evidence, which might account for the removal of the sideburns and moustache.

The third theory – though it had occurred to him – was not one that my brother felt able to pursue, involving as it did an emotional question of a certain delicacy. This task he forced upon Watson, despite the fact that Sherlock had rendered it almost impossible by his own felonious actions. The task was simply to interview Sergeant Rourke's innamorata Miss Athol and ascertain whether or not his moustache and sideburns formed an impediment to their union, or were among his chief attractions. If the former, a simple chain of reasoning existed: learning of some improvement in his fortunes, the sergeant might well have been emboldened to propose – intending to do so he would have made the personal sacrifices necessary to present himself in the most aesthetically pleasing state. I am not myself much inclined to the pursuit of the fair sex – a man my size must be most enamoured of the pleasures of the table – but surely such an act as appearing clean shaven would charm an already interested party, who had professed a disquiet in connection with his appearance, almost as much as his increased financial prospects. The murder, and the mutilation of the moustache would then be either coincidences, or, if related, would be related by a causal chain in which both were set in motion by the letter, but without being themselves connected. Alternatively, if she especially favoured his appearance unaltered, then the change wrought upon it might represent a coup carried out by a rival, or unsuccessful suitor, with the murder in that model of events being again a parallel event, unless it – in itself – formed part of the spurned lover's revenge.

Watson was – for he possesses an excellent bedside manner and all the graces of a confiding physician – able to gain the young woman's confidences, as Sherlock would not have done. She did indeed have a previously favoured man, a George Welby, who had been pressing his suite upon her for some time, but whom she had rejected when he proved to be a habitual taker of spirituous liquors. He had attempted to conceal this from her, and indeed may have been inclined at one point to attempt to set drink aside and follow her example, but he had the misfortune (as it seemed) to be taken up by new friends and in their company so to wallow in the dens of the City, so that it could not but come to her attention. Her view of the sergeant's moustache and sideburns was more than favourable, it seemed. It was one of a doting mother to a boy's first facial hair. She approved of them heartily as a sign of a virile manliness which did not require gin to set it going, nor brandy to sustain it.

This I think Sherlock should have been able to deduce without Watson's evidence – for no-one of professing an opposing view would have wished for or, having been given unwished, cherished the form of keepsake that he had earlier stolen. I confess I do not know how Holmes and Watson resolved the matter of this theft; I imagine the surreptitious re-stuffing of the bag by Holmes with some hair from a recently deceased scoundrel in police custody, and its replacement under her pillow with some embarrassment by the comfort-bearing Watson. But perhaps, after all, she did not miss it. I hesitate to conjecture about female sensibilities.

See how maddeningly my brother flounders between ideas, each one setting him on some active foray into events, when a cautious rational picture built up from item upon item of data would serve his turn so much more effectively. You can, I suppose, conclude his next step?

Quite so. Learning that the suitor Welby – now his main suspect – was prone to drink and consorted with bad companions, he began a wholesale haunting of public houses and traveller's inns, his lean body bulked up with cloth to a drunkard's dimensions and his nose reddened with rouge. Ah, what it is to be the brother of a thwarted thespian. I'd wager your own brother gave you no such trouble, personally, being a mathematician – the mildest and gentlest of professions, next to your own railway work.[9]

Thus a whole three days of time were lost, clapping men upon the back and exclaiming about this or that sporting endeavour, until Sherlock – under the barbarous name of Philip Matherhyde – was quite as boon a companion to Mr Welby as any of that young man's new friends. A telegram, meanwhile, had gone to Sergeant Rourke's relatives to discover if the mysterious message that had cheered him had originated with them, or if they could raise a conjecture as to its sender. A reply reached Baker Street by the same means, while Holmes was among his cups. The letter had not directly concerned a legacy, but it had been a turn of fortune, which might suggest to the sergeant that the time had come to actively pursue the hand of Miss Athol. The message was nothing less than the news of the death of his estranged wife, an Indian woman – whom he had abandoned on his return to England. It is perhaps surprising that a man who would readily abandon one

9 Colonel James Moriarty, though formerly in the Indian Army, was at this time employed as a railway station master. That his brother had the same name as him must have been confusing, but it is possible that they were referred to as James Senior and James Junior respectively, by a father more than usually obsessed with order and regimentation.

wife might feel a qualm in seeking to court another – but Rourke's family were Irish Catholic stock, and, whereas the leaving of a native bride was accounted a venal sin, the bigamous or adulterous acquisition of another or the horror of divorce were both to him as much an evil as the bottled demons that he attempted to wrest from the hands of his soldiers. Considering himself free, however, he had undoubtedly gone to his death in the pleasant, if deluded, mental state of one contemplating the bliss of matrimony.

Watson hurried to inform Sherlock of this, and found him in a bout of fisticuffs among drunken men, as the erstwhile Matherhyde was forced to show his metal during a bout of ribaldry. Watson's presence proved fatal to his disguise, for, as it transpired, Welby's new friends were none other than members of Rourke's own regiment, who had but a week before been questioned by Watson in connection with their sergeant's death. The jig, as the cant has it, was up. If Matherhyde's anxious friend was the well-known Dr Watson, whom could the bibulous Matherhyde be but the disguised Sherlock Holmes? The logic is not perhaps exact; Dr Watson might have many friends, but to drunken and violent men – prone to the quick reactions and suspicions of soldiers – it sufficed. My brother and his friend were bodily thrown out of the drinking den.

Only later when they compared their view of the case was Sherlock to declare that he had now, to his own satisfaction at least, determined the sequence of events, though he was doubtful of proving them in any court of England.

Firstly the presence of the soldiers around Welby was no coincidence: even before his intent encompassed marriage, Rourke desired to have no rival in respect of Miss Athol. Thus he set his men, who were keen to curry favour with him, to dog Welby's footsteps and to drag him down. It was in their company that he gained the reputation that led to Margaret Athol refusing his offer of marriage, and it was no doubt through Rourke or a third party instructed by him that Miss Athol learned of her former beau's misdeeds. Rourke then was not so innocent a victim as he might have appeared, nor were his misdeeds confined to this country, for he had left behind him in India at least one thread ending in death, which was to change his status here.

The family of his former wife was by no means rich, though, and to orchestrate vengeance across the bounds of the Empire, or over time, requires either considerable resources or passionate fanaticism, of which there was no evidence in the case.

Someone, however, had both the means (perhaps hemlock, perhaps another drug) to paralyse the sergeant, the capacity to persuade him to drink it, and – perhaps – knowledge of the shot tower. The latter requirement my brother concluded was a lesser one for he had conceived recently – a possible delusion which he has communicated to me, but which as yet I have been unable to either prove or disprove – the view that certain sorts of crime: robbery, vengeance, the more outré and unsolvable of murders, were being better planned, better executed, and rendered more baroque and elaborate in their elegance than the London criminal classes would ever manage on their own. The shot tower then might well be an elaboration of a scheme of revenge, suggested by a third party – this planner of crimes – rather than a natural thought of the murderer.

It is the shot tower that makes me call this an awful crime. To imagine Rourke, whatever his faults, lying conscious (for hemlock merely paralyses the body, it does not deaden the mind, nor, so far as I know, prevent the sensation of pain) while he was 'shot' again and again, is to imagine a mind cold and humorously evil in its planning.

You disagree? It's true, you and I, as well as Sherlock, deduced the method once the nature of the wounds was made clear to us. But to work backwards from calamity to cause is not the same as to pull the mechanism of causation from the air with a view to the causing of a calamity. That must be the mark of a brain that has teetered upon its throne of reason and begun a fall into utter blackness. A brain not unlike that of your late brother. Oh, sit down man. What good does a protest do between us?

Well, no matter. The brain that suggested the tower may be a matter for another time, but the more proximate identity of the murderer was, I'm sure you will agree, clear. Who did Rourke know with whom he might be inclined to take tea? Who would be able to persuade him to drink a herbal tonic? Who but his intended bride Miss Margaret Athol? The cause of her conspiring in his murder was partially shadowed, it was true. His treatment of her former lover? A sufficiently fanatical teetotaller might see the enticing of a man into the grip of drink as an awful crime. His abandonment of his wife? There was no way of proving that she was aware of either action. My brother, however, and this was I confess a thought worthy of us, asked himself a single crucial question.

You can't guess?

It was this: given that the method of murder – the repeated striking of shot into the body – had suggested itself to the hypothetical master planner of crime, what aspect of the request on the part of his client (whether it was Miss Athol, or not) for vengeance could have suggested to this hidden master – let us term him M – such an image? Surely the punishment must in some way have fitted the crime for which revenge was desired? An artist, a veritable Leonardo De Vinci of crime, would demand nothing less.

Once asked it is obvious, is it not? The repeated striking of shot into a victim. What was the shot tower replicating, but the action of a firing squad? A very satisfactory replication for a criminal vengeance, for it involved no living band of soldiers to shoot high from pity or to break down from guilt thereafter.

Coming to this conclusion, Sherlock sent for a copy of Rourke's military record in India – a request that I was able to facilitate – and discovered, what Rourke himself must have forgotten, or failed to connect to the prim and pretty Miss Athol of the Lady's League, his presiding presence at the court martial and execution of Private John Benjamin Athol at Benares in India in 1887. John Athol, Margaret's older brother, had taken advantage of the awful famine of that year to sell grain at inflated prices to the starving from military stores, profiteering from goods that were not his to dispose of.

My brother confronted Miss Athol with these facts and, with Watson as a witness, was present as she broke down and confessed. She defended her brother to the last, claiming that he had not sought vast wealth in gold or gems, or favours, for the grain but only desired to alleviate the horrible lack among the native population when so much was stored for the feeding of the army. My brother pressed her as to how she had arranged the murder, and how the shot tower "firing squad" had been conceived, but she refused to acknowledge any other hand in the business – although it was certain that she must have had accomplices in the movement of the body, if not in the conception of the crime. As to the sideburns and the moustache – her explanation for their removal was simple, although it struck my brother as an account she had from another mouth rather than her recounting something she had done. The falling shot had cooled insufficiently in one case during the bombardment of the body – as sometimes occurs in the process, the irregular shot so formed being discarded after passing through a sizing sieve – and a splash of still-molten metal had rebounded, catching in and singeing part of Rourke's moustache on the right side. The removal had been intended to prevent this being visible, and the removal of the rest of the moustache and the sideburns had been a matter of symmetry.

Oh, if we only knew the kind of mind that demanded such mathematical symmetry and brought such mechanical aptitude to the commission of crime, eh Colonel! A pity your late lamented brother is no longer with us; it has the feel of his work does it not, or a least a family resemblance to it.

Of course, there is no proof – but I have sometime wondered, what if a disinterested party could have spoken understandingly to your brother, before he was too far steeped in crime, could he have been persuaded to step back from the abyss? The civil service can always use a brilliant mind, and even a macabre streak need not be an absolute bar to gainful employment. Something to think about perhaps. Still, I'm rambling, and I fear I have your Queen.

A shame I never got to meet your brother, and it might be a bigger shame still if you were to have to meet mine.

PAGE TURNERS

Kara Dennison

Billy the Page first appeared in *The Valley of Fear,* the last of Doyle's Sherlock Holmes novels. While he didn't get much attention in the original canon, he was seen more in Doyle's three plays, and has appeared in a few screen adaptations. Notably, Billy was also Charlie Chaplin's first stage role, both in Doyle's *Sherlock Holmes: A Drama in Four Acts* and William Gillette's *The Painful Predicament of Sherlock Holmes.*

—Kara Dennison

You want to talk about important, right? It's all well and good to say Dr Watson's important to Mr Holmes, but he writes the stories, don't he? Of course he's going to make himself big talk in his own stories. That Lestrade fella, he shows up a lot. Probably he really *is* a bit important because he's a police sort and takes the criminals off to prison once Mr Holmes gets clever and finds 'em.

But none of them's there every morning, crack of dawn 'til whatever sound dusk makes, making sure Mr Holmes sees the people he needs to see and gets the messages he needs to get. None of these people would even see him if it weren't for me bringing 'em in, you know.

And eating; three times a day, like actual clockwork, I give a knock to let him know he needs to eat. His brain's so full of clever things, you see, he'd forget otherwise. One time Mrs Hudson roasted an entire chicken, and you could smell it all the way up in his study, and he still didn't know supper was on. She said: let him starve, the fool, but that's not my job, is it?

That's why he needs me. That's why he needs Billy. Take away Billy, and what've you got? A really canny cove who starves himself and doesn't know who's at the door.

Suppose that goes for any Billy, really. Between us? My name's Humphrey. The one before me? Alfie. But we're both Billy. And whoever comes after us'll probably be Billy, too. Easier than remembering new names every few years, I guess.

Wiggins'll have a go at me whenever he sees me, though. Thinks being a page is too soft a job. Asks me how long it takes to shine all the buttons on my jacket every morning. Talks about what he's bought with his latest guinea prize from Mr Holmes. Says he got in fistfights with big tough sorts – I don't believe that or he'd have some proper bruises, right? He's really awful jumped up, though, is Wiggins. Even more so since Dr Watson started mentioning him by name in his stories.

The other day he says – Wiggins says, I mean, not Dr Watson – the other day he says, "Maybe Holmes just don't trust you with the important stuff. That's why he keeps you at home instead of sending you off on actual important jobs." Which is not the case, thank you – and people might know that if Dr Watson ever decides to write up certain other cases. That Valley of Fear business, maybe. (People'd love that one – just a suggestion.)

Besides, how's he know? Maybe I *am* doing big, important jobs. Maybe, just maybe, Mr Holmes gives me the extra important work because he knows I won't go bragging to every last person in Britain.

Right, so this is just between you and me. I wouldn't go telling just anyone, because it ain't proper, but I know you're cast iron. You won't go blabbing about this all over the place, will you? Course not. Like I said. Trustworthy. And it's my job to know people, since I gotta let 'em in to see Mr Holmes every day.

Sometimes I get these letters to deliver that are so secret, so private, even I don't know what's in 'em. And I carry 'em! I never look, though. Never. Not even once. You ask

Mr Holmes or Dr Watson. They're sealed, and never have I ever delivered one with a broken seal. Not a one time. Not even when my life was on the line.

You take last Friday. Middle of the afternoon, Mr Holmes calls me in. He's in the middle of opening the window for some fresh air, and he hands me a letter. "This message contains sensitive information of the utmost importance," he says, all big and loud and important. "Take it to the usual recipient, and see that you're not followed. Use whatever back alleyways and shortcuts you need to, but make sure you get it to him at his practice."

"Back alleyways?" I say. "The usual recipient" is Dr Watson, see, and I'm thinking I could run down the main streets and get it to him twice as quick, maybe even take a cab if Mr Holmes'll put the money forward.

But, Mr Holmes, he knows what he wants. "You must exercise all stealth," he says. "I am unconcerned with alacrity. I can't have you being seen dashing down the main roads, and I certainly cannot have you being followed. You can make your way back here any way you please, but lie low as you go. Make sure no one sees the letter, and *definitely* make sure no one knows to whom it is headed."

Lie low as you go. "Yes, sir, Mr Holmes!" And I tuck the letter in my pocket and I'm on my way.

There's a series of back alleys and a few cuts through back gardens I can take so you'll never even see my face on the main street. That's the way I go, just like Mr Holmes asks. Not a soul back there but myself, but even so I'm sticking close to walls and shadows. Because you never know, and I follow my directions to the letter.

I'm coming 'round a corner, quiet as you please, and there's a man standing in my way. He's some toff's servant for sure. Probably a butler from how he's dressed. But he looks like he's been stuffed into that suit. There's no way he's an *actual* butler.

"Young Billy, I presume," he says, and he's giving me this look like he's deciding whether or not he's gonna skin me. "On our way on a mission from Mr Sherlock Holmes?"

I ask how he knows it's me, and he points at my jacket. "We've seen you coming and going from his rooms more than once."

Drat. That's stupid of me. I'm not lying low if I'm wearing my uniform, am I? But it's too late now. I try to sidestep him, but he follows me.

"You seem nervous," he says, but he's saying it in this really superior voice like, you know, almost like he's enjoying being a bother.

"Yeah," I say, "I've got somewhere to be and I've got a big lunk standing in my way, course I'm tense."

I figure he'll get angry at me for that, and his face does go a little red, but all he does is stick his hand out. "You're carrying a piece of correspondence. I request that you give it to me immediately."

"Nah," I say, "I don't think I will."

Now he's going *really* red. "Young boy, I fear you do not understand the something-or-other of what you're carrying." He said an actual word, but I can't remember what it was. It was one of those big expensive words like people say when they want you to think they're more important than you.

And I tell him, "I do and all, though. And I know it's not for you, so clear off."

Then he squares himself up all big, which isn't easy considering he's not really tall, and he gives me that look again but a lot worse. And he points at the letter in my hand and he says, "That piece of correspondence concerns my employer. You may have heard of her: a Mrs Henrietta Oxford."

"Never heard of her in my life."

"I find that hard to believe, as she is a match for your master both professionally and intellectually."

I laugh because *that's* not right. I've never even heard of her. There's no one's a match for Sherlock Holmes, and if there was we'd all have heard of her by now. But he ignores my laugh and just keeps talking.

"Mrs Oxford has been investigating the curious series of murders in Clapham. I'm sure you've heard about *those*, my boy."

I have and all. Gruesome stuff. Caught wind of it when Mr Holmes and Dr Watson talked about it. Men and women of any age, any class, all left dead with weird sigils carved in 'em. Some people call it religious, some go right for "occult". All I know is it gives me the shivers.

"What's that got to do with me or my letter?"

"Does Mr Holmes hire dense servants on purpose? Really. It's all anyone's talking about – the police, my employer, *your* employer…" And his eyes go back to my hand holding the letter. "If Sherlock Holmes is Sherlock Holmes, he'll know that Mrs Oxford is already on the case. And he doesn't approve of her particular methods."

"What're you talking about?"

The butler laughs at me. Actually *laughs*. Like I'm some sort of idiot. "Stop playing the fool. Mr Holmes knows already that my employer intends to take matters into her own hands, and this is his method of alerting the authorities in secret before she can act. And I cannot allow that to happen."

"Shows what *you* know. This –"

But I stop, because I remember Mr Holmes said *don't* let anyone know where it's going. This fella's obviously well off track, but I do as I'm told. Besides which, I get the feeling he'll just think I'm lying to him to put him off the scent anyway. So I shake my head and I say, "This is getting where it's going whether you like it or not!"

Now his blood's boiling, I can tell. And he makes a grab for me. Makes an *actual* grab for me! I jump out of the way and hop a fence nearby, but I don't stop there. Who knows? Maybe he can hop fences. I'm not taking that risk. I keep running down the alley, even though I can hear him scrambling and swearing and not getting anywhere, and I don't stop 'til I'm round the corner.

That's when I drop down to the ground and catch my breath. My heart's going like a bumblebee. What's in this letter that's so important? And what makes him think it's about him? I mean, maybe it *is*. Like I said, I follow directions, so it's not as though I've looked inside. I stare at the letter for a few seconds.

"You're a lot more trouble than you're probably worth," I tell it, and I shake it a bit, as though that'll help anything. Then I stuff the letter inside my jacket for safekeeping and try to get myself sorted out again. Running away from the butler's taken me off course. I can't go back the way I came, and I *really* have to keep my head down now in case he's decided to try and come at me from another alleyway or something.

Now, as I'm sitting getting my bearings, I can hear footsteps from up ahead of me. I'm about to panic, but then I realise it's not big stompy footsteps, it's little tappy ones. More like a lady's boots. And I look up and I see this woman walking towards me all slow. She's dressed nice, with flowers on her hat, and she looks sort of pretty and gentle. I don't know what a lady dressed this nice would be doing walking around a back alleyway, though.

She sees me, and she looks sort of taken by surprise and goes, "Oh, dear! Are you all right, young man?"

No one's ever called me a *man* before, so that's a bit nice. I jump up and I straighten my suit and I tell her I'm just fine, miss. Always call them "miss", not "ma'am", no matter how old they are. They like thinking you've mistaken them for really young, even if they're not. This lady's maybe my mum's age, so not *really* young, but enough that she'll still care if she's a miss or a ma'am.

She gives me this really warm, sweet smile, and she pats me on the head and asks what happened. I'm careful, obviously. I don't tell her what actually happened. Just that there'd been this terrifying sort after me and I had to get away from him.

The lady, she puts on this sad, shocked face, and she puts a hand to her heart like I've told her my dog's died. "Oh, you poor darling! I'm ever so sorry you had to go through that!" But I tell her that's all in a day's work for me, and I give my buttons a polish with one sleeve.

"Honestly, though, what would someone like you be doing running about in back alleys? There's no call for that."

"Someone like me?"

"Yes, you're Sherlock Holmes's boy, aren't you?"

Seriously? Am I this easy to spot? I really am regretting not wearing a different jacket. But I say, "If you mean am I Mr Holmes's page, then yes, miss."

"That's what I thought. You'll want to be more careful, you know. Especially considering what you're carrying."

"What am I carrying?"

"Well, I don't know. Why don't you show me?" And she holds out her hand, still smiling like there's not a single thing strange about what she's doing.

I'm about to put a hand on my jacket to cover the letter, but I shove my hands in my pockets instead. No sense giving away where it's hidden. "I don't think I ought, miss."

She laughs. It's sort of a pretty laugh, like Christmas bells, but there's also something a bit strange about it. Like I ought to be afraid of it a little. "Why not? It's almost certainly to do with me, so I should have a look, don't you think?"

"You seem pretty sure of what I'm carrying, miss. What if you're wrong?"

"Well, we can find out, surely. Is it a letter?"

I flinch. "Miss?"

That laugh again. "I suppose that's a yes. Is the name Angelina Pritchard in it anywhere?"

"I wouldn't know," I snap back, and then I add, "assuming it even *is* a letter, which I haven't said it *is*, miss."

That pretty smile is still there, but it doesn't look quite as nice anymore. It's like it went all frigid, but her face hasn't actually moved at all. "Is that so? Well, I can keep making some fairly educated guesses. I *do* love guessing games, don't you?"

"Not really, miss, no."

"Well, then." She puts a finger to her lips and looks up, like a little girl pretending to think hard. "Well, then. I can hazard a guess *where* you're taking it. The Houses of Parliament, I presume?"

...*what?!*

"Miss, I think you've got the wrong person entirely. I haven't got a clue what you're even on about."

That nice smile, even the frosty version, is gone now, and she's glaring at me like she's about to gut me. Here I'm starting to wonder if that's the only way anyone's ever going to look at me ever again. She sort of leans in really close, and I can smell her perfume, violet and something else that's giving me a headache.

"Oh, Sherlock Holmes has trained you very well, indeed, hasn't he? You're tight as a steel trap, aren't you? Well, I know better. I know he's on to me, and I know he means to stop me from doing what I intend to do."

"I don't even know what you intend to do, miss." And I'm really not keen to find out.

The lady steps back and she's still fixing me with that angry glare. "I don't believe you. I don't believe you haven't heard about me. I don't believe for one moment you haven't overheard Lord Wainwright in Mr Holmes's rooms talking about me, telling him he's *afraid* of me, of what I could do to him. And I most *certainly* do not believe the letter you're delivering isn't a warning."

Well, it doesn't much matter what she believes, does it? Lord Wainwright's a new one on me, so if he'd been over talking about being scared of anything, I certainly didn't know.

"What... *could* you do to him, miss?"

She makes a grab for me. "Give me the letter, you little whelp!"

She's awfully quick in those clicky heels, but I'm quicker, and I'm off like a shot again, running down the way she came as she takes off after me, shrieking all sorts of awful things. Worst part is, she gets a lot farther than the fella from before, and by the time I've lost her and can stop running for a few minutes, I'm well off track. I've gone in the complete opposite direction I should be going, and now I have to turn back and retrace my steps. Or rather, find some new steps. No way am I going back the same route I came. Not when I've got *two* people willing to come after me over this letter.

I know Mr Holmes said to keep to the back alleys, but as you can sort of tell, I'm not having the best of luck with those. I'm starting to think I'll hide better in plain view. Because they're all looking for me back where no one's ever looking. I know he said don't take the main roads, and I'm all about following orders to the letter… but I'm thinking maybe surviving long enough to get the letter where it's going is more important than *how* I do it at this point.

So I take a few turns and eventually make my way back out to the main road, keeping my head low and my hands in my pockets, just sort of doing my best to blend in, right? That's not too hard. There's people everywhere. And it's going to look really suspicious if anyone tries to manhandle a boy in public in broad daylight.

Ah, but you've probably already suspected that someone's going to try anyway. And you're right. Someone else walks right up to me, in the middle of everything… and he just sort of stands there. I'd try to step around him, but he's tall and wide so I know I won't be getting far unless I shoo him off somehow.

I look up at him – have to tip my head all the way back to do it. He's huge and fat, balding on top, and his face and bald pate are pinkish and gleaming with sweat, even in the cold. He's got a massive scraggly ginger beard, and this strange sort of panicked grin on his face like he's afraid his heart's about to give out at any moment but he doesn't want anyone else to know. Really, there's something so unsettling about him, I'm ready to scream for help even though he's not said anything yet.

"Hello there." His voice is a lot reedier than I would've expected it to be. And he's still smiling, fussing with his hands while he talks to me.

I give him a "Hello there" back. And he just stands there. *Smiling.* Smiling like I ought to know what to say next. I think at this point I've caught that terrified smile of his, because I can feel my face cramping up.

I try to keep my voice from going all wobbly, and I say, "You need anything, sir?"

And he sort of chuckles, like, that laugh grown-ups do when you've said something silly but they're not going to tell you *why* it's silly. He takes out a handkerchief and he dabs at his shiny forehead, but he doesn't give me an answer.

"Right, well, if you don't need anything, I'll be on my way."

I start to walk past him, and he puts a big hand on my shoulder. Not clamping down or anything, just sort of *there*, like the fact that he's done it should be enough to stop me. Granted, I'm so confused by how he's acting that it does.

"I see, you have to play dumb in public," he says, and he's trying to look all jovial, but he just looks like a sweaty, ginger St Nick. "I know how it is. Very wise of you. Don't want anyone catching on you've spotted me, do we?"

"If I knew who you were, sir –"

"Very good, very good!" He claps me on the shoulder. "You've no idea how much I appreciate your discretion, young lad. Most people would have called the authorities as soon as they laid eyes on me."

Would they? I could see someone slipping away nervously, but not much more than that. I still regret what I said next, but off I go and say, "And why would that be, sir?"

He squints at me. The smile's gone now. When he's not smiling, his face goes all threatening, like a great gorilla thinking whether it might like to squash you. "You're taking this game a little too far, boy. I might almost think you actually *don't* know who I am." He tugs on his collar a bit like it's choking him. "And considering who *you* are, and considering who *I* am, that's highly unlikely."

"Right. Well, either way, I do have somewhere to be."

"Yes." Oh, there's that grin again. Like a little boy grin. That's a grin too young to be on that old face. It's unnerving is what it is. "Yes, I know. I know, I do. You'd better run along and, er, get your message delivered."

Now at this I nearly just chuck the letter on the ground and start stomping up and down on it. *How* does everyone know? *Why* does everyone know? But I just give him a tight smile and start trying to get past him again. Except he's still got that big, flabby hand on my shoulder.

"Just… out of curiosity," he says, "what does he say about me?"

"What does who say about what?"

The hand on my shoulder squeezes. "Charles Hart, boy. Charles Hart."

"I don't know what Charles Hart says about you."

His hand is like a vice, and it nearly makes me drop. "*I'm* Charles Hart, you little —" His grip loosens and he laughs that odd strained laugh again. "Very clever, very clever. Nearly had me there. No matter, I'm sure it's about the, er, tobacconist incident."

All I want is to be away from him and his reedy laugh and his strange smile as soon as possible. So I go, "Right, right. Well, what else would it be about? Who *doesn't* know about the tobacconist incident?" And I pat my jacket and give him a wink and just hope I'm not shaking as much as I feel like I am. "Better be on my way, then."

"Yes, guess you better had." Finally his hand's off my shoulder and he gives a chuckle and shuffles off. I rub my shoulder where he gripped it, and I'm thinking maybe I should be a bit more worried about this than I am. But considering he seems *happy* thinking I'm off to report him to Scotland Yard or the Archbishop of Canterbury or whoever, I'm not going to think too hard about it.

Meanwhile, nobody else has come after me, and I'm finally starting to get closer to Dr Watson's. Can't be much longer now, surely. I know what Mr Holmes said, but I'm about finished dealing with these people, so I decide to take as straight a path possible. No stealth, no cover, no nothing. Beeline. Main streets, a hop over a fence here and there…

I'm parched.

There's a teashop just in front of me. And in front of it is a lady in a fancy black dress and gloves. She's short and skinny and sort of dark, with her black hair all piled up on her head. I'm standing there wondering about how long it took to get it to stay up like that, but then she squats down so we're eye to eye.

"You look thirsty."

I start running.

The lady starts laughing. And it's not a weird, tinkly villain laugh like the other lady, and it's not a nervous laugh like the man before. It's sort of sweet and charming, like we're old friends teasing each other. That's confused me, so I stop running and look back. And she's just smiling at me.

Now, you've heard the sort of day I've had up 'til now. Any time someone runs into me, it turns sour quickly. At this point I'm pretty sure I'll never talk to anyone ever again, save for my parents and maybe Mr Holmes. Maybe.

But there's this lady, and she's smiling and waving to me all friendly. Not examining my uniform or looking impatient. She looks really proper nice.

And I *am* thirsty.

"Come on in," she says. She's a grown-up, but her voice sounds young, sort of childish without being weird or immature. "Rest your feet. You look as though you've been running for ages."

"I have, miss."

She smiles, and it's so nice and calm and it makes me feel like maybe the whole world isn't horrible after all. So I follow her into the teashop. And barely as soon as I've sat down, there's a cup steaming in front of me and a pair of sugary biscuits shaped like flowers on a fancy plate.

"Is this your shop, miss?"

"Mm." She shrugs. "I'm here a lot, let's say."

I can see someone moving about behind the counter, but they're staying sort of out of sight. So it's as good as just being me and the lady in the show for now. She goes and picks up a teacup from another table and sits down with me.

"So, where are you off to in such a hurry?"

I tense. Is it happening again? It's happening again. "You… mind if I don't say, miss?"

The lady makes these big eyes at me, sort of pinching her mouth up, like she's confused, but then she smiles. "Of course. It's completely your own affair. I do apologise for prying." And she sounds like she means it. No, doesn't sound like – she *does* mean it, no doubt in my mind.

It's nice, this. I'm sitting, and it's comfortable, and there's hot, strong tea that's milky and sugary just the way

I like it, and the biscuits taste like cherries and flowers and shortbread. I've eaten both pretty quickly, and the shopkeeper – a small, pale girl in a black dress and white apron – comes right out with two more.

"You like those? The shopkeeper makes them herself every day."

"They're the best thing I've ever tasted, miss."

"Please, call me Maria. Surely we're friends now, right?"

"Right, then, Miss Maria."

She waves her hand, and the shopkeeper brings her over some biscuits too. So there we are, the pair of us, sitting there like old chums, eating our biscuits and drinking our tea, not talking at all. Best part is, I'm not scared for my life anymore. My heart's feeling a bit less like a hummingbird rattling about in my chest.

"Ah." It's Miss Maria, and she sounds a bit surprised. "Could you light the lamps? It's getting a bit dark out." At first I think she's talking to me, but then I see the shopkeeper start moving through the shop lighting all the lamps. I look out the big front windows and...

It's getting dark.

I still haven't gotten my letter to Dr Watson!

I jump out of my chair, nearly spilling my tea.

"Something wrong?"

"I just remembered, I have somewhere I need to be!" I'm stammering, and there's crumbs all over my face. I pat my jacket to make sure the letter's still there. It is. That blasted letter that's going to be the death of me. "So sorry. I have to dash."

Miss Maria frowns. "But we were having such fun."

"I know. It's great, really. And maybe I can come back sometime? But right now I need to finish this job I'm on."

"Oh. Yes. You were running somewhere." All the smiles are gone from her face now. She's frowning, like suddenly she's bored with me and the shop and the whole situation. It's more like the sort of look you'd see on a world-weary old lady.

"Exactly. So I should get back to that."

The door to the shop slams, and all the lamps go out.

It's happening again. *It's happening again!* I knew it! I should've listened to myself.

"You really shouldn't be out after dark, you know. A little boy like you." All of the childish sound is gone out of her voice. She sounds strangely old, even though she doesn't actually look any different. "Something could happen. You know. You've heard there's a murderer on the loose, surely."

I'm starting to get proper scared now – more than I had with any of the others. "I… may have, miss."

Miss Maria is examining her fingernails all casual-like. "Oh, you're a clever boy. You've heard. You've got that look about you – *so* proud of how clever you are." Then she's looking straight at me and she's smiling, and it's such a calm smile I'm not sure why I'm suddenly twice as terrified.

"Shall I tell you about the occult murders? Would you like to know more?"

The occult murders… all the people who've been killed and had the sigils carved in their skin. Like the butler mentioned earlier.

"N-No, Miss Maria. I don't think I would."

"Hm." She chuckles, but she's not smiling. "That's wise of you. I could easily tell you everything anyone could hope to know. I could give you enough to spare your employer weeks of work. Of course, I'd have to make sure you never leave this shop alive."

"No!"

"Just another victim. What would it matter?"

I've run for the door, but my hands are shaking too much to open it. Either that, or somehow it's locked itself tight. "I thought you were being friendly! We were eating biscuits together! You were nice!"

"Mmmmm, well, I'd *thought* I could keep being nice." Miss Maria walks towards me with a hand out. "Come, now. Hand over the letter, and I'll let you go."

"This blasted letter… It really is more trouble than it's worth. I'm about tempted to let you have it."

She smiles. "Good. I was hoping you'd say that."

"I said *about* tempted." And I grab the letter out of my jacket and wave it in front of me. "But I've a job to do, don't I? Why do you even want it so badly? How do you know it's about you?"

Miss Maria folds her arms and gives me this sort of rotten, scoffing look. "Honestly. My maidservant heard your employer through the window clear as day as she was walking down the street earlier: 'Sensitive information of the utmost importance'. Loud as you please. I'm shocked the entire city didn't hear."

Oh. "I'm starting to think it did…"

"Regardless, what else could be of utmost importance to London's finest detective save for the recent rash of unsolved murders? So hand it over. There is still a great deal yet to do."

I stick the letter back in my jacket and shrink away towards the door. "You do know that I know you're connected now, right? I don't need any letter. I could tell Scotland Yard myself!"

"Oh, darling, who would believe you?" She laughs, and

the worst part is it's not even a malicious laugh. She really is just laughing at me, like I've said the stupidest thing in the world. She reaches out her hand to make a grab for my collar–

And then she pulls her hand away and shrieks.

I look up and see her gripping her wrist and making the most horrid face. And I would be, too – she's got a bone-handled dagger sticking out of her hand. I cover my mouth and look away.

What? I can't stand the sight of blood. Yes I know I'm in the wrong line of work for that… I'd like to see *you* deal with it, though.

I hear a voice from the back of the shop yelling at me to run – is it the shopkeeper? I can't tell, and I'm in no mood to find out, so I start kicking at the door 'til it gives way, and I'm off.

No more stopping. No more waiting. No more *nothing*. If anyone even tries to stop me, I'll bite 'em. I swear I will.

And no one does. I make it to Dr Watson's practice, all out of breath and terrified and likely pale as death. That's what I'm figuring, at least, given how he's looking at me. He's packing up his kit for the day, and he stares at me like he's just gotten a surprise patient.

"Billy?"

I gasp. I grab the letter. And finally, *finally*, I hold it out to him. "Message for you, sir." Then my head feels a bit wobbly.

Next thing I know I'm lying on the floor and Dr Watson is patting my face and asking if I'm all right. Course I'm all right, I tell him, but my voice sounds all raspy.

"You fainted, I'm afraid."

That's rubbish, I tell him. Only girls faint. But he's

doing all his doctor fussing around me, making sure I can breathe, so I figure it's best to just play along.

Once I'm settled, he opens up the letter and has a read. "Very important," I tell him. "Mr Holmes told me it was of the utmost importance and not to let anyone see it."

"Did he…"

"He did, Dr Watson. And you wouldn't believe how many people stopped me along the way to try to get it from me!" I feel my head going a bit funny again, but I go on even so. "Didn't let a single one of 'em stop me, though. No, sir… Er, not for long, anyway."

Dr Watson frowns and folds up the letter. "Who exactly were these people?"

"Erm." I think back. "Well, there was the butler to Mrs Henrietta Oxford…"

"Ah, her again. Trying to compete with Holmes again, no doubt."

"And then there was an Angelina Pritchard."

I notice Dr Watson's started writing the names down on the back of the note. "Hm. What's she about?"

"Something to do with stitching up some lord or other. Winthrop? Wainwright? Something with a W."

"Really…"

"And there was a lady called herself Miss Maria at a teashop who says she knows about the occult murders."

"Miss… Maria… teashop. Anyone else?"

"Erm. Hart?… Charles Hart. Big bloke, looks like he's about to explode."

Dr Watson laughs. "God, him. He tried to shoplift a single cigar and he's been turning himself in at Scotland Yard at least once a week for it." He doesn't write anything down this time.

"So, erm… seeing as how I risked life and limb for that letter, Dr Watson, sir… d'you mind awfully if I know what the important information was?"

"Mm." He folds up the letter and sticks it in his pocket. "Holmes is going to be late to the opera tonight."

"… oh."

Dr Watson clears his throat.

"So… it wasn't about any of them."

"No, indeed. But apparently vanity runs stronger than logic in the criminal set. I shall let Holmes know that if he ever sends you on this sort of fact-finding mission again, he's to double your salary. Can you stand up now?"

I could, and Dr Watson drops a handful of coins into my hand and instructs me to take a cab home. He gets no argument from me, obviously.

…Oi. Why are you laughing?

No, I was not *duped* into anything. It was an important letter, you understand? Just because I didn't know why it was important…

All right, fine. The letter itself wasn't important. But that's not the point. Who's helped Mr Holmes crack three cases… well, two cases and some light shoplifting? Not Wiggins. Yours truly. Remember that next time Wiggins takes to bragging. Bet *he's* never seen a lady get stabbed through the hand.

…though I'm wondering if I might be clear to take a few days off before I'm given any other top secret missions.

PEELER

Nick Kyme

Though perhaps not gifted with the greatest deductive reasoning, and described equally as "ferret-like" and "rat-faced", **Inspector Lestrade** is one of the most enduring characters of the Sherlock Holmes canon, who first appeared in the novel *A Study in Scarlet*. His first appearance in *The Strand* was in the story "The Boscome Valley Mystery".

Prior to meeting Holmes, Lestrade is described as having been an officer of the law for over twenty years with his dogged determination and tenacity to thank for his success and longevity. In many respects, he is a sort of everyman, embodying a keen sense of justice and surprising compassion that, despite his ostensibly low opinion of Lestrade's intellectual abilities, Sherlock Holmes finds admirable.

Despite appearing in fourteen stories, certain facts concerning Lestrade are still a mystery, such as his first name, about which only the first letter "G" is known. During his time in the Force, Lestrade developed an ongoing rivalry with one of his fellow detectives, Tobias Gregson, and the two could not be more unalike, though they only ever appeared together once. His last appearance in the Conan Doyle stories was in "The Adventure of the Six Napoleons", after which he is mentioned again but does not feature as a character.

—Nick Kyme

I've seen things in my line of work. The things that man is capable of. True evil. Monsters. London teems with them. Sometimes I think this city has been made for them, not us, not the folk who hold the thin blue line against this tide, and those that aid us, men like *him*. I had thought myself a detective until I met him. Only then did I realise just how inept I must seem to one who possesses such intellect.

I want to save this city, but she is suffering from a grievous malady. I can smell it in every Whitechapel corpse and every swollen cadaver I've dredged from the Thames. I remember every trial, but none so vividly as the "Peeler".

A man was lying face down in an alleyway just off the corner of Lime and Leadenhall Street. I noted the time on my pocket watch, then looked up into a sky the colour of slate.

He was a rough fellow, judging by his attire. I could see it even through the window of the hansom cab. Worn shoes, faded porter's uniform with shabby broad and piping, but corpulent enough to suggest he was far from destitute.

I met Metcalfe as I left the cab, his face as grim as the morning.

"Good morning, Inspector," he said with a nod.

"It's far from good, Sergeant." I looked past Metcalfe's

shoulder. A light but unceasing rain had been falling since the early hours – I knew, because it had kept me awake – and the two constables, Cooper and Barrows, standing at the north and south facings of the street corner wore police cloaks to keep off the drizzle. Through a rising mist encouraged by a morning sun struggling amidst the grey, I saw two more men, neither of whom were Scotland Yard.

"How long has he been here?"

Metcalfe didn't turn. He had enough about him to realise who I meant. "Arrived not long after we did, sir."

A man was down by the body, crouched, but careful not to kneel on the wet road. He wore a dark woollen Ulster, scarf and leather gloves. The other remained standing, the rain trickling off the brim of his hat and onto his pale brown overcoat as he looked on.

"Keep him out, next time," I said. "Keep them both out."

Metcalfe nearly looked down to his boots, but to his credit met my gaze. "Yes, sir. Sorry, sir. He said he was consulting on a case."

I pushed on past the sergeant, resigned to the credulity of Her Majesty's Constabulary. "Of course he did. Just keep anyone else out, or I'll have your hide."

Sherlock Holmes didn't bother to look up as he heard me approach, though his companion, the doctor, gave me the courtesy of slightly tipping his hat.

"Tell me, Lestrade, what do you see?" asked Holmes, who had yet to touch the body, I now realised, but observed it intently. He had a narrow, studious face, with a thin, patrician nose and gaunt features. His eyes were always alert. I had never known them to be otherwise.

"I see murder, Mr Holmes, and a man interfering in police business."

"Now, look here–" Dr Watson began, upset at my boldness, but stopped short at his friend's raised hand. The good doctor was well groomed as always, though with a little more grey in his coiffed moustaches.

"Watson, if the good inspector wishes to admonish himself for interfering in his own duties by interrupting me, then we should allow him to avail himself of the lesson."

"Amusing, Holmes," I said, pulling up my collar as the rain grew heavier. I let him do his work, for as much as the man irritated me in his manner, I had never in all my experience met a keener or more accomplished mind. "What should I see?"

"For a start, you have not complimented Dr Watson on his fine attire. From Savile Row, no less. Isn't that right, Doctor."

"Holmes..." said Watson. I heard the warning in his tone but also noticed the doctor's fine tailoring. "Only the gloves are new," he confessed.

"Look expensive," I muttered, ruefully.

"A flutter on the ponies, wasn't it Watson? A rare triumph?"

Watson's cheeks reddened. "Holmes!"

To this day, I cannot fathom how the doctor puts up with him.

"Enough games, Holmes," I told him, "what have you found?"

"In the first instance, this," he said, removing something from Goose's person and holding it up to the meagre light.

"A key?" I said.

"Well observed, Inspector, though the question is: what does it open?"

It was small, and made of brass, though had little to distinguish it.

"Is that it, then?"

Holmes's mood darkened. "Far from it, Inspector. I see a workhouse porter and a curious predilection, I believe." He stood, looking down grimly at the man. "Lestrade, if your constable would be so kind as to turn over the body…"

I nodded to Metcalfe and he reluctantly crouched, kneeling in the blood that had pooled around the man's head. Made heavy by death and his sodden clothes, the corpse proved difficult for Metcalfe to turn but when he finally did, he gagged.

I felt a coldness seep into my gut in that moment that even my outrage could not thaw.

Metcalfe gasped. "Good Lord in heaven…"

The man had no face. His skin had been completely removed and only the red, glistening muscle remained.

"What is this, Holmes?" I asked, surprised that I rasped the words.

"Something foul, I fear, Inspector."

I almost dared not ask: "A devotee? Inspired by Whitechapel?"

"No, Inspector," said Holmes, "I think not. The victim, the method… this is altogether something else."

"Are there no depths to which man's depravity will not stoop?" said Watson. "Holmes, what need could one have for flesh taken in such a manner?"

"That, Watson, is something I intend to find out."

I returned to Scotland Yard in a Black Maria with the body. Holmes and Watson followed, but only after Holmes had lingered to make his observations. Diverted as I was by preliminary paperwork, both were waiting for me as I entered the morgue.

Holmes remained in the corner of the room throughout, swallowed in shadow like some wraith, a plume of pale blue smoke issuing from his short briar pipe. He leaned against the wall casually, though I could see little cause to behave thusly, and I was reminded again of how unlike anyone else Holmes is.

"Inspector," said Watson, standing by the slab where the faceless man now lay. A veil had been placed over the remains of his face so as to conceal his grim affliction, though the rest of his body was naked and stitched from clavicle to sternum.

"Jeremiah Goose," I said, reading from the report I had been in the middle of compiling. I had sent several constables out to canvas the streets where the murder took place, and someone had seen and recognised Goose but had not borne witness to the deed that had sent him to the morgue.

"A porter at the Alderbrook Workhouse on Lower Thames Street," said Holmes, exhaling a cloud of smoke. "I would say I knew him by his face, but that would be mildly indelicate given Mr Goose's current disposition."

"Heaven forefend you come across as indelicate, Mr Holmes," said I, turning to Watson. "What do you make of the pathologist's report, Doctor?"

"A single blow, just forward of the right temple," said Watson. He gestured to the point where the skull had been cracked open. "Killed him instantly."

"What else?" asked Holmes.

"The blow came from the front, so the killer was facing his victim. The pathologist found no defensive wounds, no bruising or lacerations of any kind, and neither can I, so we can assume our victim knew his attacker or had no cause to believe he was in danger."

"Indeed," muttered Holmes, "and you Lestrade? Have you any morsel to offer towards our understanding of what transpired?"

"A single blow, you say, Doctor?"

Watson nodded.

"Then the killer must be a man of not inconsiderable size and, presumably, height. Mr Goose must be…"

"Six foot, five inches and approximately one hundred and ninety-eight pounds," said Watson, consulting the pathologist's report. "A large man."

"So we might assume our killer was at least as large, if not larger," I said. "But why take this poor wretch's face?"

"Why, indeed," said Holmes.

"We'll learn little more from Mr Goose, I think."

"I would have to agree," said Watson.

I nodded, swallowing back the bitter tang of ammonia itching the back of my throat. "Well, I don't know about you gents, but I need some air."

I have neither the inspiration of Holmes nor the education of Watson, but I am still an inspector of Scotland Yard, and what I might lack in cognitive faculty I more than make up for in a dogged determination to see justice prevail.

With nothing further to learn from Jeremiah Goose's body, I fell back on police work. Whilst Holmes and Watson departed the Yard to conduct their own investigations, I took Metcalfe, Cooper and Barrows to follow up on the one lead I knew we had.

But by the time we got to Lower Thames Street, Alderbrook Workhouse was already burning.

The old building had gone up like dry tinder, the smoke

visible across the Thames as far as Leathermarket. Six engines circled the blaze, the firemen struggling to contain it. I saw a constable too, no doubt alerted by the shouts of passers-by, but he was on the other side of the fire and I only saw him through the heat haze. Something about his manner seemed odd, the way he just looked on at the flames, but then what else could we all do?

I stood, my officers beside me, and watched as whatever evidence may have been contained within was destroyed by the conflagration. I felt the fire on my face, such was the sheer heat, and pressed a handkerchief against my nose and mouth to keep out the smoke.

"There'll be nothing but a gutted ruin once this is done," remarked Metcalfe. I smelled something other than smoke too, and knew that not everyone within had escaped.

"What now, Inspector?"

I didn't answer straight away. Unless Holmes has found some further thread that he had yet to avail me of, I had no further leads to follow. "Question everyone at this scene," I told them. "Get help if you need to." I looked for the constable I had spotted earlier but couldn't see him through the smoke. "I'm off back to the Yard." I was angry at my own impotence and the knowledge that I was at the mercy of the killer, my only choice to wait until he killed again.

As it turned out, I did not have to wait long.

Unlike the first murder victim, the dead girl was lying on her back, not far from the Fenchurch Station, but in kind with the first, her skin had been flensed off. By the time I arrived, four constables were warning off the riffraff and Sergeant Metcalfe met me as before.

"Have you sent someone for Holmes?" I asked immediately.

Dragged to a side street cluttered with refuse and punctuated by the back entrances of shops and emporiums, the dead girl looked like she had tried to put up a struggle. She'd been hidden, at least partly, a dirty blanket laid across her legs and abdomen.

More blood this time. Less skin, though. The flesh of the shoulders and upper chest was missing. Her arms too.

Metcalfe could scarcely bring himself to look at her. He nodded. "All right," I said. "On your way for now."

Gratefully, Metcalfe went to marshal the constables whilst I got a better look at the girl. She wore a red velvet dress with a low neckline to expose the bust and shoulders. Her boots were also velvet, though in a darker red, closer to crimson, and she had a small hat with a black veil that had stayed pinned in place in spite of her violent death.

Her eyes were still open, frozen in her last moments, and I reached over to close them.

"God give us strength…"

Gradually it dawned on me, I knew her, you see, or rather knew *of* her. I had seen her face plastered around the East End and farther afield.

"Molly Cavendish." I turned and saw Holmes standing a few paces back, the doctor a respectful distance behind him.

"Did you ever hear her sing, Mr Holmes?" I asked. "She had quite the voice."

"And all of the East End shall mourn her loss, I am sure, but this is most curious…" Holmes approached to begin his examination.

"You are a cold man, Holmes," I said.

"No, Lestrade," he replied. "I am *engaged*, which is just as well for you. I fear your admirer's grief has little to offer Miss Cavendish and, if I am not mistaken, she still has something to offer us." He turned and gestured to Metcalfe. "Sergeant, as you did at Lime and Leadenhall Street, if you please."

Reluctant, but impelled by my glare, Metcalfe turned poor Miss Cavendish over. The back of her dress was torn, crudely slashed. I feared something even darker had taken place than what I had first assumed, until I realised the cut garments were merely an outer layer, an impediment to be removed before taking the skin from Molly Cavendish's back.

Holmes examined what skin remained, getting close enough to smell it. Her inspected her nails, her clothes, had Metcalfe turn her back again so he could look under her eyelids. He took a few strands of her hair, and regarded the soles of her boots. It seemed like a violation, as if Holmes were disturbing this poor girl's final rest.

"Holmes, is that enough? What more can you possibly learn–"

Holmes turned sharply. "There is always more to learn, Lestrade. You would do well to permit me, Inspector. Watson," he said to his companion. "See here."

"Bruising around the neck," Watson replied. He looked grey faced. "I would say strangulation is the likely cause of death, but the marks," the doctor shook his head, "not done with the bare hands. The discolouration, on what little skin is left, is uniform, straight." He mimicked how the murder might have happened, bracing his legs and holding out that cane he carries in two clenched fists. "Like this," he said. "I believe our killer was armed."

"Just so, Watson, just so," said Holmes. "Skin under the nails also," he added. "Miss Cavendish fought before she died."

Holmes glanced up suddenly at a noise from further down the side street. Instinctively, I reached for my gun, and saw the doctor grip his cane a little more tightly. It's for his limp, an old war wound I'm given to understand, but I'd always reckoned there'd be sharp steel inside it.

"Show yourself," I bellowed to the shadows and the warren of awnings, doorways and refuse amongst which something much larger than a rat could easily hide. "Come out now, in the name of the law."

Slowly there came a scuttling, as something small detached itself from the darkness, emerging into the grey dawn light. A girl, an urchin as filthy as the alleyway.

I lowered my gun and gestured to Metcalfe. "Bring her over here, Sergeant. Make yourself useful."

Metcalfe nodded but as he closed on the girl, she screamed. She would've run too had my sergeant not seized her by the wrist.

"Calm down, girl," he urged, as she wriggled and squealed. Metcalfe was a big man, with a full red beard. To some he might appear fearsome, I suppose, but the girl's reaction seemed extreme. He half turned, twisting as if trying to grasp an eel, "I don't know what's come over her, sir. I only–'

Metcalfe cried out, letting go as the girl sank her teeth into the meat of his hand. He turned to her, face red with anger and with a fist raised until the doctor intervened.

"Don't, Sergeant," said Watson, his hand clamped firmly around Metcalfe's forearm. There must have been something in his eyes, some remnant of the soldier he used to be, because Metcalfe retreated at once, looking sheepish.

Letting my sergeant go, Watson crouched so he was eye to eye with the girl and said something softly that made her cling to him.

"She's terrified," he said.

"Not of the law, I think," said Holmes, "or the threat of your thuggish sergeant."

"Steady on," I said, but regarding Metcalfe, I could hardly disagree that the man was brutish in aspect if not demeanour. He nursed his hand. The girl had bitten through the skin and drawn blood.

"What then, Holmes," I asked, "if not my sergeant?"

"Have you ever seen primeval fear?" said Holmes. "Note the wide eyes, the diluted pupils. Her skin, Doctor?"

"Is cold as bone, Holmes."

"Gelid," Holmes replied. "A feverish sweat dappling the brow. Bodily tremors, the fingers most acute." Indeed, the girl did shake, her hands horribly so. Holmes looked back at Metcalfe, as if seeing what I could not. Then he looked back to the girl shivering in Watson's arms, nothing more than a pallid little thing.

"What did you see?" he asked softly but without empathy. The urchin girl extended a tiny finger towards Metcalfe.

"It wasn't me," exclaimed the sergeant.

I scowled. "It's not you, you idiot."

The girl shivered harder, murmuring, "*Peeler, peeler, peeler...*" in a little rasping voice.

Holmes turned his gaze on Metcalfe and for a moment I thought he was about to declare him the murderer.

"You're right, Lestrade," he said. "It's not your sergeant, but rather his uniform."

All three of us looked at Metcalfe, at the blue of his

policeman's attire, and I felt the chill of the morning deepen and sink its teeth into my marrow.

"The murderer… he's one of ours."

I left the girl in Dr Watson's care. To take her to the Yard would only worsen her trauma and yield little, I suspected. She had done her part, giving name to a dark legend that would come to haunt my thoughts in the coming years. The irony of the killer's moniker was not lost on me, nor on any constable, sergeant or inspector of the Yard.

There were 14 inspectors, 92 sergeants and 781 constables registered to the City of London Police Force, and after ensuring the dead woman had reached the morgue at Scotland Yard, I spent most of the next few days reading through their records with the help of Barrows and Cooper, and conducting interviews. Even with a hundred constables, going through every officer in the Metropolitan Police and beyond would take months; time, I felt, we could ill afford, and so I confined my efforts to the district where we had found the victims, all of which were in the City of London.

I barely slept or stopped, save to have the odd cup of tea, even though I felt I needed something stronger. The last pot was stewed, a wince-making bull of a brew, and I had to shout at the constable who made it. I didn't recognise him, though he had an Irish lilt and more than a little cheek, and I resolved to find his sergeant and have words.

I rubbed the bridge of my nose, surprised at how little the stack of reports had thinned since that morning, and looked up from my desk to regard a map of the City of London pinned to the wall. Four marks indicated where each of the bodies had been discovered: Jeremiah Goose and Molly Cavendish and two others, a brothel keeper by the name of Vivian Dawes and a young dockhand called Edwin Buckle. They circled an area from Smithfield Market to Leadenhall Street. Metcalfe was prowling as much of it as he could with an army of constables, but had yet to uncover anything of use. Holmes, somewhat disturbingly, had not been in touch for three days, and all attempts to reach him at his lodgings at 221B Baker Street had failed. To make matters worse, both the *Standard* and *The Times*, as well as a number of other newspapers, had caught wind of the killings and that the killer was an officer of the law.

For a moment, I shut for eyes and willed for inspiration to strike and strike quickly. I had just opened them again when a knock at the door disturbed me and I gestured to the waiting constable to enter.

"Sir," said Barrows, his police helmet nestled in the crook of his arm as he leaned inside, as if afraid to step across the threshold fully. "They are here, sir." He gave a weak smile that pulled at a scar on the right side of his face, an injury sustained as an infant, a fire or some such.

I nodded, weary, and sent Barrows on his way.

The vultures of Fleet Street had gathered outside Scotland Yard in an agitated flock as I came out to meet them.

"Four dead, all by a policeman's hand," began a young-looking oik from the *Standard* called Arthur Grange, "and Scotland Yard no closer to a suspect let alone an arrest. What steps are being taken to ensure public safety, Inspector?"

"Every step, Mr Grange. My constables are at large across the city and—"

"Any one of whom could be a cold-blooded murderer," chimed a weasely fellow I didn't recognise with a trimmed beard framing his smug grin.

Before I could reply, another voice called out from somewhere in the crowd, "I 'eard he's been cutting 'em up and selling their parts as mutton!"

The vultures laughed uproariously, which only drove my anger all the hotter. I found the man amongst the crowd, an older, dishevelled-looking fellow, straight off the docks judging by his attire.

"I can assure the public, all measures are being taken to apprehend this murderer, and I would urge the good people of London to remain vigilant at all–"

"Vigilant?" asked the dock tramp, "and what will the mutton shunters be doing whilst we are *remaining vigilant*?"

"Everything is in hand," I said, in an attempt to reassert some measure of order. "Be reassured that we shall catch this heinous killer."

"Who is likely one of your own," said the weasel, George Garret of *The Times*, as I later came to learn. "An overzealous Bobby who batty-fanged some poor wretch and went too far."

"Slanderous remarks such as that, regardless of who you represent," I said, "will land you in the cells." I began to retreat, sensing an end to the conference. "I have nothing further at this time." Garret took a step towards me, intent on further questioning. "I said that's all," I warned him, "and if you take another step then I smack that door-knocker off your face and call it arrest for public disorder."

A flash lamp went off to capture the moment my humours got the better of me, and I could already imagine a headline describing police brutality or some such libel.

Garret sneered but stepped back, and I returned inside to the jeering and cajoling of the Fleet Street mob.

"Bloody circus," I remarked to Barrows, who was waiting for me. A second flash lamp hissed loudly behind me. "Ignore them, Constable," I told Barrows, who was still looking fearfully at the mob. "They'll get bored soon enough."

I was back in my office when there was a light rap on the door and I saw the dock tramp, grinning toothlessly at me through the smeared glass. Wrenching open the door, I was about to arrest the wretch for loitering when he smiled and I saw the glint in his eye.

"See, Inspector," he said, realising what the look on my face meant, "you aren't entirely without wit."

"Holmes," I replied, ushering him inside. "Why the theatre?"

"I find it useful," he said, removing the false teeth and shedding his threadbare jacket. "Few pay attention to the disenfranchised, Inspector."

"I see. Have you got Dr Watson somewhere under all of that paraphernalia too, then?"

"Ah, no," said Holmes, striking up his pipe and taking a short draw. "Watson is visiting our witness. Alas, she has said nothing since the incident, other than repeating the name of our perpetrator ad infinitum."

"So, why are you here Holmes? Is it just to irritate me?"

"As mildly diverting as that would be... no, I am here on another matter. Tell me, Lestrade, of the hundreds of officers that you are no doubt already trawling through, how many of them are or were tanners?"

I frowned, in part trying to recall, but also out of confusion. "I'd have to have a look."

"Allow me to save you the inconvenience, Lestrade.

Jacob Wainwright, aged fifty-seven, an ex-constable of your borough, now a registered tanner in Bermondsey. Discharged due to ill health."

"And he became a tanner?" I asked. "I fail to see what any of this has to do with the case, Holmes."

Holmes smiled thinly. "Should we not aim to catch him *before* the act, Inspector?"

"Very droll, Holmes." I frowned. "How did you come across the information about Wainwright anyway, might I ask?"

"Obfuscation is a useful tool, Lestrade, much in the way that *you* can sometimes be useful." I gritted my teeth. "By appearing as what is ubiquitous, one can attain a reasonable degree of anonymity. A police constable at a busy constabulary, for instance. Let us just say, I wished to experience what it was like to walk around as our Peeler does."

I was fairly sure Holmes had just confessed to illegally impersonating an officer of the law, but had neither the will nor time to take him to account for it.

"Well, Inspector?" said Holmes, with sudden verve. "Should we tarry further and let the Peeler increase his tally, or shall we make for Bermondsey post-haste?"

I wanted to tell him no, and that Her Majesty's Constabulary could catch this fiend without the aid of Sherlock Holmes but instead I called to Barrows and sent him to fetch Cooper. As he ran off, I narrowed my eyes and asked, "Holmes, what has any of this got to do with a tannery?"

"My dear Inspector," he replied, his smile as condescending as his manner, "it has *everything* to do with it. Oh, and apologies for the tea."

* * *

Few professions are as vile as that of the tanner. I could smell the dung and urine before we reached Bermondsey Leathermarket, on the Surrey side of London Bridge. London has its wretched quarters in abundance, but few are as foul as Weston Street. A grim calibre of men dwell here, a rough-handed, rough-hearted lot with all the distemper of those whose labours see them so befouled and oft reviled by fairer folk. What had brought Wainwright to such a place, I could not fathom. I knew little of the man – for I had never met him in person – save for what was in his records, the mention of an injury that had resulted in his discharge from the force. An old photograph described a thin-faced fellow with narrow eyes, his left ear with a piece missing where someone had bitten it off.

"What are we doing here, Holmes?" I asked, sitting across from him in the growler we had taken from Scotland Yard, my constables either side of me.

"Lime, Inspector Lestrade. Specifically, lime combined with small amounts of soda ash and lye. Before you wrinkle your brow, all three are used in the process of tanning and were discovered, in varying quantities and concentrations, on the remaining skin and clothes of all four victims during my initial examinations. A simple if lengthy chemical analysis confirmed it."

After leaving the growler, we approached the broad archway that led into an even broader square, arranged around which were numerous doorways. A bustling, jostling crowd filled the square. Some towed carts, others carried great rolls of hide upon their shoulders.

"Here then, Inspector," said Holmes, "and where we shall find our Mr Wainwright."

My constables turned to me. Barrows had paled a little,

and Cooper looked eager but uncertain. "You heard the man," I told them, "don't drag your feet. If he's here, we'll have him in shackles before the day is out."

Skins lay in abundance or hung from the rafters of the many warehouses appended to the square. Hides of all hue, shape and provenance were in evidence, as were the narrow-eyed merchants, smoking and glaring at the policemen in their midst. Shadows lurked within the vast stores, lit by flickering torchlight. The smell of leather was rich and heady, and men looked about furtively as my constables and I went about our business. None of them, however, were Jacob Wainwright.

"Are you sure this isn't a fool's errand, Holmes?"

"One can never be certain, Lestrade," he replied, "but I think our quarry is not far." He gave a shallow nod of the head and, as I followed the gesture, I saw a man slip furtively through the crowd. Though I caught little of his appearance through the mob I knew it was him. Older, certainly, but his chewed left ear gave him away.

"Get after him," I bellowed at my constables, and gave chase. I lost sight of Holmes almost immediately, who had gone haring off in another direction. I had no inkling, nor care, as to why. Instead, I pushed and elbowed my way through the crowd with a constable on either side.

"Move! Move in the name of the law!" Wainwright had crossed the square and scurried into the skin market. None stayed our passage, and as we gained on Wainwright, who was clad in a heavy coat, I noticed the man had a limp. He ran quickly enough though, his knowledge of the market and its secret ways giving him an advantage over my men and me.

Barrelling around the back of a well-stacked hide cart,

I lost sight of Wainwright for a moment and feared he had slipped the leash, until I rounded the cart and saw the tanner lying on his back. Standing over him was Holmes, a stern look in his eyes. Lowering the cane he had used to trip Jacob Wainwright, his gaze then alighted on me.

"Making heavy weather of it are we, Inspector?" He looked like he had been out for a gentle stroll, whereas I had sunk to my haunches as I tried to catch a breath.

"Had I the verve, Holmes," I said, brandishing the cosh, "I would use this thing on you." Barrows and Cooper joined us a few moments later, red-faced. "And don't get me started on you two," I snapped.

"I'm afraid, Inspector," said Holmes as he approached Wainwright and pressed the end of the cane into the man's chest to keep him from rising, "we have greater cause for concern."

When I had recovered and came to stand next to Holmes, I saw Wainwright properly for the first time. He was short, his shoulders narrow and his hands smaller than mine. But that wasn't the most damning thing about his appearance.

"His left hand…" I muttered, and felt frustration rise anew. It was badly deformed, and this combined with his diminutive stature led to only one conclusion. "This isn't the Peeler."

It couldn't be. A man Wainwright's size could not have overpowered someone like Jeremiah Goose, especially not with one hand. A hammer lay discarded nearby, and I assumed Wainwright had intended to use it on me or one of my men.

Holmes looked on, impassive, but I could tell he was angry.

"The Peeler is still at large," I said, leaning down to grab Wainwright. "Jacob Wainwright?"

The man nodded, scowling. "Aye, what's it to you?"

"Why did you run?"

"You'd run if someone chased you."

"A man who runs has something to hide, Mr Wainwright," I told him. "You're coming back to the station."

Wainwright's face went from indignation to fear in short order. "Bleedin' persecution, this is," he shouted to anyone in earshot. "You coming here to my place of business, chasing me down and then accusing me of God knows what."

"And what's this then?" I asked, showing him the hammer. There was a name etched into the handle, *Archie*.

"It's for tanning," he said.

"Not for breaking skulls then?" I pressed. "And who's Archie?"

"He's my cousin. He gave me the hammer when he left London."

"Left for where?" I asked.

"No idea. He came into some money, though he never gave me a penny, and left the city, left his business too. I use the hammer for trade."

Everything about this man screamed criminal, but not murderer. "And where is your place of trade, might I ask?"

I let him go so he could point in the direction of one of the tanneries. I saw a wooden sign nailed above the entrance.

"Inspector," said Holmes, "far be it from me to interrupt this expert interrogation, but we are not alone."

Wainwright's plaintive wailing had drawn a crowd. Some amongst them, the rougher sort, clutched tools and clubs as they advanced a cautious step towards us, and I was suddenly aware of how thin the blue line was here.

"Perhaps we should observe discretion on this occasion, Lestrade?" He nodded towards George Garret scribbling notes. No doubt he had followed us from the Yard.

"You'll find nothing in there but skins," sneered Wainwright as he got to his feet.

I narrowed my eyes at him. "What happened to you, Wainwright? Weren't you Old Bill, once?"

"I was," he said, with no small measure of bitterness, and slapped his injured leg and gestured to his left hand, "then I wasn't. What business is it o' yours?"

It turned my stomach to see one of our own so disaffected. "Don't make it my business," I said, with half an eye on Garret who tipped his hat and sauntered off, "because if you do, all the tanners, dockhands and scribblers of London won't keep you from the law."

As Wainwright limped away, I turned to my constables who had yet to stow their truncheons. "And you two, put those bloody things away!"

Mollified, the crowd began to disperse. Holmes was gone. I hoped, wherever he was, he was close to that one elusive scrap of evidence that would end these murders. Until then I would try and lay a trap for the Peeler.

Fog lay thick over London that night. It had done so the last four nights as I waited in the shadows of back alleys and side streets, or peered through shop windows, hoping for some glimpse of my prey. Four nights, and nothing to show for my patience but a deep chill.

"I can barely see the fingers before my face, sir," said Metcalfe.

"Keep looking," I said, squinting through the greenish pall. "He's out here. I can feel it, Metcalfe." I looked over at him. "And put your bloody hand down!"

I waited and I listened, standing in the shadows of a shop doorway on the east end of Leadenhall Street, in the vicinity of Aldgate.

"How many, Inspector?" came a voice from the shadows that gave me such a fright I almost drew my pistol and fired at the speaker.

"Hell and blood, Holmes!" I hissed at the detective as he emerged from the dark. "I almost put a bullet in you!"

"At this range, I like my odds, Lestrade."

Metcalfe had the good sense to keep quiet. I scowled, returning to my vigil of the street.

"Absent of your keeper again, Mr Holmes?"

"If you are referring to Watson, he is nearby. With half the constabulary taking to the streets these last four nights, I thought you might appreciate some assistance."

"Clandestine operation, my hat," I muttered, recalling the briefing I had given to the sixty-three plainclothes constables on the eve of this endeavour. Few were abroad this night that I had not sent out myself. Fear had wrapped itself around London like a noose, and the hangman attired like an officer of the law.

The shrilling of a whistle tore apart the night. Shouting followed, muffled by the fog but clear enough. Other whistles joined it as my constables gave out the call to arms, and I was filled with a sense of impending retribution as I ran towards the sound.

"We've got him," I said to Metcalfe, but loud enough for Holmes to hear too, "we've got him now."

From street corners and side alleys and back ways, an

army of constables spilled out into the night to chase down the fiend. I ran down Leadenhall Street, following the whistle. And then the shrilling changed, a whistle no longer but now a shout, an awful noise that sent my heart into my throat, for I recognised the voice.

"Barrows…"

I got as far as Billiter Street, and hurled my body around the corner only to stop dead as I came upon the devil himself.

Crouched apelike over Constable Barrows, he turned as he heard me and slowly rising to his full height I beheld not a man but a creature the likes of which could only be found in the Gothic imaginings of Mary Shelley. I do not consider myself a learned man, but I was familiar with such works and saw their pages given grim verisimilitude by the monstrous Peeler. His shoulders were thick and broad, with hands like spades, but it was his face that froze me to the core. Though his eyes were hooded by a policeman's helmet, I saw the skin. Pale, almost to the point of white and somehow… *ill-fitting*, as if it would slip from his skull at any moment. All the more aberrant was the fact he wore a policeman's uniform, but one large enough to accommodate his brawn. He loomed as menacing as death and just as inevitable.

As he glared at me, the same feeling returned that had come over me at the workhouse fire, and I considered with some horror that I had met this fiend before.

Only when I saw the blade, the briefest flash of light catching its edge, and knew it had been used to lay Barrows low, did I find my voice.

"Halt!" I declared, wrenching out my pistol. "In the name of the law!" I fired and my shot struck him in the shoulder, but he barely flinched and was quick to take flight. I plunged into the fog, pausing only to look upon the ruin of poor Constable Barrows, who lay dead, mired in his own blood.

I got as far as Fenchurch Avenue when I realised the Peeler was gone. As Metcalfe and the others reached me, I heard the whistles, desperate and reminiscent of screams.

Holmes and Watson were kneeling by the body of Constable Barrows as I trudged back down Billiter Street, my feet leaden.

"He was just a lad," I whispered.

"Slit across the throat, I'm afraid, Inspector," said Watson as he gently pulled aside the boy's collar to expose the savage gash.

"But that's not all, I think," said Holmes. He held up Barrows' left hand. "Skin under the nails…" he added, before pressing the fingers to his nose and inhaling deeply.

"Christ, Holmes…" I said, dismayed at such desecration.

"Pungent, Inspector. The likes of which we have encountered before, and quite recently." He stood up and began to cast about, sifting through the detritus of the street.

"Holmes, what the devil are you up to?" asked Watson.

I shared the doctor's incredulity and was about to protest when Holmes proclaimed, "Ha!"

He held something in his right hand, which looked like a scrap of cloth. It was only as he brought it closer that the grimmer truth of what it really was became obvious.

"Merciful God…" hissed Watson.

It was a face, or at least the peeled skin of a face. I recalled the pale complexion and ill-fitting nature of the

Peeler's flesh and realised he had been wearing this skin like a mask.

"A simulacrum to hide his identity and torn loose when he took flight," said Holmes.

Watson shook his head. "And yet, the lad still has his face. If this is what he came for…"

"And more besides, Watson," said Holmes. "Our man has some skill with a blade, a paring knife or some such. The cuts on all of his victims were rough but swift, hardly the act of a surgeon but more in kind with a butcher or tanner. How long, Inspector, did you hear the screaming?"

"A few minutes, no more."

"More than long enough for our Peeler to do his work. But, instead, he was given pause."

"What does it mean, Holmes?" I asked. "Tell me it means something, and that this poor lad's demise has not been for naught."

"See here…" Holmes crouched again to turn Barrows' head to the side and expose the scarred side of his face. "Flawed. And here," Holmes went on, pulling open Barrows' shirt where it had been torn. "Scarring also." He looked again at the horrific mask, the skin, I now realised, had come from the dead porter. "The late Jeremiah Goose, his death mask entire." His gaze then flicked to Watson. "I can think of only one reason for such scrutiny and discernment. Watson, if you please, would you surrender your gloves."

The doctor got to his feet and looked at his hands.

"What for, Holmes? It's freezing out here in this fog."

"Your gloves…" Holmes repeated, "if you please."

By now, several of my men had gathered at the scene. Metcalfe was doing his utmost to marshal them, but curiosity had gotten the better of some. A few carried lanterns and tried to shine a light on poor Barrows so the detective could do his work.

Watson did as he was asked, carefully removing the garments and handing them to Holmes who promptly threw them into the gutter.

"Holmes! What the devil are you—" Watson began, but Holmes had already snatched a lantern from one of my constables and smashed it against the doctor's gloves. I have never seen Watson so apoplectic. "Good God, man! They were almost five pounds from Savile Row!"

Oil and flame eagerly spread across the leather. The fire quickly took hold, blackening and curling the leather and giving off a most noxious stench. I knew the smell, a noisome odour. It reminded me of the workhouse fire at Lower Thames Street and the men and women I knew had been trapped inside, cooked alive. Watson knew it too, I suspect. A man who had spent any time on a battlefield will be all too familiar with the reek of burning human skin.

"Good God," said Watson, paling as he pressed a hand against his mouth, "is that… ?"

"Long pig," Holmes replied, nodding. "Indeed, they have been fashioned from human skin. We should speak with your tailor, Watson, though I suspect I already know the name of his supplier from Bermondsey."

Watson appeared only to be half listening. "The sheer devilry of it," he breathed, transfixed by his burning gloves.

"Rest assured, justice will find him, Doctor," I replied, "Then, it'll be the noose for this fiend."

Holmes's prediction about the Savile Row tailor was accurate, and not long after dawn, I brought an army of constables down on Bermondsey and the tannery of Jacob Wainwright. Holmes and Watson had joined us, observing a grim silence. I crossed the threshold to declare, "Jacob Wainwright, you are under arrest!"

No answer came, and the darkness inside the tanner's warehouse made it hard to see much of anything beyond the shapes of hanging hides. The stench was palpable enough, though. I had drawn my pistol and used it now to urge my men inside.

"Find him, and take him. Alive, if you please gentlemen. I have questions I will have answered." Over thirty constables rushed into the tannery, brandishing their truncheons. "I'll have this dog, Metcalfe," I swore to my sergeant. Before Metcalfe could reply, a shout from within got the sergeant running and me with him. One way or the other, I would get Wainwright to talk, and there would finally be justice for the dead.

The hanging body put paid to that belief. Stabbed through the chest and hung up on a hook like the rest of the meat, I did not need Metcalfe to lift the dead man's chin to know this was Wainwright.

"He's dead, sir," said Metcalfe.

"This is *him*, isn't it," I said, not needing to be a detective the calibre of Sherlock Holmes to realise this was the Peeler's doing. Wainwright's feet dangled over a foot off the ground, and with the strength it would require to impale a grown man like that...

Holmes agreed. "It can be no other, Lestrade."

As he crouched down, ferreting for something beneath the hanging body, I heard Watson enquire, "What is it, Holmes?"

"Burnt offerings, Watson," said Holmes, holding up a

scrap of blackened material to the meagre light before showing it to me.

"He had some kind of fire? I don't see the significance."

"Did you find anything resembling a lockbox or perhaps a safe?" asked Holmes.

I frowned. "Nothing of the sort."

Holmes did not elaborate, but instead gestured to the scrap of material. "If you'll permit me, Inspector Lestrade?"

I couldn't care less. "Be my guest, Mr Holmes," I said, and turned to Metcalfe and my waiting constables. "Tear this place apart. If there's anything that will help us stop this man, I want it found!"

The tannery yielded nothing but the skewered remains of Jacob Wainwright, certainly no lockbox or safe, and, as his body lay in the grim accommodations of the Scotland Yard morgue, I began to believe we might never catch the Peeler. Surely now, with Wainwright dead, he would go to ground, and we might never learn his true identity or the reason, if one existed, for his crimes. I could only assume Wainwright had been his accomplice, for surely there could be no other explanation, and the Peeler had turned on him and ended any chance we might have to question him.

After several hours of searching, I left Wainwright's empty-handed. Holmes and Watson had long since returned to Baker Street and I had little choice but to go to my office, my cohort of officers disbanded, and review what little evidence remained. It was a surprise, then, that when I did return I found the detective and the doctor waiting for me.

"Both of you impersonating officers now, are you?"

Watson answered as Holmes smiled thinly. "Your desk sergeant was kind enough to accommodate us, Inspector."

"I see," I replied, making a mental note to reprimand the desk sergeant later. "So, are you here to gloat?" I asked, going to my desk drawer and the bottle of Lea Valley malt whisky I kept there for occasions such as this. Having poured my own, I offered both a cup but they declined.

"I prefer different vices, Inspector," said Holmes.

"And it's a little south of the yardarm for me," added Watson.

"Please yourselves," I said, taking a chair. "I hope you're here with good news. I could use it."

"Indeed, Lestrade," said Holmes, "and I believe we have it."

I sat up in my chair, my cup forgotten for the moment. "I'm listening."

"It was the mask, Inspector, when I first began to form suspicions. The dead flesh of Jeremiah Goose staring through hollows instead of eyes, it kindled a theory I have been harbouring ever since we met Jacob Wainwright." He struck up his pipe. "There can be no doubt that Wainwright is not our murderer, but I believe he knew him, and has done for several years." Holmes then produced a sheath of papers from his jacket pocket that looked suspiciously like a police document and set it down before me.

"I took the liberty," he said, "of having a look in the Scotland Yard archives and found something that piqued my interest."

I looked down at the document, a sergeant's record, the man declared dead several years ago.

"Has it ever occurred to you, Inspector," said Holmes,

"that our Peeler, who wears the flesh of dead men, might in fact be a dead man himself? At least," he added, "according to his official police record."

I read some of the details aloud. "Morris Duggen, killed in the line of duty, 6th June 1891."

"His partner that fateful day was a Constable Jacob Wainwright," said Holmes. "Both were involved in the foiling of a robbery at the Whitechapel branch of the London and Westminster Bank, which resulted in the deaths of several men, one of whom was Morris Duggen. This, Inspector," said Holmes, "I garnered from my own extensive archives and from the scrap of material I recovered from Wainwright's tannery." He brandished it again. "A piece of artist's canvas. It is difficult to discern, but a faint signature is just visible at the burnt edge. *The Duchess*, a lesser known but valuable piece, kept at the London and Westminster Bank on account of the previous owner's unpaid debts. Its seizure was mildly scandalous at the time. All of which led me to recall a report of the robbery in *The Times* that named both the dead officer and one Barnabas Fenk, a former army man with moderate expertise in explosives. I say moderate because the explosives he used to breach the London and Westminster's vault detonated prematurely and the aforementioned deaths occurred."

I leaned back in my chair, availing myself of a warming sip of the malt. "Fascinating as all of this is, Holmes, what has this got to do with our skinner?"

"Barnabas Fenk spent some time in Alderbrook Workhouse where, no doubt, his path would have crossed with a certain porter."

"Jeremiah Goose," I said, setting my cup down again.

"Just so. I believe Mr Goose knew of, or was involved

somehow in, the robbery of the London and Westminster. Several thousand pounds remain unaccounted for, as well as *The Duchess*, believed lost in the fire that broke out following Fenk's botched incendiary device, the self-same blaze that crippled Wainwright and supposedly killed Morris Duggen."

"Except Duggen survived," I said, "and you think both he and Wainwright were somehow involved in this robbery? Duggen survives, escaping with the stolen monies, and Wainwright is honourably discharged. Fenk is dead, so there is no one left to contradict Wainwright's story. Except Jeremiah Goose. But what about Duggen's body? There'd need to be one if he was assumed dead."

"Archibald Drew," said Holmes. "Wainwright's cousin, believed to have left London for brighter prospects elsewhere."

"Archie," I realised, nodding, "from Wainwright's hammer. He took him on the robbery too."

"Indeed. Wainwright was too frugal to discard a perfectly good stupa."

"Drew's body, all burned like that. Wainwright could have said it was anyone and make up any story to explain his absence."

"And did so, Inspector."

"Jeremiah Goose, he found out somehow," I said. "And Duggen killed him for it, even took his face."

"This is not a rational man we are dealing with, Inspector," said Watson.

"But Lestrade is right," added Holmes, "though I suspect Goose did more than merely threaten to expose Wainwright and Duggen for their crimes. I believe he stole some of their ill-gotten gains, and Duggen went looking for them."

"The Alderbrook fire."

Holmes nodded. "Enraged when he couldn't find what he was looking for, I think he set the blaze to deny anyone else getting their hands on the money. Furthermore, unsettled by his recent encounter with the law, I believe Jacob Wainwright took steps to rid himself of any damning evidence in his possession, hence the fire at the tannery. The canvas and a sum of money that, at the least, would raise questions."

"And Duggen killed him for it."

Holmes nodded. "Judging by the condition in which we found the body, I believe he tortured Wainwright, who knew Goose, and found out about the lockbox."

"The key," I realised.

"Precisely, Inspector. Stitched into the lining of his jacket, which is why Duggen missed it."

"He's gone back there. To Alderbrook," I realised, catching up to Holmes's train of thought at last. "It's empty on account of the fire, but he'd still need to wait until after dark. He's still after the money."

"Trusting to Goose's lockbox to have protected it from the blaze," said Holmes.

"He's still there, he must be," I said, grabbing my coat. "I'd wager my reputation on it."

"A modest bet, Inspector," said Holmes, "but a hansom cab awaits to take us."

By the time we reached Lower Thames Street, the day had almost ended and night was creeping in. What scant light remained made a hollow of the old workhouse, burnt and blackened. Roof beams had become exposed to the elements, jutting outwards like rib bones. Rats and vagrants made their lair here now, and somewhere amongst them was Morris Duggen.

"Shouldn't we wait for your men, Inspector?" asked Watson as we paused at the threshold. I had sent Cooper off to find Metcalfe and have him rouse as many constables as he could.

I shook my head. "I won't risk him getting away again," I said. "We'll have to be enough to apprehend him."

Holmes nodded, having drawn a pistol. Both Watson and I were also armed. "Then let's be at it, gentlemen," said Holmes, and we entered the ruins of Alderbrook. It was dark within, and we dared not risk any light for fear of alerting our quarry, so we made do with what little illumination penetrated from the outside.

The entrance hall was deserted, and I saw Watson move off to the right to look through a gutted doorway. He shook his head, indicating that the room beyond was empty. Holmes took the left as I pressed ahead to the stairs. It was then that we heard it: a faint scuffing against the wooden boards. It was coming from above.

"I don't think he'll be expecting us," said Watson.

"Then let's keep it that way, Doctor," I replied and advanced up the stairs.

I led us on. As we ascended a stairway with a broken railing, I saw what looked like an office at the end of a long gallery and realised that this was where the scuffing sounds were coming from. Doors, some shut, some black and broken, led all the way down on one side. On the other, the railing continued, some of its balusters burnt down to little more than nubs.

Here in its upper reaches, Alderbrook was open to the

sky, and I felt the wind catch my overcoat and the rain against my face as I approached the office at the far end of the gallery. The door to the room was open, broken on its hinges, and I could see a shadow moving around within. As we got closer, I thought I saw it pause, only to continue whatever it was doing a moment later.

"Are you gentlemen ready?" I asked as we neared the open doorway. Both nodded and I stepped through, preparing to render unto Duggen the full justice of the law, but something struck my weapon, wrenching it from my hand before I could shoot.

A hand clamped around my wrist and I was yanked off my feet, into the office and against the facing wall. Pain tore through my shoulder as it bore the brunt of my fall, and I collapsed in a heap.

I saw Duggen. He glanced at me once, a snarl on his shapeless lips, and I beheld a face so monstrous I now knew why he chose to hide behind a dead man's skin. He had a melted lockbox under one arm, a chisel in his hand, and he barrelled out of the room like a Smithfield bull.

I saw Watson raise his pistol but, upon seeing the horror of Duggen's face, delayed his shot. The bullet struck Duggen in the same shoulder where I had clipped him before – even in the dismal half light, I saw the spurt of blood – but as before he barely slowed, barging Watson off his feet and sending him crashing through the blackened balustrade.

Holmes cried out, "Watson!" and there was a second shot.

I thought the doctor had been pitched over the edge to his certain death until I saw Holmes scrambling to grasp Watson's wrist as he clung on perilously.

Duggen left them, limping now, and I realised Holmes must have clipped him before going to the doctor's rescue.

I got to my feet, still groggy from being thrown across the room. Duggen had left a gaping hole in the floor from where he'd smashed through to claim the lockbox. I staggered to the doorway, remembering to retrieve my pistol.

"Holmes?" I asked, seeing him slowly wrenching Watson to safety. Duggen meanwhile was fleeing across the gallery.

"All is in hand here, Inspector," Holmes assured me breathlessly. "To your duty."

I went after Duggen and got halfway down the gallery when I held my pistol outstretched and declared, "Halt! In the name of the law, halt or I *will* shoot!" I wanted to kill this man for all the ills he had inflicted upon London, and most especially for the death of Constable Barrows, but I would have justice not revenge.

Duggen stopped. With his limp slowing him, we were but a few feet or so apart. I heard the floorboards, so ravaged by fire, creak ominously beneath us and knew I had to get him down quickly.

Then he turned.

A malformed face greeted me. Its flesh was raw and twisted, and reminded me of melted wax. He didn't speak, and it occurred to me he might not possess the faculty to do so, given the severity of his scars. But instead of holding up his hands, he brandished the chisel and took a step towards me.

"Halt! I warn you, Duggen!"

Duggen kept going, limping towards me at a steady pace. I fired, or would have, but the pistol clicked deadeningly in my grasp and despite my frantic efforts I could not get it to shoot. Duggen grinned as he advanced on me, his red raw lips peeling back over his teeth. I drew my cosh, preparing to defend myself…

I felt the slightest tremor run through the wooden boards underfoot. Duggen felt it too and reached out to grasp the balustrade, dropping the chisel as his grotesque face contorted. I kicked the railing, hard enough to split it from its foundations. Duggen stumbled as the railing collapsed in his grasp. He teetered, one arm flailing, the other cradling the lockbox until at last pitching over the edge.

"Holmes?" I yelled.

"Here, Lestrade."

"And the doctor?"

"Present, Inspector," said Watson.

I carefully went over to the broken balustrade and looked over the edge. Morris Duggan lay broken on the floor below, his neck twisted at an awkward angle. The lockbox had split apart as it hit the ground and the stolen notes from the London and Westminster still fluttered in the wind before finally settling on the corpse.

"He's dead," I told them, and only then felt my hands begin to tremble. I sagged against a doorway as the shouts of Sergeant Metcalfe and my constables appeared below, and murmured gratefully, "the Peeler is dead."

I saw little of Holmes and Watson after that night. After several days of gruelling police work, all of the flesh garments wrought by Duggen and sold by Wainwright were recovered and destroyed. Though it could not be proven, it was widely believed by those involved in this investigation that Morris Duggen had used the skin of several other men and women in his wretched flesh trade, but post mortem.

Only the larcenous deeds of Jeremiah Goose had brought the killer out in him, though I suspect it would only have been a matter of time regardless. It turned out, Goose did know Wainwright, the latter owing gambling debts to the former and hence Goose's desire for recompense that in the end led to his death.

The stolen money was returned to the London and Westminster, a modest sum, but it had been enough for Duggen to kill his partner. In the end, through perfidy and misadventure, both men were spared the noose, a fact that rankles me but also lets me sleep more soundly knowing they are dead.

London grinds on in their absence, though it has no shortage of monsters still and horrors to spare, I am sure.

About the Editor

George Mann is the author of the *Sherlock Holmes: The Spirit Box, Sherlock Holmes: The Will of the Dead*, the Newbury and Hobbes and The Ghost series of novels, as well as numerous short stories, novellas and audiobooks. He has written fiction and audio scripts for the BBC's Doctor Who and Sherlock Holmes. He is also a respected anthologist and has edited *Encounters of Sherlock Holmes, Further Encounters of Sherlock Holmes, The Solaris Book of New Science Fiction* and *The Solaris Book of New Fantasy*. He lives near Grantham, UK.

About the Authors

Jonathan Barnes is the author of three novels: *The Somnambulist*, *The Domino Men* and *Cannonbridge*. He contributes regularly to the *Times Literary Supplement* and the *Literary Review*. He has written numerous audio dramas for Big Finish Productions, including a cycle of new Sherlock Holmes stories, starring Nicholas Briggs and Richard Earl.

Simon Bucher-Jones, like Mycroft, is a civil servant. Unlike Mycroft, he has permitted his well of intellect to be befouled with the creation of fiction. He's written or co-written five novels relating to or spinning off from Doctor Who, two books of poetry, a cursed verse play, a novel concerning Dickens' trip to Mars in 1842, and a steampunk version of *A Christmas Carol*. This is his first piece of Sherlockiana.

Kara Dennison is a writer, editor and illustrator born and bred by the Chesapeake Bay. A graduate of the College of William & Mary, Kara began her career as a journalist and localisation expert, serving as a feature writer for *Otaku USA* magazine, Crunchyroll News and others. Her work can be seen in the Obverse Books anthology *The Perennial Miss Wildthyme*, multiple volumes of the *You and Who* line, and the upcoming light novel series *Owl's Flower*, illustrated by Ginger Hoesly. She lives with four guinea pigs, whom she occasionally upsets when she leaves home to serve as a host and interviewer at (Re)Generation Who, Intervention and other conventions in the eastern US.

Ian Edginton is a *New York Times* bestselling author and Eisner Award nominee. He is currently writing *Batman '66* meets *The Avengers* (Steed and Mrs Peel, not the other ones!) for DC Comics as well as Judge Dredd, Stickleback, Helium, Kingmaker and Brass Sun for *2000AD*.

Other titles include such iconic characters as Wolverine, Batman and the X-Men. He has also worked on a number of film and television properties including Star Wars, Star Trek, Aliens, Predator, Terminator, and Planet of the Apes. In addition, he has written the audio adventures of *Doctor Who: Shield of the Jotunn* and *Torchwood: Army of One.*

He has adapted into graphic novels works by bestselling Young Adult novelists Robert Muchamore, Malorie Blackman and Anthony Horowitz as well as literary classics, *Pride and Prejudice*, *The Picture of Dorian Gray*, *A Princess of Mars* and the complete canon of Sir Arthur Conan Doyle's Sherlock Holmes novels. He has also written several volumes of Holmes apocrypha, *The Victorian Undead*, has adapted H.G. Wells' *The War of the Worlds* and written several sequels, *Scarlet Traces*, *Scarlet Traces: The Great Game* and *Scarlet Traces: Cold War*.

He lives and works in Birmingham, England.

Lyndsay Faye is the internationally bestselling author of five novels. Her latest, *Jane Steele*, reimagines Jane Eyre as a heroic vigilante killer. *The Gods of Gotham*, the first book in the Timothy Wilde trilogy, was nominated for an

Edgar Award for Best Novel and translated into fourteen languages. She is the author of numerous Sherlock Holmes pastiches, including the critically acclaimed *Dust and Shadow* and the forthcoming short story collection *The Whole Art of Detection: Lost Mysteries of Sherlock Holmes.*

Jaine Fenn is the author of numerous short stories in various genres and of the *Hidden Empire* series of character-driven space opera, published by Gollancz.

Nick Kyme is an author and editor who lives and works in Nottingham in the United Kingdom. He has written over fifteen novels and novellas based in the fantasy and science fiction worlds of Warhammer 40,000 and Warhammer Fantasy Battles, published through the Games Workshop imprint, the Black Library. His novella *Feat of Iron* featured in the *New York Times* bestselling novel *The Primarchs* for The Horus Heresy series, for which he has also edited several collections. He has written many short stories, one of which, "Forgotten Sons", was part of the *New York Times* bestselling anthology *Age of Darkness,* and his short story "Tempest" featured in the *Sabbat Crusade* anthology edited by Dan Abnett.

Regarding Sherlock Holmes, he wrote the short story "The Post Modern Prometheus" as part of the *Encounters of Sherlock Holmes* collection, published by Titan Books.

As well as novels and short stories, he also has worked in the video games industry and consulted on the acclaimed *Freeblade* by Pixel Toys.

Andrew Lane is the author of some thirty-three books ranging across fiction & non-fiction, adult & young adult, historical & contemporary and crime & science fiction. He has been occupied recently with a series of YA novels investigating Sherlock Holmes as a teenager and with building up enough Conan Doyle pastiches to eventually fill his own anthology.

James Lovegrove was born on Christmas Eve 1965 and is the author of more than fifty books. His novels include *The Hope*, *Days*, *Untied Kingdom*, *Provender Gleed*, the *New York Times* bestselling Pantheon series – so far *The Age Of Ra*, *The Age Of Zeus*, *The Age Of Odin*, *Age Of Aztec*, *Age Of Voodoo* and *Age Of Shiva*, plus a collection of three novellas, *Age Of Godpunk* – and *Redlaw* and *Redlaw: Red Eye*, two novels about a policeman charged with protecting humans from vampires and vice versa. He has written three Sherlock Holmes novels, *The Stuff Of Nightmares*, *Gods Of War* and *The Thinking Engine* for Titan Books, and a Holmes/Cthulhu mashup trilogy; the first volume – *Sherlock Holmes and the Shadwell Shadows* – is due out in November 2016. His latest series is the Dev Harmer Missions, an outer-space action-adventure series, beginning with *World Of Fire* and *World Of Water*.

James has sold well over forty short stories, the majority of them gathered in two collections, *Imagined Slights* and *Diversifications*. He has written a four-volume fantasy saga for teenagers, *The Clouded World* (under the pseudonym Jay Amory), and has produced a dozen short books for readers with reading difficulties, including *Wings*, *Kill Swap*, *Free Runner*, *Dead Brigade*, and the *5 Lords Of Pain* series.

James has been shortlisted for numerous awards, including the Arthur C. Clarke Award, the John W. Campbell Memorial Award, the Bram Stoker Award, the

British Fantasy Society Award and the Manchester Book Award. His short story "Carry The Moon In My Pocket" won the 2011 Seiun Award in Japan for Best Translated Short Story.

James's work has been translated into twelve languages. His journalism has appeared in periodicals as diverse as *Literary Review*, *Interzone* and *BBC MindGames*, and he is a regular reviewer of fiction for the *Financial Times* and contributes features and reviews about comic books to *Comic Heroes* magazine.

He lives with his wife, two sons, cat and tiny dog in Eastbourne, a town famously genteel and favoured by the elderly, but in spite of that he isn't planning to retire just yet.

William Meikle is a Scottish writer, now living in Canada, with twenty novels published in the genre press and over 300 short story credits in thirteen countries. He has Sherlock Holmes's collections and novellas available from Dark Regions Press, and a variety of his Sherlockian stories can be found in anthologies. He lives in Newfoundland with whales, bald eagles and icebergs for company. When he's not writing he drinks beer, plays guitar and dreams of fortune and glory.

Tim Pratt is the author of over twenty novels, most recently *The Deep Woods* and *Heirs of Grace*, and many short stories. His work has appeared in *The Best American Short Stories*, *The Year's Best Fantasy*, *The Mammoth Book of Best New Horror*, and other nice places. He's a Hugo Award winner, and has been a finalist for World Fantasy, Sturgeon, Stoker, Mythopoeic, and Nebula Awards, among others. He lives in Berkeley CA and works as a senior editor at *Locus*, a trade magazine devoted to science fiction and fantasy publishing. He tweets a lot as @timpratt, and his website is www. timpratt.org. He publishes a new short story every month for his Patreon supporters at www.patreon.com/timpratt.

Number one bestselling author **Cavan Scott** has written for such popular series as *Doctor Who, Star Wars, Vikings, Highlander, Judge Dredd* and *Blake's 7*. His first Sherlock Holmes novel, *The Patchwork Devil*, was published by Titan Books in 2016.

Jeffrey Thomas is an American author of horror and science fiction, the creator of the dark future setting Punktown. His novels include *Deadstock* and its follow-up *Blue War*, from Solaris Books, *Letters From Hades, Monstrocity, Subject 11, Boneland*, and *A Nightmare on Elm Street: The Dream Dealers*. His short story collections include *Punktown, Ghosts of Punktown, Thirteen Specimens, Nocturnal Emissions, Worship the Night, Unholy Dimensions,* and (with W. H. Pugmire) *Encounters With Enoch Coffin*. His stories have been reprinted in *The Year's Best Horror Stories* edited by Karl Edward Wagner, *The Year's Best Fantasy and Horror* edited by Ellen Datlow, and *Year's Best Weird Fiction* edited by Laird Barron. Thomas lives in Massachusetts.

ENCOUNTERS OF SHERLOCK HOLMES

Edited by George Mann

The spirit of Sherlock Holmes lives on in this collection of fourteen brand-new adventures. Marvel as the master of deduction aids a dying Sir Richard Francis Burton; matches wits with gentleman thief, A.J. Raffles; crosses paths with H.G. Wells in the most curious circumstances; unravels a macabre mystery on the Necropolis Express; unpicks a murder in a locked railway carriage; explains the origins of his famous Persian slipper and more!

FEATURING ORIGINAL STORIES FROM

MARK HODDER • MAGS L HALLIDAY
CAVAN SCOTT • NICK KYME • PAUL MAGRS
GEORGE MANN • STUART DOUGLAS
ERIC BROWN • RICHARD DINNICK
KELLY HALE • STEVE LOCKLEY
MARK WRIGHT • DAVID BARNETT
JAMES LOVEGROVE

TITANBOOKS.COM

FURTHER ENCOUNTERS OF SHERLOCK HOLMES

Edited by George Mann

Once again the spirit of Sherlock Holmes lives on. Wonder at how the world's greatest consulting detective plays a deadly game with the Marvel of Montmartre; investigates a killing on the high seas; discovers Professor Moriarty's secret papers; battles a mysterious entity on a Scottish mountain; travels to the Red Planet to solve an interplanetary murder; and solves one last case with Dr Watson Jr!

FEATURING ORIGINAL STORIES FROM
PHILIP PURSER-HALLARD • ANDREW LANE
MARK A. LATHAM • NICK CAMPBELL
JAMES GOSS WILLIAM • ROY GILL
SCOTT HANDCOCK • GUY ADAMS
LOU ANDERS • JUSTIN RICHARDS
PHILIP MARSH • PATRICK MAYNARD
& ALEXANDRA MARTUKOVICH

SHERLOCK HOLMES
THE WILL OF THE DEAD

by George Mann

A rich elderly man has fallen to his death, and his will is nowhere to be found. A tragic accident or something more sinister?

The dead man's nephew comes to Baker Street to beg for Sherlock Holmes's help. Without the will he fears he will be left penniless, the entire inheritance passing to his cousin. But just as Holmes and Watson start their investigation, a mysterious new claimant to the estate appears. Does this prove that the old man was murdered? Meanwhile Inspector Charles Bainbridge is trying to solve the case of the "iron men", mechanical steam-powered giants carrying out daring jewellery robberies. But how do you stop a machine that feels no pain and needs no rest? He too may need to call on the expertise of Sherlock Holmes.

SHERLOCK HOLMES
THE SPIRIT BOX

by George Mann

German zeppelins rain down death and destruction on London, and Dr Watson is grieving for his nephew, killed on the fields of France.

A cryptic summons from Mycroft Holmes reunites Watson with his one-time companion, as Sherlock comes out of retirement, tasked with solving three unexplained deaths. A politician has drowned in the Thames after giving a pro-German speech; a soldier suggests surrender before feeding himself to a tiger; and a suffragette renounces women's liberation and throws herself under a train. Are these apparent suicides something more sinister, something to do with the mysterious Spirit Box? Their investigation leads them to Ravensthorpe House, and the curious Seaton Underwood, a man whose spectrographs are said to capture men's souls…

For more fantastic fiction, author events, competitions,
limited editions and more

VISIT OUR WEBSITE
titanbooks.com

LIKE US ON FACEBOOK
facebook.com/titanbooks

FOLLOW US ON TWITTER
@TitanBooks

EMAIL US
readerfeedback@titanemail.com